CRAVE

Jennifer Dawson

This is a work of fiction. Names, characters, places, and incidents either are the product of the author's imagination or are used fictitiously, and any resemblance to actual persons, living or dead, business establishments, events or locales is entirely coincidental.

The author has asserted their rights under the Copyright Designs and Patent Acts 1988 (as amended) to be identified as the author of this book.

Copyright © 2015 Jennifer Dawson
Edited by Mary Moran
Cover Design by Alvania Scarborough

All rights reserved.
This book, or parts thereof, may not be reproduced in any form without permission.

Dedication

To my husband, who has loved and supported me, and all my craziness, for over twenty years.

To Lizbeth, our walk and talks gave me the strength and peace of mind to walk this path.

Special Thanks to Alvania Scarborough.

No book is created alone and that is especially true here. Thank you for holding my hand, walking me through this crazy process, believing in my writing, and the thousands of conversations we've had over the years that brought us to this point. You're the best!

Praise for Jennifer Dawson

"TAKE A CHANCE ON ME is a captivating, lighthearted story from the first page to the last."- Cocktails and Books

"Witty repartee, memorable secondary characters, and powerful attraction skillfully handled will have readers eager for the next in the series" TAKE A CHANCE ON ME– Publisher Weekly

I loved this novel (Take A Chance on Me). Mitch and Maddie are perfect together, and their story is a feel good, sexy read. – Love Reading Romance

"THE WINNER TAKES IT ALL was pure bliss to read. I loved the writing, the dialogue, the banter and I absolutely adored the characters." - The Sassy Booster

"If wicked banter, a little heat and family gatherings make you smile, I totally recommend the Something New series."- Caffeinated Book Reviewer

"I loved **Cece and Shane** together. From their first scene in this book (Winner Takes It All) their connection and chemistry was evident"- A Fortress of Books

"Dawson draws a clear picture of a high-powered romance…The titillating sex scenes feel like lost souls coming together." THE WINNER TAKES IT ALL – Publisher Weekly

Welcome to Crave, the first novel in the Undone Series

I vow. I crave. I give in.

I used to be a nice, normal girl. I had dreams. Good, happy dreams of a white picket fence, 2.5 kids, and a fairytale love that lasts forever. Nobody ever warned me that sometimes, the prince dies three weeks before the wedding.

Like any addict, I swear this time is the last….

Now, I go through my days, a shadow of my former self. I pretend I'm okay, and the people in my life pretend to believe me. But, sometimes, when I can no longer stand the craving, I roam an underground sex club looking for my next hit. It's dirty and wrong, but I can't stop, and my only line of defense between them and me, is the rules I've designed to keep me safe. The men always abide by my rules. Until I meet *him*.

And, like any addict, I'm wrong.

I don't question the instincts that tell me to run. One look at him, standing there, power radiating off him in waves, tells me all I need to know. He will make me crave those happy dreams I've left behind. And that is not an option.

Other books by Jennifer Dawson

Something New Series

Take A Chance on Me
The Winner Takes It All
The Name of the Game (coming September 2015)

Undone Series

Crave
Sinful (coming Fall 2015)

1.

Eleven P.M.

Two months. Five days. Twenty-one hours.

It's my new record although I have no sense of accomplishment. No, I'm resigned as I walk down the dark, deserted alley. The heels of my knee-high, black patent boots click against the cracked concrete in echo of my defeat. The distant sounds of the bass thuds in my ears in time to the heavy beat of my heart.

My own personal staccato of failure.

I'm not sure why it's always a surprise. Maybe because, at first, my conviction is so strong. By now my pattern is long and established—I vow, I crave, I give in.

Rinse. Repeat.

But, like any good addict, I always swear this time is the last.

Of course, I try. My therapist has given me "management tools" to get me through the hard times, and like a good patient, I follow her instructions to a tee—I meditate, do yoga, and write all my crappy feelings in the journal she insists I keep.

Only, it's backfired and become part of the ritual. When the cycle starts, it's a matter of time before I end up here.

I'm sure when John brought me to this underground club the first time, he'd never envisioned I'd be back on my own, wandering through the crowds, looking for my next fix. The club reminds me of him, and I wish I could go somewhere else so I wouldn't be confronted with my betrayal, but I don't have a choice. There aren't ads for places like this. Or maybe there are and I don't know where to look.

Swift and sudden, anger clogs my throat, and for a split second I hate him for changing me so irrevocably, and leaving me so permanently. Fast on the heels of anger, the guilt wells, so powerful it brings a sting of tears to my eyes. In the pockets of my black trench coat, my nails dig crescents into my palms.

I push away the emotions. Exhaling harshly, my breath fogs the air as I spot a hint of the red door that signals both my refuge and my hell. I hear the muffled hum of music that will crescendo once I'm inside to pump through me like a heartbeat.

My pace quickens along with my pulse.

As much as I hate giving in, I can't deny my relief. Once I step through that door, I don't have to pretend. I don't have to be normal.

The tension, riding me all day, distracting me in meetings, making me wander off in the middle of conversations, ebbs. A twisted excitement slicks my thighs as the bare skin under my skirt tingles.

I haven't bothered with panties. It makes things easier, quicker. Less about getting off and more about taking care of business.

I have on my usual club fare: short, black pleated

skirt that leaves a stretch of thigh before my stockings start. A sheer, white silk blouse that's unbuttoned low enough to show the lace of my red demi-bra. My lips are slicked with crimson and my dark chestnut hair is a tumble of shiny waves down my back.

My outfit is carefully orchestrated. I leave as little to chance as possible.

No leather or latex. I'm not into bondage. Chains and rope do nothing but leave me cold. Once upon a time I loved to be restrained by fingers wrapped tight around my wrists, digging into my skin, but now I can't handle even a hint of being bound.

I reveal plenty of smooth ivory skin, my clue to guys into body modification or knife play to stay away. I like fear, but not that kind. I want my bruises and scars hidden away, not worn like a badge of honor for the world to see.

My wrists and neck are free of jewelry so the Masters don't confuse me with a slave girl. I tried that scene once, thinking all their hard play and intense scenes would focus my restless energy and make me forget, but there is no longer anything submissive about me.

I don't want to obey. I want to fight.

2.

The scream leaves my throat, echoing on the walls of my bedroom, as I start awake. I jerk to a sitting position, sucking in great lungfuls of air. Drenched in sweat, I press my palm to my pounding heart, the beat so rapid it feels as though it might burst from my chest.

I had the dream again. Not *a dream*—dreams are good and full of hope—no, a nightmare. The same nightmare I've had over and over for the last eighteen months. An endless, gut-wrenching loop that fills my sleep and leaves my days unsettled.

I miss good dreams. Miss waking up rejuvenated. But most of all, I miss feeling safe. I'd taken those things for granted and paid the price.

Lesson learned. Too late to change my fate, but learned none the less.

On shaky legs I climb out of bed and pad down the hallway of my one bedroom, Lakeview condo and into the kitchen, my mind still filled with violent images and blood trickling like a lazy river down a concrete crack in the pavement.

I go through my morning ritual, pulling a filter and coffee from the cabinets. Carefully measuring scoops of ground espresso into the basket as tears fill my eyes.

I blink rapidly, hoping to clear the blur, but it doesn't work, and wet tracks slide down my cheeks. But even through my fear, my ever-present grief and guilt, I can feel it. It sits heavy in my bones, familiar and undeniable.

The want.

The need.

The craving that grows stronger each and every day I resist. That the dream does nothing to abate the desire sickens me.

I know what Dr. Sorenson would say: I need to disassociate. That the events of the past, and my emotions aren't connected, but she can't possibly understand. Throat clogged, I brush away the tears, and angrily stab the button to start the automatic drip.

My phone rings a short, electronic burst of sound, signaling an incoming text. I'm so grateful for the distraction from my turbulent thoughts I snatch up the device, clutching it tight as though it might run away from me.

I open the text. It's from my boss, Frank Moretti. *CFO is leaving to "pursue other opportunities". Need to meet 1st thing this AM to discuss.*

I sigh in relief. As the communications manager at one of Chicago's boutique software companies this ensures a crazy day I desperately need. Frank will have me running around like a mad woman. I take a deep breath and wipe away the last of the tears on my face.

Salvation. I won't have time to think. Won't have time to ponder what I'm going to do tonight. I type out my agreement and hit send, hoping against hope I'll be too exhausted this evening to do anything but fall into a bed, dreamless.

Too tired to give in to my drug of choice.

※

My morning is filled with back-to-back meetings and I don't sit at my desk until eleven. On autopilot, I make my way through voice mails, jotting down the calls I need to return. All the while the all too familiar ache has only grown more insistent.

The morning's pace has done nothing to ease the tightness in my chest, or curb the craving. Other than momentary periods of respite, it's distracting me.

Reminding me in countless little ways I can't resist.

My sister's voice comes over the line, ripping me away from my thoughts. Tone light and happy, she tells me she's looking forward to our lunch at noon. I dart a quick glance at the clock on my computer and groan.

April is the last person I want to see.

Not that I don't love my sister, I do. She's great. It's just that being around her reminds me of all I've lost and how I'll never be the person I was again. Today, I can't bear to witness that look of expectation my family gives me, like they're waiting for the Layla Hunter I used to be to show up. I hate the disappointment, the loss, shinning in their eyes when they search and don't find her.

I don't know how to tell them I miss that girl as much as they do.

This is not a good day to remember. Not when I miss John so much it's a physical hurt. If he hadn't died, I'd have been married a year and a half now, living the younger woman's version of April's life. Despite our dirty little secret, John and I were like every other couple we'd known in our late twenties, living in the city, having as much fun as we could before I got pregnant and we moved out to the suburbs to claim our white picket fence, four bedroom, and two and a half bath dreams.

Unlike me, my sister's path didn't deviate, falling perfectly into place as she'd planned all along. Her successful executive husband adores her; my twin nieces are right out of a stock photo they're so cute. Beautiful, golden-haired angels that break my heart every time I see them they're so precious. April even has my dog, the Golden Retriever John and I said we'd get the second we moved out of the city and had a yard.

His memory is close today, and with April's call, I can see it—that charmed, blessed life I'd believed I was entitled too. A life where the evils of the world were so out of my hemisphere I'd never dreamed they'd happen to me.

Obviously, I was wrong.

Panic fills my chest, breathless in its intensity. I look down to realize I'm clicking the button on the top of my pen over and over. Stilling my restless fingers, I take a deep calming breath. Counting to twenty as Dr. Sorenson has taught me.

I can't go to lunch with April. Not today of all days when I need so badly what John used to give me that it's a dull, persistent ache.

I dart a quick glance at the clock and pick up the phone. I might be able to catch her. But then I recall I canceled on her two times before. My sister might be a happy little homemaker, but she's no pushover, if I cancel again, she'll come drag me to lunch by my hair.

I swallow all of my turbulent emotions threatening to bubble over and drop the receiver back into its cradle. Resigned.

༄

I spot April already waiting for me in the little French bistro two blocks away from my work. She wears a worried, uneasy expression as her gaze darts around the room. As soon as she spots me she beams, flashing her trademark, million-dollar smile.

My stomach tightens as I walk toward her. She looks gorgeous and the sight of her makes me feel like a poor carbon copy of my former self.

While we have the same clear, sky-blue eyes, she's a California blonde to my brunette. Today she's wearing a casual dress the exact color of red autumn leaves falling to the ground outside. The simple cut, and jersey fabric, skims her body kept toned by walks and grueling sessions of hot yoga. It highlights golden skin, sun-kissed from her recent four-day jaunt to Naples, Florida, for a little alone time with her husband, Derrick. She radiates good health.

In essence, my complete opposite.

She throws her arms out in greeting and I begrudgingly step into her embrace.

"You look wonderful," she says, squeezing me tight.

Liar. I look horrible. Lifeless and flat in the light of her glowing, earth goddess warmth.

"So do you," I mummer back, except I mean it. I suck in her scent. She smells like flowers and sunshine. Achingly familiar, so reminiscent of a time hovering out of my reach, I want to stay in her embrace forever.

But, of course, I don't. I break away and step back. Her lightly raspberry-stained mouth tucks down at the corners, her hands still resting on my arms as though she means to pull me in for another hug.

I tug away, retreating to the safety of my seat.

Her lips press together, but then she flashes me another brilliant smile, and settles into the chair across from me. She lays her crisp, white linen napkin daintily across her lap before looking at me. And I catch it, the hope shining in her eyes.

I pick up the menu resting across my plate and

stare at the words without reading. An awkward silence, which never existed between us before, fills the empty space.

April clears her throat. "How are you?"

"Good." Another lie. Today, I am drowning. "Work's crazy."

"I'm glad you were able to get away, you need a break, Layla."

I put down the menu. "I'm fine."

I want to reassure her. If we have a good lunch, she'll be able to report back to my mother that I'm making progress. Peace might elude me, but I want it for them.

The frown makes another appearance, but before April can say anything, our waiter comes over and places a big bottle of sparkling water down on the table. Young, with a mess of golden-streaked hair, and the chiseled bone structure of a model, he's all fresh-faced innocence. "Can I get you something to drink?"

My sister orders a glass of white wine.

I shake my head and he disappears into the lunchtime crowd, leaving us alone with our uncomfortable silence.

I manage a smile and settle on the safest possible subject, one guaranteed to make my sister forget her worry. "How are the girls?"

Her whole face lights up. "Their dance recital is in a couple of weeks and they love their costumes so much I can't get them to take them off." She picks up her phone and swipes over the screen before holding it out to me.

I take it and the image of my two nieces, Sasha and Sonya, fill the screen. As soon as I see their precious little faces, decked out in lavender leotards with matching tutus accented by pale green bows, I realize I'm longing for information about them. They're so adorable it brings a sting of tears to my eyes that I blink away.

Technically, when I find myself on the verge of uncontrollably crying throughout the day, I'm supposed to call Dr. Sorenson for an emergency session, since it's a trigger for my unhealthy behavior.

But I already know I'm not going to do that.

I'm ready to fall. Crave it in that way nobody could talk me out of.

I straighten in my chair and hand the phone back to April. "Text me the picture."

"I will." She drops the cell onto the table and places her hands in her lap. "They'd love it if their Aunt Layla came to their dance."

An image of sitting in the audience fills my head. My parents, April and Derrick, and me, sitting next to some stranger where my husband is supposed to be. It's a selfish thought and I immediately dislike myself for it. This isn't about me. It's about my nieces.

I nod. I will not disappoint April, not in this. "Of course, I'd love to come."

She clasps her hands together in a gesture of prayer. "Thank you so much, they'll be so excited."

I'm sad she views this as a major accomplishment, and I renew my vow to spend the rest of lunch being a good sister.

Thirty minutes later, April has filled me in on every aspect of her life—from the petty women in the PTA, to her vacation with Derrick. I've done a good job, made all the right noises and gestures, laughing in all the right places. She's satisfied. Relaxed.

The waiter walks away with our empty plates and April puts her elbows on the table and leans forward. "I want to ask you something."

Spine stiffening, I'm immediately on high alert.

"I don't want you to say no right away." April's

gaze looks just past me and she nibbles on her bottom lip.

All my good intentions fly out the window and I say in a hard voice, "No."

April sighs, folds her hands on the table, her two and a half carat ring glitters in the sunlight streaming in through the window. "You don't even know what I'm going to say."

I shake my head, one hundred percent certain I don't want to hear it. "I don't have to."

Her blue eyes fill with a shiny brightness. "Please, won't you please hear me out?"

Do I want to ruin her whole lunch? I grit my teeth and nod.

She twists her ring, a sure sign she's nervous, and my stomach sinks. "There's a man, he works with Derrick—"

"Absolutely not!" I'm unable to hide the shriek in my tone. How could she even suggest it?

She holds up her hand. "Layla, wait, just listen. He's a great guy. His name is Chad and he's an IT Manager."

"Stop." My voice shakes. "How could you?"

She runs a hand through her golden hair, and the waves rustle before falling perfectly into place at her shoulders. "I only want what's best for you. Tell us how to help you."

"And you think going on a blind date would be helpful?" The words are filled with scorn. I'm unable to hide my sense of betrayal.

"Layla, it's been eighteen months," April says, her voice soft.

I look down at the table, staring at the leftover basket of half-eaten artisan breads, as I swallow my tears. Why does everyone keep saying that? Is eighteen months really that long? Is there an expiration date on grief? On fear?

"We all loved John, you know that," my sister continues without mercy. "But you're still young with your whole life in front of you. He's gone. It's time to move on and put your life back together. I don't think he'd want you suffering like this."

I put my hands in my lap and clench them tightly, so tight my nails dig into my skin. So brittle I might break, I look at my sister. My beautiful, thirty-five-year-old sister, who's never even had a bad hair day.

"Someday," I say, my voice cracking. "I'm going to ask you if you think eighteen months is a long time, and we'll see what your answer is."

She pales and reaches across the table, making me jerk back. She slides away. "I don't mean it like that."

"You do." A cold, almost deadly calm fills my stomach. "You keep waiting for the girl I was before to show up, and that's never going to happen."

She presses her lips together, and tears fill her eyes, turning them luminous. "I miss you."

"I miss me too." And it's the truth. All pretense of faking falls away. It's impossible to maintain the mask, not with my emotions so close to the surface. So raw.

April picks up her white linen napkin and blots under her lashes. "I can't pretend to know what you are going through. And with," she clears her throat and her chin trembles, "what happened..." She trails off and looks beyond me, over my shoulder.

A smug, selfish satisfaction wells in my chest.

"Look at you," my tone filled with an ugly meanness I want to control but can't. "It's been *eighteen months*, April, and you can't even say it."

Emotions flash across her face—worry, sadness, and lastly guilt. "I'm sorry."

Remorse weaves a fine crack through my heart, but it doesn't break me, because I've spoken the truth. None of them can even bring themselves to mention that night. They avoid it. Pretend only John's death is the issue. I can't say I blame them. Where we live, bad things happen to other people. They're ill prepared for tragedy.

I abruptly stand. I need to get out of here. Escape. I glance at the large clock hanging on the wall. Ten hours. It seems like an eternity until I can go to that one place where I'm free to be as fucked up as I want and don't have to apologize. I grab my purse, slip out two twenties, and throw them on the table. "I need to get back to work."

There will be no good progress reports today.

"Wait, please." April's tone is pleading. "Don't go."

"Text me the details about the twins recital." My voice is as cold as I feel.

"Layla." A big fat tear rolls down my sister's cheek.

I turn to leave before I confess my biggest secret, not to cleanse my soul, but out of spite. I've shielded my family from the worst of that night, the true extent of what happened and how it damaged me. Not because of some misguided notion of protecting them, but because, in truth, I'm no better. I also want to pretend.

Only, my nightmares won't let me.

3.

This long, dreadful day is finally over and I've ended up exactly where I predicted. I didn't stand a chance.

Every person in my family has called today—the news of my lunch with April having made the rounds—but I've ignored them all. Instead, I plowed through work, staying late as not to face a dinner alone in my condo. After my boss finally hustled me out the door, I ate takeout and wandered restlessly until it was time.

Tonight, unlike others when I'm in full denial mode, I ignore everything in my real life with the ease of shedding my trench coat that I hand to a girl behind the counter.

A Goth girl with black lipstick, equally dark hair, and tattooed sleeves running the length of her thin arms, left bare by a black leather bustier. Once upon a time this girl would have seemed like an alien she was so far outside the realm of my white picket fence life, but now, she's as familiar as my own reflection.

She juts her chin toward the long, narrow stairway leading to the underground club. "Good crowd for a Thursday."

I give her a small smile and begin my descent.

Cool air hits my bare thighs as someone comes in behind me. The night air brushes my overheated skin, reminding me of the near desperate anticipation riding me hard. Now that I'm committed to my perversion, I'm anxious to get the show on the road. Once I take care of business I'll be filled with conviction to start anew and the process will begin again.

But for those first few weeks, I'll have peace. Or as much peace as my life allows. And I crave that as much as I crave the release I get from my seedy activities.

I follow the sounds of bass; pounding so loud the lyrics to the music are indecipherable. Lights flash varying degrees of bright as I step into the main room filled with nameless, faceless strangers. Eleven o'clock is still early by club standards but the crowd is electric. The room pulses with energy, it sucks me into its world, and the Layla Hunter everyone knows disappears.

I slide up to an empty spot against the wall, seeping into the shadows to survey the landscape. People litter the small dance floor occupying the center of the room, gyrating to a pulsing techno metal, but they don't interest me. I don't like exhibitionists. I'm interested in the men lining the interior, watching and waiting for someone just like me.

My thighs clench as my skin heats. I'm too on edge, too anxious and filled with impatience. Tonight, all I want is to take care of my itch and get the hell out of here. I know from experience this is not a good place to be. No matter how subtle, people pick up on desperation and it's never attractive. This is the downside of too much self-denial but I'll forget this lesson as soon as I get what I came for.

I always do.

I scan the mill of bodies, littering the main room in the flash of bright lights, accompanied by moments of darkness. The area is small, giving the illusion of throngs of people, when really there can't be more than a hundred or so. The gathering area looks like any other club or bar in Chicago. It's the *getting to know your neighbor's kink* place. The real action happens in the specialty rooms—the private playgrounds, the voyeur's paradise, the dungeons, and medical examination rooms—the places you go when you've met your perverted match.

But I don't go into those rooms anymore. Not since John.

No, I stay right here. This suits me just fine with its dark nooks and crannies. I don't need the intimacy of those places. The reminder. All I need is rough, mean sex, and a lot of filthy language to create the illusion I'm getting what I need, all while remaining safe. In control. It's not perfect, but it's enough to tide me over. Besides, I won't allow anything else.

Against the wall, arms crossed, I scan the crowd. A man on the dance floor, not too far away, attempts to catch my attention. Hips swaying, he crooks his finger and motions me close.

He's handsome, slick, and all wrong.

I shake my head. His jaw hardens and he motions me more firmly.

Absolutely not. I turn away, knowing that will be the end of it. Guys like that want their women compliant, to abide by the rules they set. Not a game I play.

No, I set my own rules and don't break them for anyone.

My gaze skips over a submissive guy with a dog collar around his neck and bare chest.

I dismiss the man in latex.

The guy with a Mohawk and too many piercings.

The man with broad shoulders and wife beater T-shirt.

Wrong. Wrong. Wrong. They are all wrong.

My stomach turns heavy as I scan a group of men dressed in business suits but none of them suit me, besides they're window shoppers and probably half of them are married.

There are a few clean-cut types, in jeans and polo shirts I don't even consider. They remind me too much of John. He was that type. All American, boy-next-door good looks, so nice and considerate everyone thought he was an angel. And, he was, unless he was fucking.

Then, a different John came out.

Of course, I didn't know that when we'd met. Our relationship hadn't started out deviant. We'd just become that way over time. Slowly but surely John instilled cravings in me I hadn't even imagine existed, although he claimed I'd had them all along.

And who knows, maybe he'd been right. Remembering the first time John and I had sex way back on his narrow dorm bed, the signs had been there, I just hadn't recognized them.

When we'd met my sexual experiences had consisted of a few clumsy attempts at sex that left me wondering what the fuss had been about. Our relationship started like any other college romance. Downright normal. We'd met at a party through mutual friends. Flirted, drank too much, made out in the corner like the kids we were.

But from the beginning, John wasn't like other boys.

Other boys hadn't cared about my pleasure, and I'd thought that's how it was supposed to be. But John had cared. Back then I was shy, and since I hadn't responded to anyone else, I was sure it would be the same with him. So when we fooled around, I'd focused all the attention on him. Other guys ate it up like a hot fudge sundae, but John wouldn't have it. He kept trying to touch me, and when he did, I'd struggle. Resist. Endlessly I attempted to divert him by turning the tables. He never fell for it, and I couldn't seem to stop trying to control the experience. This went on for weeks, until the struggle became part of our foreplay. The first time he made me come, he forced a screaming orgasm out of me as he held a viselike arm over my belly so I couldn't move.

It had been like crack for both of us. Although, I'd learned later he'd always been drawn to more sadistic acts. When other teenage boys had been watching choreographed porn of blonde girls with overly plump, glossy lips and blow-up tits, give messy blowjobs, he'd been watching girl's getting tied up and spanked until they bruised.

Back then none of this concerned me because I believed we'd be together forever, and it was such a gradual process I never thought it was wrong. John and I loved each other. We were great together. We wanted the same things out of life, had the same values, work ethic, and desires. And we were lucky enough to burn up the sheets. Who cared if it was a little perverted? Certainly not us. We loved our secret.

I remembered how we'd go to parties: that sly, smug look he'd give me from across the room. Sometimes we couldn't wai—

With a violent shove, I slam the door shut to the past. If I slip into my memories of him, it will be impossible to ignore that this little ritual I've created pales in comparison to what we had.

My nights alone are for my memories. Tonight is to get my fix and be on my way.

I force my attention back to the present and

methodically start making my way around the room, mentally trying on each man before dismissing them.

I will not think about John.

I catalog each man as frustration grows like a knot of thorns. I want to scream. None of them have that *feel* I'm looking for. That click of recognition.

Just as it starts to feel hopeless, my attention stops on a biker type in heavy leather.

I pause, consider, some of the tension unraveling enough for me to think. He's not my normal type, but something about him snags my interest. He's big and bald with arms the size of my thighs.

Nothing like John, he'd leave no room for confusion.

The man's already engaged in a conversation with a blonde woman in a red corset and little else. She's pretty and petite with full breasts, a minuscule waist and toned legs. He runs a finger over the curve of her smooth, pale cheek. As attractive as she is, she doesn't concern me.

In a place like this, talking means nothing.

I continue to watch him. He's wearing a black vest, no shirt, leather pants and motorcycle shit-kicker boots. He could work. He looks mean enough.

I drop my arms and undo another button on my blouse, letting it gape open and expose the swell of my cleavage in my red bra. I wait. My gaze direct and heavy, I will him to look in my direction. At some point he'll sense my heavy attention.

I bide my time and focus.

At long last, he lifts his head as though he's scented something in the air. Distracted now from the woman he's been talking to, he slowly cranes his neck and catches my stare.

My breath stalls.

From across the room our eyes lock.

My heart gives a loud thump against my ribs.

He gives me a long, slow once over, followed by an appreciative nod.

I slowly expel the air from my lungs. Deflated.

It's wrong. I don't know how I know, I just do.

The moment fades like a mirage.

He turns back to the woman he'd been talking too, and I move on.

⁂

Fifteen frustrating minutes later, when I feel like I've checked out every man in the room, I make my way to the bar for my first drink. The ache between my thighs a constant reminder I might not find what I need. That I'll go home alone and be forced to try again another night.

That's not an option.

I take a deep breath, reminding myself to stay calm. It's early. There's time. I haven't been here long and there's still people coming down the stairs. I have to be patient. Not my strong suit at the moment.

Throat dry, I sidle up to the bar and pull a twenty from the inside pocket of my skirt.

I wave the bartender over. He nods and thirty seconds later he's in front of me, grinning his boyish, got-to-love-me grin. He's young and cute, with mussed brown hair, and dancing blue eyes. He reminds me of one of those Abercrombie and Fitch models with a finely built body and jeans slung so low on his hips you can see the cut of bone. He looks like he's never had a complicated thought in his life.

"How's my girl tonight?" he asks, gaze sweeping over me with obvious appreciation.

Inwardly I cringe at the "my girl" reference. It was a favorite of John's and he's already on my mind far too much. So close I have to resist the urge to turn and look for him.

I nod as way of greeting and say, "Good, thanks,

I'll have a Grey Goose and cranberry."

A girly drink, but it's quick and it gets the job done. Besides, I don't like the taste of alcohol.

The bartender pulls a glass from under the counter and free pours the vodka a third of the way before filling the rest with Ocean Spray. "Good crowd tonight."

"Yeah." My gaze darts up and down the bar, searching for the one guy that pings me the right way, only to come up empty. I blow out a hard breath.

"Tough day?" He slides the drink in front of me.

I stare at the pink liquid and tiny ice cubes bobbing in the glass. I share nothing about my personal life here. I push the twenty toward him. "I'm good."

The bartender winks and flashes his killer smile. "It's on the house."

We've fucked before. One time about six months ago on another night I couldn't find the right person. The way he's practically undressing me with his eyes, he's more than agreeable to another round. I find myself mildly tempted—not because I want him—but because he's easy. Uncomplicated. Quick.

Only, if I hook up with him, I'll break my one-night rule. While he's hardly a threat to my emotional health, he doesn't really satisfy my needs. Oh, he knows all the right words and actions, but lacks the pure menace that really flips my switch. Merely, he'd be a temporary fix.

I take a sip of the pink liquid and push the twenty back. "No, really, I insist."

He takes the money, eyes still twinkling with mischief, as though I hadn't rejected him at all. A few moments later he's back with my change, which he slips next to my palm before rubbing a thumb over the back of my hand.

I pull away.

He gives me a nonchalant shrug. "If you change

your mind, you know where to find me." Another sly smile flirts over his lips and he disappears to the other end of the bar.

If only things could be that easy.

Out of nowhere loneliness wells inside me. A pang of longing clogs my throat and tightens my chest with an almost unbearable ache.

I scoop my drink up and turn away, taking a long gulp. The tang of cranberry bursts over my tongue and some of the god-awful weight pressing against my ribs eases. With sudden clarity, I know I'm going to go home tonight empty-handed. I'm in the wrong state of mind. My emotions are too raw. My need too prickly.

No one will do because, tonight, I miss John. I want *him*. I miss the connection, and I can't find that in a seedy, underground club with a random, nameless stranger.

I take another sip, forcing myself to swallow past the lump in my throat, before putting the glass down on the bar.

It's time to go home and call this night for the disaster it is.

A shift of movement catches my eye and I peer past a group of men who look like they've just come from a board meeting. Past a woman gyrating her hips over the lust-dazed guy sitting underneath her, and a couple making out.

And, then, I see him.

My heart slams into my chest, my pulse kicks up, and something akin to panic rushes across my skin.

He's staring right at me.

My throat dries up like the Sierra and every cell in my body knows he's *the one*.

He's tall, well over six feet, with broad shoulders and a strong chest that fills out a tight black T-shirt before tapering down to a narrowed waist. He's wearing a pair of jeans that hug lean hips and encase powerful thighs. And while his body is spectacular, his face is something altogether different.

Like nothing I've ever seen before.

From the distance, I can't see the color of his eyes but his gaze is so hot on me, so intensely focused, I flush with desire. With short brown hair, an angular jaw, and full sensual lips, his features are strong. Powerful. Masculine. He's not exactly good looking, in fact, he wouldn't be called handsome on his best day, but there is something about him that is downright sinful. Pure, evil wickedness. Sex appeal pours off him in waves, lapping at me like a touch.

I shiver as my blood quickens and I respond to him like he's my own personal homing device.

I want him. More than I've wanted anyone in a long time.

I swallow, my thighs instinctively clutching together, I can already feel the slickness between my legs, the beading of my nipples. My skin pulls tight, warms. I clench my hands into fists as my breath comes a little faster.

I'm not sure I've ever had such a visceral response to a man, not even Joh— I stop the treacherous thought, unable to believe it even crossed my mind. The thin threads of anxiety weave an intricate pattern through my case of instant lust.

I turn away from his magnetic presence.

Fear coats the back of my throat. No. He's not for me. He's too intense. My body's response is too strong. In that one look I know he will give me *exactly* what I've been craving, but the price is too high. This is not a man that will abide by my rules.

I stare down at the gleaming dark wood of the bar, reaching for my drink with shaky fingers.

I feel the pull of his gaze. The weight of his stare. His desire at my back, crowding me from across the room. The lace of my bra becomes an irritant, and I suddenly wish I had panties on. I need any protection I can get.

Goose bumps pop along my skin and the compulsion to look back gnaws in my stomach.

I want him. Want what I *know* he can give me. No man, in the year I've been coming here, has ever come close, but somehow I know the man across the room is the one. The one I've been both desperately searching for, and terrified I'd find.

I imagine his gaze skimming over the lines of my back, the curve of my hips, the length of my bare thighs.

He is not safe.

The bartender walks past me, delivering another knowing wink on his way to service another customer, and suddenly his safety and simplicity doesn't seem so bad. My one-night rule isn't for men like him. He's not a risk.

I bite the inside of my cheek. I want to look back. At *him*.

I take a deep breath, hating the thought that's taken root in my mind—that the man across the room wouldn't be a substitute for the man I love—he'd never let another man overshadow him. In that distant, logical part of my brain I understand I'm attributing traits to him I can't possibly know, but the logic doesn't stop the certainty. Or the panic.

There is only one, viable option. I need to leave. I will allow myself to look one time, then I will go up those stairs leading to the outside world, and climb into a taxi. Once I'm back in the safety of my own home, I will change into sweats, wash my face, put my hair in a ponytail, and cry until there are no tears left.

It calms me. Settles my ragged nerves.

One look, then I run. Hopefully, I'll never see him again.

Slowly, as casually as I can muster, I crane my neck

and peer over my shoulder, searching out the space along the wall he occupies.

It's empty.

My stomach drops like a lead weight.

He's gone.

I swing around, searching the perimeter of the club, but he's nowhere to be found. Desperation churns inside me, and I pick up my drink. Raising it to my lips, I down the last of it in one long gulp, appalled at my disappointment.

It's for the best. I'm sure it's for the best. I replay the mantra in my head over and over, hoping I'll believe it.

He is the most dangerous kind of man—one that can make me forget. It's for the best he's gone. Moved on.

I put the empty glass on the bar. It's time to go home. I shouldn't have come. Like today, everything about tonight is all wrong.

I turn around and slam right into him.

On a quick intake of breath, I sway on the heels of my knee-high boots.

Strong hands clasp my hips, his fingers a tight hold that makes a shiver run down my spine, even while he settles me. I don't know whether I'm relieved or in full-blown panic mode. I look up, and up, into a pair of darkly amused hazel eyes.

I attempt to pull out of his grasp but his grip tightens, his fingers on my hips digging into me. Pure electricity jolts through me. A normal woman would be disgusted by the blatant display of arrogance, slap him or fling her drink in his face, but, I'm not normal. And his handling of me excites me to an almost dangerous level of lust.

Irises of green, mixed with gold, meet mine. The smug knowledge and blatant challenge clear in his gaze. He will give me *exactly* what I need. I haven't had what I've truly needed for a long, long time.

It scares me.

I want to flee. I want to stay. The sane, rational Layla whispers in my ear that he's a threat, and not in that good way we like. We need to run.

Places like this are for ignoring sanity.

My tongue darts nervously out to wet parched flesh. I take a deep breath and say as calmly as I can, "What do you think you're doing?"

That wicked mouth quirks into a grin that does nothing but increase the pure sex and menace pouring off him. I respond like I've just taken a hit of crack. "Please let me go." My voice quavers, betraying me.

His gaze drops to my lips, before rising to meet my eyes. "You didn't think I was going to let you run, did you?"

4.

My reaction to this man is so strong; my thighs start to quiver. I swallow hard, striving for the icy nonchalance so easy in my prior interactions. In my most haughty tone, I say, "There is no letting me."

His palm, hot on my hip, slides up the curve of my waist, his touch light but firm at the same time. Showing me in that one proprietary movement how easy control is for him. "Is that so?"

"This doesn't actually work, does it?" My voice is far too husky for legitimate disgust.

His other hand slips loosely around my neck and his thumb presses into my hammering pulse. Giving him all the answers he needs. "What's your name?"

To my astonishment, I open my mouth and my name almost slips past my lips. Jaw snapping shut, I press my tongue to the back of my teeth.

I *never* make that mistake. Ever.

My only excuse is his presence has thrown my hormones into such overdrive, habit has taken over. I shake my head. "No names."

Those unusual hazel eyes flicker and one dark brow rises. "Really now?"

"Yes," I say, my chin lifting into the air. Most men don't care about particulars like names when they think they have access to easy sex, but stating this requirement of mine feels silly. Since he's the kind of man I created my list of rules to safeguard against, I'm all the more determined to stick by them.

Gaze intent on mine, as though he's studying me under a microscope, his lips once again twitch with the hint of a smile. "The name's Michael."

I knew it. Knew he'd never abide by the rules.

"I said no names." My tone sharp with agitation, I push at his broad chest. The unmovable muscles under my fingers set off a riot of indecent thoughts. I could fight and struggle as much as I wanted and he wouldn't break.

A shiver races down my spine while goose bumps explode over my skin.

"I'm not real good at following instructions." One hand still a vise on my hip, he drops the other and traces a finger along the swell of my traitorous flesh. Saying without words that my body is giving him all the signals he needs.

I press my lips together at the almost irresistible urge to lay myself in front of him, and offer whatever he wants as long as he takes me, rises in my throat. At my waist, he strokes over my silk-covered skin, as though sensing my distress. My resistance wants nothing more than to melt away as desire slams through me.

He's so very dangerous.

It's more important than ever to be level headed. I clear my throat. "Then that's going to be a problem because I have some rules."

He chuckles, a low rumble of a sound that actually

raises the fine hairs along my nape. His thumb returns to play over the delicate cords along my neck, as though he has every right to touch me. "Somehow that doesn't surprise me, sugar. Let's hear them."

Detailing my rather stringent set of rules is the first thing I do with a prospect. If they don't like them, they walk away, and I move on to someone else.

Staring into his not quite handsome but strangely compelling face, I find I'm reluctant. All of the sudden embarrassed.

This is bad.

The silk of my blouse shifts over my back and I realize I'm sweating. My throat constricts, locks up tight, making it impossible to speak.

"You're one of those overthinkers, aren't you?" Amusement gleams in his gaze as his lips lift in a half smile that makes me want to take a bite out of him. He steps closer, his presence surrounding me, blocking out the people in the club, the flashing strobe lights over the dance floor, even dimming the music. In the sea of bodies, it's as though we're entirely alone.

I need to leave.

He shakes his head. "No, you're not going anywhere."

It's like he sees right into me. "This is a mistake." My voice a hoarse croak that reveals everything.

"Is it?" The smug amusement disappears, replaced by an intensity that hardens his jaw, and carves out his cheekbones. In that instant, I understand the amusement is an act to disarm me. This man, Michael, wants me as much as I want him. I have no idea how I know, but I do.

"Yes." The word a mere whisper.

He leans in close, so close I feel the heat of his mouth against mine. "Liar."

My breath stalls in my chest. If I move a half an inch, his lips will touch mine. I can picture the kiss.

The hot melding of mouths and tongues. I want it so damn bad I could weep.

Since John died, I've fucked more than my fair share of men. I've had men's hands on my breasts, on my clit, inside me. I've been spanked, bruised, and violated. I've been taken hard on my knees with my ass in the air and my face pressed into the ground.

But I have never been kissed. The use of mouths, anywhere, is forbidden. It's too intimate. Too reminiscent of what I shared with John. It's a right I reserve only for the man I love. A small concession for my betrayal.

That I would kill to have Michael's mouth on mine terrifies me.

His thumb once again pushes into my ragged pulse. He steps closer.

I step away.

He advances.

I retreat.

His touch is like a brand on my skin.

My back butts up against the bar and there's nowhere left for me to run.

"Please, don't." My voice is filled with thick need. Between my legs I'm so wet, a trickle runs down my inner thigh. My heart slams against my ribs.

His large body, so powerful and strong, presses into mine, crowding me. Overpowering me in a way even my roughest bouts of sex haven't.

My lips are so parched I'm desperate to lick them, but I can't, because if I do, my tongue will touch his. And that would be a disaster. I want to feel his lips on mine too badly. His mouth is beautiful—full and masculine—almost cruel. His mouth could make even the purest women have illicit thoughts, and I am nowhere near pure.

Reflexively, I clench my thighs as my belly jumps with desire.

"Spread your legs." His tone is a low, guttural rumble that is like a stroke against my skin.

Panic. I shake my head vehemently.

"Spread them."

"No."

He kicks my feet apart effortlessly. I teeter on my pointy heels but manage to remain upright by the strength of his grip alone.

I tighten my muscles, desperate to hide how much I want him. Even though he certainly knows his effect on me. But, if he doesn't have evidence, I can delude myself into thinking I'm still in control. It's one of those ironic twists of fates—as much as I cling to my control and the rules I've created—I crave the release he can give me like an addict craves their next hit.

But instead of heroin, I crave complete depravity. Delicious chaos.

No one has even come close to delivering. What I've been doing is a Band-Aid fix, like methadone.

But Michael, he will deliver. And I'm scared. Exhilarated. A mess of vacillating emotions I can't even begin to decipher. All I know is that right now every single one of my senses is on full alert, and my flight-or-fight response is fully engaged.

In my head, flight is winning. I believe this absolutely until I press my palm against his stomach and whisper a need-soaked, "Stop."

His head lifts and those strange hypnotic eyes meet mine. "Give me another word."

I finally dart my tongue over my dry lips. He tracts the movement like a predator lurking in the jungle, ready to strike. Even though I know what he wants, I stall, not ready to make a decision and end this agony and ecstasy of suspended anticipation. Not when it's been so, so long.

Breathless, I ask, "What?"

"Say another word, sugar." One long finger slips

past the silk of my blouse and circles my nipple through the lace of my bra. I jolt, the pleasure so exquisite it borders on pain. Under normal circumstances this type of behavior would be obscene, but here, in this nameless club anything goes except outright force.

And anyone watching us wouldn't dream of intervening.

Another slow, torturous circling of puckered skin. I have a sudden, startling image of his mouth on my breast, sucking hard. That mix of wet fabric, hot mouth and teeth. I shiver and manage another feeble protest. "No."

Jesus, I have to fight to keep my head upright. The rounded edge of the bar presses firmly against my back as the heat of his body intoxicates me.

He pinches the hard bud and rolls it between his thumb and forefinger. My nails curl into the black cotton of his shirt and he lets out a low sound of appreciation. His knee slips between mine. Both a threat and a promise. A tug on my nipple, I gasp and force my eyes to remain open. I try again. "Please stop."

He gazes hungrily at my mouth. "We both know for a woman like you, please, no and stop don't mean the same thing they do to other women. You want me to stop, give me another word. Any other word but the ones that keep making those pretty blue eyes of yours dilate and those throaty little moans escape from between those very fuckable lips."

Unable to stop myself, my tongue darts out to wet my lower lip at the mention of my mouth.

A safe word. That's what he wants. That magic word that stops everything. Of course, I have one, it's in my long list of rules, picked with John long ago. Asking for a word lets me know Michael is one of the good ones. That he's responsible and understands the game we're playing. That my safety and comfort matter. But the word is a life preserver that puts the decision in my hands.

I hate it.

It's wrong. I know it's wrong but I can't help it. I want to be powerless here. To have no control. My choice stripped away. To be overpowered so I won't be responsible. If I don't tell him my safe word, I can ignore that I don't want to say it. That I want what he'll give me, more than I want to walk away.

My mind goes unbidden to that night when John died—when I'd had all those choices stripped away from me. That I want them now fills me with shame.

Instantly, my eyes well.

All at once, Michael transforms in front of me. His knee moves from between my thighs. His hand on my waist gentles and his tortuous fingers leave my breast. He steps away but brushes away the tears that have slipped onto my cheeks. "Those will work too."

I blink, my throat closing over. "I'm sorry."

"Want to tell me about it?" His voice is soft, but it still sends another wave of tingles down my back.

I shake my head. "I need to leave."

"Why?" His large palm slowly slides up and down my spine, and I want to melt into him.

"Because this is wrong." I order my feet to move away, but they stay rooted to the floor as though nailed into the concrete.

"Don't bullshit me."

The sharpness of his tone has my head jerking up and my sadness retreating to the background.

His gaze narrows. "It's right, and that's what's got you so spooked."

Of course, he's correct. The chemistry between us is so strong it crackles like electricity, but I can barely admit it to myself, let alone him. Instead, I offer up a feeble, "You don't know anything about me."

"I know what's important." He leans in close and I suck in the scent of him, noticing for the first time he smells delicious. An intoxicating mix of spice, sex and danger that makes my head spin.

"I can give you what you need." His fingers twine around my throat and squeeze. Not hard enough to hurt, but enough to feel the threat, and respond with another surge of powerful lust.

"Not what you want—" His mouth dips perilously close to mine. "What you *need*."

It takes every ounce of willpower I have not to lift my lips the rest of the way to his, which my instincts warn he's waiting for. I manage to resist.

In the end, it's the image of John's face that stops me.

"And it scares the hell out of you," he murmurs in a low tone that rasps along my nerve endings.

His accuracy is dead-on and it fuels my determination to get back on firm footing. I steel my spine. "You don't know anything about what I need."

Liar.

His palm, so hot it almost seers my skin, grasps my bare thigh. I bite my lower lip so I don't moan in ecstasy. He squeezes, and then roughly shoves his fingers between my legs. My cheeks heat as he glides over my soaking flesh. Those hazel eyes meet mine. "Yeah, I can see that."

The muscles in my legs relax fractionally, almost against my will. I want his touch so bad it's like an ache. His hand is big, his fingers thick and slightly callused. Rough, worker hands that feel like heaven on my skin.

I gasp with pleasure as his thumb strokes my clit. "Do you taste as good as you look? As you feel?"

In the distant recesses of my mind I try and formulate a sentence that will make it clear mouths aren't on the table, but my thoughts scatter every time his thumb circles the hard bundle of nerves between my thighs.

As odd as it sounds, I rarely come from my trips to the club, yet out of nowhere the orgasm rises in me like a tsunami. Panic sweeps through me, combining with my desire as his movements become rougher. Harder. More insistent and controlling. That he manages to handle me so effortlessly frightens and excites me to an almost unbearable pitch. My eyes go wide and like a compulsion, I meet his intent gaze just as the climax starts to swell.

Abruptly, he pulls away and the wave that would push me over the edge recedes. He slowly raises glistening fingers to his mouth and sucks.

I pull in a deep breath, taking in the scent of my arousal that clings to the air. It should look cheesy and pornish, but he manages to make it look like the most erotic thing I've ever witnessed.

When he's finished, he reaches for me, curling his hand around my neck. His thumb brushes first my cheek and then my lips. The essence of my desire seeps into my skin and I'm completely hypnotized.

Another stroke of his thumb over my overheated flesh. "We're not gonna play by your rules."

It's like a slap in the face.

I viciously pull away, batting at his hands. The reasons for my rules come crashing to the forefront. They serve a vital purpose. They're for protection. From men like *him*.

"My *rules* are the only ones that matter." My voice shakes with the force of my fear. Fear that he'll stay. Fear that he'll leave. I shouldn't want him to stay. That I desperately do causes me to add rashly, "If you don't like them, you can leave."

His lips curve into a cruel smirk. "Sugar, if I leave, you'll be hating yourself in an hour."

I square my shoulders and my chin tilts with

defiance. "In an hour you'll be replaced."

He laughs. Actually laughs.

Anger is added to my already volatile pile of emotions. "You don't think I'll do it?"

He shrugs as though completely unconcerned. "Even if you do, it will leave you empty and unfulfilled."

"You can't possibly be that arrogant."

"I've seen you. I know how you operate."

The admission surprises me. I've never seen him and he'd be impossible to miss. "Have you been watching me?"

His eyes flash, turning them more green then gold. "I've been biding my time."

Before I can get lost pondering what that could possibly mean, I force myself back on track. "Then you understand it's my way or no way."

The statement hangs in the air, suspended between us.

His lips quirk. "All right, no way it is."

My heart hammers against my ribs as though pounding to get free and stop this madness. The urge to take it all back clogs my throat. I grind my teeth to keep the words where they belong.

He turns away.

My stomach drops, churning. I clench my hands into tight fists to keep from reaching for him.

He's leaving. His absolute control over the situation infuriates me.

Just as I want to scream, he swings back around.

I feel a split second of overwhelming relief that's quickly dashed by the hard jut of his chin. That is not the face of compromise.

"Saturday night." The words a clipped, almost military command.

"What?" I sputter.

"Be here, Saturday night."

"I won't." Goddamn him. Again, he's making it up to me. My decision.

His jaw firms into a hard, unforgiving line. "You will."

My fucking choice. "This is your only chance."

"You keep telling yourself that."

I hate him. And want him. "I won't be here."

I can't be.

"We'll see who's right Saturday." And with that, he walks into the crowd without a backward glance.

I search the throngs of people that have somehow materialized while I was lost in my own little world, but he's gone.

And, once again, I am alone.

5.

By noon the next day I'm a wreck.

He was right. Within an hour I hated myself. I'd gone home alone, just as he'd predicted. After my encounter with him, no one else would do. The second I walked through the door, I collapsed on my bed and rubbed my clit frantically to an explosive orgasm, so powerful my hips came off the bed and I cried out.

After, I sobbed.

I hadn't thought of John. Not even for a moment.

I'd thought of cruel lips, strong, high cheekbones, and hypnotic hazel eyes. I thought of his calloused thumb moving in deliberate circles, and how he sucked his fingers clean. I thought of his hand on my throat. The tight grasp on my hip. And how much I wanted his mouth on mine.

For the first time, I had an orgasm that hadn't included John. The guilt is like the dull blade of a knife. I've shattered the connection between us and I want it back. I need it.

The pull of Michael is too strong. He's like a drug, and I cannot prove him right. Not again. I haven't felt this volatile since John's death, and the fact that I didn't get my fix isn't helping matters. Maybe it wouldn't be so bad if I'd gotten some relief, but instead, I'm almost manic in my desperation.

I need a plan of action, because I cannot be at that club tomorrow.

Impulsively, I schedule an emergency session with my shrink. Not because I think Dr. Sorenson can help, but because she's the only one I can tell the truth. The only one who knows my dirty little secret. She's my confessional. My nonjudgmental calm in the eye of my emotional storm.

After I get time on her calendar later this afternoon, I pick up the phone and quickly dial my best friend, Ruby Stiles. She picks up on the second ring and I get straight to the point. "What are you doing tomorrow night?"

"I have Nanna's eightieth birthday party." Her voice has a smoky rasp that perfectly complements her femme fatale dark-haired looks.

"Shit!" The word a hard, angry bite. Too late I realize my reaction is out of proportion to a night spent alone. My usual preference.

"What's wrong?" Since my friends normally have to drag me out by my hair, she naturally assumes something is amiss.

She's right. Not that I'd dream of telling her why. She might be my best friend, but she has no idea about my late-night activities. And despite Ruby's live-outside–the-box philosophy, I doubt she'd understand.

"Nothing," I answer quickly, wanting to reassure her, but my frantic impatience bleeds through.

I have to find something to do. There is no way I can sit home by myself.

"Where were you last night? I called." Her tone is

filled with concern.

I never looked at my messages. I should know better, considering I'm on the watch list. Not wanting to raise any additional suspicions, I lie. "I was home. I didn't feel like talking."

That's entirely within character.

"Are you sure? You sound strange." Ruby and I met our freshman year of college when we were paired as roommates. Two good girls from the suburbs on our own for the first time, we were fast friends and she knows me better than anyone. But, like the rest of them, I've hidden the full extent of what happened, and what I've become as a result. She's always been there for me. Even during the worst of my grief, she held my hand those first few months, staying over, shaking me awake from my violent nightmares and soothing me back to sleep.

I blink, taking in a quick intake of breath. I hadn't dreamed last night.

Why hadn't I dreamed? I *always* have the dream.

"Layla?" Her voice even more worried now that I failed to answer.

"I'm fine. What's Julie doing?" Not a close friend, but she knows all the best hot spots and is able to walk right into any club, regardless of the line. A luxury afforded by her father's name and her gorgeous, Nordic good looks.

A long, silent, assessing pause. I've gotten use to them. It's what people do when they're deciding whether or not you're too fragile to push. Finally, after what seems an endless wait, she says, "You want to go out…with Julie?"

"Yes," I snap, no longer caring that I sound like a lunatic. "Is it so hard to believe I want to go out and have a good time?"

"Well, yeah."

I don't blame her for this. Everyone assumes I

spend all my nights home in isolation, refusing to get on with my life. Which is what I normally do, except for when I cave. "I want to go out. You should be happy, isn't that progress?"

In my desperation, I'm not remotely convincing.

Another long stretch of dead air. "Layla, *what is wrong?*"

"Nothing!"

"Look, I'm singing tonight over at The Whisky, meet me there and afterward we can talk."

I blow out a hard breath filled with frustration. Tonight doesn't solve my problem. An image of Michael's face fills my mind; so crystal clear I can almost reach out and touch it. Unlike my fiancé's image that grows more and more fuzzy as the days drag on.

What I need is a plan for tomorrow because I *cannot* go to the club. Obligated to appease Ruby's concern, since she's tried so hard to help me, I'm trapped into agreeing. I don't want to raise any more suspicion. "Yeah, sure."

"Okay, I go on at nine. Don't blow me off."

She knows me too well. "I won't."

As soon as we hang up, I scan through my phone's contact list, searching for someone—anyone—to go out with. I start making calls. One by one I'm met with sad, I'm-so-sorry-I-have-other-plans-already responses.

I want to scream in frustration.

It's like the gods are conspiring against me—which makes no sense—I have zero willpower right now, why aren't they helping? Don't they understand how important it is that I stay strong? If I can just get through Saturday night, I'll never see him again. It's forty-eight hours. Then, after it's over, and the threat of him is gone, I can relax and start again.

With someone safe. Who will stick to my rules and won't make me forget.

All of my options exhausted, I'm near frantic. I have to do something. Anything. I'd go to my parents' house, but they go to bed at nine, and that's too much time left on my own. I will cave. I'm too weak to resist, and Michael is too addictive to ignore.

I already miss his hands on my skin.

The notion of missing any other touch but John's is so jarring, one last-ditch, desperate option comes to me. It's the worst option, but still, better than the alternative.

Besides, it will help my family, and that's worth something.

I pick up the phone one last time.

This has to work.

My sister answers in a half of a ring, rushing headlong into contrite. "Layla, thank god you called, we've been worried sick about you."

In my panic, I've forgotten all about the calls from my family, each one more anxious than the last. "I'm fine."

How many times have I uttered those words? Too many times to count.

"You were so upset. I'm sorry I pushed you. It's just that we're all so worried about you."

"Don't be worried. I'm fine. I'm the one that should be sorry. You were only trying to help." I was cruel to her yesterday. Needlessly harsh. But I'm about to make it all up to her. I take a deep, cleansing breath and try to calm down, unable to believe I'm about to do this.

But there's no other choice.

"We only want what's best for you," April says, in her soft, apologetic tone.

"Sure, I know." I don't want to go into this right now. My mental health, the state of my grief, I'm just so sick of it. I rush headlong into the purpose of my call. "Listen, about yesterday." The words are like tar in my throat, but I manage to spit them out. "You mentioned Derrick knows a guy at work."

The line becomes so quiet you could hear a pin drop. "Yes, Chad."

"If he can get together tomorrow night, I'll go."

※

"Something's happened." The first confession of my inner turbulence lightens some of the tightness in my chest. Just saying it, and getting it out of my crazy head, is a relief.

I'm on Dr. Sorenson's subdued, sage couch as she sits across from me on her swivel chair, notebook in hand, pen at the ready. A nonthreatening, attractive champagne blonde in her mid-forties, she flashes me a pleasant, closed-mouthed, professional smile. "Go on."

I lower my gaze to my lap and twist the thin silver, etched band around my right finger. John gave me the ring for my college graduation. I put it on to help me reestablish the threads of connection broken last night. To remind me of what's important. "I went to the club."

I hear the scratching of ballpoint pen across paper and imagine her writing something like—*Still no progress!* Triple underlined.

I swallow and go on. "I…met someone…someone dangerous."

"Dangerous?" she asks, her tone banal.

I glance back at her, and she appears completely unruffled. Her hair is in a smooth, sleek ponytail, her makeup neutral, warm brown tones that match her knee-length rust-colored skirt and cream, button-down blouse. There's no alarm on her face, no surprise. Her expression gives away nothing.

"I felt…" I trail off, not sure how to explain.

"You felt?"

I swallow hard. "Threatened. Unsafe."

She shifts on the chair, and leans forward ever so slightly. "Did it bring back the flashbacks of the attack?"

I shake my head. "No, that's not what I mean."

Her head tilts to the side, encouraging me without words to continue.

"I met a man, and I felt something." Such inadequate words to describe what went down with Michael last night.

"Go on." One of her favorite phrases.

"He made me forget. About—" tears well in my eyes, "—John."

She expertly plucks a tissue from the box sitting on the coffee table that separates us and hands it over to me. "And how did that make you feel?"

"Like I betrayed him."

"How?"

She already knows, but I suspect she wants me to sort out and unravel all of my complicated emotions. I realize my cheeks are wet and I swipe them with the Kleenex. "The club isn't for feelings."

"I see." She once again leans back on her high-back leather chair. "And what is it for?"

Punishment. The word pops into my mind like blown glass, so startling and contrary to anything I ever thought, I can only freeze in the face of it.

A second later, the idea shatters into a million shards.

It cements my determination to stay far away from the club, because in that one moment of absolute clarity, I can see how Michael will change me on a fundamental level.

And I can't have that. Not with someone like him.

6.

Apparently, my brother-in-law has good taste in men, because Chad Fellows is a dream of a blind date. Across from me, at a small round table, in an out-of-the-way Italian restaurant, the incredibly good-looking Chad is sitting with an easy smile on his lips. He's clean cut, with short hair the color of melted caramel and blue eyes that dance with amusement.

At six-one, he's not built like a guy that spends all his time behind a computer. His shoulders are broad, his body fine, and after the time I've spent with him, I'm positive he doesn't get his sex from a World of Warcraft game.

To my surprise, I find myself attracted to him, but it's easy and nonthreatening, nothing like the intense rush of lust and panic I experienced with Michael.

And thank god for that. There's room for John here.

Over the course of the evening, I've found myself relaxing. Chad feels like something I understand.

Comforting and hot, with a bit of bite. I genuinely like him. It's unexpected. And welcome.

The gods have delivered the perfect distraction after all.

We agreed to meet for drinks, but quickly moved on to dinner. Two hours later, the pasta dishes cleared away, we're making our way through our third bottle of wine.

I've only thought about Michael and the club every five minutes or so. Not bad, considering he's fast becoming an obsession I can't control. Which is why I need him out of my head for good.

Instinct tells me Chad could help, and for that, I'm grateful.

"Layla?" Chad calls from across the table, pulling me from my thoughts.

I blink, snapping out of my fucked-up head. "Sorry."

"Where'd you go?" His long, tapered fingers slide up and down the length of the wine stem as though he's caressing a lover.

Not wanting to make an excuse, I tilt my head to the side, narrow my gaze and divert. "Why doesn't a guy like you have a date on Saturday night?"

He laughs, the sound as deep and smoky as the red wine we've been drinking. "A guy like me?"

I'm perched on the edge between buzzed and drunk. It's a nice place to sit and it makes flirting with Chad easy. Sitting right here, I can almost forget. Almost touch that time in my life when I was just a girl on a harmless date.

With a smile, I shake my head. "Don't even try that on me."

He shifts in his chair, and placing his elbows on the small round table, he leans in. Cast in the dim warm glow of candlelight, the sleeves of his white shirt are rolled up, and the muscles in his forearms cord and flex, drawing my attention to his lightly tanned skin.

I'd expected this date to be a complete disaster, but it's not. I have no desperate desire to escape. In fact, I feel a sense of safety. Like I'm cocooned in a warm glow. It's such a relief after the violent, visceral, blood-pounding, heart-racing desire of Michael.

Why do I keep comparing Chad and Michael? When I should be comparing Chad to John? I hate it. Hate Michael for preoccupying me.

"Why are you frowning?" Chad asks.

I quickly and expertly smooth my distressed expression into what I hope passes for pleasant. "Sorry, I wasn't meaning too."

"What are you thinking?" Chad's gaze dips suggestively to my mouth.

He might not be in your face about it, but the guy has sex appeal in spades. I take a sip of my wine and let the smooth liquid slide down my throat. "Why are you diverting?"

He gives me a long, assessing look as if deciding something before an easy smile flickers across his lips. "Truth?"

I nod. Chad makes me long for normal. It's so easy to pretend with him.

Then, the man waiting for me in dark shadows pops unbidden into my head, tempting me with all the things I've been craving.

Stop thinking about him, Layla. This, right here and now, is what's important. I've been delivered my salvation, my escape route, and I will focus on that.

Chad scrubs a palm over his stubbled jaw. "I did have a date. I canceled on her."

Somehow this doesn't surprise me; he's not the kind of guy who sits home by himself on a Saturday night. "Why's that?"

"Derrick made it sound like a one-shot deal." His expression turns sheepish. "I'm shallow and I saw your picture."

It sounds good, but somehow I doubt it's the full story. "And?"

His attention slides away, settling on a spot over my shoulder.

"Tell me," I insist, already knowing the real reason, but wanting him to say it, curious if he'll be honest.

He shrugs. "I owed Derrick a favor. He called it in."

The truth it is. My respect for him raises another notch. A hard, bitter-tinged laugh escapes my lips. "That must have been a great selling point."

He grins. "I wasn't lying, I am shallow. I saw your picture, so I knew at bare minimum I'd have something pretty to look at."

I raise my glass and take another sip of wine. It tastes like heaven now and every drink coats my raw nerves like a salve. "You must have been terrified about what you were getting into."

"I'll admit I wasn't looking forward to it." His voice is strong, unapologetic. "But honestly, were you?"

I suck my lower lip between my teeth as an image of Michael's hypnotic eyes elicits a shiver. I shake my head.

Across from me, Chad studies me, watching and waiting patiently for me to continue. I'm not sure I can elaborate. The truth isn't an option, but there's something about Chad that makes me not want to lie.

He leans farther over the table, the dim votive candle casting his skin in warmth. "My plan was to have a drink or two then meet up with the girl I was supposed to go out with."

His answer makes me like him even more. "That's honest."

"What was your plan, Layla?"

The way he says my name, something in the tone

or inflection, jingles the faintest bell of recognition. I avoid his question. "Why didn't you?"

"I'll let you evade." He flashes his white teeth, so even and perfect they could have only come from the orthodontist. "For now."

I blink, as a quick flash of instinctive heat warms my skin. The wine must be going to my head, because I'm imagining something that can't possibly be there. I clear my throat. "So, what happened?"

He shrugs. "You're an interesting woman. I like interesting. After fifteen minutes I knew I wasn't going anywhere. When I got up to use the bathroom, I called her and told her something came up and I'd have to cancel."

I want to tell him how thankful I am, but that would sound odd, so instead I ask, "Was she upset?"

"She wasn't happy."

"Do you think she'll forgive you?"

He chuckles. "Probably."

"Why are you telling me this?" It's an odd strategy, but one I appreciate.

His gaze skims over me in such a way I find I have to make a conscious effort not to shift in my seat. "If you were a different kind of woman, I'd give you a story."

I like his bluntness. It's something I understand. "A different kind of woman?"

He nods. "One who hasn't seen so much."

My shoulders slump as reality comes rushing back. Of course he knows, I'd just deluded myself that Derrick hadn't told him because I wanted to believe, if only for a moment that I was a normal girl, on a normal date, filled with possibilities.

The loss of the momentary dream is an ache in my chest.

The waitress, who's been circling our table, appears. "Can I show you the dessert menu?"

"We're not ready yet." Chad's eyes don't leave my face.

She disappears into the crowd.

In that split second, what's been tugging at me all evening, reaches out and slaps me. Chad is dominant. It's softer than the raw, brute force of Michael, but it's been there the whole time and I've been ignoring it. He's more like John. Oh, sure, I don't know if Chad's preferences are the same, but he's got that same understated, quiet confidence about him. The same easy manner. I'd bet money that, like John, Chad sheds the mild manner the second the bedroom door is closed.

My gaze widens and I shudder, my body's instinctual recognition and response.

His expression flashes and I know he's been waiting for this. That, somehow, he's known all along. I'm not sure why this surprises me. Is real life any different from the club? Like gravitates toward like, without fail.

Needing to fill the silence, I ask a question I already know the answer to. "Did Derrick tell you?"

"Yes, Layla, he told me." His tone now holds a cadence I'd have to be blind, deaf and dumb not to understand since it's staring me in the face.

"I wish he hadn't." My voice is suddenly thick.

"Why? It's part of who you are."

Exactly. It permeates my life. It's always there, whenever anyone looks at me. It's in the way they talk. How they respond. Sometimes I want to scream at them to stop being so nice, to stop treating me with kid gloves. But I never do. I can't hurt them any more than I already have.

It's why I started going to the club in the first place. To remember what it's like when people don't know. And I need the freedom to be as fucked up as I choose without apology.

Chad's waiting in that patient way good dominants have. He's not afraid of this conversation, of my past. Unlike me. I look into his steady blue eyes and find myself giving him an honest response. "It changes how people see you."

He laces his fingers in front of him. Those strong hands look capable, and somehow safe. "I imagine it would, but tell me how it makes you feel."

I frown, taken aback, only Dr. Sorenson asks about my feelings and I'm not prepared to talk about them out in the open. I cross my arms protectively. "I don't want to."

To my shock, he laughs.

It breaks some of my tension and I find a smile quirking. "I guess that sounded pretty petulant."

He holds his thumb and forefinger an inch apart. "Just a little bit."

This man across from me feels familiar, and good. If only I could give in. But that would require something I can't give Chad, something that's missing inside me. Besides, I can't break my rules, and this isn't the club, it's not like I can lay them out on the table without him thinking I'm a nut case.

Besides, he deserves better. He deserves someone like the old Layla, someone shiny and fresh, full of wonder and life. Not my pale, lifeless self.

I realize Chad's staring at me and I quickly offer an apology. "I'm sorry."

"Don't be. It's kind of cute." His attention intent on me, he continues, "Do you still miss him very much?"

My throat tightens. No one ever asks me. Not ever. For the most part, no one talks about John at all. It's like he's a ghost that only I remember.

Something about Chad invites honesty and I confess, "Yes, every single day."

"There aren't really words to make it okay, are

there?"

I shake my head. "No. How much did Derrick tell you?"

He laces his fingers on the table. "Only that your fiancé died a couple of weeks before your wedding."

So my brother-in-law didn't reveal all my secrets. "I see."

"Is there more?"

"Nothing I care to talk about." That little bit is enough to make me feel vulnerable and exposed.

He sighs, and takes a long gulp of wine. "I wish Derrick hadn't pushed so hard and maybe waited a year from now."

"Why's that?"

"You're exactly my type. But sadly, I think we both know you're not ready to date."

And just like that, poof, the dream is over. "You're right, I'm not." Even if I was, it's Michael I burn for. Unwanted tears well in my eyes. "I'm sorry. I'm a total wreck."

"I don't think so. I think you're stronger than you realize." His expression is still relaxed, as though I'm not crying. It's one of those good things about guys like him—they don't fall apart at the first sign of tears the way most men do. "I apologize for bringing up a painful subject."

Not sure what to say, I pick up the white cotton napkin and twist the heavy cloth and blurt out, "I'm not your type."

He reaches over the table and strokes a finger over my knuckles. "Be still."

Instantly, without thought, I stop my fidgeting, and a second later I know I've confirmed his suspicions.

A slow smile spreads over his handsome face. "Oh, I think you are."

Throat tight, I am unable to do anything but shake my head.

"You never answered my question."

I swallow hard, searching my mind for his question, and coming up blank. "What question?"

"Why'd you agree to this date when you're clearly not ready?"

I look into his blue eyes, his gaze so steady and sure, and it strikes me how much Chad reminds me of John. This should be disconcerting, but strangely, inexplicably, I find it comforting. It makes John feel close when I need him so badly.

I can't lie to Chad and give him the truth. Or at least my watered-down version of it. "I needed something to occupy my time this evening."

"Why's that?" His voice is quiet, but edged with that tone.

I can't very well say that sometimes I go to an underground club and get my brains fucked out by strangers, and one of these strangers makes me want him so strongly it's taking every ounce of strength I have not to go to him.

It makes me sad. In another life, Chad and I are probably soul mates. He's a reminder, a sign that all is not lost. It should be a ray of hope, and it is, but it doesn't change anything.

I'm not ready. And I still want Michael's mouth on me. It would be somehow more tolerable if I just wanted him to fuck me, but it's so much more than that.

"Layla?"

My throat is tight but I manage to say, "I didn't want to be alone."

"I think there's more."

I bite the inside of my cheek and shake my head.

"I won't press." He studies me for a long, long time and I resist the urge to fidget. "I'll be your company tonight."

Relief sweeps through me. I'll never be able to

express my gratitude and can only whisper, "Thank you."

His lips curve into a smile and he leans across the table and clasps my cold hands. "But, maybe someday, we'll have a chance to try again."

If only that was true, but it's not. Men like Chad don't last long and some lucky girl will snap him up. But I nod in agreement.

I'll save my arguments for another day when I'm not so desperate.

After a chaste brush of Chad's lips across my cheek, and a promise that he'd see me again, I make my way into the safety of my condo, dead bolting the door behind me. I kick off the heels I've been wearing and practically crawl onto my couch. A soft, dove-gray suede that's both modern and comfortable. John picked it out. I hadn't liked it at first, it didn't look cozy, but he'd talked me into it.

Of course, he'd been right, it was a dream of a couch.

I remember the day it was delivered. The guys had left, and before the door even clicked shut, John had my jeans stripped to my knees and me flipped over the arm. He'd teased me that day. Held me down and forced me to come over and over again until I was sweating and exhausted. After he declared the couch perfect for his purposes, I'd curled up under a white fluffy cover, so soft and luxurious it should be labeled illegal, and slept for hours. It was a good afternoon and this couch is still my favorite piece of comfort furniture.

Although neither of us could have predicted it would see more tears than laughter.

I glance at the clock, modeled after the one in Grand Central Station: it's twelve o'clock. The witching hour.

I've done it.

I've managed my way through the night. With the help of Chad, someone I actually like, that gave me a tiny sliver of hope for the future. And I'm thankful.

I close my eyes, anxious for those first moments of sleepiness to creep over me. But they don't come. Instead, an image of Michael, a man I have no business thinking about, fills my mind.

The lust and the want, peaceful the last couple of hours, roars back, erasing any chance of sleep in an instant. My nipples bead and my belly heats, and it comes, that inner demon that lives inside me.

It's not too late. An evil whisper tangles me in its twisted thoughts.

I suck in a breath. No. It is too late. He's gone, and even if he's not, I'm not going.

But now, the thought's in my head, taunting me.

I want to be strong, but he's like a compulsion.

What if he finds someone else? What if he picks some other woman? One that wouldn't dare resist?

I can see it, the pretty blonde girl in the red corset from the other night. But this time, it's not the big biker running his finger down her cheek, it's Michael. His mouth skimming down her neck, licking at her pulse. Their lips fused together.

The image of his mouth on hers is so vivid, so powerful, I bolt upright, my heart pounding.

No. It's too late.

It doesn't matter. If he finds someone else, I'm saved.

It's what I want.

I glance at my front door. My black stiletto heels are discarded on the floor.

Don't do it. The sane, rational part of me begs. But I already know the truth.

It's too late. I have to see.

Turns out, I've failed after all.

7.

My mad dash to the club has left me breathless, but at least I've stopped thinking. Stopped thinking about consequences, the angst, and just committed. It's the wrong decision, but a decision nonetheless.

That's what the craving does, makes nothing else matter.

The truth is I don't even know what I'm going to do when I see him, if I see him. I fly through the room, trench coat half hanging off my shoulders, ignoring the people, the flashing lights, the writhing bodies on the dance floor and the bass too loud in my ears. Finally, after what seems like one of those action dream sequences in movies where the corridor gets longer and longer the faster you run, I'm standing by the bar, in the exact spot I stood Thursday night.

Sweat trickles a fine path down my spine as I scan the room frantically.

There's no sign of him and my heart is pounding nearly out of my chest. I'm not sure if I'm terrified I will see him, or that I won't. Most likely both.

The place is in full swing, packed with a sea of bodies, making it impossible to find him in the crowd. I crane my neck, but I don't see anyone who looks like him. No one who makes my blood race or my knees weak.

Everyone I see looks ordinary. Not him.

I take in a deep lungful of humid air, thick from the press of too many bodies packed together. I wait.

And wait.

Sure if he sees me, if he's looking for me, he'll look here first.

One techno electronic song turns into another. Several men pass me by, looking me over, but I barely notice, they're simply white noise.

I wait some more.

Irrationally, I'm now in a panic that I'll never find him. My feet are restless to move, and I can no longer stand one more second of inaction. I have to look for him. I'll walk the perimeter until I'm satisfied I've lost him for good. Unsteady on my heels, I walk toward the farthest corner of the room and start making my way through the crowd.

What if he's in one of the theme rooms with someone else? What if I've been replaced by a girl not as complicated and fucked up as I am? What if I never see him again?

I forget all about my earlier resistance. Forget that I'm getting exactly what I wanted. Instead, I'm propelled by my need, and I focus on nothing but my search.

Face after face passes me—some young, some old, some handsome, some ugly—but none of them his.

What if I'm too late? Or simply, he decided I wasn't worth the effort. Which I'm not… I'll never be carefree and easy again. It's why I had to turn down someone as great as Chad. He deserves someone better, who doesn't have all my issues. He deserves a nice girl, although for his sake, I hope she's at least a little perverted.

Maybe Michael found someone just like that, and he's forgotten all about me. I don't know what to do with the knowledge or how the thought makes me sick to my stomach.

I make my way around a corner and my gaze inadvertently snags on a guy in his mid-thirties. He's got that mean look in his eye, that casual dismissiveness I usually glom on to. He's exactly the kind of man I'd normally go for. I can practically feel his coldness. How emotionally remote he is. How safe.

As I pass, he reaches out and grabs my arm. "And who do we have here? Aren't you a pretty little thing."

Before, I'd have gone right into mode, flashing him my cool, distant smile, engaging him just enough to give me the opportunity to outline my requirements. Momentarily, I still, thinking it through.

This man is not a threat. Michael is. Doesn't it make more sense to abandon this crazy search and go with the safe bet? This guy could give me what I've been getting from the club since the first time I showed up here—a calculated interaction filled with cruelty that will leave me empty and defeated.

My punishment.

There's that word again. Is that what this has been? Does it matter?

This man before me is the only thing I've ever wanted from this club, what I still want, but somehow, I can't. Can't force myself into the act one more time.

I pull my arm away. "Thanks, but I'm not interested."

His eyelids dip; casting his dark eyes in a hooded gaze that I'm positive drives women mad. "Are you sure about that? I can make it hurt real good, baby."

Sadist. A hard-core one, I'd guess.

"No, thank you." I move away before he can say anything else. Before he thinks I'm just being coy and want him to give chase.

Suddenly, I'm overcome by a deep sadness that sinks down so far inside me I feel like I'm drowning in it. My throat tightens, and I turn away, not sure where I'm going.

And, once again, I smack right into Michael.

I teeter, and his hands grasp my hips to steady me. His palms are so hot they're like a brand on my skin, burning me through the red jersey dress I wore tonight.

I stare at his chest, as broad and strong as I remember, in a black knit V-neck shirt. My relief is so powerful it scares me, and my flight response kicks into high gear even though I know I'm not going anywhere.

I steel my spine, pulling myself together to prepare myself for the smugness I'll find on his face. I look up and finally meet his hazel-eyed gaze.

The arrogance I'm expecting isn't there. I search and search, but can't find it. Instead, he studies me intensely, his brow furrowed in what I can only assume is concern.

He's here.

I blink.

And burst into tears.

"Sshhh," he murmurs, pulling me into his embrace and cradling me close. He strokes my hair before gliding down my spine. "It's okay, sugar."

I'm mortified. I should pull away, should run but I don't, I curl in deeper and suck in his spicy masculine scent.

"It's okay," he says again, his hands moving a slow path up and down my back.

It's not okay. With him, it will never be okay. I've come to him. I've broken the most important rule of all—never, ever get emotionally involved.

The lights and music pound away at me, beating to the frantic pace of my heart, throbbing against my temples.

My hands curl into fists so I'm not tempted to clutch at him. I want to trace the lines of his muscle, run my palms over his sure-to-be warm skin. I want his mouth all over mine. I need it. At the wrongness of my desire, I punch at his chest as I accuse, "You knew."

"Yes," he says, his tone soft as he wraps me up tighter. "I knew you'd come."

I want so badly for him to be annoyingly arrogant and filled with bluster, but he's none of that. He makes his statement as the simple truth. Nothing more. Nothing less. "How?"

"For the same reason I would have sat here and waited for you until the last person left and they kicked me out, locking the door behind me. Because sometimes you have no other choice."

I am shocked at his bluntness. That he would admit such a weakness. With tears still clinging to my lashes, I meet his gaze. "Why?"

"I don't know why." His voice is so confident and filled with strength I want to curl into it for a million years. He feels like safety and danger, all rolled together. His thumb swipes across my cheek, wiping the wetness away. "I only know when I look at you, you feel like you belong to me."

No! No! No! I shake my head, and move to step away, but, of course, he won't let me. I tilt my chin and say with as much determination as I can muster, considering I'm a watery, tear-streaked mess, "I can't belong to you, not now, not ever."

"You're wrong." Simple, sure words.

"No. I belong to someone else."

Hazel eyes flash with bright bits of green, before

they narrow. "And where is he?"

I blink, and another tear slips free. "He's dead."

The statement hangs in the air.

I can't believe I said it. That I've told him. It's another rule broken.

"I'm sorry." His fingers curl around my neck. "But you're still here."

I shake my head, but I'm not. That girl I was, the one I recognize as me, she's gone. I'm broken now, and momentary fleeting bits of lust and need are all I can manage.

Michael's lips brush my ear. "You are and this is real. Flesh and blood. You're not going to be able to escape it."

In that instant, everything inside me flares to greedy life. I bite down on my lip to keep from moaning. When I think I've got myself under control, I say, "Please, you need to leave me alone."

Someone bumps into us, jostling our bodies so we're pressed closer together. His erection brushes against my belly and my core gives a hard clench of demand. My body doesn't care about practicalities such as emotional danger.

His hand grips my neck tighter. "Is that why you're here, for me to leave you alone?"

"I don't know why I'm here." I only know I'm not strong enough to resist, which leaves his willpower as my last refuge of hope.

"Don't you?" His voice turns harder now, losing that soft edge of concern, and reminding me he expects to be in control.

"No."

He suddenly jerks, and the next thing I know I'm being pushed backward. He's walking so fast, practically carrying me as I stumble to keep up. I almost fall but the wall of the club catches me.

The cool of the building's concrete is a heady

contrast to the heat of Michael's strong, hard body. His entire length presses into me. Trapping me. Exciting me. Desire obliterates my fear as that feeling of helplessness takes hold of me.

His fingers encircle my wrists and I flinch away. "No, please, anything but that."

His gaze narrows, then he releases my hands. "What happened?"

"I can't." I shake my head, fighting the sudden, violent slash of images assaulting me.

Please, no, not now. Anything but this. The strobe lights over the dance floor flash before my eyes, disorientating me. I snap my lids close and feel the sting of a fist on my jaw.

Don't think about it. Don't. But it's too late.

The cold of the concrete at my back, it's just like before. I'm trapped. John crumpled to his knees.

I shudder.

The tight bind on my wrists. I can't move. I'm helpless.

My palms slick.

The duct tape over my mouth.

I can't breathe. Adrenaline races through my body, a mad rush that crushes my lungs.

I'm going to pass out.

The river of blood. John's blood and mine, mixing together, our lives joining for the last time.

My heart is going to explode. I'm going to die. Right here in this god-awful place.

A rush of panic consumes me, dulling my vision, putting me back in that alley, bruised and broken.

John's head on my lap. His vacant eyes staring up at me.

I want to scream, but nothing comes out. I cover my face and whisper, "No, no, no."

Over and over.

Suddenly, I'm ripped away from the brutal scene as

someone shakes me by the shoulders.

I lower my hands and clutch at a broad chest. Solid strength. Real. I gulp for air, the tight constriction binding my ribs loosens. The attack recedes and I'm once again in reality.

The music comes blaring back, anchoring me.

I blink. Look up.

It's Michael.

I feel vulnerable. Stripped and shaken. I peer into his not quite handsome face, with his compelling green-gold eyes, and his expression is filled with concern.

I'm shocked at the words that leave my lips. "Please, help me."

I have no idea what I'm asking for, only that I need something from him.

"I will, sugar." Gently, with the upmost care, he wraps me up in his arms. "Let me get you out of here."

I start shaking my head before he even has the sentence out. "I can't."

It's exactly what I want, but I can't. It's against the rules. I'm afraid. If we leave here, then he means something.

"You can, and you will." He leans away, and keeping one arm around my waist, he tilts my chin. "We're leaving. I'm going to take you to the little coffee shop a couple of blocks from here and we're going to sit down and talk like regular people."

No! I can't do that. I need to keep this contained. Isolated in this club. The room, the press of bodies, the loud music jacked up to accommodate the Saturday night crowd, the flashing strobe lights, I need all of it to maintain the façade. It's a layer of protection I've grown dependent upon.

In a flash, I realize, I don't want to be here. I fucking hate this place. My own little masochistic torture chamber. The knowledge doesn't change that I have to keep Michael here. Where he belongs. Locked away with the other nightmares.

He crooks my chin higher. "I'm not asking. I'm telling you."

All the noise in my head quiets. I can't think of a way to argue myself out of this. So I divert, ignoring the issue altogether. "What's wrong with you?"

He chuckles, and I realize how crazy that sounds, since I was the one in the middle of a full-blown panic attack. Steady now on my feet, some of my defensiveness rears up. "Are you some sort of glutton for punishment?"

His lips quirk. "Let's just say a damsel in distress appeals to me more than it should."

"So you have a hero complex."

He shrugs. "I'm a cop, it goes with the territory."

I jerk back, my eyes going wide in shock. This disturbs me on some deep level. I don't want to know anything about him—let alone to find out he's a cop. I don't like cops. They didn't help me. Or John. They ask questions. Questions that make you feel unclean. "You are not."

He reaches behind and pulls out a badge, handing it out to me. "Detective Michael Banks."

I take the badge and trace the line of the engraved star with my fingers. The words Chicago Police curved over the top and the word detective, plain as day, underneath.

This is the last thing I want him to be. I hand it back. "I should go."

"You're not going anywhere without me."

"You can't stop me."

One dark brow rises. "You sure about that?"

No, I'm not sure at all. Right now, I don't think there's anything he couldn't talk me into except handcuffs, which is why I need to leave. I'm already starting to feel as though he's a real person. That he's more than an object, existing only in this darkened room, to cure me of my cravings.

"Here's how we're going to do this," he says, his tone slightly amused but with an edge of command. "We are going to leave and walk to the coffee house. When we get there we are going to sit down and have a cup of coffee. This isn't open to debate. I won't touch you, but you are going to talk to me. Do you understand?"

I know how silly it sounds. How crazy it is to someone who doesn't have my tendencies. But his absolute certainty that I should obey, the perception that I don't have a choice in the matter, frees me in a way nothing else has in eighteen months. If I weren't so stripped away, so beaten, I'd ask him what would happen if I didn't understand or something equally sassy. But today, I don't have any fight left. I've been fighting him, our chemistry, my reactions and raging emotions for two long days, and I'm done. I've got nothing left.

I nod, and look over his shoulder. I'm breaking another rule. Because of him.

"Good." He grips my jaw and forces my gaze back to his. "Now, tell me, what is your name?"

Transfixed, I stare at him for a long, long time. The moment suspended. Freeze framed.

His attention doesn't waver from my face. I can't hide the truth, or myself.

Written in his expression, I know not telling him will be a deal breaker. If I want him, I have no choice. If I don't concede, I won't get another chance. That he has no need to explain this to me is a measure of his confidence, and of his certainty that in the end, I'll comply.

Which is why I didn't want to come to the club tonight in the first place. Detective Michael Banks is too impossible to resist. And furthermore, right now, I don't want to.

I take a deep breath and lick my parched lips. "My name is Layla Hunter."

8.

He knows my name. I can't believe I told him.

I sit across from Michael in a tiny, dimly lit, late-night coffee house at a complete loss for what to say. We'd walked in silence, ordered coffee in silence, and are now sitting in silence. I suspect he's giving me time to mellow out before he starts asking questions like the detective he is, and I appreciate the time, even while it grates on my nerves.

In the corner, next to the picture window overlooking the street, a guy with long blond hair, a graphic T-shirt, and jeans plays an acoustic guitar, singing *Hey There Delilah* in a smooth, mellow voice. I watch him with rapt attention, unwilling to look at the man I've broken so many rules for. Who's stripped away so many of my defenses.

I have no idea how to act out here in the real world. Michael is part of my dark, secret life, and sitting here with him evokes an irrational fear that everyone scattered about the cafe knows all of my secrets.

The night has been endless. Wrought with unexpected changes and outcomes. I feel like I've traveled a thousand miles since my date with Chad, who now seems like a distant dream. When I'd raced to the club, I'd convinced myself it was for sex, to satiate the need clawing away inside me. I still want to believe that, but how can I with Michael across from me, and I'm still untouched?

Out here in the real world, he's even more overpowering. He seems to fill up all the free space, but instead of the panic I should feel, I feel protected. And that scares me even more.

"Are you going to pretend you're sitting here alone?" Michael's deep voice reaches into my thoughts and pulls me back to the coffee shop.

I glance at him, and then look quickly back to the singer, tucked neatly into the corner. While it's one thirty, it's Saturday night, and we're in the heart of Wicker Park. The streets are still bustling from the bar crowd. A group of girls pass by, arms locked at the elbows as they wobble on too-high heels. They look happy and carefree and I find myself wistful for when I was just like them.

"Layla." Michael's tone is commanding, speaking to that twisted part inside me that feels compelled to obey.

I've fought enough. I have no sass in me. I reluctantly turn my attention away from the slice of normal life to the man that threatens everything I've come to depend on.

The round table, cluttered with our two cups of coffee, looks far too small for him. Almost like he's sitting at the kid's table. Anxious to focus on something innocuous, I tilt my head, and ask, "How tall are you?"

He smiles. "Six-five."

I'm five-seven, hardly short, but I feel positively tiny next to him. "That's tall."

"Yeah, it is."

John was an average five-ten.

What would it be like to have Michael's big body moving between my legs? His size alone is enough to threaten. Intimidate. My thighs squeeze involuntarily as the image fills my head. I should be thinking of John, not Michael. I glance down at my coffee, staring at the creamy leaf design made from skim milk by the barista, bleeding into the darker liquid.

"What we're you thinking, just then?"

I shake my head. No way will I make that confession.

He chuckles, the sound low and sexy, sending goose bumps racing over my skin. "All right, sugar, I'll let you have your secrets."

Since my panic attack has worn off, and I've recovered, all of my physical responses are flooding back. Somewhere, I find a bit of defiance hidden in some secret reserve. I cup my hands around the warm cup. "This is a one-time thing."

"No, it's not." There's still none of that cocky arrogance I'm used to hearing from guys like him, Instead, he states everything as fact, as though I have no say in the matter.

Of course, that the presumption flips my switch, as much as it irritates me, is just another example of life's twisted sense of humor. I take a deep breath and try to get this situation under control. "Look, thank you for helping me, and I'm sorry I freaked out on you, but I don't see people outside the club. Not now. Not Ever."

He leans back in his chair and I try desperately not to stare at the expanse of his chest, or the flatness of his stomach. Even through the thick cotton of his black shirt I can see how hard his muscles are. How defined. "I don't doubt that's true, but you're going to be seeing me outside of that club, so you might as well get used to it."

"No." I shake my head, scowling. "You don't understand."

"I understand more than you think, Layla." The chair squeaks across the floor as he leans over the table. "I told you, warned you, that first night, we're not playing by your rules."

I straighten, snapping back, "What makes you think you have a say in what I do?"

His jaw hardens, transforming into that stubborn line that sends my blood racing. "Coyness doesn't suit you."

"I'm not being coy."

"Bullshit." His gaze narrows, turning dangerous and mean. The air practically sparks with electricity. "I might not know much about you, but don't kid yourself into thinking that I don't know exactly how you're wired."

I can't figure out if I'm plain stupid or insane, but I find I want to push him. I tilt my chin high in the air. "You don't know the first thing about it."

A muscle in his jaw jumps and those hazel eyes flash. He flexes both hands. "I can't wait until I take you over my knee. Because I am going to smack the hell out of you."

My whole body flares to life like a match. I gulp.

He leans closer, and my breath stops. "Maybe I should take you into the bathroom and do it right now, just so I can get it out of my system." Another flex of those long fingers.

Yes. I shift, already able to feel his palm on my skin. The pain and searing heat of that first strike. The image is so vivid I can almost feel the wetness that would trickle down my thighs as I pray for him to stop, and beg for him to continue.

It's been so, so long since I felt that indefinable *it*. Since I wasn't going through the motions like I was doing penance.

His gaze dips to my mouth. "You'd like that, wouldn't you? You can already feel my hand on your ass."

I have no words to speak. I'm completely mesmerized. My nipples pull into tight peaks and that slow, insistent ache fills my lower belly.

I want him. So badly it terrifies me.

He gives me a slow, wicked once-over that feels like a tease against my skin. "I'd take you by the hair and force you to watch every single reaction in the mirror."

My pulse pounds. I want, no…need, everything he's describing. I lean into his words as my fingers grip the ceramic mug hard enough to shatter.

He pulls back, reclining lazily in the chair. His expression turns arrogant, sly. "Yeah, I don't know shit, do I?"

I grit my teeth to fight against a wave of frustration that makes me want to scream *I hate you* at the top of my lungs. I force the words back into my throat and purposefully relax my hold on the cup, and say flippantly, "Nope, nothing at all."

He laughs, an amused, hearty, good-natured sound. That one response says so much about him. It tells me that he doesn't take himself too serious. That he's confident in his control. And most importantly, that he can handle someone like me, who will never follow every command, even if I want to.

The struggle is part of my nature, it's always been that way, and I don't expect it will ever change. I need dominance. Need to be controlled and forced. But sitting at some guy's feet, serenely staring into space as I wait for my next order is never going to be my thing. I will not go gentle into that good night.

I blow out a breath I hadn't realized I held. Part of me hoped for a different response, one that would make him less irresistible, but I can see nothing with Michael will be easy.

He grins, and it transforms his face into something rakishly charming and equally lethal. "You know, Layla, you don't have to angle for a spanking."

I get a quick flash of what it would be like to be with him. Really be with him. He'd be fun, infuriating, intimidating and always get his way.

Not happy I can see it so clearly, I frown. "I'm not!"

His grin grows even wider, and his attention drops to my lips. "Give me what I want, and I'll give you what you need."

"What do you want?" I cringe, hating the desperation in my voice.

"You."

That's what I was afraid of. Because he doesn't mean my body, he means me, stripped away and raw, completely exposed. And that's something I can't ever give him. I shake my head. "You don't even know me."

"Maybe not yet," he says, and that sureness I hate, but need, is back. "But I will, soon enough."

I have no idea what to do. I'm totally lost. I can't put him back into a box. He'll never be contained, and I don't know how to resist him. I only see one option—to tell him the truth. To lay myself bare for one fraction of a moment so he'll see, and rightly leave.

My throat constricts and I force myself to meet his gaze even though I can already feel the welling in my eyes. "You don't understand." My voice cracks. "I am a total, fucked-up mess. Sometimes I can barely make it through the day. I have nothing to give."

His jaw hardens, and he places his elbows on the

table and leans close. "What happened?"

I have to tell him at least the bare minimum. "My fiancé died three weeks before our wedding. The grief..." I swallow; my throat so full it feels like it's been stuffed with cotton. "I'm having a hard time moving on."

It's enough to scare most people away. To make even the most tenacious think twice.

His expression turns suspicious and I have no trouble picturing him as the cop he is. "There's more."

I don't want to continue down this path. "Isn't that enough?"

He focuses on me so directly he may as well have pinned me to the chair. "I'm a homicide detective; you don't think I recognize the signs of trauma when I see it?"

I flinch, suddenly cold. I pull my trench coat from the back of my chair and wrap it around my shoulders.

"What happened?" he asks, continuing ruthlessly.

I press my lips together not wanting to speak the words, but knowing I have to, as surely this will make him drop it. "He was murdered."

Michael's eyes turn a cold shade of greenish gold. "How?"

The alley. The blood. John's head in my lap. My restrained wrists. The cold concrete. The pain. It all flashes through my mind in nightmarish vividness. "I don't want to discuss it."

I see the exact second comprehension dawns. He shakes his head as though filled with disgust. "Fuck. You were there, weren't you?"

He doesn't need to know the rest, that's enough for any sane man to run for the hills. I curl tighter into my coat, my chill bone deep. "I don't want to discuss it."

Michael studies me for a long, long time, then reaches across the table and takes my ice-cold fingers in his.

His hand is warm, almost hot. Big and strong and oh so capable. The veins weave an intricate path under his skin and I long to trace them, to know him. His fingers are long, his nails blunt and clean. He has the kind of hands that makes a girl feel safe. It makes me all the more vulnerable as I desperately miss feeling safe. My own fingers twitch, I want to take hold and never let go, so I force myself to remain limp.

"I'm not going to push you tonight, Layla." His voice is achingly soft. "But someday, you're going to tell me."

I can see it. See how he'd wrap his arms around me and keep the nightmares away. I shake my head. "That day will never come."

He shrugs, and squeezes my fingers. "I'm not going to waste my breath arguing with you when I know I'm right."

Why is he so damn sure? Why can't he see I'm too broken to ever be put back together again? I pull my hand away and shove it under the table where he can't reach me. "What do you want from me?"

"I want to know you."

"There's nothing to know."

"You're wrong."

I blow out a breath of frustration. "There are a million girls out there, ones that will give you want you want without any trouble or complication at all."

He smiles. "If I didn't like complication, I'd have gone into finance like my dad wanted me to."

My head snaps back, so taken aback by this slice of normalcy I ask stupidly, "You have a dad?"

He laughs. "Of course. I also have a mom and two sisters."

"You do?" I don't know why this astounds me. What did I think, that he was hatched? It just seems so…ordinary.

"I get up, put my pants on one leg at a time. I hang

out with friends, work too much, and go to my parents' house for Sunday dinner." He leans forward and says in a mock whisper, "I even have a dog."

"Really?" In my head I've built him up into some sort of rogue fallen angel sent from hell to torture me.

"Really." He takes a sip of coffee before reaching into his jean's pocket and digging out an iPhone. He works his thumb across the screen then hands the phone to me. "An eighty-pound mutt who thinks she's a lap dog."

I stare down at a picture of one of the ugliest dogs I've ever seen. Big, with mangy fur of black, brown and white, the dog sits with its head resting on its paws, looking up into the camera like the most pitiful creature ever. The image is calendar-worthy adorable.

"I found her scrounging through my garbage one morning near starving."

I give him back the phone. "She's cute."

He grins, his expression one I've seen my brother-in-law wear when looking at his daughters. Complete, blind devotion. "She's a total con artist."

"What's her name?"

"Belle. Amy, my niece, named her. Belle is her favorite princess."

He even has a niece? I can only blink at him, amazed. Not sure if I'm terrified or happy to find out he's human after all.

He holds his hands wide and shrugs. "See, I'm just a regular guy."

I want to shove him back into the mold I cast for him, but I can't. Instead, I can't stop picturing him with that mangy-looking, adorable dog sitting on his lap.

He leans back on the chair, completely relaxed. "What about you?"

I'm so taken by this domestic image of him, I have no idea what he's talking about. "What about me?"

"Do you have family?"

Off in the corner, the guitarist strums the first few notes of *Here Comes the Sun* and a chill races down my spine. He needs someone perfect to complete the image, but it's not me. I long, more than ever, to be that girl I once was.

I push a lock of hair off my cheek. "You should go find yourself a nice girl."

"I don't want nice," he says, his voice dropping an octave. "I want you."

"You don't know me." Attempting to appeal to his logic. "It's the chemistry messing with your brain."

"I will know you." He gives me a lazy smile. "And don't knock it, mad, crazy chemistry doesn't come along very often, which is why it's impossible to ignore."

I fight the urge to slip into normal girl mode and pretend, if even for a second, but I can't. It's too dangerous. And he's too tempting. "I'm damaged."

"Yeah, I know," he says, like it's no big deal.

Suddenly, I remember his story of how he came to own his dog, and I bristle. "Is that your thing? Rescuing strays? Because I want no part of it."

"Yeah, I know that too, you'd rather wallow in it." There's no softness or apology in the words.

I've become so use to people tiptoeing around me, I snap back as though he's slapped me. "Fuck you. You don't know the first thing about it."

I am *not* wallowing.

My outburst doesn't appear to faze him because he looks as calm as ever. "It's not going to work, Layla."

"What?" I'm so stung with hurt I can barely croak out the question. It's so easy for everyone to say, but they don't have to live with it. They can escape, forget, pretend but I don't have that luxury.

"You're not going to scare me off," he continues without mercy. "You, your story, whatever happened to you, it does not scare me. I see horrible, inhumane shit every day. I'm not squeamish. So you'll have to think of something else to push me away."

I feel beaten, bruised and so damn fragile I want to scream. I stare into the coffee I haven't touched and whisper, "I want to go home."

I need to curl up on my comfort couch.

I steel my spine, waiting for an argument that doesn't come. "All right, I'll take you home."

Because I'm twisted, and clearly insane, bitter disappointment stings the back of my throat. I shove my arms in my coat. "No thanks, I'll find my own way."

"You will not." That hard, determined do-not-fuck-with-me tone.

"I will." It's bad enough he knows my name; I can't let him see where I live.

"Layla, look at me." He's speaking in a voice I can't resist.

That part of me I've never been able to understand, is compelled to respond. I obey, but make no effort to hide my defiance with a sullen twist of my lips.

"I'm bigger than you, and stronger," he says in an implacable, reasonable voice. "I will pick you up and carry you over my shoulder to the car if I have to and no one will stop me. Now are we going to do this the hard way, or the easy way?"

I am at his mercy. I want to be strong and walk away, or at least try, but deep down I know the truth. As furious as I am, I don't want him to let me go.

It kills me to admit, even to myself.

I throw up my hands, trying to save face and snap, "Fine, but don't touch me."

An amused chuckle, that sounds like nails on a chalkboard, even as it heats my belly. "Done."

I blow out an exasperated breath. "You are so twisted."

"Sugar, you have no idea."

Twenty minutes later, I'm standing in front of my front door irrationally irritated I'm untouched. The tension between us is pulled so tight it might snap at any moment. I spent the drive home in a state of deranged flux, ranging from bursting into tears, starting world war three, or climbing on top of him and begging him to fuck me.

He, on the other hand, couldn't have seemed more relaxed. He'd kept the conversation light and easy, sticking to banal subjects like the weather and the current political scandal. He didn't seem like he struggled at all to keep his promise.

Which, of course, just makes him all the more irresistible.

I fumble for my key, silently swearing. I want him to force me. Force his way into my condo, into my bed, and into my body.

Into my life.

But he won't. And I hate his ironclad control almost as much as it excites me.

I slip my key into the lock and twist, opening it a fraction of an inch, before he covers my hand and pulls the door shut.

My heart starts to pound. I'm no longer strong enough to deny him. I want his mouth on mine. My head tilts, and my loose hair spills to the side, exposing my neck. Breath stuttering, I close my eyes, almost able to feel the first brush of his mouth on my skin. The heat of his body warms me through my coat and I have to lock my legs to keep from leaning back.

That's all it would take. One. Lean. Back.

My lids snap open and I rush back to reality when he presses a small card into my palm. It's a department-issued business card with all his information on it. It has his work number, cell, and in black ink written in strong, bold script is his home number.

He braces his hand on the side of my doorframe, crowding me without laying one finger on me. "If you need to reach me."

"I won't," I say automatically, but take the card anyway.

"You will need me," he whispers, raising the fine hairs along the nape of my neck. "But I know you're too stubborn to call."

"Then why give me your numbers at all?" I close my eyes again, not wanting to go inside and end this yet, but I'll have to soon enough. Selfishly, I just want to enjoy this, his body close, the desire and anticipation zinging between us, if only for a second.

"Because, I hope I'm wrong."

"You're not."

"I know." He presses closer, but still manages to keep the smallest of space between us.

It's so frustrating I could scream. If I just lean back, he'd take it as the surrender it would be. But, as he already explained, I'm too stubborn for that.

It's why I need to be taken and forced in the first place.

So here we stand, so close, yet not nearly close enough. Our breathing seems to synchronize into short, agonizing puffs of air.

"I want to touch you, Layla." His voice a low rasp.

I squeeze my eyes shut tighter.

"I want to flip up that dress, rip off your panties, and take you right where you stand."

I bite my lip to keep from groaning.

"Jesus, I don't think I've ever wanted a woman this much. You're like a fucking drug."

I blink my eyes open, unable to believe what I'm hearing. I grit my teeth as I watch his fingers flex on the doorframe as though he means to rip the wood from the wall.

"But, I'm keeping my promise. Not only to show you I always keep my word, but also to teach you to be careful for what you ask for." He bends his head, and I can feel his breath as his mouth trails down my neck. I grind my teeth in frustration as his lips graze over the finest of hairs, but never make contact.

Sensation explodes over my skin and I gasp as an inferno builds between my legs. I whisper an urgent, "Please." Not sure if I'm asking him to stop or continue.

"No," he says.

The disappointment that washes over me gives me my answer. I want him to continue. I feel empty knowing he won't. I lean my forehead against the door. If I don't get space, I'll start begging, so I manage to croak, "I need to go in now."

He shifts behind me, and I have no idea what he's doing until thirty seconds later he holds out a small pad of paper and a pen. "Give me your home and cell number."

I can only stare at the offending objects. "No, I can't."

"I'm not asking. Give them to me, or I'll get them myself, but understand you will be hearing from me."

I grumble and take the pen, scribbling my numbers on the paper like a good little girl. "There, are you happy?"

"Yep," he says simply and the pen and paper disappear.

Out of nowhere, surprising me as nothing else about this night has, a smile twitches at my lips. A real, genuine, spontaneous smile that hasn't graced my face since John died. I clear my throat, as a small bubble of laughter fills my chest. I cough it down. It unnerves me, frightens me.

I've barely thought about John. Even worse, I don't want to think about him.

"Turn around and look at me," Michael says, and again, it's not a request.

Once I have my stoic mask back on, I don't even bother trying to fight, and turn around.

His hazel eyes flash with what I can only assume is approval. "I'm on call the next five nights, but Friday, you are mine."

Heat and desire flare to life. "And if I say no."

He bends at the knees so his face is close to mine. "Sugar, no isn't an option here."

Something entirely devious tickles my belly. "No."

He grins. "Someday soon you're going to have to start paying up on all these challenges."

I cross my arms over my breasts, hoping to hide my beaded nipples. "It's not a challenge. It's a refusal."

He laughs and chucks me under the chin. "Friday night. Seven o'clock."

He turns and starts to walk away and I call after him, "I won't be here."

He swivels around and walks backward toward the elevator, giving me an obscenely, exaggerated perusal. "Yes, you will be."

Yeah, he's right, I will.

9.

"So, how'd it go?" April asks, a big, goofy grin on her face. She's practically giddy with excitement, standing in her expansive dream of a kitchen, filled with all the latest commercial stainless steel appliances, custom distressed white cabinets, and Italian marble countertops. April and Derrick live in a six thousand square foot house in Barrington. Land of the one acre lots and open concept floor plans.

My brother-in-law lounges on the couch in the great room, watching the football pre-shows before the Sunday game starts, while my nieces build a city of pink, green and white Legos on the coffee table.

They're the perfect picture of domestic bliss.

My sister decided to throw together an impromptu brunch and my parents should be here any minute. I wanted to say no, but couldn't. I'd said no the last three times and that's my quota. Besides, my family is worried about me, and this visit will assure them that I'm not about to slit my wrists.

I'll never tell them that wasn't always the case, it would break their hearts, and I can't bear that. They'd never rest easy knowing how many times those first six months I sat huddled up on the shower floor with a razor in my hands, the sharp edge gleaming under the rainfall of water. But I've come through that hurdle. I guess that's one good thing about me, through it all, I could never put the blade to my wrist. Even at my absolute worst and most desolate, some part of me clung to life.

"Come on," April says, pulling me back from those dark times. "Don't leave me in suspense."

My brow pulls together. I have no idea what she's talking about, and in a moment of pure panic, I think she means Michael before logic prevails. There's no way she could know about him. I search my mind and come up blank, finally asking, "How'd what go?"

She blows out an exasperated puff of air. "Your date with Chad."

Oh, that. My date seems like a lifetime ago, and my head is so full of Michael, I'd forgot all about him.

I look at my sister, standing with her hip propped against the counter in her skinny jeans, knee-high Frye boots, and winter-white sweater. Her hair is pulled back into a ponytail, and her sky-blue eyes are even more vivid with artful makeup in shades of brown to complement her fading tan. She looks fresh faced and gorgeous, like an advertisement for upscale, weekend casual.

Her expression is so painfully hopeful; I can't help but throw her a bone, especially after our disastrous lunch. "It went really well. He's great. Your husband has good taste in men."

It's the truth. That I'm conveniently leaving out my desperate lust for a homicide detective that eclipses every man I know, including my dead fiancé, is despite the point.

Derrick, my handsome brother-in-law, with his sandy-blond hair and brown eyes, holds up a beer bottle in salute, never leaving his position on the couch. "See, I told you that you were worrying for nothing."

April clasps her hands together in what can only be glee. "Oh, Layla, I'm so glad. I drove Derrick crazy all night."

He finally looked away from their sixty-five-inch flat screen to grin at me. "I had to pry the phone from her hands more than once."

I roll my eyes and shake my head. "He was a perfect gentleman and very nice company. There was nothing to worry about."

A timer dings and April flits over to the stove to remove her homemade cranberry muffins. "Are you going to go out again?"

"I don't know," I say, evading. I don't want to give her false hope but I don't want to cruelly dash it either. To divert her attention, and mine, I glance around. "Is there anything I can do?"

April places the steaming muffin pan on the Viking range to cool. "Nope, everything is ready to go."

Of course it is. My sister inherited the domestic goddess gene from our great Aunt Betty, whose parties are still legendary in some circles. All the food is already in various ovens and warming drawers, the mimosas are chilling in the fridge, and April's table is already set.

The center of the dining table holds a magnificent arrangement of fresh flowers in different shades of light green and creamy white. I'd bet a million dollars April arranged them instead of a florist. They're packed with flowers, with zero filler, and have her signature all over them. Crystal candlesticks, with lime-green pillars flank each side and various baubles adorn the table. Cloth napkins rolled around silverware and decorated with rings of glitzy green and silver beads lay across crisp, white china plates. Each place setting has a crystal champagne flute and matching water glass.

Her table looks ready for a Martha Stewart photo shoot. Better actually.

Would I have been like this if John hadn't died? Would I be designing my own tablescapes by now? This thought sends me tumbling head first down the "what if" path. Would we have moved out of the city into a starter-size version of this one? Would I have been pregnant by now? We'd loved kids and neither one of us had wanted to wait long. I can almost picture him here, sitting on the couch with Derrick, discussing the upcoming games. I place a hand to my flat belly and experience a pang of loss so deep it takes my breath away.

I want to be normal again.

A soft hand cups my shoulder. So deep in thought, I jerk back and find April staring at me with a frown of concern. "Are you okay?"

"I'm fine." My standard white lie nobody believes. I blink, and clear my throat of its sudden tightness.

She searches my face, and opens her mouth to speak, but before she can say anything the front doorbell chimes, and my parents call out in greeting.

Saved by the bell from further probing.

My two darling nieces jump up and race to the door squealing, "Grandma, Grandpa." They adore my parents. As well they should.

My mom bustles into the room followed by my dad, their arms filled with bags and a big white box obviously from a bakery.

Sonya claps her hands and yells, "Doughnuts!"

Sasha tugs at her Grandmother Clara's hand. "Did you bring chocolate?"

My mom, still an attractive woman at sixty with her artfully highlighted blonde hair and blue eyes that match her daughters, smiles in obvious delight. "I did."

"And powdered sugar?" Sonya asks about her favorite.

"Of course," my mom says.

April shakes her head. "You shouldn't have. I've got plenty."

Clara waves her away, giving her a quick kiss on the cheek before putting the boxes on the island.

Sonya turns to my dad. "We built our Lego friends you gave us for our birthday. We have a whole town."

My father laughs, and ruffles her spun-gold hair. "Sounds impressive."

My parents, expressions filled with happiness, turn and see me. Instantly, their faces transform into twin masks of concern. Like all the joy has been sucked out of them.

My stomach twists.

It's how they look at me now. It's not their fault. They don't mean it. In truth, they probably don't even realize it. They're so worried about me all the time they can't help themselves.

I ignore how it hurts me, how responsible I feel, and determinedly plaster a smile on my face. "Mom, Dad. How are you?"

"You came." My mom's tone clearly states she wasn't expecting me.

"Yeah," I say lamely. "I missed the last few."

Robert, my father, gray and partially bald now, walks over and pats me awkwardly on the shoulder. "It's good to see you. You look well."

"Thanks." It's a lie. I look horrible. The mirror this morning wasn't kind. I can no longer hide the dark shadows under my eyes with makeup. I'm pale and wan, my cheekbones too defined, making me appear gaunt. My clothes, a pair of baggy jeans and long tunic, hang on my frame. I look unkempt, like I'm recovering from an illness. And standing next to April with her fresh, golden beauty, that screams vitality and health, I'm positive the difference is quite startling. Quite concerning.

My mom frowns even while she gives me a hug and a kiss on the cheek. "I'm so happy to see you, my baby."

"Thanks, Mom. You too."

Now that the pleasantries are over, an uncomfortable silence permeates the kitchen before my mom shifts her attention to the twins. "Come, Sasha and Sonja, and show me what you built."

My nieces are only too happy to drag them away.

I watch them, feeling wistful, as Derrick gets up from the couch and shakes my dad's hand before hugging my mom.

It pains me that my parents don't know how to talk to me anymore. I can't blame them. I don't make it easy on them. They don't know what to say to this damaged daughter that's replaced their fun, happy one.

What happened, it's like an elephant in the room, sitting there blocking all the light. My family thinks I avoid them because it's too hard for me, and I'm too desolated by grief to make it through a family event. And that might have been true at first, but now, I just can't stand how uncomfortable I make them.

When I'm not around they can forget, be happy. I want that for them.

They think this is all about John, but they don't understand, when I lost him, I lost them all.

I'm a stranger now, walking among them, but essentially alone.

It's nine thirty on Sunday night and I'm lying in bed, curled under the covers trying desperately to think of John and failing miserably. It's Michael who's captured my attention and he's pervasive. All consuming.

Just thinking about him makes me wet and I've been resisting the urge to rub my clit and quell some of this god-awful desire. I don't know why I'm resisting. It's silly, considering he'd never know, but that stubborn part of me doesn't want to give him the satisfaction, even though I'm only hurting myself.

My nipples pull tight, taunting me further.

I try and focus on the time John made me go to work with no underwear and tortured me the entire day with dirty text messages and even dirtier phone calls. I try to recall how he sent me to the bathroom over and over again to bring myself close to orgasm but never go over.

But the image doesn't stick.

Michael's face keeps replacing my fiancé's and I hate him for that. Even as my body burns. I'm not even thinking of anything kinky or obscene, instead I can't stop obsessing about his mouth. I've memorized its shape, the fullness, the cruel curve of his upper lip. The way he smiles.

How would his mouth feel on mine? His tongue. The scrape of his teeth on my soft flesh.

I groan and give in to temptation, pulling at the hard buds through my nightgown. My head relaxes into the pillow as I picture his lips tugging at my breasts.

I want to think about John, like I always do when I'm desperate to come and needy, but I can't.

Instead, I replay my encounter with Michael in the hall. What would have happened if he touched me? Would he have fucked me right in the corridor where any of my neighbors could have seen? Would I have wanted him too?

Right now, my body on fire, the answer is yes. I've always liked danger. Liked the risk of public disclosure. My fingers slide down my belly. I can't resist.

The phone rings, and I let out a startled scream, my palm covering my suddenly pounding heart. I look at the caller ID—private. It's possible it's a telemarketer, but I already know it can only be one person.

I press my lips together.

It rings again.

My fingers clutch the sheets. *Ignore it.*

Another ring.

One more and it will go to voice mail.

After a quarter of a ring, my willpower crumbles and I snatch the phone from the receiver. My voice is entirely too breathless when I say, "Hello."

"Hello, Layla." It's him. Of course, it's him.

"Why are you calling me?" I snap rudely, ignoring the leap of excitement at the sound of his voice.

"I told you I would."

Irrationally, I feel like he can see me, that he knows I was about to touch myself while thinking about him. "You said you were on call."

"I am," he says, the deep rasp of his voice causing a shiver down my spine. "I just got home."

I can't help but wonder what home looks like. Is he sitting on his couch? Lying in bed? Is the TV on in the background? I hate that I'm so curious about his life. I don't want to be, but I can't help myself. I want him back in the club, where he belongs, but refuses to stay put.

I've known him four days and he's already invading my life.

"Are you tucked into bed like a good little girl?" His tone amused.

I shift, sitting up and leaning against the headboard. "It's early." I refuse to acknowledge the little girl comment.

"Too early for bed?"

I glance around my bedroom, unable to shake the feeling he's spying on me and knows all my secrets. "I don't want you calling me."

"Liar."

I bite back a growl of irritation. Because, of course, he's right. I was preoccupied all day wondering if he'd call. At April's house I kept my cell phone in the back pocket of my jeans instead of stuffed in my purse like normal. When I went to the bathroom, I'd checked to make sure it hadn't switched to vibrate, and then got completely annoyed at how much I cared. Earlier this evening, I couldn't stop shooting sidelong glances at the phone or the anxious welling of hope that I'd hear from him. When I picked up the phone to make sure it had a dial tone, I gave up and went to bed.

Not that I'd admit any of this in a million years.

Instead, I say haughtily, "Has it occurred to you that I haven't thought about you at all?"

He laughs, a low rumble of a sound that races over my skin as though he's touched me. "No, not even for a minute."

He's baiting me; I know he's baiting me. It's a tactic John used to employ all the time. I shouldn't rise to the bait but, for a girl like me, it's impossible to resist. "Are you really that arrogant?"

"Of course." There's a pause over the line. "But that's not why."

"I'm not going to ask." I hold my breath, wanting him to push on.

"You don't want to know?"

"No. Don't bother." So stubborn. John used to say it was my biggest weakness, what he could count on to be my undoing.

I haven't changed.

A long pause. "Have it your way."

I want to scream in frustration. He knows I want to know, but now I've gone and trapped myself, which he probably anticipated all along. I shake my head. "You're impossible."

"You're not exactly a cake walk, sugar."

I find another wayward smile tugs at my lips. Am I enjoying this? No. I can't be. I quickly transform the quivering of my mouth into a frown. "Then you should make it easy on yourself and walk away."

"Tell me the truth, Layla," he says, his tone dropping an octave. "Do you really want that?"

Yes, of course. I need to stay safe and he's not safe. He's dangerous. He's already making me forget. I believe this wholeheartedly and I want to say the words, but they stick in my throat and refuse to budge.

"You don't," he continues, so sure his confidence practically reaches through the phone and grabs me. "So be a good girl and stop pretending otherwise."

The sound of him calling me a good girl sends a shock wave through me, heating me in a place I thought long dead. I let out an exasperated screech. "Do not call me good girl."

He just laughs, obviously enjoying himself.

Through gritted teeth I spit out, "Can I help you?"

"Yes," he says, his amusement clear as day over the line. "Tell me what you did today."

"Why?" I ask, instantly suspicious.

"Because I want to know how you spent your Sunday."

My stomach takes a wild jump. This is too normal of a discussion. Too innocuous. I'd be more comfortable if he'd talk dirty to me. I can't pretend this is impersonal if he asks me about my day. "What does it matter?"

"It matters, because I say it does."

A spark, one I haven't felt in a long, long time ignites. I'm not sure what it is, interest, life, or just plain hope. The last thing I want to do is look too deep, because I'm not sure I'll like the answer.

I bite the inside of my lip.

"Layla," he says, his tone losing all traces of

amusement. "It's a simple question and I expect a simple answer."

I remain silent. Why can't he just stay in the box I put him?

It's subtle, this interplay between us, but he's once again backed me into a corner. I recognize this is my fault for making a big deal out of the question in the first place, but now that I have, I'm stuck. If I answer, I give in. If he lets me slide, he gives in.

He waits.

I wait.

The desire to give him what he wants fills me like an ever-expanding balloon. I grow tight with the need to burst. I close my eyes, breathing into the phone. If I answer, I instinctively know all bets are off. Acknowledging without words my rules no longer matter. That I'm in this, and he has power over me.

Finally, I hear a sigh and my lids snap open. Did he break?

"Are you going to tell me or not?" He doesn't sound happy.

My heart starts to pound and I lower my head. I can't do it. I can't give in. This time it's not stubbornness, it's because I want it so bad. Michael makes me remember what it is like to live. And I'm afraid.

Since I started going to the club I've never had a problem walking away. If a guy wouldn't do what I wanted, I didn't look back, just moved on until I found someone who would. Having real control over me, having a say, that's reserved for John. And only John.

That I want, more than anything, to open my mouth and speak the answer Michael is waiting for is why I must say nothing.

"Goodbye, Layla."

His words startle me, although they shouldn't have. A needy, desperate panic speeds through me, and I immediately want to take it all back, but it's too late.

He's already gone.

When the dial tone rings in my ear, I finally put down the phone only to realize tears are streaming down my face. I've broken my rules for him, I've come for him, and now I've wept for him.

But it's done, and I don't have to worry any longer.

Tomorrow, I'll be relieved, but tonight, I cry.

10.

I was wrong. I'm not relieved. In fact, I'm more lost than ever.

My breath steams the air and I shiver in the cold. It's autumn and the weather holds the first hints of winter. The sky is gray with a heavy cloud cover and everything has turned from the lush colors of fall to a bleak and dull monotone.

Appropriate, considering I'm standing over John's grave.

The last time I was here was two months ago with his mom. We celebrated his thirty-second birthday together. The flowers have changed since I was here last. Dead brown, gold, and red Gerbera daisies, replaced the white roses we'd brought. John's mom has been here. It reminds me I need to call Mary, my mother-in-law-to-be, and invite her for lunch. After, we'll visit this cemetery and have our own private mourning ritual where we can talk about him without judgment.

I suck in a deep breath and let the cold do its work, numbing me. This wasn't how I'd intended to spend my lunch hour, but I feel so far away from John. So alone, and I need him. Need to remember how easy it was between us. How right.

We might have burned up the sheets, but our relationship had been easy. Nothing like the volatile, chaotic storm of emotions I experience with Michael.

How it was with John, that's the way it's supposed to be. Roller coasters are only fun when you know you're safe, and only John can give me that. Michael is like taking a ride on the X-flight without a lap harness.

A hot tear slips down my cold cheek as I stare at John's name scrolled across his gray tombstone with blurry vision. The word *Beloved* is under the dates of his life and death. When he died he wasn't a husband, but we were so close to the wedding he was no longer just a son. In the end Mary and I decided on that one simple word. It encompasses all that he was to us. The date of his death mocks me. It's so final and absolute. No amount of wishing or longing will ever bring him back.

His life is over, all because of a stupid, selfish mistake I made. By all rights I should be lying next to him. That was the plan; the knife had been at my throat. My attacker had already made a nick, taunting me, as his friends held me down. John lay dead, sprawled across the concrete. Once the worst was over they were quick to finish the job. The first trickle of blood had run down my neck, and I'd been prepared to welcome death.

Only fate had saved me.

The first swell of panic threatens to engulf me. Consume me in its fiery, insistent fear. I recognize the signs now, the rush of adrenaline, the too fast beat of my heart, the crushing of my lungs, but knowing stops nothing. Unsteady, I take deep, huge gulps of air, bracing my hand on John's grave as I start to hyperventilate.

I'm going to die.

I'm right there, back in that alley with a knife at my throat and I'm going to die. I shake my head, willing the images that bombard me to abate, focusing on John's name etched in stone.

But it doesn't work.

I'm there.

I can smell the stale cigarettes on their breaths.

Hear the tear of fabric as they shred my blouse.

A scream wells in my throat, coming out as a strangled sob.

I close my eyes and see…Michael. His image slices through my panic and shakes me from the memory. Reality rushes back like a freight train and I'm once again standing in the cemetery with the gray, cold sky above me. I'm breathing fast. Too *fast*. I'm lightheaded and my vision swims. I force myself to slow down so I don't pass out. In my head, I chant the calming mantra Dr. Sorenson has given me to help manage my attacks.

My free hand covers my face as I weep. I've cried entire rivers and I wonder if I'll ever run dry. When my heart rate finally begins to calm, John's grave comes back into focus. Residual anxiety still courses through my veins, my body not quite caught up to the fact that I'm not in danger, but I'm once again grounded to the earth instead of lost in that nightmare.

A persistent thought I don't want to acknowledge niggles at me, growing stronger and more insistent until I'm forced to recognize it.

Michael's face brought me back.

Not John and his memory. In that moment of pure hell I wanted Michael, not John.

I scrub away my tears.

How could I think such a thing? I blame the way Michael held me at the club. The feel of his arms wrapped around me is fresh. When, even on my best day, I'm starting to forget the way John felt.

But still, that's no excuse. I'm standing over his grave, for god's sake.

It's the worst kind of betrayal.

I begin cleaning the fallen leaves scattered over the dull grass, pulling up the abandoned flowers, and wishing I had fresh ones.

I don't even know Michael. How could I think of him? I don't know him. I will never know him. He's gone. I made sure of it. I've pushed him away and guys like him don't come back. I've succeeded. I wait for that protected, numb feeling I've kept wrapped around me like a second skin this past year, but it doesn't come, instead the tears rise once again.

Furious, I brush them away, my fingers cold against the hot tracks on my cheeks. Then, my stride angry, I turn and walk briskly to a trashcan. I toss the dead foliage away, and return to start the process all over again. Focusing on John, and not the card tucked into my bedside table, with Michael's numbers. Trying not to remember how many times I've run my finger over the strong, black script, or how I memorized the numbers without meaning too.

He's gone…and someday soon I'll forget.

That night, exhausted, but restless, I'm lying in bed with Michael's card in my hand, staring at the bold numbers scrawled across the bottom. After a long day of work, and even longer night sitting mindlessly in front of my TV watching reruns of *The Walking Dead*, I admit my defenses are down.

I want to call him. It's like an ache inside. He's like an itch, deep under the skin I can't scratch. I need him, just like he predicted. I pick up the phone and dial the first three digits before hanging up.

And just like he predicted, stubbornness won't let me.

I've been trying to convince myself he doesn't want me anymore, that if I called, he wouldn't welcome it. I don't quite believe it.

I blow out an exasperated breath. Unable to stand the crushing silence and mental angst one second longer, I pick up the phone and call Ruby.

She picks up after the first ring. "Layla, where have you been?" Her voice is irritated and filled with a coldness I haven't heard since Robby Benson liked me, instead of her, freshman year.

My brow furrows. "Where I've always been, at home."

"You don't even remember, do you?"

I race through my mind unsure of what I've forgotten. The only thing I know is that I didn't forget her birthday; she's a Christmas baby. But, otherwise, I'm at a loss. "I'm sorry. What did I do?"

She *tsk*s. "Friday night. You blew me off. You were supposed to come to The Whisky at nine."

Shit. I sit up in bed and put Michael's card on my bedside table. I completely forgot I'd agreed in my manic desperation to stay away from the club.

"I've left messages for you and you haven't returned my calls," she says in a shrill tone.

My thoughts are so full, my emotions so raw, I've been avoiding everyone. Including her. I'm a horrible friend. "Ruby, I'm sorry."

She huffs and blows out an angry sigh. "I know how busy you are, holed up in your house like a hermit, and I've tried to be patient. We all have, but honestly, Layla, this is getting ridiculous."

She's really mad, and I can't blame her. My personal tragedies don't excuse me from poor behavior. "I'm so sorry. Please, tell me how to make it up to you." Guilt has my hand curling into a fist. What kind of friend am I anymore? What kind of person? I barely remember making the promise that was clearly important to her.

A long pause falls over the line. "You don't get it, do you? It's not about making it up to me. It's about you rejoining the land of the living."

I pinch the bridge of my nose and stifle the urge to cry. I wonder if there will come a point where I'm not constantly disappointing people. "I'm a shitty friend."

"Yeah, you are." Ruby's voice is full of frustration, and she's not pulling any punches. "But worse, you're hurting yourself. You have to stop pushing everyone away."

"I'm sorry."

She lets out a loud screech and I can just imagine her throwing up her arms. "I don't want your stupid sorries. That's all you ever say anymore. Fuck, every time I talk to you I feel like I've kicked a puppy. Scream, tell me you hate me, rage at the world but please…" She trails off and follows with a heavy sigh. "Stop this."

My jaw clenches tight and I bite my lower lip. I don't know what to say, because the only thing that springs to mind is another apology.

When I don't speak, she continues, "I want the old Layla back. I miss my friend. The one that fought back. The one that wasn't afraid all the time."

"Don't you think I want that too?" That's what everyone wants, that old Layla, but I don't know how to find her again. She's a dream now, hovering so far out of reach, I can barely see her anymore.

"I believe you think you want that," Ruby said, her voice resigned. "But you've just given up. I hate it."

I swallow past the lump in my throat. "It's so much harder than you think, Ruby."

"I know," she says, her tone softening.

"But that's just the thing, you don't know, nobody

does."

"I'm not saying I understand, or pretend to know what you've been through, I know it's hard but you've got to find a way to come through this. You need to fight."

"I'm trying. I know it doesn't seem that way to you, but I am." Have I though? Other than going to Dr. Sorenson, what had I really done? Michael's words about how I choose to wallow come back to me. I frown, is he right?

"Let us help you," Ruby says. "Let *somebody* help you."

I take a deep breath and run my hand through my hair. I used to be social and outgoing with plenty of friends, but most of them have dropped off over time as I've become more and more reclusive. But not Ruby, she'll stick it out with me until the bitter end. In this way I'm blessed. I need to do better, for her. And for my family. The ones that care about me no matter how I act. "I promise I'll try. I'm so sorry I forgot, Ruby. Please, I know you don't want my apologies, but I was wrong. Let me make it up to you."

"It's not about making it up to me."

"I know, but I still want to. I'll do whatever you want. I promise."

A long silence ensues and I bite my lip, afraid she's going to tell me she's had enough. I wouldn't blame her, and I realize I care. That I don't want to be alone anymore. "I want to make it better."

She finally lets out a long sigh. "John wouldn't want this, LayLay." She uses his nickname for me and I want to throw up. "I know he was yours, but he was my friend too. I knew him, and I promise you, he'd hate that you've let this beat you. That you've given up."

She's right. He'd hate this. I'm not the girl he fell in love with. I don't even think he'd like me. I croak out,

"I miss him."

"I miss him too."

"I want him back." My voice catches as the tears well in my eyes and I admit something to my best friend I've never admitted to another living soul. "I'm scared, he's starting to feel like a dream."

She doesn't speak for a good fifteen seconds and then I hear her blow out a hard breath. "You know, I know how it was between you."

I blink, her statement shaking me out of my misery. I'm so startled by the unexpected change of topic, I blurt, "What?"

She sighs. "I'm not stupid. I know you guys didn't have a regular sex life."

I'd never told anyone. Way back when, I'd talk about sex with my girlfriends, and like most women, shared way too many details, only I'd stick to the semantics and not the intent. "How would you know that?"

She huffs. "Duh, I was your roommate. Do you know how thin those walls were? You don't think I heard stuff? I wasn't trying to listen, but there were a lot of strange noises coming from your room. After a while, I pieced it together."

My cheeks heat and I'm not sure why I'm embarrassed. "I never heard you."

She laughs and the tension between us lifts considerably. "Well, I'm not prone to screaming like you are."

I. Am. Mortified. How foolish of me that I never considered this before. My only excuse is John made sure I only focused on him, and orgasms. I never thought about the screaming and moaning coming from my room.

But our prior sex life is hardly relevant. I clear my throat. "Well, I can't see what that matters now."

"It matters," Ruby continues, her voice strong.

"Because you and I both know that John would *never* allow this. You want to respect his memory, respect that."

I suck in my breath; my chest tightening like someone's squeezing my heart between a fist. She's right. I'd never thought of it that way before, but she's right. John wouldn't have tolerated this.

I take a deep breath. "I'll try."

"You'd better," she says, her tone lightening. "Or I'll come over there and beat your ass myself."

I didn't think it was possible, but I laugh, and the band around my ribs loosens. "It doesn't quite work like that."

"Ah, laughter, that's a sound I haven't heard from you in too long."

God, I'm so lucky to have her as a friend. I don't appreciate her enough, but I make a silent vow to change that. "Ruby, I am so sorry I blew you off. Please forgive me."

"You're forgiven. And if you want to make it up to me, Ashley roped me into going to O'Malley's tomorrow night. It's league night, and someone told her that's where every hot guy in the city is. You could come and keep me company while she does her thing."

Ashley's another college friend who hung out in the same crowd as us. A blonde, busty cheerleader type who loves men, and they love her right back.

Something shifts inside me and the heaviness in my chest lightens. I want to go, not because of obligation, but because I want to see Ruby. To make it right between us. To prove I can do something normal. Even if that means I have to watch Ashley's shameless flirting in a too-tight, sports-themed, baby-doll tee. I smile. "That sounds horrible."

Ruby chuckles. "Exactly."

In that moment, I know that everything is going to be all right between us. "I'm in."

11.

Once again, I'm sitting on Dr. Sorenson's couch, trying to recapture some sense of equilibrium. I swallow hard as she sits across from me, looking ever so patient. The silence is growing, becoming uncomfortable as she waits me out.

Absently, I wonder if shrinks take some sort of class in waiting. She must have because she's a master at it.

Unable to resist any longer, I blurt out, "I've had two panic attacks in the last week."

Her pen scratches across her notepad, and in my head, she's judging me. After all these months she must be tired of hearing me whine. I wouldn't even tell her, but I've hidden my attacks from my friends and family, so she's the only person I can confess to about my backward slide.

I frown, finding the notion that the only person I can talk to is my shrink, disconcerting. How fucked up is that?

Her lips press together, and she nods. "They'd been under control for a while now, what do you think has changed?"

"I don't know," I lie. I'm sure they're related to Michael. All the violent emotions he evokes within me aren't allowing me the numbness I was afforded before. But there's no need to talk about him. He's gone. And he's not coming back. It's been sixty-seven hours since we spoke, clearly, he's moved on. Talking about him will make him real, and I need to forget.

"Tell me about the first one," Dr. Sorenson says in that calm tone she has, interrupting my obsessing.

If I talk about that, I'll have to talk about Michael, so I skip it and head straight to the latest, more explainable one. "I had one Monday, when I went to visit John's grave. While I was standing there, I had a flashback about the attack."

"Understandable." She's nodding and writing again. "And the other?"

"I was at the club." How to explain?

She looks at me, and one dark blonde brow rises in question.

I lick my lips. "Someone...grabbed my wrists, and it happened then." I don't want to talk about this so I change the subject. "Don't you ever get tired of my lack of progress?"

She rests her pen on the pad before tilting her head to the side. "Why do you think you haven't had progress?"

I throw up my hands and I raise my voice without meaning to. "Um, because I haven't. Nothing has changed. This is pointless."

"And, yet you keep coming back. Why?"

I bite my lower lip, hard enough to sting. "I don't have anyone else to talk to. Everyone else has moved on."

My throat closes over, and before the first tear even

falls, she plucks a tissue from the box on the table and hands it to me. "Tell me more."

I dab at my eyes with the soft cotton, before pressing my fingertips to my temple. "I'm tired. All these months later and I'm still having nightmares, still having panic attacks, still crying at inappropriate times, still fucking random guys. When is it going to stop?"

"There's no timetable on grief, Layla."

I stare at my gray-and-black tweed skirt until my vision blurs.

"You have to remember, your situation isn't as easy as laying a loved one to rest. You didn't just lose John," she continues, her voice soft and so empathetic, I want to crawl into it. "You suffered a trauma."

I blink and a fresh wash of tears slide down my cheeks. "Aren't you frustrated with me?"

"No, I am not."

I look up; surprised she's given me a straight answer.

She points a manicured finger at me. "But you are, and *that*, is progress."

12.

After my early-morning session with Dr. Sorenson, I haven't had time to think, as my day has been filled with one meeting after another. My small company just won a major client and is going through their millionth restructuring while they shuffle things around to accommodate the business. I'm missing lunch, needing to get the first draft of my communication plan to my boss, by the end of the day. But I don't mind, I need the constant buzz of activity to keep from going insane.

As though I've conjured him, Frank leans over the side of my cube. "How's it going?"

In his late-forties, with a salt-and-pepper buzz cut, and dark brown eyes already deeply lined with crow's feet, Frank Moretti reminds me of a mobster crossed with a newspaper man from the comic books.

"Good." I shrug one shoulder. "At least I don't have to start from scratch. I'm just modifying the com plan from the last go around."

He nods. "At least it's good news."

One thing I've learned in the year I've been working for the boutique software industry is that they love change. Ironically, considering my love of keeping everything the same, I find the frantic pace suits me. I use to work for a large, Fortune 100 company, but when John died I quit, unable to stand being around so many people who knew what happened. When I finally hit the market this job fell into my lap as one of the head software developers, Doug, is a good friend of my brother-in-law. At the time I wasn't in a position to be picky and it all worked out in the end. I'm a department of one, and my salary is enough I'm able to pay the mortgage on my condo in comfort. I've learned to live with, and even appreciate, the chaos.

It allows me the luxury of being able to avoid my own.

I turn my attention back to Frank. "I should have a solid draft to you by two."

"Fair enough," he says, then juts his chin toward the direction of his office. "If you need Judy's help, I've already told her to give you whatever you need."

"Thanks, I'll take you up on that." Judy, Frank's admin, is a whiz at PowerPoint in a way I could only dream about.

He turns and leaves, and I, once again, immerse myself in my document. Fifteen minutes later, my cell phone rings and I answer without looking at the caller ID. "Layla Hunter."

"What did you do on Sunday, Layla?" Michael's deep voice washes over me and I'm so relieved if I'd been standing it would have brought me to my knees. My mind goes blank and my mouth instantly dry. He's been nagging in the back of my mind all day but, convinced I'd never hear from him again, I refused to let him in.

I don't even want to think about how happy I am.

How glad I am to be wrong. "Michael." My tone is breathless and filled with a hope that makes me cringe.

"Do I have to go through this whole cycle again?" That voice. So deep and rich, every time he speaks it's like a stroke against my skin.

"No." I manage to croak out. He's called and my stubbornness is already melting away.

"Well?" While the word is a hard bite, I can make out a faint undercurrent of amusement.

He knows he's got me.

I press my lips together and take a deep breath. Answering this question means things will change between us. And as terrified as I am, I'm unwilling to let him go. I will, someday soon, but not today. I exhale. "I went to my sister's house, she had a family brunch."

"Good girl," he says and my whole body quivers with the impact of those two little words. "Tell me who was there."

My work phone lets out a loud shrill and I jump in my seat, quickly identifying the caller as the Director of Operations, and ignoring it. Not even the CEO herself could pull me away from this call. "My sister, obviously, her husband and my twin nieces. And my parents."

"How old are your nieces?" He sounds completely normal, as though we're actually discussing our day. As though nothing monumental has happened and I haven't taken this gigantic step.

I'm not sure if I'm happy or irritated. "They're five. They just started kindergarten."

"Cute," he says. "And that reminds me, how old are you?"

"I'm thirty." I can't stop my heart from pounding too fast. I can feel sweat slick my palm as I hold the phone far too tightly. "How old are you?"

"Thirty-three." He chuckles and it's as sinful and

decadent as I remember. "Wanna know my birthday?"

I wipe my clammy palms across my black skirt. "Yes, please."

"November thirteenth. What about yours?"

I swallow hard. I'm doing it. I'm having a normal conversation. "April fifth."

"I feel like we're supposed to say something about our signs, but I don't know anything about that stuff."

I laugh and the knot in my stomach loosens. "Me either."

"Did you have a good time at your sister's?" he asks.

I decide to be honest. I don't really know why. Maybe because I'm too tired to pretend any longer. Just so damned tired of holding it all in. "No."

"Why not?"

I take another deep breath, hoping to slow my pulse. "They're all waiting for me to go back to normal and I always end up disappointing them."

"You're never going to be normal, sugar." His voice is soft, almost consolatory.

"Yeah, I know." What else is there to say?

"Is that a bad thing?"

"I don't know. I think they think it is."

There's a pause and I hear the buzz of activity through the line, before finally he says, "Something to talk about another time when I'm not sitting in the middle of the station. So tell me, was it really that hard to answer the question?"

I nod, and then remember he can't see me. I clear my throat. "Yes."

He laughs. "Your honesty is one of the things I like best about you. I was going to call yesterday but I got caught at a scene and didn't get home until two in the morning."

I frown, picking up a pen and holding it tight. Not liking the reminder of his profession. I clench my teeth, it doesn't matter what he does. Regardless of what I've agreed to in the present, he's still temporary, and eventually I will get him out of my system. He's not a replacement for John. "I didn't expect to hear from you at all."

"Did you really think I was going to give up that easy?"

"I don't know you." I pause and weigh my answer carefully. "But you seem like the kind of guy who doesn't waste your time."

"Layla, you might be a pain in the ass, but you're not a waste of time."

A smile tugs at my lips before I'm able to help myself. "What is wrong with you?"

"Nothing at all." His voice drops. "I like a good challenge and I'm not about to skip out before we've had the chance to do battle."

I can't stop the gasp or help how my blood picks up speed, heating in an instant. I lick my dry lips, wanting to come back with a witty retort, but I'm unable to think of a damn thing. All I can think of is the hot delicious rush of anticipation at the thought of going toe to toe with Detective Michael Banks.

"Would you like to know where we're going on Friday?" His tone is amused, knowing and smug.

I narrow my eyes. "How do you know I don't have other plans?"

He laughs, an evil sound that girls like me recognize in an instant. It sends a spike of desire through my veins like I've just taken a shot of tequila. "If you do, I expect you to break them."

"Don't you think that's a bit presumptuous?"

"I think it's a lot presumptuous, but the statement still holds."

"And you think you have that right?" I can feel it, that stir of excitement I haven't felt in forever. Betrayal takes a vicious jab, but I ignore it, because my craving for Michael is a real tangible thing, while betrayal is a familiar friend I'll meet again.

"Do you want to know where we're going or not?" Completely disregarding my attempt to bait him.

I mutter a curse under my breath.

"What's that?"

"Oh, nothing," I say with a tiny kernel of satisfaction.

"I guess you don't want to know then."

"Wait!" I have to know how to dress. I might be half dead but I'm still a girl. "Go ahead and tell me."

"Aww, sorry, sugar, you missed your chance."

I shiver, my heart and body falling into the game, and welcoming it with open arms, even as my brain protests. "You're evil."

"It comes with the territory. You know that." His voice drops to a husky rumble. "Don't make me keep repeating myself and I won't have to pull rank."

"You don't have rank!"

"Christ, I can't wait to make you eat those words."

The heat between us, present every time we interact, flares from a smolder into a hot lick of flame. I smile, a real genuine smile that warms something inside me that's been long cold. "At least tell me if it's fancy, casual or somewhere in-between."

"It's casual."

"There, was that so hard?" I use my sweetest, most cloying voice.

A long, long pause filled with promise. "You are just begging for it, aren't you, Layla?"

I feign complete innocence. "I have no idea what you're talking about."

"You—" A beeping noise goes off in the background and he mutters something under his breath. "I'm sorry, I have to run. Duty calls."

"Okay," I say, trying not to think about how disappointed I am. How that long-forgotten girly part of me wants to talk to him for hours.

"Tomorrow, seven o'clock."

"All right." I hang up and stare at my computer monitor until the pretty blonde HR Generalist, Priscilla, stops at my cube.

"Hi, Layla, all ready for our eleven thirty."

I blink at her, completely confused.

She points down the corridor. "I reserved conference room A."

"Oh, right." I straighten and start scooping various meeting materials into my arms.

"Are you okay?" Priscilla asks, and waves a hand in my direction. "You're all flushed."

"I'm fine." I just agreed to an actual date. With Michael. In less than twenty-four hours.

I should be obsessing about the implications of what I've done, what it means, how I'm breaking every single one of my rules, or how I've barely thought about the club that I fixated on all last week.

But I don't think of any of those things, all I think is…what am I going to wear?

O'Malley's is beyond packed with wall-to-wall people. Every single woman in Chicago must have heard the same thing as Ashley, because there's just as many girls decked out in their finest casual clothes as there are guys in various sports jerseys and backward baseball caps.

I'm thankful Ashley insisted we get here early because we're lucky enough to have a table. With the crush of people, free flow of alcohol, and sweaty men, standing in the middle of the commotion would have been too much for me. The last thing I need is another panic attack.

No, I'm fine right here, tucked into the corner, and nursing my third round of the bar's local autumn ale.

"Having fun," Ruby shouts into my ear.

"Oh, tons," I yell back, grinning at her so she knows I'm not being sullen.

She looks amazing in faded, distressed skinny jeans and a tight white T-shirt. She did her famous smoky makeup, and her bright blue eyes are a stark contrast to her ivory skin, and shiny black hair swinging around her shoulders. As always, she manages to be stunning without appearing like she's trying way too hard.

"Thanks for coming, I had no idea how crowded this place would be. Are you okay?" she asks, brow furrowing in concern.

My fingers tighten around my beer. After my talk with Ruby last night, and my call with Michael today, I'm actually feeling decent. Even a bit hopeful, and for tonight, I don't want anyone reminding me of my past. Tonight, I want to have fun. That is, if I remember how. I pull at the red jersey top I'm wearing, and ignore how humid the air is. "Don't worry, I'm fine."

From across the table, Ashley cups a hand around her ear. "What?"

I wave a hand through the air, gesturing it's not important, and to minimize my screaming so I'm not hoarse for my work presentation tomorrow.

Unlike Ruby's not trying too hard, Ashley is the exact opposite, in a faded blue V-neck adorned with the Cub's vintage logo. The top is so tight it might as well have been painted on, and her jeans ride low enough to show a strip of skin between the hem and waistband of her pants. Her one concession to the casual, after-the-game vibe the Irish pub has going on, is her sleek, blonde ponytail. I have to admit it's an effective look, with her cute face, dancing brown eyes and absolutely killer rack she's perfectly positioned to capture the attention of the Chicago jocks.

Ashley fans her face and leans across the table. "Have you ever seen so many hot guys?"

She's right; there are a lot of hot guys. Of course, no one pings my radar, and even if they did, Michael's an impossible act to top. My mind drifts to our date tomorrow night and at the reminder of all the possibilities, my stomach flutters.

I'm not sure if my exhilarated anticipation terrifies me or not.

I yell, "Yeah, it's great."

Ashley gives me a speculative once-over. "Are you ready to get back on the horse?"

I issue a fierce, "No!"

At the same time Ruby says, "Ashley!"

She shrugs one shoulder. "What? It's a logical question."

I take a deep breath. This is what I wanted, for people to treat me like I'm normal, and that's what Ashley is doing. I can't fault her for that. I shake my head. "I'm just trying to get out of the house a bit more."

"And I bribed her," Ruby says.

But Ashley has already lost interest, her attention fixed past Ruby and me. A mega-watt smile lights up her whole face. A healthy flush fills her cheeks and she practically screams, "Oh my god, Tyler's here."

Ruby and I groan in unison.

Tyler is Ashley's kryptonite. The baddest of bad boys, who's supposed skills in bed are only rivaled by his legendary California good looks. At six-two, the bone structure of a model and a body to match, even I have to admit he's gorgeous. Although he's not to my taste and I've never quite understood the appeal. Of course, that could be because John used to joke that he was a closet sub, so every time I see him I get a mental image of him in chains at the stockade.

Ashley, however, has different ideas and goes crazy anytime he comes within a mile radius. The two of them have been hooking up for far too many years to count. This wouldn't be a bad thing; except Ashley deludes herself into believing he'll change for her. That someday he'll realize what a catch she is and put a ring on her finger. The chances of this happening are less than zero, and someday Ashley will understand that Tyler is doing her a favor. Guys like him are never faithful.

As her friend, I'm duty-bound to at least object to the mistake she's about to make, even though she'll never listen. I tap Ashley's hand on the table and shake my head. "Don't do it."

"She's right, Ash," Ruby says, backing me up. "You know what happens."

But Ashley is ignoring us, her gaze on the man of her dreams.

Ruby sighs. "Do you see why I need you?"

Ashley pulls down the hem of her baby-doll tee, making sure to reveal maximum cleavage. "He's coming over."

Of course he is, she's a sure thing. I want to say this, but hold my tongue. I'm not telling her anything she doesn't already know. Besides, who am I to judge? Every sane, rational brain cell I have tells me to run from Michael as fast as I can, but I haven't been able to resist him.

Chemistry, real or perceived, isn't good for thinking straight.

Tyler, and three of his buddies, make their way over to stand at our table. As they crowd in, they take up all the available space, blocking out some of the light and making me feel enclosed. All four of them look like a bunch of college frat boys with slick smiles that don't reach their eyes.

I can't help it—my mind flashes back to that alley and the men crowded around John and me. I tense, experiencing that momentary sense of adrenaline racing through my blood.

I need to remain calm. These guys are not a threat, and I'm not alone. Nothing is going to happen to me. I take a deep, shaky breath and will my pulse to slow.

Ruby nudges me. "Are you okay?"

I nod and gulp for air, steeling my spine while forcing my body to relax.

Tyler bends his head in greeting to Ruby before shifting his attention to me. "I haven't seen you in a while, Layla."

"Hey," I say, not inviting conversation.

He points to his friends and rattles off their names but I'm not paying attention. I'm concentrating on air and taking slow breaths.

Ruby nudges me again. "Do you need some fresh air?"

This time I don't resist her offer to help. If I step out into the cold night, I'll be able to compose myself and continue my night out as a normal girl. "Yeah."

She grabs my elbow and yells across the table. "We'll be right back, are you okay on your own?"

Ashley waves us away, her hungry eyes never wavering from Tyler smiling down at her. He's already cupping the back of her neck and leaning in close.

One of his friend's, a boyishly cute *GQ* type I've never seen before winks, flashing me a smile filled with perfect white teeth. I push my way past him but before I can slip away he slides an arm around my waist. "Where are you off to?"

His touch makes me recoil, not because there's anything wrong with him, but because there are too many people, it's too loud, and the air is thick and hot. The bar smells like sweat and beer and the last thing I need is some guy groping me.

I jerk away and force a smile on my lips. "We're just getting some fresh air."

His gaze drops to my mouth. "Hurry back."

I remind myself this is what guys do in bars,

especially in places like this, swarming with too much testosterone left over from whatever game they've been playing.

Ruby grips my arm as I push my way past the hordes of people while trying not to think about the bodies pressing too close into mine. Strangers. I'm normally okay in a crowd but this place has to be over capacity and I feel like I'm suffocating.

Not a great feeling on the verge of a panic attack I want to control.

I press my lips together, and regulate my breath in an effort to remain calm, as I focus on the front door. Off to the left something familiar catches the corner of my vision. I turn my head and come to a dead stop so quickly Ruby runs smack into me.

"What?" she asks from behind me, but I barely hear her.

I blink. It's Michael, standing not ten feet away from me.

He's with a girl.

13.

Nausea rolls through my stomach in a cruel wave and I break out into a cold sweat. For a moment, I think I'm going to throw up the beer I've drunk, but I manage to push it back down.

He's standing close to an extremely cute, tall brunette with long wavy hair wearing a black sleeveless top, tight jeans and knee-high black boots. Michael puts a hand on her elbow, laughing at something she says, and she grins up at him.

They look like a couple.

I'm definitely going to be sick.

How could I have been so stupid? How could I have gotten sucked in? He made me believe, even if only for a fraction of a second, and I hate him so much I want to claw his eyes out. My hands curl into fists as my nails bite into the skin on my palms.

Ruby pokes me in the ribs, prodding me forward.

But I can't move, I can only stare in horror.

"Layla," she yells over the crowd.

The sound of Ruby calling my name must have carried through the short distance because his head jerks up and his gaze locks instantly on mine.

In that one moment all the noise—the crowd, the bar, the beginning stages of my panic attack—disappears. I'm left with one thought—he gave me hope.

Hope I wanted no part of. And I will never forgive him.

Some drunken guy jostles me, propelling me into action. I begin walking as fast as I can away from him. Away from this godforsaken bar. And most certainly away from the tiny glimmer of life growing ever larger each day.

"Layla," Michael calls.

But I'm already leaving, practically running as fast as I can in my high-heeled boots.

He calls again, but I shut him out.

I'll never let him in again.

I can't believe it. I care. I'm fucking jealous.

I hate him.

Never, *ever* again.

"Layla." It's Ruby's voice this time but I don't even slow, just push my way past the people like I'm a bulldozer until I finally reach the front door.

I break free and race outside. The cold air hits my too hot cheeks and I suck in great gulps of air.

I squeeze my lids shut tight. This is my fault.

This is why my rules are so important. They were designed to keep me safe, and now I've gone and blown them all to hell.

How did this even happen? I've only known him a week. A week! He owes me nothing, least of all loyalty. But logic doesn't matter.

In my heart, buried so deep I didn't recognize it, I'd believed I was special somehow. That he was charged with the same violent rush of emotions as me.

But it was just a game. A challenge.

And I fell for it. How could I be so stupid? How could I betray John? For something so inconsequential.

Ruby comes rushing out, spots me, and puts a hand over her heart. "Jesus, Layla, what the hell happened back there?"

"Nothing." Nothing, I'd made into something.

"Who was that guy?" She point in the direction of the bar, as if I need some sort of reminder of whom she's referring to.

"No one." I lean one shoulder against the side of the building, trying to collect myself. My voice is dead calm, conveying nothing of the turmoil rioting inside me. "I'm sorry, Ruby, I don't think I can go back in there. It's too crowded."

"All right, I understand. I'll go back in and grab our stuff then we can go hang out at The Whisky and talk. Okay?"

I betrayed John.

I nod and close my eyes. I'm going to have to think of something to tell her, because this time there will be no letting me off the hook. Ruby will want answers.

A big hand grips me by the elbow. I'm hauled off the wall and swung around.

Michael.

I try and pull away but his grasp is firm. Not hurting me, but forceful enough to let me know I'm not going anywhere until he's ready.

"Hey!" Ruby yells. "Don't touch her."

Next to him is the girl, arms curled around herself to protect against the cold, her brow furrowed. She's even prettier than I'd thought in the bar.

"Let me go." My words are filled with venom. How could he bring her out here?

"Layla," Michael says, his tone filled with that hard command custom designed to make me stand up and take notice.

My traitorous body responds with an answering shudder.

"Let her go, asshole." Ruby steps toward us, ready to take him on.

He ignores her and issues the girl forward. Of course, she obeys. Like me, she probably doesn't have a choice. "Layla, I'd like you to meet my *sister*, Jillian."

Every tense muscle in my body uncoils and I blink at the girl.

His sister? She's tall for a woman, maybe five-nine and her hair is the same dark brown as Michael's.

She smiles and steps toward me. Her face illuminates in the glow of the street lamp and I see she shares the same unusual striking hazel eyes as her brother. "Hi, you must be Layla. I know this because I heard Michael yell your name about five hundred times."

I glance at him, and he nods. His fingers relax fractionally on my arm. Not enough to set me free, but enough to know he no longer considers me a flight risk.

She turns and gestures behind her and for the first time I see there's another man there. A cute, Italian-looking guy with black hair and dark eyes. "This is my boyfriend, Leo."

Leo grins and it transforms his face from cute to devilishly handsome. He swings his arm around Jillian. "I work with Michael. I can vouch that she's definitely his sister."

Michael's gaze narrows and a muscle jumps in his jaw.

I'm still not able to speak. Now that the mad rush of emotions is over, I can't help but see how crazy I acted. Embarrassment washes over me like a hot wave. What have I done? I've given away my true feelings. Revealed how much he means to me.

In front of everyone, including Ruby.

Michael releases his hold on my elbow and grips my chin, forcing me to look up and meet his gaze. I resist, closing my eyes, not wanting him to witness what I've given away. I've only known him a week. I've stayed protected for so long, built my walls so completely, how did he get past them so quickly?

I can no longer deny he's gotten through all of my toughest defenses.

His fingers slip down the curve of my jaw to wrap gently around my neck. His thumb presses into the pulse beating far too fast and my lashes flutter open in response to the subtle pressure. I shiver involuntarily.

His hazel eyes flash with something that looks a lot like satisfaction. "My sister, Layla." He strokes over my skin then his hand falls away.

I press my lips together and nod. I cross my arms, hugging myself tight against the crisp nighttime air. It's one thing to agree to go out with him. On a date, I could still maintain indifference.

But he knows now. I can't hide or pretend otherwise. He has power over me.

I search his expression, looking for the arrogance that has to be lurking there, but he only looks concerned, with a frown on his lips, and narrowed eyes that study me far too closely. Dangerous, cop eyes.

"What is going on?" Ruby's voice shakes me from the spell Michael has me under.

I glance around to see Jillian and Leo grinning at me, expressions filled with avid interest. I can feel a hot flush spread over my cheeks.

"I'm Michael." He holds out one strong hand and Ruby reaches out, her face filled with questions. As her palm slips into his grasp, I watch my regular and secret life collide.

I can do nothing but stand there and watch it happen.

She nods at Michael. "I'm Ruby."

The second he drops her hand she turns to me. "Is everything okay?"

No, everything is not okay. I've been caught having a jealous fit over some guy I barely know, that Ruby's certainly never heard of, when I'm supposed to be in deep mourning over the love of my life. Of course, I can't say that, so, I do what comes natural and avoid. I toss a furtive glance at Michael. "Ruby's my best friend."

Michael flashes her a killer smile filled with charm that actually makes me go weak in the knees. "Do you think you could give us a couple minutes here?"

Ruby crosses her arms. "Layla, who is this guy?"

"Um…" I lick my lips and everyone watches me expectantly. "Um…he's…just someone I know."

Leo laughs and Jillian nudges him in the ribs with her elbow.

One brow rises up Ruby's forehead. "Yeah, I can see that." Her tone is acid and I can tell she's hurt.

I don't blame her; I'm already breaking the promises I made the night before. I grit my teeth and decide I'm going to tell her at least some version of the truth. I owe her that. But first I need to deal with this disaster I've created.

I put my hand on her arm. "It's fine, I promise."

She scowls, not at all convinced. "But—"

Michael cuts her off and reaches into the pocket of his jeans, pulls out his badge and hands it over to Ruby. "I'm a cop. Nothing is going to happen to her while she's with me."

I bite my lower lip. One part of me recognizes him as the most dangerous thing out there, while another is wrapped up in a blanket of security I haven't experienced since before the attack when I believed nothing bad could happen to me.

She studies the badge then slowly hands it back to

Michael.

I turn to her, needing some way to make it up to her. "I'll explain everything as soon as I get back inside."

"All right," she says, looking at me like I'm a stranger. "I'll be at the table."

I nod, and she turns to walk away.

Leo and Jillian, however, stay firmly in place, watching us.

Michael juts his chin. "Go."

Jillian flashes a grin. "I can't wait to tell Mom."

Leo slides his hand into hers. "Hell, I can't wait to tell everyone."

Clearly disgusted, Michael shakes his head, grips my elbow and starts tugging me down the street in the opposite direction of the bar and the crowded sidewalk in front of the door where people stand to smoke. "Jesus Christ, they're pains in the asses."

I'd smile at his brotherly disgust if only it wasn't a harsh reminder of how wrong I was and how much I'd given away. My thoughts of embarrassment fade into the background, when ahead, I catch the first glimpse of the alley waiting for me. Tendrils of darkness seem to creep onto the street, encroaching into the glow cast from the streetlights above.

I stiffen.

"What's wrong?" he asks immediately, missing nothing.

My pace picks up as my throat seizes. "No alleys."

He says nothing but his expression hardens and he quickly sidesteps around me, placing himself between me, and the long dark corridor that fills my nightmares. "Better?"

"Yes." It's a small gesture—and maybe any guy would do it—but with Michael my tension abates and the warmth envelops me.

When he takes my hand, the part of me that wants

to remain protected and insulated from feeling anything but my loss, resists, but I curl my fingers around him anyway. I try not to pay too much attention to how strong and solid his grip is, or how much I crave his arms around me.

I'm in way over my head. If I'm not careful, I'm going to start needing him. And that can't happen, I may have given up the fight to stay away, but this is still temporary.

We walk a half a block before he pulls me into a deserted vestibule of a closed dry cleaners. He maneuvers me into the corner, standing in front of me so he blocks most of the autumn wind.

With any other man this position would terrify me, but with Michael, I can't deny I feel safe.

He rubs my arms. Since my coat is inside with Ashley and Ruby, I can feel the warmth of his palms through the thin jersey of my red top. I want to protest, but find I don't have the energy. Or, maybe, I miss the sensation of being safe and protected too much to refuse.

"Are we okay, sugar?" he asks. With the shimmer of the streetlights behind him, I can see him searching my expression in that slow assessing way he has. Looking for clues, like the detective he is.

I lower my gaze and stare at his broad chest. The navy cotton of his long-sleeved shirt stretches over muscles obviously honed to perfection. He's built so different than John, who was lean, almost slight. I wonder what it would be like to lay my head against Michael's chest and listen to the steady, sure beat of his heart. My fingers itch to touch him, and if it was just for sex, I'd be okay, but it's not. I lust for the comfort he gives me as much as his body.

He's impossible for me to objectify. To use. He'll make me forget John and I can't have that. I gather what's left of the last shreds of my defenses and steel my spine. "There is no 'we' and I'm fine."

His gaze narrows and his jaw hardens. "It's not going to work, Layla. So don't even bother trying."

My chin tilts with a defiance I don't even come close to feeling. "I'm stating a fact."

"You're stating what you'd like to be true." His hand moves up my arm to stroke over the exposed skin of my neck. "There's a big difference, isn't there?"

I can't stop the shiver that races along my skin like lightening. "Why are you doing this? Can't you see I don't want this?"

"No, I don't see that at all. I think you want it far more than you can admit."

My throat closes over, and I want to look away, but can't.

"When I first met you, I thought about it," he says, and the admission spikes hot panic through me. "But, I'm sorry, I can't let you run."

I shake my head and cross my arms protectively around my chest, hating the rush of relief at his words. "Why?"

His thumb presses into the curve of my jaw, forcing my head and my gaze to meet his. When I finally look at him, his expression is deadly serious, holding not even a trace of lightness or amusement. "Because there's something between us I can't ignore and neither can you. And I'm not talking about lust, which is like a kick in the fucking gut every time I even think of you, I'm talking about something more. You sense it too and you're terrified."

I want to protest everything he's saying, but I can't. I can only stare at him, unblinking.

The hard line of his jaw relaxes, and his thumb moves to brush softly over my cheek, he leans in close. "The truth is, it scares me too."

"It does?" The question slips from my lips as I forget I'm supposed to be denying our involvement.

"Hell, yes," he says, the amusement creeping back into his voice. "But you and I, we're fighters and a little fear isn't going to stop us."

"I'm not a fighter." Doesn't he understand how I've given up?

"You're wrong. And someday, you'll see that." Before I can say anything, he grips my chin, holding my gaze steady. "I will pick you up tomorrow at seven."

I nod, giving up the pretense of walking away. At least for tonight.

Ruby and I sit at a back table of The Whisky, sipping glasses of red wine and listening to the bluesy singer taking center stage. I have no idea what song the African-American woman is singing, but her voice is hauntingly soulful, and when she hits certain notes, chills race along my skin.

The atmosphere is completely different from O'Malley's frantic crush of people, pheromones and desperation. A welcome relief. The Whisky is our spot of choice when we just want to hang out and talk. It's mellow, darkly lit, and intimate with great live music. I find myself relaxing for the first time all night, even though I know I have to talk to Ruby about what happened.

After Michael and I walked back inside, he promptly delivered me to a narrow-eyed Ruby and astonished Ashley before he took his leave. I don't know if he went back to his sister or left, but in the thirty minutes we waited for the dance between Ashley and Tyler to be complete, and for her to ditch us so we're free to go, I couldn't help scanning the bar. I never spotted him. I found myself missing his company. That sense of safety he gave me mixed, ironically, with the white-hot desire that sparked like something alive and tangible between us. He'd yet to really touch me since the first night we met, but I already craved his hands on me like a drug. Instinct told me the wait would be over tomorrow, and like any addict, the closer I get to my fix, the more anxious I become.

But first, I have to talk to Ruby.

I dart a quick glance in her direction. Her attention is focused on the singer. She hasn't pressed, but she is waiting. If I don't provide an explanation, this night will widen the distance between us, instead of closing the gap as I'd intended. I will not allow space to grow back into our friendship. She's too important to me. I'd been searching for an explanation that would satisfy her, but all I can think of is the truth.

I sit with this a while, as I let the music wash over me, and come to the conclusion that I can't think of anything because I no longer want to lie to her.

Sudden tears come to my eyes. I want my best friend back. I suppose I can thank Michael for this, he's stirring renewed life inside me, making it impossible to go back to that dark place I came from.

I'm scared as hell. My heart pounds fast as my palms turn clammy, but I don't want to lose this desire and miss being close to her, so I take a deep breath and say, "John and I use to go to this club."

Ruby's focus shifts immediately to me, eyes widening as though she's surprised, but she doesn't speak, just tilts her head to indicate she's listening.

There's nothing to play with at the bar table where we're sitting and I wish I had something to occupy my hands. I settle for the stem of my wineglass, running my fingers nervously up and down the smooth stem. "It's this underground club we use to visit every once in a while when we wanted to spice things up." A nice way of saying we wanted to add an element of exhibitionism and danger into our sex, but I don't think Ruby's ready to hear that.

Besides, she's a smart girl; she can read between the lines.

"What's it like?" She blinks, as though startled by her own question. "I mean, that is, if you are okay talking about it."

I shrug. I don't know if I'm okay talking about it, but I'm going to anyway. Not only for Ruby, but for me. "It's kind of a mishmash of kink. It's not a leather club, or a straight-out BDSM club, but basically, anything goes. They have a main room and then they have theme rooms. I've seen people there that don't look any different than you and me, and I've seen people there covered in head-to-toe latex. John always liked it better than BDSM clubs."

"Why?" Her attention seems absolute and I think she's legitimately curious.

I take a sip of my wine to compose myself before continuing. "That wasn't his thing. While he was dominant, he didn't like all the ritualistic stuff, and didn't care for a lot of props."

Ruby leans forward, placing her elbows on the table. "Props?"

I study her. She's interested, and not in that mildly curious way, but in that way John would have called telling. I stifle a smile and say, "Oh you know, whips and heavy restraints, Saint Andrew's crosses and things like that. He didn't like"—I make air quotes—"scenes. He didn't want me to call him master or sir, he just wanted, what he wanted, when he wanted it and didn't expect to hear no from me."

She leans in even closer and if the table wasn't there she'd have tipped over. "And if you said no?"

A smile tugs at my lips and it occurs to me I'm talking about him and it doesn't feel like a big, gaping wound. It's still a deep ache in my heart but it doesn't feel fresh. For the first time since he died I let some of my good memories in. "Well, then he would have changed my mind."

She opens her mouth but then snaps it shut and shakes her head. "It's so hard to believe, even when I kind of knew what was going on, John was so mild mannered."

"Yeah, he was." I grin at her. "Except when he wasn't."

I shiver as I think of it. God, it was a beautiful sight to behold. He'd give me a hard-eyed, stern look. That certain expression—I can still picture like it was yesterday—would slide over his face, turning him from boyishly handsome into something dangerous.

Ruby's gaze darts away and a faint splash of color fills her cheeks. "Can I ask you something I've always been curious about, but isn't really any of my business?"

I take another healthy gulp of my wine and nod. "Of course."

"If you don't want to answer you don't have to."

"Ask," I insist, curious in spite of myself.

"Okay, what was going on between you at Carlo and Angela's party that one time?"

I'm so surprised I burst out laughing, shocking myself. It's been so long I'm rusty. Of course, I know exactly what party she's talking about. John had been in a real mood that night. I point to my glass. "We might need a lot more drinks before I can talk about the details and you probably would too, and we both have to work tomorrow."

"But I'm right, aren't I? There was definitely something going on."

"Oh yes. What I will say is by the time I left that party I'd been violated in many different ways, I couldn't sit down, and I'd had about four orgasms."

"Wow," she says the word and sounds almost wistful, before she shakes her head. "It's always the quiet ones, huh?"

"Yeah." John hadn't been quiet but I knew what she meant, he'd had an innocent look to him that made him very affable and charming. Most people wouldn't have guessed that he fucked like the devil and was twice as mean.

Not like Michael. I can't imagine a woman alive would think he took his sex nice.

I wait for the hard slap of betrayal I experience every time I think of John and Michael so close together, but it doesn't come. In fact, I'm more relaxed and mellow than I can ever remember being since before John died.

Dr. Sorenson may have had a point when she'd said that talking was good, and part of the healing process. The wine is starting to go to my head, making me nostalgic and fuzzy. I smile at Ruby. "Thank you, I miss talking about him."

Her brow furrows and she covers my hand. "I'm sorry, I didn't know. I don't bring him up because I don't want to upset you."

My eyes well with tears, but it's different this time, it doesn't have the same sharp edge of grief. I wipe under my lashes. "I know, but no one even says his name anymore, it's like he's disappeared from everyone's mind but my own."

She squeezes my fingers. "No, never. I—" she shakes her head and her own eyes grow bright, "—I never thought of it like that. You've been so cut off, so remote, I didn't want to do anything that would push you farther away."

I squeeze back, and it's like a dam breaking between us, and all our emotions gush out. "I've been so horrible. I didn't mean to, it's just everyone wants me to be like I was before, and I can't be. I constantly feel like a disappointment."

We both start crying in earnest and she looks at me

all watery eyed. "I don't expect that, Layla, I know this past year and a half have been harder and more painful than most of us will experience in our lifetimes, but don't shut me out. You scare me when you do."

I brush away my tears and nod. "I won't, I promise." Never again.

Our waitress, Milly, comes over with a pile of napkins, slides them onto the table and pats Ruby on the shoulder before wandering away.

I grab a napkin and wipe my cheeks while Ruby does the same. When we're under control, she covers my hand with hers. "I miss him too and I'll talk about him whenever you want."

"Thanks," I say, my voice a little shaky.

Her hand slips away and she grabs her wineglass. We spend several minutes watching and listening to the singer's rendition of Etta James's, *At Last*. When she sings the last lines of the song in that haunting voice of hers, a powerful chill sweeps over me, and for a fraction of a second I can feel John in the shift of the air and breath of my body.

I freeze, wanting to soak up the warmth that's so distinctly him, but then it's gone and I'm back in The Whisky. A peace settles deep within, and I'm so grateful for that one moment, I could weep.

The last notes of the song fade away and Ruby turns back to me. "So? Are you going to tell me or not?"

And, at last, we're at Michael and the strange whisper against my skin dissipates into the ether. I'm at a loss for what to say—not because I don't want to tell her—but because I don't know how to explain. So I decide on the simplest form of the truth. "The club I told you about, sometimes I still go there. I met Michael there about a week ago."

Had it only been a week? It feels like a lifetime.

"And?" she prompts.

I shake my head. "And I don't know. I want to stay away, that's my intention, but I haven't been able to. Tonight, well, tonight was a strange coincidence."

Her brow furrows. "He doesn't seem like your type."

A smile flirts at my lips then falls away. "I suppose that depends on your definition of type."

Comprehension dawns across her face. "Ah, so he's…um…that way."

I nod. I might not know the particulars yet, but Michael is most certainly "that way". I take a deep breath and confess, "I'm going out with him tomorrow night."

She straightens in her chair. "Like on a date?"

"Yes." Then it's my turn to blush. "I'm not sure how I ended up agreeing."

"Do you trust him?"

It occurs to me that it never crossed my mind not too. How strange. Curious as to why she seems worried, I ask, "Why do you think I shouldn't?"

She shrugs. "Well, I don't know, he's so big…and scary."

"Yeah, he is." And yet, I've never felt safer. I give her a reassuring smile. "He's trustworthy. I promise."

Brackets of doubt form on either side of her mouth. "Just because he's a cop doesn't make him trustworthy."

"Yeah, I know. And that's not why."

"Then why?" She leans forward.

"Experience, mainly, but it's more than that, he's responsible. Safe and level headed."

"How can you possibly know that?" Her tone is filled with incredulity.

I laugh, and the edges are a bit bitter. I pat her hand and assure her. "He's had to be to deal with me."

14.

I am so nervous I'm practically motion sick from all the jumping my stomach is doing. After an endless day at work, where the clock seemed to tick by, second by excruciating second, I made it home, took a shower and have been stressing about my wardrobe ever since. I'm on my fifth outfit change and sixteenth phone call to Ruby, who at this point, must wish I'd go back to being a reclusive mute.

Somehow, in my mind, I'd imagined being calmer. Cool and nonchalant about the whole thing. After all, it's not like I haven't had any contact with men since John died. Only, as I stare at my flushed cheeks in the mirror, I'd forgotten they didn't mean anything.

With Michael, I care way too much.

I blow out a hard breath, sending my long side-swept bangs into flight before they settle back into place. I wore my hair in loose curls, the flow haphazard and tousled over my shoulders. Bedroom hair. A look effected by a two-inch curling iron and

Bumble and Bumble's shine serum. I kept my makeup neutral, but my blue eyes look bright and excited. I need to find a way to calm down, or I'm going to hyperventilate and pass out.

I glance at my clock and let out a shriek. It's six forty-five, and I'm standing here in my underwear. Thank god I've at least decided on the set. I went with silk, edged with lace, but in a neutral boring color. Pretty, but not suggestive, it seems safe enough.

I take a deep breath and, this time, instead of starting with the outfit, I begin with the shoes. Shoes should be easy to pick out. He said we were going somewhere casual, so fancy high heels are out. The nights are cold, so anything open toed is abandoned as well. I search through the contents littering my closet floor and finally settle on a pair of distressed, brown knee-high boots in soft, buttery leather. They have a three-inch wedged heel, with hooks and eyes that lace up the front.

They're perfect.

I sigh in relief as it narrows down my outfit choices considerably. I flip through several dresses before settling on a cream sweater number with a low scoop neck. As soon as I slip it over my head, I know it's right. It drapes my body and manages to hug my curves without clinging. I look good, but not like I'm trying too hard.

The longer it's taken me to get ready the more concerned I've become about trying too hard. The irony isn't lost on me.

But now I have another problem. The Chicago weather and weight of the fabric demands tights. An item of clothing I can't wear. The sound of tearing nylon rips through my head, and my muscles contract, like the elastic is still rolled up and tight against my waist. I close my eyes and feel a wash of panic that has nothing to do with Michael.

No! No! No!

I won't let the horrid images invade my thoughts. I take a deep breath and steady myself, counting slowly in my head until I settle. Once the image subsides, I refocus. I'm making too big a deal out of this. I can wear my normal thigh highs and Michael won't think anything of it.

Another minute ticks by.

I could change into pants. But then I would have to change my shoes.

Maybe I should call Ruby again.

The intercom buzzer rings.

My heart leaps into my throat, as my stomach gives another lurch. I pick up my phone, and let the doorman buzz him in.

It's too late to change again.

I quickly pull on a pair of cream, thigh-high tights, zip up my boots and stand back to survey the results. Besides my cheeks, which are marred by two splotches of bright pink, I look pretty good.

I fan my face but it has no effect.

The doorbell rings.

My breath quickens as the nerves stomp through me, but I manage to walk out of my bedroom, and to my front door.

Heart racing nearly out of my chest, I open the door.

Michael fills the space and I can only stare. All other frantic thoughts still in the face of him. I don't know what I was expecting, but it wasn't this. How was it possible I didn't think he was handsome? He might not be a traditional pretty boy, but the man is downright gorgeous.

He stands there with his wicked smile, delectable in a black V-necked sweater that's pulled tight across the broad expanse of his chest, his hands tucked into a pair of gray, casual flat-front pants. There isn't even an ounce of stress visible as he props against my doorframe. "How's my girl tonight?"

Oh god. I think I might swoon.

The way the "my girl" rolls off his tongue is enough for the desire to surge through me. I want him. Just looking at him is making me weak in the knees.

This is going to be a disaster.

He straightens and takes a step toward me.

Involuntarily, I retreat.

Hazel eyes darken and he comes toward me again.

I move back.

He shakes his head. "You're not going to bolt, Layla."

I stop in my tracks, and take a deep breath. "Okay."

He comes to stand in front of me and reaches out to stroke one finger over my cheek. His hand is cold from the outside on my overheated skin. "Nervous?"

I nod, not able to pretend otherwise.

"Is this the first time since your fiancé died?"

The question trips me up. I frown, not knowing how to answer. Surely he must know I haven't been a saint.

"Not counting your self-punishment at the club."

My confusion lifts and I say, "Yes, although I did recently go on a blind date arranged by my sister. I met him out and, um, it wasn't the same."

A smile lifts the corners of his full, masculine lips. "And how'd that go?"

I decide on the truth. With him I always decide on the truth. "It would have been great if I hadn't met you first."

He laughs and shakes his head. "You never fail to surprise me, sugar."

I bite the inside of my cheek, unsure and awkward. I haven't been on a real date since I was nineteen. I have no idea how this is done.

He cups my neck and his thumb brushes over the skin on my throat. It calms me, centers me and I'm grateful. "You are one gorgeous girl, Layla Hunter."

I swallow. "Thank you."

A muscle ticks in his jaw, and I watch his Adam's apple bob as he swallows. "Everything we've been dancing around over the past week is going to get dealt with, one way or another, tonight."

I gulp. That's what I was afraid of. And desperately hoping for.

He presses into my pulse point. "My way. My rules. You don't have to worry about anything. Understood?"

Relief, and the loosening tension in my body, doesn't lie. It's what I want. To hand responsibility over to him. "Okay."

His hand tightens around my neck. "I'm going to kiss you."

My heart skips a beat then resumes the pounding of a galloping racehorse.

He leans close, but unlike the first time, when we'd only just met, I tilt my face to greet him, breathless with anticipation. Right before his lips touch mine he stops and says, "I only hope we survive."

The first brush of his mouth is like an electric shock to my system. He doesn't plunge as I expect, considering the heat between us, instead he gently sweeps across my lips, frustrating me.

I haven't kissed anyone but John in too many years to count, and I thought it would be strange to have another man's mouth on me. But it's not. And Michael is not some other man. He feels right.

I'm suddenly greedy.

I want more. Need more.

I put my hand on his biceps and rise to my tiptoes, hungry for the taste of him.

But he still doesn't deepen the kiss, just teases me

with a flick of his tongue.

I plaster my body to his and his erection presses against my belly. I arch into his cock as my fingers curl into the fabric of his sweater.

He takes my hips in his hands. They're so big and strong I want to melt into him, but he doesn't allow that, instead he lifts his head and sets me back.

I glare at him. I've resisted all this time and when I finally give in he gives me the equivalent of an air kiss.

He grips my chin. "Stop trying to control everything, Layla."

I blink, and try to pull away, but can't. "I'm not."

His eyes narrow menacingly and I can't deny the leap of excitement tinged with fear that zings through me. He lets me go, juts his chin towards the door and says, "Let's go."

I blow out an exasperated breath and turn away, stomping to my closet to angrily jerk my coat from its hanger.

Behind me, he chuckles. "Impressive tantrum."

Cheeks burning in humiliation, I swing around and point a finger at him. "I. Am not. Throwing a tantrum."

One dark brow cocks. "Really now? You could have fooled me."

He's infuriating. Unable to control my agitation, I yell, "You think you know everything but you're not half as smart as you think you are. This is a big deal for me."

A huge deal, breaking my cardinal rule for him.

"Yeah, I know," he says mildly, looking unimpressed.

I shove my arms into my coat, already hating him, even as I burn. I button my coat and tie the belt with a hard yank, cinching my waist way too tight.

He walks over to me, grabs the belt, and unties it before redoing the knot so it rests comfortably around my waist. When he's done, he looks at me, his expression unreadable. "You've been controlling every single thing since your fiancé died. And while it might make you feel safe, it will never make you happy."

I feel small, vulnerable and scared. I cross my arms protectively over my chest. I drop his gaze and study my hardwood floors and say softly, "One of my rules was no kissing of any kind. No man's lips have touched me, or any part of my body, since he died."

"Ah, I see," Michael says, but doesn't sound all that surprised. He wraps his arms around me and it's like being wrapped up in the most heavenly blanket. "Can you at least trust I know what you need? And how to give it to you?"

I'm so tired of trying to hold together my crumbling armor. It's bone-deep exhausting. For the moment, I give it up, and put my head on his chest. I could stay like this forever. "Yes, I think so."

"I suppose that's good enough for now." He rubs my back and I press closer.

My lashes want to drift shut. I could sleep with him. He might even keep my nightmares away.

"Ready?" His embrace loosens.

I nod, and reluctantly step away. I turn toward the door and put my hand on the knob, opening the door a crack.

He comes up behind me and puts his palm against the door. It snaps shut. He sweeps my hair to rest on one shoulder and leans down, brushing his mouth against my neck.

I shiver, and lean back against him.

"I want you, Layla." His voice is a husky whisper in my ear. "More than I have ever wanted anyone." His tongue flicks across my pounding pulse and I bite back a moan as his teeth scrape over my skin. "Now is not the time to kiss you the way that I want, because I swear to god, if I do, you'll end up fucked in whatever position is most convenient."

Jesus, the heat, it's like an inferno. I want to scream in frustration. That's how much I want him. It's like an ache. A craving that overpowers anything I've ever experienced.

His lips skim over the line of my jaw. "And call me old-fashioned, but I'm going to at least take you to dinner before I violate the hell out of you."

The images that flash through my mind are so explicit, so carnal, I gasp.

He grips my chin, twists my head and claims my mouth in his.

It's the kiss I've been dreaming about. Hard and aggressive. Powerful and commanding. He takes complete control as his tongue sweeps along mine.

I moan, and attempt to twist in order to get better access, but he stops me with one arm wrapped around my waist, holding me in place. White-hot desire beads my nipples and I can feel the heat between my thighs.

Then, just like that, it's over.

I'm left dazed, breathless and wanting more.

Low in his throat, he growls, kisses me again with a fast, brutal press of his mouth. "Let's go."

I don't want to, but obey, because that's what he wants and what I want too.

After a nearly silent drive over, where I think we were both trying to settle our raging hormones, he guides me into one of Chicago's most sought-after hot spots. From where I'm standing, it doesn't look like there's an open table in the large, loft-style restaurant, and there's people milling around the front door and at the bar. The crowd parts for Michael as we walk, seamlessly falling away as though by magic, and as soon as he gives his name to the hostess we're taken right to a table.

It's a spacious booth tucked into the back corner. I slide into the prime location, and Michael takes the seat adjacent, which allows us the intimacy of both looking at each other and being close. His knee touches mine. With a grin he reaches under the table, shifting my legs to rest against his as though he has all the right in the world.

I contemplate moving away, but don't, tonight I want to surrender. Besides, I like the way his muscled thigh feels against my leg, that perfect mix of danger and safety. After the hostess hands us our menus, featuring the latest trend in "small plates" and leaves, I turn to stare at him.

"How did you get reservations here?" It's a six-month wait for a table on the weekend, and we've known each other a week. "Did you already have another date planned? Or is this an example of police corruption?"

He chuckles, shaking his head. "Did anyone ever tell you that you have a smart mouth?"

"Yes, as a matter of fact." The memory of John creeps in and my shoulders slump a bit. "But not for a long time."

He smiles and puts an arm around my shoulder, tugging me close. "I think I'd like your fiancé. What was his name?"

I stiffen against him. How can he be so casual? I swallow and answer, "John."

"Where did you meet him?" His thumb rubs slowly up and down the curve of my neck.

"What does it matter?"

"It matters because he's part of who you are, and your relationship with him is important."

I can't talk about John, not tonight. It's too hard, when the guilt of wanting the man across from me, threatens to overwhelm. I don't want to remember what it was like between us. It's too much like infidelity. I deflect, and pull back, shaking my head. "Who are you? I thought cops were supposed to be all blunt force and hot tempered, why are you always so logical and reasonable?"

He grins. "That's Hollywood cops, if real cops acted that way, they'd end up dead. A cool, level head keeps you alive."

My throat goes dry at the mention of his profession and I realize too late I've been avoiding it, pretending it didn't exist. He comes in contact with violence every day. I pick up my water glass and chug down half of it. He could be killed.

Murdered.

Just like John.

The waitress comes over, interrupting the dark path my thoughts are taking, and bringing me back to the present. She looks like a hipster with curly brown hair, a face scrubbed free of makeup, and a mellow smile. She starts to speak but Michael shakes his head. "Give us a minute."

"No problem," she says and walks away.

"What is it?" Michael asks, studying me intently.

I press my lips together and rub my clammy hands on my dress. Michael's profession doesn't matter. This date is temporary insanity, not a relationship. I'll be long gone before anything can happen to him.

"Layla, answer me." His voice is hard.

I straighten my shoulders and say as lightly as I can, "I don't know, sorry. It's silly but it only just hit me that your job is violent."

His expression softens, and once again his thumb starts that slow stroking. "Yeah, it is. But probably not as dangerous as you think if you remember I'm an after-the-fact guy."

I tilt my head, my brow furrowing. "What do you mean?"

"It means I usually get called in after the crime's

already committed. I'm not first response, at least not anymore."

He has a point, but I don't want to think about his job right now. I want to bury my head in the sand and give myself this one night without worrying.

It's not too much to ask, is it? Not too much of a betrayal. John wouldn't begrudge me this one night.

Before I can speak, a tall, willowy, stunningly gorgeous redhead, wearing a tight black tee, emblazoned with the restaurant's logo, and matching skirt walks up to the table with a huge smile on her face, her gaze trained on Michael. She holds out her arms. "You made it."

Smooth as silk, he slides from the booth, leaving a cold spot in his wake. He hugs her and they kiss each other on both cheeks. "Thank you again."

"Of course, you know I'd do anything for you."

I can only stare, and focus on making sure to keep my mouth shut, instead of gaping open.

Michael turns to me, gesturing in my direction. "This is Layla Hunter. Layla, this is Gwen Johnson, she owns the place, which is why we have such a great table."

Gwen gives me a mega-watt, supermodel smile, and reaches over to shake my hand.

How can a restaurant owner be so thin?

And why am I jealous?

I cover my awkwardness with a bright smile of my own. "It's a pleasure to meet you."

"You too." She's got those really light, striking blue eyes that redheads sometimes have, and they dance with mischief. She gives Michael a sly glance. "So this is the one Jillian told me about?"

Michael rolls his eyes and says to me, "Jillian and Gwen are best friends."

I'm starting to relax and the knot in my stomach loosens. "Thank you for the table, I've never been here before and, like everyone else in Chicago, have heard nothing but raves."

She puts her hands together. "Oh…a newbie…I love it." She turns to Michael. "Let me put your order together."

Michael shifts his attention to me. "Well, what do you think?"

A meal specially prepared by one of the tops chefs in the city, I can't possibly refuse. "That'd be wonderful."

"Fabulous." Gwen looks me over. "Any allergies or things you hate?"

"Nope, I'm not at all picky and will try anything once."

Gwen winks at me. "A girl who lives on the edge."

I have to stifle my laugh, if she only knew.

Michael slides back in the booth and narrows his eyes on Gwen. "Try not to hover."

Gwen laughs. "Oh, all right. I'll be good, but I'm still reporting to Jillian."

She leaves, motions to the waitress, and the two of them head off to what I presume is the kitchen.

Michael's voice shakes me from staring after them. "Do you see what I do for you?"

My brows knit. "I would have gone anywhere."

He crooks his finger, urging me closer, and, of course, I comply. "But I wanted to impress you."

"You did?" I'm surprised.

"Yes, Layla, I did."

"Why?" I don't know why this so hard to believe. He seems so confident and sure, it's hard to imagine him trying at anything.

"Because I need to overshadow the things you don't like…the things about me that scare you." He brushes my hair off my cheek.

His answer makes my breath catch and my heart pound a bit harder. When I think I can speak without my voice cracking, I say, "You always know the right answer."

He laughs. "Trust me, I'm bound to fuck up eventually, and when I do, hopefully there will be enough good things you'll be able to forgive me."

I don't know what to think of the suggestion of a relationship, and what it might mean. I need to believe this doesn't mean anything. That he doesn't mean anything.

I tilt my head to the kitchen. "So you know the owner? That's convenient."

He nods. "Jillian and Gwen have been best friends since birth. Her family lived next door."

So he lived next to that gorgeous woman? I push aside my jealousy.

"Where'd you grow up?" It feels as though I met him a lifetime ago, but really I don't know much about him. I'm curious, and suddenly want to know everything, so my knowledge matches the depth of my emotions.

"Evanston." He names one of the diverse, well-off, lakeshore suburbs on the north side. "How about you?"

"Wilmette."

He smiles. "That doesn't surprise me."

"So I take it you don't come from a family of cops."

He laughs, outright. "God no. My parents were horrified."

The waitress comes over and puts a martini glass filled with something the color of blue sapphires in front of me, and what looks like plain old whiskey or scotch in front of Michael. "Gwen said to give you these, but if you don't like them, let me know and we'll get you something else."

"Thanks." Michael wraps his fingers around the rocks glass.

"Sure thing." She nods and offers her mellow smile. "Your first course will be right up."

I stare at the drink. I'd never seen a cocktail quite that color before. It's almost too pretty to drink. "What is this?"

"God only knows. I stick to Glenlivet, but I'm sure it's trendy and delicious."

I take a tentative sip, and close my eyes in pleasure, as the faint hints of rum, lime and other flavors I can't even begin to identify hit my taste buds. I take another drink, this time more healthy, resisting the urge to down the to-die-for concoction in one gulp.

"Good?" Michael asks, clearly amused.

"Heavenly." I swipe my finger along the glass's edge, rimmed with black sugar, and lick. I seriously don't think I've ever tasted anything so good. I take another drink, and sweep my tongue over the rim—it's sugar, but there's something else in there too. "Gwen is a genius."

When Michael doesn't respond I look at him and find his gaze hungry and hot on my mouth. He leans in and flicks his tongue along my lower lip, shocking me still.

"I could watch you drink those all day." His voice is rough. The air crackles with sex. He rubs his lips over mine and it's like a bolt of lightning straight through me. "You taste delicious." Another lick. "Maybe I'll bring some home so I can lick it from your clit later."

I gasp, my cheeks heating from his words, and the alcohol shoots straight to my head after a day of not eating. My breath turns shallow and fast as I'm caught in his magnetic presence.

The waitress returns with a long, flat wooden board filled with various breads and dips, breaking my trance. Reality floods me with a whoosh.

Michael turns and thanks her, so casually, it's as

though we'd just been discussing the weather.

She puts down the tray, and starts describing each item, but I don't hear a word of it because blood is rushing in my ears and I'm throbbing.

As she keeps talking, Michael slips a hand under the table, and onto my knee. I stiffen, and his fingers play over my tights. My entire focus is on his hot palm.

Oh god.

His hand creeps up my leg, agonizingly slow.

I hold my breath. Anticipating the climb of his fingers. I can almost feel it, the shock of his hand on my bare skin, the slide of him brushing over the silk of my panties. His fingers working their way past the elastic to touch moist, hot flesh.

Unable to resist, I arch, my legs parting of their own volition. I stare fixedly at the board of breads in front of me, but my rapt attention is on him.

He stops.

I bite my lip.

He toys with the lace edge of my tights, running his thumb along the edge. I shift again. Urging him to go farther. It's been so long. So incredibly long since I've done anything like this, and only now do I feel the depths of how much I've missed it. How much I need it.

His hand squeezes my leg, goes a tiny bit higher, and then retreats to a respectable level.

I want to scream.

He does it again.

I clench my teeth to keep from moaning.

And again.

Sweat beads my back. I'm mentally willing him to go higher. To, please, touch me.

But he never does.

He just makes me want. Need. Crave it like the addict I am.

After what feels like an eternity, the waitress finally

finishes her speech and leaves.

I fight to keep from panting like a dog in heat.

His hand falls from my thigh, and I have to stop myself from crying out in disappointment. He reaches for a slice of bread then covers it with a creamy spread. He holds it out to me. "Here, you'll like this."

"What is it?"

He gives me his most evil grin. "Weren't you paying attention?"

I snatch the bread from him. "Don't be cute."

He knows just what he's doing and it both irritates and enflames me.

He laughs, the sound wicked and amused, and it rolls through me like a wave.

To keep from saying something stupid, I take a bite of bread, which turns out to be pretzel bread topped with something laced with honey, and is utterly divine. I moan in pleasure as I chew slowly and deliberately, savoring every bite. It's like I've woken up from a long famine and I'm tasting everything for the first time. Which, actually, isn't that far from the truth.

He laughs. "Thank god you're not one of those girls who hates to eat."

I take another bite of the bread and close my eyes in pure bliss. "No way."

I look down at my plate; while caught up in my food porn, he'd put another one of the breads in front of me. I hurry to take another bite. This one is as good as the last and filled with cranberries and nuts mixed with something sweet.

I'm suddenly starving, for the food, for him, for life.

15.

I'm as greedy for information about him, as I am for the food in front of me, and I ask, "Why were your parents horrified about you being a police officer?"

He studies me and when I start squirming, a smile ghosts his lips. "Because the Banks are investment bankers. That's the family tradition, unbroken for generations until my sisters and I came along."

"Goes with the name, huh?" I laugh and it occurs to me it sounds almost natural.

He picks up my martini glass. "Have another sip."

It's too delicious to refuse, and I drain the rest of what's left of the drink, licking the mystery-flavored sugar from my lips.

His gaze darkens while his hand slips under the table to rest on my thigh.

I have to force back the gasp at the contact and quickly say, "So your sisters aren't investment bankers either?"

"My sister, Sara, her husband is a partner in my

dad's firm, but she stays at home with my niece. That's as close as my dad's going to get with this generation of rebels." He strokes the inner part of my knee with slow deliberateness. "Jillian is an artist. Or at least that's her claim this month."

The touch is innocent, but oh so distracting. I long to open my thighs wide in invitation, but tonight, I'm like a schoolgirl on her first unchaperoned date. Every move and action seems portent with meaning and innuendo. "Is artist better or worse than law enforcement?"

His hand leaves my leg, picks yet another piece of bread, and slathers it with a brownish dip before handing it to me. "I suppose it depends on who you ask on what day."

"Does it bother you?"

"Nope. They've forgiven my choice of profession. Sure my mom gets scared and my father worries about how I'll get by on less than three hundred thousand a year, but it's just normal parent stuff." There's no bitterness in his words, actually he sounds downright good-natured about the whole thing.

I take the flat bread, and bite into some sort of balsamic and truffle bruschetta, which is as divine as everything else I've tasted tonight. "Three hundred grand, huh?"

"Sometimes I want to take him into the middle of a high-crime, poverty-ridden area and drop him off for a few hours so he can gain some perspective." His tone is a mixture of exasperation and amusement, and I'd bet money that they have a solid relationship.

I chew slowly and when I swallow, I ask, "How'd you discover you wanted to be a cop?"

"It was a fluke. I had a football scholarship to University of Pennsylvania. I was enrolled in all the standard business classes, ready to walk in my dad's footsteps, and I took a law enforcement class on a whim as an elective." He shrugs, picks up a lock of my hair and twirls it around his finger. "It was love at first sight."

"You played ivy league football?" He's big enough, and smart enough, but it's so hard to imagine him as an eighteen-year-old kid roaming the campus quad.

"Yeah." He leans close to whisper, "You've stopped flinching when I touch you."

Faint heat fills my cheeks, and I say as lightly as I can muster, "I didn't realize I did."

As if to emphasize his point, he strokes a path over my jaw. "Only when you weren't expecting it, but you're getting used to it now." He brushes a kiss across my lips. "Progress."

When he pulls away I fight the urge to chase after him. "Is that why you keep touching me? To get me use to it?"

"I touch you because I like touching you. Your skin is soft and your hair feels like silk." His eyes darken. "But mostly I like how you respond, the little gasps of surprise, how you shiver in excitement, how your pupils dilate when I wrap my fingers around your throat."

My blood heats at his words.

He rubs a finger over the pulse picking up considerable speed in my neck. "Like right now, you're that perfect mixture of terrified and aroused."

I swallow, my thighs clenching. I know what that look does to someone like him; the same thing being called a good girl does to someone like me. Instant hunger.

Our waitress comes over with another platter of food, breaking the spell. She puts down a plate of ahi tuna made three different ways, explaining them to us in a hurried manner that makes it clear she realizes she's interrupting.

Michael is nothing but gracious, thanking her,

before ordering us another round of drinks.

After she leaves, he takes a fork and cuts into the seared fish and holds it up to me, his gaze hot on mine. "Take a bite."

It's an order, delivered softly, and with no particular significance, but an order all the same. My brain wants to resist, but my desire for him overrides it. I open my mouth, and he slides the fork between my lips. The hard crunch of the sear gives way to tender flesh that melts over my tongue. "It's good."

He picks up another piece and takes his own bite. "Yeah, it is."

I move to grab my fork but he covers my hand and shakes his head. "No. I'll do it."

My fingers move relentlessly over the tines, but I nod. He spears the next piece and holds it out. Our eyes lock as he places the cool metal against my lips. "Open."

I obey.

"Take it slowly with your tongue."

My whole body flushes, even as I inwardly cringe at what he wants. Being fed by someone is an intimate act, especially the way he's doing it with that look in his eyes, and we're in the middle of a crowded restaurant.

I give in to natural instinct and shake my head.

"Yes." That's all he says. No bark of command, or inflection in his tone. Straightforward. Simple. Impossible to ignore.

The waitress returns, and out of the corner of my eye, I see her put the drinks down in front of us.

My cheeks burn, certain she knows everything that's going on, but Michael's gaze does not waver from mine.

"Do you need anything else?" The server's voice is hesitant.

"No." Michael's answer is clipped and she moves

away. He motions with the fork, but says nothing else.

I swallow hard. I've engaged in my fair share of sexual activity back in that underground club, done things that would give most normal people pause, but since John died, this is my first real submissive act. Everything else, even at its roughest and most extreme, was play-acting. Trying to get my fix in the safest way possible. I haven't risked anything.

This one simple gesture, taking a piece of food off Michael's fork, will be the first risk I've taken since I walked into that alley and my life changed forever.

I'm terrified.

He nods. "You can do it, Layla. You want to."

He's right. Beyond the fear and anxiety, I'm beyond excited. Wet and hopeful, filled with that indescribable exhilaration I thought I'd never experience again.

I take a deep breath and do as I'm told.

As my tongue curls around the fish, Michael's own pupils dilate. "Good girl."

Although I'm sure it's delicious, I don't taste it, as my insides have turned to mush. Molten lava. My breath catches in my throat.

He leans in.

My lips part. I want this kiss. I need it.

"How is everything?" A female voice breaks the spell and the entire restaurant rushes back.

Michael jerks back and glares at a wide-eyed, innocent Gwen.

"Fine." The word coming out like he chewed it between his teeth first.

The mood shatters and I straighten in my seat to say politely, "Everything is beyond fine. Your food is incredible."

"Thank you." She beams at me, and then her smile shifts to something sly as she turns to Michael. "Are you bringing Layla to Jillian's birthday party?"

I tense, all that languid heat cooling as I look at

Michael in horror.

Michael covers my knee with a hand. "Go away, Gwen."

She huffs, but I can see her amusement. "Is that the thanks I get?"

"Goodbye, Gwen."

She tosses her hair. "No biggie, I'll just go call Jillian for a chat."

I can't help the smile that tugs at my lips when Michael waves her away. "Have fun."

He shakes his head. "Did I mention they're a meddlesome bunch?"

"So far, the food has been more than worth it." I shrug, watching the gorgeous Gwen disappear between double doors. I can't help being the tiniest bit curious. I say in a light, breezy voice, "With her culinary skills, I can't believe you haven't swept her up long ago." Not my most subtle inquiry.

He laughs. "Jealous?"

"Of course not," I say primly. "Merely curious, she's quite beautiful." Which is actually an understatement.

"She's also a pain in the ass." He sighs. "But, truth be told, we did secretly go out on one date."

A lump forms in the pit of my stomach. Why did I ask? "Secretly?"

"At one point, our families were really pushing us, and it made sense, I suppose. So one night, drunk on too much tequila we agreed to go on a date, just to see." His fingers trace a slow path over my knee, as though he's not talking about some other woman. "Yes, she's beautiful, as my friends routinely inform me, but I don't know. I watched her grow up; she's my baby sister's best friend, and I could never work up any enthusiasm for her. But, I decided what the hell."

His hands inched up my thigh and I can't deny I want to spread for him, regardless of the subject matter, but my legs stay firmly clasped like any good, normal girl. "So what happened?"

"We had fun, but I have more chemistry with dirt. We actually made fun of it the entire time."

I'm a lot happier than I should be, but tried to put on a sympathetic face. "That's unfortunate."

His hand slips another inch up my thigh, thankfully still covered by my thick tights. "Not really, even if we had chemistry it would have never worked out and we would have ended up ruining a good friendship."

"Why's that?" My muscles tremble from the exertion of staying shut.

"Well for one, I'm a cop, and she's a restaurant owner. Between the two of us it's a scheduling nightmare." His gaze drops to my lips then raises back up to meet my eyes. "But more important, she's not submissive."

The word hangs in the air, flustering me as nothing else could have. Which is ridiculous since it's been between us from the beginning. I can only sputter, "How do you know?"

His fingers creep higher, until he hits the wedge of my clasped thighs. "Same way you do, sugar."

Like attracts like, without fail. Every time. I know this, so I can't explain why I say, "I don't know what you mean."

He squeezes my leg. "Open."

My legs stay firmly shut.

His attention locks on me. "That night we met, I watched you searching, sizing everyone up, before dismissing them. But the second our paths crossed, you knew. How'd you know, Layla?"

I swallow hard. Sixth sense. "Instinct."

"Exactly." His fingers dig hard into my flesh, until the pressure and need to obey becomes too much. I relent, and open. His hand relaxes and stays right where it is, frustrating me when I want him to go higher.

But, of course, he doesn't, and I know why, because he wants his victory to sit between us.

My throat is dry, and my body on fire. I need it. I need him. Need that indescribable feeling of being controlled. So I open my mouth and say the stupidest thing I could to a dominant. "I'm not really that submissive."

He laughs. "Call it whatever you want. It's all semantics."

I experience a vague sense of disappointment, and realize too late I'm baiting him, wanting him to show me how wrong I am. I lick my lips. It's stupid of me, because it will surely backfire, but I'm unable to stop the path I'm on. "I'm just trying to explain I don't like all that lord, master of the underworld, scene stuff."

"I already know what kind of girl you are, Layla. And I sure as hell know what you need."

My chin tilts as a distinct surge of defiance pulses through me. "I hate all that Dom stuff, all those rituals and protocol."

He raises a brow, but says nothing, and my mouth runs away from me.

"You might know the basics, but I yield for no one." I hold my breath. I'm playing with fire and I want to get burned.

The waitress comes to our table with another plate. Michael waves her away. "No explanation is necessary."

She doesn't even hesitate, just turns and scurries away.

He shifts his attention back to me and pins me with a stern look that has me sitting straighter in my seat. "I know what you're doing, and it's not going to work."

Petulant, I cross my arms over my chest. "I'm not doing anything."

"You're impatient, and trying to force me to exert

my dominance over you."

Shit. I've tried too hard and overplayed my hand. My only excuse is I'm out of practice.

"You need to understand two things: My control over you is already firmly in hand." His hand slides up the length of my thigh, to rest on my overheated bare flesh. "And I'll fuck you when I'm damn well good and ready and not a second before."

I stare down at my plate, chastised and wanting. It's hard to explain to someone who doesn't have my tendencies what a statement like that does to me. How the reprimand mixes with anger and humiliation, becoming a powerful cocktail of arousal. How it both puts me in my place and makes me wet and free. It's what I need, what I've been longing for all this time. Unbearably missing since John died.

The memory of what it was like whispers over my skin, light, but achingly familiar. I've tried so hard to forget, so hard to resist, I'd almost forgotten the most important part.

When I finally surrender the battle, I am free.

He strokes my thigh. "Tell me what you're thinking."

I take a deep breath and tell him the absolute truth. "This is real."

His hand falls from my leg before he slides an arm around my shoulder and tugs me close. He plants a kiss on my head then whispers in my ear, "Yes, Layla, it is."

"I don't know if I can. Not anymore."

He cups my jaw and forces me to meet his gaze. "All you need to worry about right now is dinner. That's it. Nothing else. We're going to eat and talk. I'm going to touch you. I'm going to kiss those lips that drive me crazy whenever I want. I'm going to play with you and make you wet. And I'm going to learn you. That's all. It's that simple. You can do that."

There is nothing simple about it. I can only turn pleading eyes on him.

His thumb brushes over my mouth before he leans down and licks my lower lip. "I know what you want, sugar, and I'm going to give it to you. I'll fuck you hard and rough. I'll take you. Possess you. You'll fight me and I'll win because it's what we both want. But tonight, right now, here in this restaurant, I'm going to be soft. Because, even though I know you don't want it, I think you need soft."

My throat closes over because he's so perfectly described all the frantic, mixed-up emotions running rampant in my brain. It makes me think of John. How it really was between us, not the bastardized version in my head. That mix of hard and soft. The gentle danger. It's a part of me I've only shared with John and as much I want to, I'm not sure I can with anyone else. I croak out, "That belongs to him."

"Yeah, it does." Michael brushes my cheek. "Giving it to me doesn't negate that."

Of course, the tears come. I can't stop them; no matter how hard I try. "He didn't like to share."

A smile flickers over Michael's lips. His cruel, beautiful mouth I want more than I want my next breath. "I can't imagine he did. We're alike that way. I don't share either."

I pick up my napkin and dab under my eyes, hoping I'm not ruining my makeup. I laugh, and it's brittle and bitter. "This is some date, huh? Isn't this what every man wants? A girl crying all over him because of her dead fiancé."

"Hey," he says, his voice hard. "Stop that. I'm exactly where I want to be. I knew what I was getting into, Layla. There are no surprises. And I'm a patient man."

"I can't give you what you want." I wave my napkin at him, agitated now.

"What do you think I want?"

I raise my gaze to meet his. "You want me to open up and bleed for you and I can't do that. Not now. Not ever."

He is silent for a very long time, his expression unreadable. His hand drops away and I miss his heat. He scoots back, putting distance between us, and places his arm on the back of the booth, not touching me. He juts his chin toward the entryway. "Walk away, Layla. You can forget all about me and go back to your safe, grief-stricken bubble where you'll never be hurt ever again."

My heart starts to slam in my chest, pounding in my throat. Panic washes over me, so fierce my vision dims.

Ruthless, he points to the door. "You keep saying you want me to let you go, that you can't, so here's your chance to run. Leave. I'll never bother you again."

My hands curl into fists as I blink at the door. Patrons are pouring into the already crowded restaurant while only a few strays venture out into the cool Chicago air. I bite my lower lip. I can't.

As much as I know what I am supposed to do, as much as I need to stay true to John, I can't pry myself out of this seat, even if he came in and sat down next to me. I start to cry and I shake my head, unable to speak.

Michael once again slides close and pulls me into his chest. "You're afraid, and overwhelmed, but you don't want to leave. Can you at least accept that?"

I'm trembling; I tilt my face up to his.

He rubs his thumb over my lower lip. "Trust me enough to keep you safe. Will you do that?"

I think of endless nights stretched out, lonely and without him, as I troll through the club, punishing myself with random acts of cruelty. I can't go back. I don't want to. I want what Michael is offering. I nod.

"Yes."

This isn't about sex. This is about surrender. To him. To myself. To the possibility of what we may become.

16.

The rest of the night had played out exactly as he'd said it would, but he hadn't touched me since we'd left the restaurant. I knew why. Sex and tension pulsed between us like a heartbeat, threatening to consume us.

And now I stand at the edge of Michael's king-size bed, my gaze darting nervously around the room, looking anywhere and everywhere but at his headboard. An intricate, iron scroll pattern that, combined with the rich, velvety chocolate-brown comforter, gives the bed a medieval flair.

All that iron. All those different ways to tie a girl up.

Jealousy storms inside me as I imagined the women he's laid across that bed, arms stretched wide, wrists manacled to the iron. Pale skin against cool metal.

And I wasn't just jealous of their existence, but that they'd had what I never could. My fingers play over my wrists as images of that night flood into my memory. Assaulting all my senses, overtaking me.

The rush of terror pulls me into the abyss so quickly I'm powerless to stop the onslaught. There's no chance to calm my breathing. To count.

In a flash, I'm back in my own private nightmare.

The darkness. The duct tape cutting into my skin. My smothered screams. My helplessness as I watched John's battered body slip to the ground, his blood slowly seeping out as his life drained away.

The panic storms relentlessly over me, and my breath becomes a rapid shallow pant as blood pounds through my ears and my vision blurs.

The alley.

The shadows.

The damp smell.

The rusty taste of blood.

It's all I can see. All I can hear, taste, and feel.

"Layla!" A sharp, male voice behind me.

I don't respond. I'm paralyzed. The fear a hard, angry vise that won't let go. My heart rages in my chest, threatening to burst. Adrenaline is a hot rush along my skin.

I can't breathe. I'm going to die.

"Layla." Strong hands clasp my waist, turning me.

I scream.

"Layla." The utter calm of my name on Michael's lips shakes me from the memory.

Reality floods back and the vision fades, leaving behind a metallic taste in my mouth. Covering my face with my hands, I fight to remember my breathing exercises as my heart races, not cued into the fact that I'm not in danger.

Count.

I'm supposed to count.

Palm on my belly to regulate my breath.

Inhale.

Exhale.

Michael pulls me close and I sink into his hard

chest, closing my eyes. His hands stroke my back. He murmurs nonsense, soothing me with his hands. I lock on to his voice, the slide of his palm on my back, until my breathing slows. I have no idea how long we stand like that; it could have been five minutes or five hours, but finally my heart rate calms and the panic retreats.

I shudder from the leftover anxiety and swallow hard.

I don't know how to do this anymore. But I can't let him go. I clutch tighter. "I'm sorry."

"Sshhhhh, you have nothing to be sorry for." His voice is so soft and warm I want to curl into it.

"It's getting worse instead of better." I'd thought the panic attacks were the one thing I had under control, but I was wrong.

He traces a finger over my jaw before gripping my chin and raising my gaze to his. "Since you met me?"

Unable to speak, I nod.

His unusual hazel eyes steady me. Calmness settles inside me, and my muscles ease.

He toys with my hair, his other hand still skimming over my back. "Have you considered it's because you're not repressing your emotions?"

It's what Dr. Sorenson had said. "Yes."

"Sit down on the bed." He gently lowers me to the mattress and I cling to his arm, not wanting to let him go. "I'm not going anywhere."

I reluctantly release him, wrapping my arms around myself in a hug as I shiver.

He walks over and picks up a chair that's sitting in the corner, pulling it over to the bed where he sits in front of me. He takes my hands, rubbing my ice-cold fingers between his hot palms. We sit like that, knees touching, fingers clasped for a long time until all my vital signs return to normal and my core temperature warms.

Finally, he asks, "Better?"

I nod.

He squeezes my hands. "I need to tell you something, but you're not going to be happy about it."

Alarm bells clang in my head again, I try and pull away, but he doesn't let go. "What's wrong?"

"Nothing is wrong." His expression is a hard line of concern. "I didn't want to bring it up tonight, but I see now I don't have a choice. I only hope you'll understand."

I lick my dry lips and look at him expectantly. "I'm listening."

He takes a deep breath and slowly exhales. "I read your case file."

It's like a slap in the face. My head snaps back and I jerk my hands away. This time he releases me. He has those images of me in his head now. It's the last thing I want. Betrayal rings clear in my tone as I ask, "How could you?"

He rakes a hand through his hair before putting his elbows on his knees and placing his open palms on my legs. "I understand you're not happy and I don't blame you, but I didn't read it to appease my curiosity. I had to know, because you're not ready to talk about it, and I couldn't risk triggering you."

I look down at the floor. He knows. Only the doctors, the police, and Dr. Sorenson know the whole truth, but they don't count. They aren't part of my real life.

Gently, he runs his thumb over my wrists. "I won't tie you to the bed, Layla. I won't restrain your wrists in any way, not even with my hands."

Tears slip down my cheeks and I nod, my throat too tight to speak.

"Is that the worst trigger? Or are there others I should know about?"

I sit in silence for a long time but finally I manage to strangle out the words. "I don't like anything tight on my waist."

"Okay," he says, his deep voice soothing. "What about your throat?"

I swallow. "That's okay."

"Your mouth?"

"I don't know. My mouth has always been off limits." They covered my mouth with duct tape so I wouldn't scream, but the thought of Michael covering my mouth makes me shiver in awareness. Since it's always been one of my rules I'm not sure how I'll react.

"We won't test it out now." He presses foreword, his knees bracketing mine. "I will be very careful, Layla."

I can only nod. In this, I trust him. He's proven he'll care for me, that he has my best interests and wellbeing at heart. My hands curl into fists and I bite my lip. I need him to be careful, but I don't *want* him to be.

That he understands this speaks volumes.

He continues, breaking through my thoughts. "You'll stay here with me tonight, that's not negotiable. But if you're not ready, sex is off the table."

Hanging my head, I close my eyes. I take a deep breath and admit the truth. "That's not what I want."

"And what do you want?"

"You. Tonight. Now." Something deep inside me needs to feel whole again, and he can give me that.

He reaches for me, and tilts my chin until I meet his gaze. "Are you sure?"

"Yes." And when he doesn't look quite convinced I add, "I haven't been this sure of anything in a very long time."

The concern clears from his face, but he remains serious. "I violated your privacy and I'm sorry."

I wait for a bit…but he doesn't offer an additional excuse. I blink the tears from my eyes. "I didn't want you to know."

He smiles, all warm and tender. "I think, deep down, you know that's a lie. Because you have to know, sooner or later, I would have gotten the truth out of you."

It's true. He's not the kind of man that let's secrets go. If I spend enough time with him, eventually, he will know everything about me. I nod again.

"And just because I know doesn't mean you don't have to talk about it. We *will* talk about it."

"Why? It's the past and I can't change it. I can't go back."

He reaches out and touches my jaw before tucking a lock of my hair behind my ear. "It's time to start healing, Layla."

"Do you think you can rescue me?" I believed I couldn't be saved, but now I am not so sure, because with him, anything seems possible.

"No, I think you will rescue yourself." He leans forward and brushes his lips against mine. "I'll be there to hold your hand, but the hard work is up to you."

The words make me stronger somehow, more in control. "I don't understand what personality defect you have that makes you want me. But, tonight, I'm glad you do."

He laughs, shaking his head. "This is a real thing for you, isn't it?"

I shrug, not wanting to admit the truth. It is a thing for me, I keep waiting for him to figure out I'm not worth it. That I'm too much effort and not enough reward.

He sighs and once again clasps my hands. "I'm not an easy road kind of guy. I never have been. When you meet her, you can ask my mother, but the easy way is not in my nature, much to her distress. Even when I was a kid, when my friends and I would climb a tree, my friends would climb the easiest path, but I'd stand back and figure out the hardest way and take that route. When I played football my coaches would get pissed because I'd try and plow through the swarm of uniforms instead of taking the hole up the right side. When I could have followed in my dad's footsteps, I became a cop. I could have gotten a job in his firm, with a nice plush six-figure salary the day I graduated, but I couldn't do it. Even though every person I knew tried to talk me out of it. The easy way has never interested me."

"So I'm a challenge?" When I ceased to be so, would he let me go? The thought scares me more than I can admit.

"God yes," he says, squeezing my hands. "But it's more than that. I want you like I've never wanted anything in my life. There is something about you that reaches inside and won't let go."

It's the exact words I've thought about him. No matter what, I can't seem to turn away. And I'm exhausted keeping up the façade that I want to. I swallow hard. "In the restaurant, would you have really let me go?"

His hands slide around my waist. "No."

He spreads my knees and lifts me, pulling me on top of him. My dress slides up to rest high on my thighs, and I wrap my arms around his neck.

"But, I'll confess, it was easy to make the offer, because I knew you couldn't leave." Hands gripping my hips, he tugs me forward so I rock against his erection.

I bite back a moan at the friction.

I'm instantly hot, all his teasing at the restaurant rushing back. I admit something to him I've barely been able to admit to myself, and my voice cracks. "I've never felt like this before."

His big hand slides along my neck. "I know, sugar, me either."

My fingers tangle in his hair, and I press closer, whispering my secret in a trembling voice, "I need you. I'm afraid of how much I need you."

His free hand moves up my thigh and settles on my hip. "I'm not going anywhere."

I rock into him, circling my hips so I rub against his cock. He squeezes my ass, hard, and it ignites me to instant, greedy lust. Then he tugs at my dress and says in that voice that drives me mad, "Lift your arms."

I do and he peels my dress over my head and it falls to the floor. A second later my bra follows. His gaze locks on mine as his fingers hook into the sides of my lace-trimmed panties.

Anticipation roars through me as he pulls at the strings at my hips, his eyes never leaving mine.

The fabric snaps.

That special brand of electricity we generate fills the room. I lick my dry lips, unable to look away.

With one hand still on my hip, he gathers the bit of silk and lace, then tugs, so the material slides over my ass, before dragging over my clit. I shudder, clenching my jaw at the torture. He tosses the scrap of cloth on the floor.

I'm naked, except for my boots and thigh-high tights, while he's completely clothed.

Maybe a normal girl would be embarrassed by the vulnerability, but I'm not normal, and sitting here like this has me so aroused I might spontaneously combust.

The vulnerability, the disparity, is part of the allure.

He hisses out a breath, drinking me in. He rubs his thumbs over my nipples.

I gasp as it shoots straight to my clit.

"Fucking gorgeous." His voice is a low guttural growl. He pulls me closer and his lips claim mine.

And this kiss, it is a claiming. Pure, primal possession. His tongue sweeps in, demanding everything, and I don't resist. No, I just surrender to the force of him, the chemistry, and to my own desire.

Our breaths quickens as our mouths turn frantic. Hot and hungry. Unleashed with the passion that burns between us. His hands cover my breasts and he plucks at the sensitive buds. Needy desperation takes over, clouding any and all thought. My hips circle, riding his cock through his pants, wanting closer.

He pulls away, his lips gliding down my neck, pausing to scrape teeth against my pounding pulse, before he continues on, still lower, until his mouth covers my nipple and he licks.

There is no buildup. It's just instant overload.

"Michael." I grip his hair, pulling him close as he tugs at my swollen flesh. It's been so long since I've been touched like this, and only now do I realize how desperate I've been for it. How much I've missed it.

His lips move to my other breast, treating it with a type of gentle brutality, as his fingers move over my exposed wet nipple.

Blood pounds in my ears in rhythm to my demanding desire, and I wantonly start grinding against his erection.

He lifts his head and puts his hands on the curve of my hips, stilling me.

I blink at him, dazed and uncomprehending.

His hazel eyes have that look now, filled with power. He slowly unbuckles his belt and my fingers twitch, but he shakes his head and I swallow hard. Knowing something is about to happen, that he won't allow a simple bout of sex.

No, he'll make me work for it, because it's what we both need.

He unzips his pants and nods at my arms. "Put your hands on my knees."

With that voice, I don't even think about disobeying.

The action thrusts my breasts out, and he palms my nipples. "I want to watch you come."

His hands drop from my breasts, and he shifts his body, just enough to pull his pants and underwear down, and for his cock to spring free.

My mouth actually waters as the sight of him. Hard, long and thick. All I can think about is how much I want it. I can practically feel it filling my throat, hot and slick.

He growls, grabs a fist full of my hair, and jerks my head up, covering my lips with his. His tongue enters my mouth with a demanding thrust, but as soon as I move my arms, he pulls away. "Don't move."

I freeze, my breath fast, my excitement building to an impossible pitch. He grips my hips and yanks me forward, shifting until his cock rubs my clit.

I tremble, gasping as pleasure races along my skin.

He reaches between us, spreads me wide, and I think he's finally going to fuck me but instead he positions his shaft flush against my swollen, wet center.

I look at him, expectantly.

"Make yourself come, just like this. I don't want your hands to move." That control he's been containing all night is now thick in his voice, thrilling me.

He grips the back of the chair, lacing his fingers along the legs, making it clear he'll offer no assistance. His expression is hard, the dominance that rolls off him in waves, amplified.

My breath hitches. To do what he's wants, I'll have to work myself along his length, with no help from my hands, or his.

It's hard, what he's asking. It requires a certain amount of desperate wantonness.

I meet his gaze and his hazel eyes burn with an almost feral desire. He wants me. Wants this. My muscles tense and he gives a small thrust. The head of his erection nudges my clit. "You're so wet, sugar. Let me see how much you want it."

I groan, my fingers tightening reflexively on his knees. My attention never leaving his, I lick my lips, and circle my hips.

He lets out a hiss.

His response increases my confidence and I repeat my actions.

His jaw tightens, muscles flexing as he grips the chair.

And I feel it—it rushes over me in a great wave—power.

The power I'd believed I'd buried along with John. It's different, but no less compelling and addictive. I thought I'd lost it forever. It washes over me, cleansing my grief and making me pure instead of twisted.

I look into Michael's eyes, hot with lust, and a smile breaks across my lips.

His cheekbones become even more prominent, and the full weight of his control is unleashed. "Get a move on, sugar."

I slowly, deliberately, drag along his cock. First up. Then down.

A muscle in his jaw jumps.

With the excitement of the game I'd thought I'd never play again, I grow bold. Daring. "I think I can break you."

A cruel smile sends my heart into overdrive. "You won't, but you're welcome to try. You're so primed you won't last long."

I circle my hips. I'm so wet I glide effortlessly along his erection without the least bit of resistance. "And you're not?"

His gaze flicks casually down my body. "As much as I want to bury myself inside you, and fuck us both into oblivion, you're not going to win. You're far too needy."

Of course he's right. I can already feel the desperation clawing away inside me, but I don't care, I don't really want to win. As he well knows.

But I want him to suffer with me. I want him to fight for it. Fight for me. I shrug. "I'm not too worried."

He laughs. "I've never met a woman who angled so hard for a spanking."

In answer, I give him my best sassy smile, and rub along the length of his shaft.

One dark brow cocks, seemingly unimpressed. "Put your money where your mouth is, girl."

And I do.

I start slow. Driving myself near mad as I work my way up and down his cock. Reveling in the feel of him. The rush of power that enflames me. The thrill of the game. The competition.

And the inevitable consequence of where this will end.

My head falls back as I ride him. I'm so slick, so slippery, the glide of my clit over the hard press of his cock is the most exquisite sensation I have ever felt in my life. My hair brushes over my hands as I arch my body, circling and grinding my way along his length. A fine sheen of sweat glistens on my skin. My breath is a hard pant. All rational thought drifts away and I lose myself in his control.

I give him quite a show as the girl I thought I'd lost forever breaks free.

His own breath turns labored, urging me on, propelling me further.

I tease the head of his cock with my clit.

I jerk, moaning, as need spirals tight in my belly.

The climax swells hot and insistent, and I stop moving, willing my body to calm.

"What do you think you're doing?" His voice a

harsh, menacing rasp that sends tingles down my skin.

I raise my head, blinking at him.

His expression is hard, determined. He shakes his head. "There's no recovery time in this game. No cooling off. Move."

I swallow hard and work my hips. Immediately, the orgasm threatens to overtake me. I'm out of practice, if I can't stop, I won't be able to stave off the inevitable. The only chance I have is to let go, lose control, and hope he follows. I begin to move in earnest. Never breaking eye contact, I grind up and down his shaft in a hard, frantic rhythm.

I'm so damn hot.

His eyes burn into me.

So damn ready.

His jaw clenches.

The orgasm grows.

Tightens.

His temples bead with sweat.

The climax swells.

I clutch his knees as I work my clit along him.

"Michael." His name a desperate plea. I'll think about the permission I'm asking for later, but now I just need it.

He nods.

And I break, my head falling back, as the orgasm rips through me, shattering me into a thousand different pieces. I moan, my fingers digging into the fabric of his pants, as I writhe on top of him, lost in the first real climax I've had since John died.

"Fucking hell," Michael says, and lifts me with the tremors still shuddering through me.

He throws me on the bed, rips off his shirt, makes quick work of a condom, and drives inside me. The shock of his entry sets off another wave of contractions and he growls, a feral sound.

His hand clamps around my throat and his mouth

covers mine. Consuming me as he slams inside me. His thrusts powerful. Driving me to a fit of passion unlike anything I've ever known. His kiss takes everything from me as his fingers tighten around my throat and his big body covers mine. Relentless, he pounds into me, and even though I came hard, lust consumes me.

I rise to meet him. My nails raking down his back as I fight to get closer.

Animalistic in his determination, he takes me ruthlessly.

And my starving body drinks it all in.

The bed rocks hard into the wall, the loud noise, the groan of the mattress in rhythm to our matching pants, only heightens our out-of-control passion.

He tears his mouth away, and pounding into me, he growls low in my ear. "Mine."

Yes. As the word tears through my mind, an orgasm assaults me, near blinding in its force.

He's claims me as I need to be claimed. By him.

My vision dims as the pleasure crashes through me. I cry out, shaking as the contractions storm through me.

A second later, he roars loud enough to shake the rafters and shudders, following me into oblivion.

I don't know how much time passes before I finally drift back into reality, but when my eyes flutter open I find him watching me. He smiles, and pushes my hair back from my face before brushing his lips over mine. He's moved to the side so he wouldn't crush me, but he still covers me, and I feel warm and safe.

Happy. It's been so long since I felt happy I want to sink into it and stay here forever. I snuggle in deeper, glad he'd insisted on me staying, because I couldn't pry myself out of this bed with a crowbar.

His fingers brush over my jaw. "That was, by far, the most gorgeous thing I've ever seen."

I flush, remembering my wildness there at the end. I turn into him, burying my face in his neck.

He laughs, stroking my hair. "Are you embarrassed?"

I nod.

He crooks a finger under my chin and tilts my face, forcing me to look at him. When I meet his eyes he says, "Would it make you feel better if you knew how close I was?"

I blink up at him, heating with pleasure this time. "You were?"

His eyes blaze. "The only reason I didn't break the chair was because the legs are iron."

A wide smile spreads over my lips.

He wipes a thumb over the swollen flesh. "Laugh now, sugar, but remember payback is a bitch."

A giggle escapes me, a real honest to goodness giggle, and he squeezes my ribs, making me jump and squeal with laughter.

"That's it," he said, rolling me over and throwing his leg across mine. He tickles me, until I'm squirming and laughing so hard tears stream down my face as I beg him to stop.

He shakes his head. "Nope you're a very bad girl and have to pay the price."

He's deliciously relentless. Slowly, the tickling turns into soft caresses. A thumb circling my nipple. His tongue licking across my skin. The laughter dies away, replaced by soft moans and cries of ecstasy that last for hours, wrapping me up in a hazy cloud of exquisite pleasure I never want to end.

17.

Empty lifeless eyes stare up at me.

I brush John's hair back from his forehead as best I can with my bound hands.

The slow trickle of blood over concrete.

A cry shakes my body and I wake with a start. Terror crests over me like a wave before I startle to reality.

It's a dream. Just a dream.

I slow my breathing as I try and orientate myself to my surroundings.

It's dark. Unfamiliar. There's a heavy arm under my ribs. The night with Michael comes rushing back to me.

I'm in his bed. I've slept naked in his arms. How had that happened? The last I remember, I said something about going home.

I barely move, listening to the sound of his heavy, rhythmic breath, thankful he's still asleep. At least I didn't wake up screaming with tears streaming down my cheeks.

Restless, I fight the urge to fidget under him. I should leave, but somehow I don't think that would go over too well. Michael is not the kind of man you sneak out on in the middle of the night.

But I need to get up. Breathe and watch mindless TV so I can shake off the nightmare. As quietly as I can, I move, slipping out from under him and rolling out of the bed where I'd experienced so much pleasure. The room is dark, and I feel around, finally touching a T-shirt of Michael's he'd abandoned on a chair in the corner. I throw it on and sneak out.

I wander into the living room, flick on the light and scream, my hand flying to my chest.

There's a dog sprawled on the couch.

The big mangy mutt's ears perk, she lifts her head and then bounds off the couch.

"Belle, no," Michael says from behind me, and I let out another yelp in surprise. His arm encircles my waist as the dog dances excitedly around me.

I remember the picture I saw in the coffee shop. My heart rate slows. I hold out my hand and the dog sniffs and slobbers all over it. "Where'd she come from?"

"Sometimes my neighbor watches her for me when I'm going to be gone for a long time, I picked her up after you fell asleep."

The dog jumps up, planting her big paws on my chest.

Michael lets me go and barks out, "Down, Belle."

The dog completely ignores him and licks my face. I laugh and scratch up and down her back as she whines happily.

"She's the worst trained dog in the world." Michael pulls her down before straightening. His hair is a mess, his chest bare and beautiful. "I'm sorry she scared you."

"It's okay." I walk over and sit down on the couch. With an excited wave of her tail, Belle jumps up next to me, and nuzzles her head on my lap, gazing up at me adoringly. I pat her head, and she burrows closer, making me laugh with her greedy bid for attention. My fingers smooth over her soft, shaggy fur and my heart melts.

She squirms and twists in her attempts to get closer, and I smile at her cute antics, letting her climb all over me. I hug her as she licks my face.

"She likes you," Michael says, he's thrown on a pair of workout shorts that hang low on his hips.

Belle, halfway in my lap, rolls over and sticks her legs straight up in the air. I giggle, and give her belly a rubdown. She's better than therapy. "I'm in love, can I keep her?"

Slowly, he shakes his head. "Nope. Sorry. If you want to see her, you'll have to come here."

I put on a mock pout. "Pretty please?"

His gaze drops to my lips. "You know I'd do anything for that mouth, but you can't have my dog. I need her."

I can't blame him. I wouldn't give her up either. Hugging the dog, I close my eyes, laughing again when Belle gives me a big, sloppy kiss on my cheek.

"That's a good sound, sugar," Michael says, his voice husky. He walks over to the couch, affixes a stern gaze on Belle, and points to the empty end of the couch. "Move."

Belle's tongue lolls to the side and she stays right where she is.

I repress a smile.

Michael scowls and points again. "Belle, off."

Belle ignores him and puts one paw on my chest. I don't know where it comes from, but I say in my most serious voice, "It must be quite hard for you to live with a female that doesn't snap to your every command."

He sighs and sits in the empty spot. "The irony is not lost on me."

A bubble of laughter escapes my throat.

"Layla," Michael says, his tone warning, but amused.

I can't help it, and I burst out into giggles. Belle wags her tail, catching my happiness. "Come on, you have to know how funny it is."

He grins, shrugging. "If her blatant disregard for any order I give her puts that smile on your face, it's worth it."

I have a sudden urge to lean over and kiss him, full on the mouth, then crawl on top of him. Instead, I stay right where I am and say, "She's wonderful."

"Did you have a nightmare?" he asks, changing the subject.

I think about avoiding but dismiss the idea. I'm so tired of hiding all my cracks. I nod. "I'm sorry I woke you. I tried not to."

"How do you feel now?" His expression is intent on mine.

"Pretty good, actually." I play with Belle's soft, floppy ears.

"Do you want to tell me about it?"

I shake my head and say softly, "I don't want to ruin the night."

He crooks his finger. "Come here."

I don't even think of refusing, because he's the only place I want to be. I extricate myself from Belle, stand up and walk around the dog before standing in front of him. He puts his hands on my hips and squeezes. "I like you in my shirt."

He pulls me down and I tumble into his lap. When I settle into a spot, Belle turns around and puts her head on Michael's knee. He sighs. "She's an attention hog."

"She is, but she's so cute, it's hard to mind." I put my head on his shoulder, and it suddenly strikes me how domestic this is. How right it feels to be cuddled up in his lap, with his dog by my side.

I tense. The familiar betrayal slicing through me.

He trails his palm over my bare thigh. "What?"

"Did anyone tell you how annoying that is? Picking up every nuance?"

"Occupational hazard. Comes with the package of dating a cop."

At the mention of us doing something as normal as dating, I pause; worried the idea no longer terrifies me. "Is that what we're doing? Dating?"

"Yes." His tone doesn't invite debate.

The guilt, however, still comes. This was supposed to be reserved for John. I'm not supposed to feel this way about anyone. I clear my tight throat. "I never intended to date anyone. Let alone a cop."

He tilts my chin, and gazes deeply into my eyes. "You loved your fiancé very much."

"I did." Frightened that I used the past tense, I instantly correct myself. "I do."

He nods. "Then ask yourself, if the situation is reversed, is this what you'd want for him? To spend his whole life mourning you?"

Muscles rigid, I clench my hands in my lap. "No, of course not. It's just…" I trail off, unsure how to explain. I owe it to John. It's the only way I can make it up to him.

Belle nudges my fingers with her nose and I smile, automatically releasing my death grip to stroke her soft head.

I take a deep breath and try again. "I don't want to forget him. I'm afraid if I move on, I will. I have to remember. His death has to mean something."

Nobody understands this part, but it's crystal clear to me.

He tucks me under his chin and squeezes tight. "Dying right along with him isn't the way to make sure it means something, sugar."

A spike of anger, like a hot poker, has me straightening, pulling back from him. "You don't think I know that? Everyone always says that like it's so easy, but it's not. You haven't walked in my shoes, you don't understand."

He makes soothing sounds, but it doesn't calm my frustrated rage. I glare at him. "It's not that easy. And the heart doesn't listen to logic."

He doesn't look impressed; instead he nods, matter of fact. "I'm not saying it's easy, Layla. I'm saying you have to start somewhere."

I scramble from his lap and Belle lets out a little whine. I put a hand over my chest and yell, "You don't think I'm doing that? Every instinct I have tells me to stay away from you. I've broken every single rule I have, because of *you*. Do you understand how hard that is for me? Even worse, you did it effortlessly. You didn't even have to try. I've done all the hard work here, not you. Me. And then you act like I'm not even making an effort?"

He shifts on the couch and plants bare feet on the floor before placing his elbows on his knees and lacing his fingers. "Don't twist my words to suit your argument."

"I'm not. I've taken a huge step. I'm sleeping in your bed." I lower my head and stare at the hardwood floor. The rich, dark brown blurring through the tears welling in my eyes. My anger abates and sadness takes hold. "I fucked plenty of men after he died but you're still the first."

"I know." His voice is soft.

I blink away the wetness. "I didn't even think of him."

"I know," he says again. He pauses for a few beats

before continuing, "I'm not sorry. Maybe that's selfish of me, but I can't be sorry."

I nod, at a loss for what to say.

He continues in a soft, soothing voice. "I'm not saying it's easy. Now, come back here. I don't want to talk with you so far away."

So tired of standing alone, I brush the tears away and return to him. I can't deny the relief and safety I experience when his arms hug me close.

He brushes his lips over the crown of my head. "I understand this is a big deal. I know you're scared. I'm merely suggesting you think about what he would want for you the next time you feel guilty for being alive. You survived, Layla, and I know sometimes that's worse, but don't let *that* be for nothing."

"I'm trying." I rest my head on his chest.

"I know, sugar." Another kiss.

We sit like that for a long while, my ear pressed against the steady beat of his heart, his knuckles running up and down my arm.

"It's not effortless, you know. You are far from effortless," he says, breaking the peaceful spell.

It's true most men would have given up, but that's not really what I meant. "I have no defenses against you. I never even got to lay out my rules and you were breaking them."

He tilts my chin, forcing me to look at him. "Do you know how hard it was for me to walk away from you that first night?"

I shake my head. "You didn't even look back."

He smiles, his expression rueful. "If I'd looked back, I would have turned right around. I'd been biding my time with you and I was already on edge. It was hell to walk away. Especially when your body was so damn ready for me, but I had to risk it. I promise you it took every inch of self-discipline I had to do it."

The statement reminds me of that first night, when

he'd said he'd watched me. I can't resist touching him and I place an open palm against his hard chest. "You never told me what you were doing in the club. Or how long you'd seen me before talking to me."

"The first time I went to the club was about a year ago. I was following a lead for a case I was working that wound up a dead end. Being a small world, the owner of the place ended up being a friend from college. We'd lost touch over the years, but reconnected after the case wrapped and started hanging out again." He grins. "We, um, have similar tastes."

I laugh. "What a shock."

He shrugs and the muscles under my hands ripple. "I've never been much for the club scene, but I'd go hang out there sometimes, mainly shooting the shit with my buddy with an occasional hook up."

I ignore the jealousy trying to worm a hole in my belly.

He strokes a finger over my cheek, as though sensing my unspoken distress. "I saw you the first time around six months ago."

I blink. How was it possible I'd never seen him with the way I comb through the room? "But, how? I never saw you." Surprise made me honest. "And you aren't someone I would have skimmed over."

"I'm a detective. You didn't see me because I didn't want you to."

"But why?"

"Instinct, I guess. The first time I saw you was after you hooked up with that bartender who's all wrong for you. I watched you leave, and when you returned he tried to touch your arm and you flinched, and then looked at him like he was a rapist. When you turned away your expression was filled with anger, and disgust. I couldn't help wondering why you'd done something you so clearly didn't want, or what put those deep shadows under your eyes."

This news unsettles me and, unsure how to respond, I accuse defensively, "So, what? You were waiting your turn?"

Lines bracket the corners of his mouth and he sighs. "I promised myself if you ever asked, I'd tell you the truth."

My stomach plummets to the floor. Nothing good ever comes from those words, but I don't back away. I'm equally terrified and hopeful the confession will somehow break his hold over me. "What truth?"

His gaze slides away from mine. "I wasn't waiting my turn. I wanted nothing to do with you."

My mouth drops open. It was the last thing I expect him to say. "What?"

"I took one look at you and every instinct I had told me to stay the hell away from you."

Irrationally, this annoys me. So much for him pining for me from afar. "I see."

He shoots me a crooked grin. "In fairness, can you say your first reaction was far off?"

My first reaction was instant, all consuming lust…followed by terror. I blush.

He cocked a brow. "What was that thought?"

"Nothing. Go on."

He narrows his eyes. "Tell me."

"I will not."

He grips my chin. "You will. Or suffer the consequences."

I shiver at the thought, I've yet to feel the sting of his hand on my ass and I still long for it. But that's not the point. I pull out of his grasp. "That's not fair."

"That's what you signed up for, sugar, you know that."

Of course he's right, I don't want fair, but that doesn't mean I have to admit it. I huff. "Please go on with your story about how you couldn't stand me."

He flashes me an evil grin. "Don't misunderstand, I wanted you like a son of a bitch. But my first instinct warned me off. Now tell me you didn't feel exactly the same."

I bite my lip and concede. "You're right, my first reaction wasn't far from that. I perceived you as a threat. Even as my body knew you could give me what I'd been craving."

"Good girl." He squeezes my hip, and I experience a flash of heat at his words. "I didn't see you for a couple of months after that, but the next time I did you were wearing red lipstick and a short black dress that looked painted on. I never wanted to fuck a woman more. But it wasn't like normal desire, it bordered on violent."

I lean in, greedy for information. "Like what?"

His attention shifts to my mouth. "You were leaning over the bar getting a drink and I had the most uncontrollable desire to walk over there, shove that dress up your hips, and take you in the meanest, most visceral, most public way possible. I've never been much for public displays and my desire wasn't about voyeurism. It was about ownership. Pure and simple. Possessive—she's mine—ownership."

I can picture it. I want it. I lick my suddenly dry lips.

"I ended up leaving to get away from you." His voice drops, becoming smoky.

It's tendrils curl around me. "I know that dress."

He grips the back of my neck in an almost feral display of dominance. "You can wear it the next time we go to dinner. Don't bother with panties, because I'm going to do the most depraved, twisted things to you."

My breath comes fast. "Yes."

There's a flash in his gaze and his free hand circles my nipple. "Are you on the Pill, Layla?"

"Yes." A stuttering gasp.

"I'm going to come inside you."

It's a statement of fact but he pauses, giving me time to protest. I've never wanted anything more and I'm unable to pretend otherwise. "Please."

In an instant, everything changes between us as the chemistry we both fought against once again overpowers us.

He shoves his hand between my legs, pushing my thighs apart to slide over my swollen clit. "What's making you so hot? The thought of what I'm going to do to you? Or that I want to fucking own you?"

My inner muscles clamp down on his fingers as soon as he says the word *own*, betraying me. I gasp, moaning.

His lids hood, giving him a dark, sinister look, as he hooks into my G-spot. "That's right, girl. You're mine."

I cry out, clutching his shoulders, hanging on for dear life as a climax builds strong and swift inside me.

He bites my lower lip. "Mine."

"Yes." A distant part of me is horrified I agreed, but I couldn't stop it. Couldn't deny what I so clearly want.

He growls, low and deep. Before I come, he pulls away and lifts me, yanking my hips so I straddle him.

We're all hot, panting breaths and fumbling hands. There's no build up. No foreplay. No kissing. This isn't about that.

This is about him taking what he wants and my surrender.

I'm desperate for it. Need it more than my next breath. I tilt up just enough for him to slide his shorts down. His beautiful, hard cock springs free.

All I want is to feel taken by him, to turn his words into reality.

He slams into me and my head flings back as I

arch.

He grips me around the throat, his grasp tight and commanding.

The possession wraps around me. More. So much more.

I ride him, hard and fast.

His free hand clamps down on my hip, his grip like a vise. Pain and pleasure collide.

"Mine." A hard bark as he pummels into me.

"Yes." I answer back the truth. Not willing to hide.

We're fucking so hard, the couch is protesting and Belle has taken off for parts unknown.

I dig my nails into his skin. Gasping as he tightens his hold on my throat and hip. I might be on top, but he's in control and making sure I know it.

It makes me hotter.

Wetter.

I forget all reason, all thought, all shreds of innocence and propriety.

I am wanton need.

A fierce storm of lust.

Our breaths are nothing but pants.

Our bodies slick with sweat.

His cock driving so hard into me I cry out.

It's so damn good.

It's too much and not enough.

His grip shifts and he fists my hair. He releases my hip and clasps my waist, the angle forcing my clit into greater contact with his pelvis.

I'm going to come. I don't want to, not yet. It's been so long since I felt claimed.

I try and hold back, not ready for it to end.

He kisses me, a brutal brush of his lips before he whispers, "I own you."

I lose the battle. I climax so violently my whole body shakes with the force of it, as wave after wave crashes through me.

He groans, takes my hips and slams into me as he follows. On a final thrust, I collapse against him; my heart beating so hard and fast I fear it might burst.

He pants out, "I'm glad we got that settled."

A laugh gasps from my chest.

He rubs my back. "You'll spend the day with me tomorrow."

Bone-deep satisfaction settles inside me, making me sleepy. "Yes, Michael."

"Good girl."

I melt. There's really no other option.

18.

The day is perfect. Too perfect.

I can't help looking over my shoulder, waiting for the other shoe to drop.

From the moment I woke up this morning, it's been heaven. The nightmare hadn't returned; as though Michael were a knight that could magically protect me.

I'd stretched awake, his big arm thrown over me. I'd turned to look at him, still sleeping. The bright sun streamed through his bedroom window to fall across his perfect face and body, casting his features in a soft glow. Unobserved, I watched him, the light playing over his skin taunting me to reach out and touch him. Everything felt so right, as though waking in his bed was the most natural thing in the world.

He'd sensed me watching him and his thick lashes fluttered open, his hazel gaze steady and sure. I'd taken a deep breath, and he sucked me under, obliterating all my fears as he took me.

When we'd finally made our way out of bed, we went to a little breakfast diner right around the corner from his apartment. We took showers, got dressed and took Belle for a walk down by the lakeshore before stopping at the dog park to let her roam wild and free. We ate lunch. Talked. Laughed. Fucked in a Starbucks bathroom, our movements rushed, jerky and frantic.

Absolute perfection.

The whole day I could only be amazed at how normal I felt. How good. The way his hand fit perfectly, his strong fingers wrapped around mine. The way he looked at me.

But most of all I felt safe. Safe in a way I hadn't for such a long time I'd forgotten it even existed. That he gave me even an hour of reprieve from the desperate, worried fear that plagued every moment of my life, let alone a day, made me so grateful I wanted to weep with it.

But, surprisingly, I didn't. I hadn't cried all day.

I had, however, smiled so much my muscles ached from overuse.

Now we stood in a two-block line at the new, trendy cupcake place, holding hands, my face tilted to the late-afternoon sun.

He tucks a lock of hair behind my ear before pulling me close, his arm slipping around my waist. "You look good wearing that flush I gave you."

I duck my head as my face heats in remembrance.

He chuckles, pressing a kiss to the top of my head. "I particularly enjoyed the look of disapproval that woman gave us as we walked out of the bathroom together."

"I was mortified." The words losing their force as laughter bubbles in my throat. Of course, I was mortified, but in that way girls like me are addicted to. The old woman with iron-gray curls and mean eyes had threatened to tell the manager and Michael had just shrugged nonchalantly and told her to go ahead before pointing him out.

His fingers curl around the nape of my neck. "I can tell by how hard you came."

"You're the worst," I say, my breath catching in my throat because I already want him again. Even with all the sex we've had, there is an insatiable desire that permeates the air between us. Our chemistry almost a live, tangible thing.

He grins down at me. "You need the worst."

I do.

He leans down and brushes a kiss over my lips.

And that's when it happens.

The other shoe I've been waiting for.

"Layla!" My sister's voice rings through the air, full of surprise.

Panic washes over me as I jerk back from Michael, turning in horror to find April and Derrick in front of me, their expressions wide with shock, their mouths hanging open. My heart starts to pound as my mind goes blank, searching for some reasonable explanation as to what I'm doing with another man that's not my fiancé.

Michael's hand curls around my waist, and he squeezes my hip lightly as though attempting to steady me, as the four of us all stare at each other in silence.

I flush, what I'm sure is scarlet, and mutter, "April, what are you doing here?"

My sister blinks at me, her gaze darting to Michael. She blinks again, shifting her attention back to me.

Derrick clears his throat and holds out a hand to Michael. "Derrick Murphy, I'm Layla's brother-in-law."

I glance away from April's questioning expression.

Michael nods and shakes Derrick's hand. "Michael Banks."

He doesn't elaborate on who he is.

"Layla?" April asks.

I lick my lower lip and Michael squeezes my hip again. "Um, Michael is a...um..." I dart a pleading glance at him.

He smiles and takes pity on me. "I'm a friend of Layla's."

April cocks a brow. "A friend?"

Michael gives her a smile so dazzling it makes me weak in the knees by proxy. "Among other things."

Another flash of heat layers on top of my already overheated cheeks.

Derrick chuckles, clearly amused, unlike my sister whose brows only furrow deeper together. "What other things?"

My brother-in-law, god bless his soul, encircles her waist and pulls her close. "Now, honey, that's really none of our business."

April frowns, her gaze shifting back and forth between Michael and me. "But—"

Derrick cuts her off. "Layla's a big girl and can take care of herself."

I'm so off balance I can't help but lean into Michael, instinctively seeking his warmth. I'm unable to meet my sister's eyes but can feel her questions bearing down on me. Questions I have no answer to.

Derrick turns to Michael. "I have to meet some clients for a drink, but after we were going to grab dinner, why don't you guys join us."

Oh no. God, no. My mouth opens to protest but before I can speak, Michael is nodding in agreement. "That'd be great, name the time and place."

I clench my hands, my nails digging into my skin. We *cannot* go to dinner with them. But as much as I want to protest I can't open my mouth to speak. Unconcerned, Michael and Derrick are busy making arrangements while my sister and I silently stare at each other.

Then, the moment has passed, and Derrick is pulling April down the street, with her looking back at me. Derrick calls out, "See you later."

When I can no longer see them, the words finally come, and I turn to Michael, furious and accusing, "How could you do that?"

One dark brow rises up his forehead. "Should I have said no?"

"*Of course* you should have said no." My voice is several octaves too high.

The line moves several steps forward.

Michael shrugs. "I was going to meet them anyway, and it seemed like the perfect excuse to get it over with so you wouldn't have to worry."

Meeting my family was a million steps away from where I am. I'm just trying to get through the day without worrying I'll be attacked, without screaming myself awake, and without dying of guilt.

I shake my head. "No, you weren't going to meet them."

His gaze narrows in a way that has my spine straightening, and when he speaks there's that distinct *you're treading a fine line, girl* tone. "I understand the lies you tell yourself so you can go on pretending that this isn't happening. You can tell yourself whatever you need to. Pretend all you want, sugar, but you and I are happening. And all that comes with it."

Frustration eats away inside me. "You don't understand."

"Explain it to me." That damned implacable voice that drives me crazy.

Exasperated, I throw up my hands. "Three weeks ago my sister was begging me to go out on a blind date and now she finds me on the street with a guy she knows nothing about."

The line moves another couple of feet, and when we come to a stop he cups my jaw and lifts my face to study me. "Did you go?"

I nod. "I mentioned it."

"So you've already broken the seal, only the guy has changed."

"Don't be reasonable."

A curve of his lips. "Someone in this relationship has to be."

I push at his chest. "Don't say that word."

His thumb runs along the side of my jaw. "You're mine. And that includes me meeting your family."

"I'm not ready," I say, but my voice is already softening.

"Layla, it's done. They've already seen me. You won't be able to pretend." He leans down and brushes his lips against mine. "Believe it or not, I agreed for your own good."

"How?"

His tongue flicks over my lower lip. "They're going to question you, right? Regardless?"

I nod, not understanding where he's going with this.

His fingers slip over my throat and I can't help the shiver that speeds through me. "Well, I don't want you alone when they do. Period. End of story."

Stunned, I blink up at him. I'd forgotten what it was like to be protected. All my anger drains away, replaced by a new kind of warmth. "Oh."

"You're not alone anymore," he whispers then kisses me.

Lashes drifting closed, I melt into him, forgetting the people milling around us.

Because, for the first time in eighteen months, I actually believe it.

After the pleasantries were over, and we're settled into a booth at Joe's Stone Crab, the four of us stare at each other in the loud restaurant. My sister's gaze sharp and speculative on Michael and me.

Derrick clears his throat and offers his trademark smile. "So, Michael, how did you and Layla meet?"

Anxiety zings through my blood, making my heart beat fast. I tense, my mind an utter blank for a proper answer. All that comes to me is the truth. Under the table, Michael puts a hand on my leg, his fingers gently squeezing my thigh in reassurance.

In direct contrast to my bundle of nerves, he is completely relaxed. Dressed in a charcoal V-necked sweater, with a white button-down underneath, that he's rolled up to his elbows, exposing his powerful forearms. I focus on the way his muscles flex under his skin. Remembering how those arms held me down while he'd brought me to orgasm three times before we'd left for dinner. Powerful, forceful orgasms that ripped through me and left me exhausted. A relaxation technique, he'd told me later with a grin. It worked, for at least the cab ride over.

"We met at O'Malley's a couple of weeks ago," he says, the lie effortless on his tongue.

I instantly ease, catching my sigh of relief just in time. Of course, he wouldn't out me. Or himself. The fear that he would is irrational, but in my experience, fear has no rationality.

Derrick nods and takes a sip of his Scotch, ordered neat. His drink of choice. He darts a glance in my direction. "I'm surprised. Layla hasn't been very social lately."

A subtle ploy to see how much Michael knows of my past. The tragedy nobody talks about, but hovers over us like a dark cloud.

Michael shrugs, and his fingers stroke over my thigh, just below the hem of my tights. Another distraction technique. He offers a charming smile. "It wasn't an easy chase."

My sister seems to come to life at that moment, taking her attention off me and putting it onto Michael. "What do you do for a living?"

Michael turns his direct gaze on her and says in a steady voice, "I'm a homicide detective."

April gasps, her hand fingering her necklace. "I see."

I know what she's thinking. How tangled and twisted it is that Michael's profession is so closely tied to John's death. A violent, dangerous profession. The kind I should stay away from. The kind that should make me run, but that would mean running from him, and that's no longer an option. I can't explain to my sister his real draw or make her understand why that makes his profession a moot point.

I can see her sizing Michael up, trying to figure out how this man across from her would possibly hold an attraction to me. I get it. And it's not that Michael isn't a gorgeous man, because he absolutely is. He's tall and broad, with a face carved from stone. He has a powerful, magnetic presence that, after spending the day with him in public, isn't lost on the female population. It isn't his looks.

It's that subtle, indefinable sense that there is something different about him.

On top of that, he's nothing like John, who might as well be Michael's polar opposite. John was cute, affable, and charming. Everyone loved him and with his relaxed, easy manner he could put anyone at ease. Nobody would have ever guessed how he was in bed. The things he liked to do with me. But there is no way to explain to April that beyond the surface, John and Michael share one thing that is like crack to a girl like me.

Derrick tilts his head to the side. "Interesting. How did you get into that?"

Michael tells him the story of his Ivy League school

and how he fell into law enforcement. And, in turn, asks Derrick about his job. The two men fill the awkward silence between my sister and me. Of course, the conversation turns to football and they are off, engaged in an in-depth conversation about this year's Bear's team.

The universal conversation filler between men who are strangers.

In the meantime, April and I face off across the table. My shoulders tense, my teeth grit, and I fiddle with the napkin on my lap. I have no idea what to say to her.

This beautiful sister of mine, whom, after we got through being teenage girls together, used to be one of my best friends. There never used to be silence between us. We used to spend endless days together.

Once upon a time, she helped me pick out the items on my registry, after John begged off when I was unable to stop agonizing over what china pattern to pick. Looking back, I can't believe how silly I was, worrying over plates that would have most likely sat in a cabinet, rarely used.

My sister and I would make a day of it, and she'd laugh, good-natured and understanding, as I suffered terrible indecision over which placemats to choose. Back then what placemats would tie my table together was my biggest worry. Somehow, it never occurred to me during those endless hours that I could just go out and buy a second set once I grew bored. But April and I had loved every minute of our days together. We giggled and laughed our way down Michigan Avenue, stopping for tea, and then drinks as we talked houses and babies. Like regular people.

At the memory of us combing the streets of Chicago, it crystalizes, the problem between us. The gap that divides us so completely. She's still that regular girl.

I'm not. And I probably never will be again.

I resent her for asking it of me. Of wanting it. But I'm jealous too. I can feel it, twisting and turning, just below the surface.

She's the lucky Hunter girl.

Everything she's wanted has come true. She got it all. The great husband, the adorable kids, the dog, and the McMansion in the suburbs. She gets to spend her days going to the gym, attending playgroups for the twins, and planning her next tablescape with her perfectly coordinated placemats.

She has all the things I believed I was entitled to. That I took for granted.

And I hate her for it.

Like most of life's revelations, my understanding doesn't float over me like a gentle breeze, but more smacks me in the face, sucking the air right out of my lungs. This whole time, I've been blaming her for the distance in our relationship, but really it's me. I'm to blame.

Through no fault of her own, I'm furious at her. An angry, ugly fury that she got everything I wanted. That she's living the blessed life that's supposed to be mine.

I swallow the lump in my throat, and blink back the sudden tightness in my throat. And here I thought today would be the first day I didn't cry.

Don't count your chickens before they hatch, Layla, as my mom used to say.

I had. I'd made that mistake with John. Thinking we were on the path to that perfect life. I'd been so cocky and sure, and I paid the price for my arrogance.

The thoughts become tangled in my head.

The what-ifs that all lead back to me. So many of my choices and decisions that led us to that dark alley. There are things I can't even think of, and hundreds of inconsequential things too. Like the cancelation of another wedding that had opened up our dream venue. What difference did a week make? But if we'd gotten married just a week earlier, like we'd originally planned, we'd have been on our honeymoon, and he'd be sitting here with me right now.

The notion disorientates me, because Michael has been consuming my thoughts and body all day.

I don't know which I want more. John or Michael. It's a terrifying thought.

And I feel it. The first swells of a panic attack. My heartbeat starts to pound furiously against my ribs. My head swims as an icy sweat breaks across my temples and down my back.

There's a shift in the air, sudden and swift, like a summer storm blowing in from out of nowhere.

Michael breaks off mid-sentence, and pins me with his stare. His hand slips from my leg to curl around my neck. "Layla."

I clutch my napkin in my clammy hands.

April leans against the table. "Layla. What's wrong?"

Michael's strong fingers squeeze my neck. "Look at me."

Like I'm drowning, I do, clinging to his steady gaze like a lifeline.

"You're okay. You're safe." His voice soft and sure. So steady and calm. "Breathe, girl."

It's an order. I suck air into my lungs as the adrenaline speeds through my blood.

"Slower." His thumb strokes over my rapid pulse. "Nice and easy."

I do as I'm told, slowly breathing in and out, my gaze locked on his. I don't know how long we stay like that, the table silent, but the panic finally recedes to a low-level hum.

When I'm once again centered in reality, I bite my lip. "I'm sorry."

He shakes his head. "You've got nothing to be sorry about, sugar."

I'm embarrassed, and I turn to find April and Derrick gaping at us with wide, stunned eyes. April is clutching her husband's hand, her knuckles white and I know I've scared her.

"I'm sorry, I'm okay. I just…" I trail off, unsure what to say.

April's mouth curves into a deep frown. "Maybe we should go to the bathroom."

Before I can speak, Michael says, "No. She stays here."

I stare down at my lap; unable to process that he's being so overt. John wasn't like that, anytime we were with friends and family our power dynamic was very undercover.

"She's my sister," April says, the words a hiss of indignation.

"Honey." Derrick pats her shoulder.

Expression set in a stubborn line she shrugs him off. "No. Something is wrong with her. I don't know this guy, and we're her family. Not him."

The adrenaline exiting my system has left behind an undercurrent of nausea. I take a sip of my water, the condensation on the glass cold on my overheated palm. I manage to mutter, "I'm okay."

Michael shakes his head. "I apologize if this is a shock to you, I have two sisters I'm fiercely protective of, so I understand. I can only promise you I have Layla's best interest at heart. But, I'm afraid I can't let her out of my sight until I'm assured her panic attack is under control."

April's expression turns hostile, and she opens her mouth, but then her face twists into concern. Her gaze flies to me. "You have panic attacks?"

Oh no. She knows now. I've been hiding them all this time and now she knows. Soon my whole family will know. I will be forced to deal with all their questions. I need to make light of it, and I shrug. "Sometimes."

Michael gives me a sharp, narrowed glance. "You never told your family?"

I shake my head.

"Oh Layla," April says, her eyes filling with tears.

Derrick puts an arm around his wife's shoulders and hands her a napkin.

"I'm sorry," I say, ashamed I've once again managed to ruin everything.

Michael sighs, and turns to my sister and brother-in-law. "After what's happened to her, panic attacks are common, hopefully they will get better over time, but there's a possibility she'll have to deal with them long term."

April's brows rise up her forehead as she delicately wipes under her lashes. "You know?"

Michael nods. "I know."

There it is. The truth. My hidden panic attacks. The lies I tell my family. The truth of who Michael is, and what he means to me. It's all out there in the open for them to see.

And I feel...relieved. Blessed liberation.

There, under the last remnants of the panic attack, all my worries and fears, another broken piece of me falls into place, and heals.

19.

"You're staying with me." It wasn't a request. It was a statement.

We're in front of my building, and Michael's parked in a loading zone. I look out the car window and stare at the front door leading to my condo.

It's been a strange evening. After the panic attack, the night had calmed down. Derrick and April's shock had worn off. My sister stopped watching me with wary, concerned eyes. I relaxed. Eventually, the awkwardness ebbed as the men in our lives kept the conversation light and engaging.

To my surprise, we'd gone on to have a good time. We ate too much food, drank too much wine, talked a little too loud.

And I laughed. Real, belly-clenching laughter that made my cheeks ache.

I pretended not to notice the flickers of relief on April's expression, and she pretended not to notice that it had been far too long since she'd heard me sound happy.

As the evening wore on, I watched my sister and brother-in-law fall hook, line and sinker for Michael. All his brains and charm. His easy confidence. The way he handled me. By the time dinner had ended, Derrick and April looked at him the same way I did, as my salvation.

It makes me nervous. Wary. If I let him, Michael would slip effortlessly into my life. Staying with him again only makes it that much easier.

I'm at a crossroads. Or, at least, that's the way it feels.

Even without looking at him I can feel his heat. His power. And I want it so damn bad I can taste it.

I swallow hard. "I don't think I should."

A beat of silence. "Why's that?"

Because I want to, far, far too much.

If it was just for the sex, that would be one thing, but it's not. It's what I want after my insatiable craving for him is satiated that frightens me. I want to curl up on his couch. I want to pet Belle while her head rests in my lap. To laugh at bad TV, his arms wrapped around me. To drink coffee in the morning, the sun streaming through the windows as we talk.

I want the little things. The normal, couple things I've only done with John.

But I can't say this. Instead, I lie. "I have a headache."

He doesn't speak for a moment, and the air grows thick. "Let's go upstairs."

It's not a concession, but I take it. It seems the safe choice. I nod my agreement and we climb out of the car.

On the sidewalk, he takes my hand, and I don't pull away.

He leads me inside and while we're waiting for the elevator he looks down at me. "You survived dinner."

"I did." My fingers clench on his. I don't want to let go.

"And I was right, about being there, wasn't I?"

My brows knit, unsure of where he's going with this. I shrug. Of course, he was right. It was better.

The elevator chimes.

His grip tightens. "Answer me."

My throat tightens even as my belly heats at the command. I bite the inside of my cheek. "It was."

I can't lie. Not about this.

"I'm right about this too." The doors open.

I press my lips together. I have no argument as we enter the car in silence.

The second the elevator closes he's on me, pushing me against the wall, his mouth on mine.

His kiss. It's like nothing I can even describe. Hot. Consuming. It obliterates all my worries and fears. It makes me forget everything and anyone but him.

It's all I want. *He's* all I want. His control. Possession.

His tongue sweeps along my lips, demanding entrance.

I don't resist.

He twines his fingers with mine, then raises our clasped hands above my head, his large frame immobilizing me.

Yes, yes, yes. I bow my back, arching to meet him.

He kicks my feet apart, his powerful thigh slipping between my legs, before he tears his mouth away. "You don't have a headache."

He presses against my clit, rotating his leg to increase the pressure.

I moan at the friction. I need his mouth on me. Need to be swept away. I tilt my head up, offering my lips, but he doesn't give in.

He pushes me harder against the panels. "Tell me."

The dominance. The force, it only increases my

need. I shake my head. "No, I don't."

"You want to stay with me, don't you?" The cadence in his voice a warning not to evade.

"I can't." It is the truth. Just not the explanation.

"That's not the question I asked, Layla."

I stare at him, stubbornly unable to admit how much I want to sleep in his bed. My reaction is why he's so dangerous. Why I must say no. I take a deep breath, desperately trying to figure a way out of this. My mind so filled with the truth, evasion escapes me.

And then, the elevator saves me.

It shudders to a stop and Michael pulls away as the door slides open. One of my elderly neighbors gets on. Sure my mouth is as swollen and wet as it feels, I flush from embarrassment. My hair is most likely a mess. My eyes glassy. I say primly, "Good evening, Mrs. Klosen."

Her eyes widen at the sight of Michael before shifting back to me and going as big as saucers. "Hello, dear. How are you?"

Michael works his way under the hem of my sweater, and strokes across the base of my spine. I shiver at the contact. "Good." I clear the sex from my throat. "Where are you off to so late?"

"Shirley Hanson in 15B is having a midnight tarot party." She casts a sidelong glance at Michael; the question as clear as day. She was one of the first neighbors John and I met when we moved in. She welcomed us with homemade cherry pie that John ate off me later that night.

"Sounds fun." I squeak as Michael's hand slips down my skirt and his fingers brush the crease of my ass.

Something flickers across the older woman's face and then she turns pointedly to Michael. "I'm Iris Klosen."

Smooth as silk, he holds out his free hand.

"Detective Michael Banks."

Her wrinkled, arthritic hand meets his, and it makes him look even more strong and powerful. She smiles at me, and nods. "Good for you."

Michael chuckles.

I blush, and stammer. "Ummm…"

The elevator dings and stops blessedly on my floor. His palm falls away, but the heat remains, like a brand on my skin.

Michael winks at Mrs. Klosen. "Have a good night."

"You too, dear."

And we step into the hallway and once again, we're alone.

"She seems nice," Michael says as we walk down the corridor. For a split second I think he's forgotten about our conversation, but he quickly dashes that hope when he continues, "I believe we have a question on the table."

I pull my key out of my purse and unlock my door, flicking on the light to step over the threshold.

The place looks just like I left it this afternoon when I'd come home to change and get ready for dinner, Michael had been with me then too. I'd walked into the living room to find him stretched on my couch, an iPad in his hand. The sofa had been too small for him, and his feet had hung over the edge. I'd experienced a stab of guilt that I liked the look of him on John's favorite piece of furniture.

But it had been daytime then, and the room had been bright, not dark and cold like it was now. I scan the room and emptiness sweeps over me.

It feels frozen in grief. Nothing like the warmth I'd experienced at Michael's.

It scares me. Forces me to acknowledge the truth I've been avoiding.

I've barely left this apartment in a year and a half.

It's been my safe place. My haven. Filled with both my memories of the man I loved and the nightmares of his death.

Every inch is coated in my despair, my tears, and sadness.

And I don't want to be here.

The thought of climbing into my bed alone is too much for me to bear. But I don't know how to say the words.

In the end, I don't have to.

I look at Michael. My face must be as pleading as I feel, because he frowns, juts his chin toward the hallway leading to my bedroom, and says, "Get your things, Layla."

I turn, and do what I'm told.

A week later, we're walking Belle through the city streets after dinner. Belle tugs at the leash, anxious to get to the dog park where she can run after being cooped up all day. Michael yanks the leather handle and scowls at the dog. "Belle, heel."

She ignores him.

I duck my head, smiling. I've stopped insisting I need to go home and as a concession, Michael hasn't forced me to talk about the state of our relationship.

I still tell myself this has to end. Not today. Another day. At some point I'll gather enough strength to walk away. But today, I just want to be with him, walk his dog together, and sleep in his bed.

"Belle!" Michael barks out in his most menacing voice as she tries to leap excitedly at a poodle passing her by.

A laugh bubbles from my throat. Michael might have domination down to an art form, but his dog is clearly the boss of him. Every time she disregards his orders, I'm filled with a giddy delight.

He squeezes my hand. "Are you laughing?"

I grin up at him. "Who me? Would I do that?"

He gives me his most dangerous glare. "Absolutely."

Slowly, as the days pass, more and more of my natural personality is starting to peek through, and I can't help but tease him. "I'd never. She's clearly well trained."

"She listens…" He sighs as she lunges down the street. "Sometimes."

I nod. "Thirty percent isn't bad."

He laughs. "Brat."

I slip out of his grasp and curl my hand around his arm, pressing close as we walk. I love how he makes me feel safe. Love how I don't worry about dark shadows when he's with me. He can protect me. He's armed and dangerous, and if anyone fucked with me, they'd be dead. The knowledge gives me a twisted satisfaction that makes his job almost worth it.

We stop at a light and I put my head on his arm, resting against him, sucking in all his strength and warmth. "Maybe all she needs is some discipline."

He chuckles and kisses the top of my head. "Are we still talking about Belle? Or you?"

I thought I was teasing about the dog, but now I realize that wasn't at all true. I've worked myself into a nice comfortable corner I've refused to test, even as I strain at the confines. He hasn't pushed. But I want him too. He's been in absolute control, but whatever sadistic streak he possesses has stayed firmly under wraps.

I want it. Crave it. And I'm scared.

I suspect my fear, and the trauma I suffered, is what stops him from unleashing on me what I so desperately need. The acts I'd preformed with the men in the club don't count. I'd let them hurt me because I'd wanted to hurt. To suffer.

With Michael I want the cathartic release of it. Believe it will somehow cleanse me. But as much as he teased me, he'd yet to deliver.

I know why. I've learned how he operates. He wants me to need it. Wants me to break free from the box I've created, to take back another piece of myself.

He's waiting for me to ask. But I don't know how to say the words. With John I never had to, I'd just angled and bratted it up until I got my way, and he turned me over his knee.

But Michael isn't like that. There is no topping from the bottom with him.

So I've taken to skirting around the issue, only to back away the second he calls me on it. Which is exactly what I'm going to do now. I clear my throat and say lightly, "Discipline? Me? I'm a perfect angel."

"That you are," he says. The light changes and we start to walk again. He's silent the next couple of blocks and the butterflies in my stomach fade away. When we reach the dog park Michael lets Belle off her leash and she sprints away, racing around the open field like a lunatic.

I laugh. I love her. She's helped me heal almost as much as Michael. I cast a sideways glance; he's standing there, an amused expression on his face.

I bite my lip. I'm worried. I think I might be halfway in love with him. Maybe more…maybe I'm all the way and I can't admit it. That sounds like me.

He catches my stare and raises a brow. "And what was that thought?"

I flush, thankful for the cold and my already pink cheeks. "Your dog is crazy."

Michael watches her tear around the park. Eventually she calms down and then we throw the long ball to her for a while before heading back home. "Yeah, she is. She's worth every second of the trouble."

Before I can stop the words, they are out of my mouth, hanging in the air between us. "Are we still talking about Belle? Or me?"

I frown, chewing on my lower lip. Why did I say that? I advert my attention to the dogs roaming in the park.

He runs a hand down my arm and when I still don't look at him, he grips my chin and forces me. When I meet his gaze, his hazel eyes are absolutely serious. "You are worth it, Layla."

My throat tightens and I nod. It's hard. It's baby steps, and I sometimes feel like I'm standing in place. I'm getting frustrated. I want to be worthy of him. To be the woman he deserves. Once upon a time I was.

Another thing that night stole from me.

He leans down and brushes my lips with his. "You're worth it."

"Okay." In that moment, I believe.

He tucks a lock of hair behind my ear, and bends down to whisper, "You know what you need to do, girl."

"Yes." Hot, wanton need warms my belly.

"Just say the words, and I'll give you what you've been craving since the moment we met."

I put my hand on his chest to steady myself. I want him so badly my legs are quivering. "Why?"

There are a million questions in that one word.

Another brush against my lips. "You know why. It has to be your choice."

My fingers clench on his coat and I sniff from the cold. "But you already know."

A smile lifts the corners of that beautiful, cruel mouth. "I do, but it doesn't absolve you from making the choice."

My teeth clench. This is what's so frustrating about him. And me. All I need to do is ask and we'll both get what we need. Because as much as I need it, he needs it too. His craving is just as strong. I know this. Sometimes, when we're lying there, I can feel all his power leashed just under the surface, straining for freedom. But there's one thing I've learned about Michael.

He never, ever breaks.

As much as I want to say the words, they stick like molasses to the sides of my throat. I growl. "Why do you have to make this difficult?"

He shrugs, not seeming the least bit stressed. "I'm greedy. I want to hear the words from your lips. I want you to ask me." He leans down again and nips my earlobe. "I want to hear you beg."

20.

Tonight. Seven o'clock. Black dress. No panties. A car will be waiting.

That's all his text had said.

The Uber car he'd arranged had driven me to another trendy hotspot restaurant, and now I stood in front on the sidewalk.

I take a deep breath. I don't know why I'm nervous, but I am. Maybe because this was the first time he'd given me such a direct order, and that order could only lead to good, but scary places.

A symbol of our progress in the relationship I refuse to name.

Since his message earlier this afternoon I'd been a mess of anticipation and now, hours later, I was on edge, nervous with excitement. As prepared as I'd ever be, I swallow hard and walk inside.

A pretty blonde hostess smiles as I enter. "Can I help you?"

I glance around at the patrons scattered about but

don't see Michael in the crowd. "I'm supposed to meet someone."

The hostess looks at the screen in front of her. "Your name?"

"Layla Hunter."

She scans the computer and nods. "Yes, your party is waiting. Let me take your coat."

I wasn't late, so that could only mean he'd gotten here first to watch my entrance.

Licking my dry lips, I shrug off my jacket, smoothing down my miniscule skirt. I feel vulnerable and exposed, which, of course, is his intention. This was exactly the kind of depravity that works girls like me into a fevered pitch.

The message hadn't specified what black dress, but I knew he'd meant this one. The one he'd seen me in all those months ago when he'd watched me, unaware. I filled it out better than the last time I'd worn it, the sharp angles of my bones disappearing as my appetite returned.

I follow the woman, scanning the dining room for the man that had taken my heart and refused to let go.

When I spot him, my breath catches in my chest, and my heart seems to stop. He's in a corner booth, dressed in black, his attention locked on me. The expression he wears reminds me of the first time I saw him, intense and powerful. Completely mesmerizing.

My body responds, just like it had back then, springing to furious life, as every cell screams—*this one.*

My heart beats nearly out of my chest as his gaze slowly, deliberately scans down my body.

He lingers on my lips.

The curve of my neck where my pulse beats wildly.

My breasts, heavy and tingling with awareness.

The swell of my hips, and unbidden, an extra sway goes into my step.

My thighs, quivering in anticipation.

His gaze doesn't leave me during my entire walk through the restaurant, an eternity where the room went silent and the other people ceased to exist.

It was just us. Michael and me. Alone in the chaos.

When we reach the table the hostess gestures to the open seat and I move toward it only to freeze when Michael shakes his head.

His attention shifts to the pretty blonde and she stands a bit straighter in his presence. Michael nods. "Thank you."

That's all he needs to say to make it clear it's time for her to go. A flush stains her face, and she darts a furtive glance in my direction. I can't tell if she's terrified for me, or jealous. Probably a bit of both.

She turns and scurries away.

I suck in a breath before taking a step toward the table, but again he shakes his head. "No. Let me look at you."

My own cheeks heat at the display, but I stand in place, as though rooted to the floor.

That cruel smile lifts the corners of his lips and he raises one finger and makes a twirling motion.

I lick my lips, darting nervous looks around the room to see if anyone is watching. Michael is much more blatant than John, and I'm still not used to it.

Although I can't deny it excites me. I'd always had a secret thing for private acts played out in public. The danger and threat of getting caught. I didn't want to be on display, per se, but more I like the thrill of fear.

It wasn't John's preference, but he indulged me. I frown; it's that desire that caused my life to change so dramatically.

I've kept it carefully under wraps, but of course, Michael has figured it out. But, unlike John, it is very much his thing. While this is the most overt he's been, it's always there, prowling just below the surface.

A dark brow rises. "I'm waiting."

Again, I glance around; positive everyone knows what's going on between us. I suck in a lungful of air, and then slowly turn around in a circle.

When I once again come to a stop, he nods. "Good girl."

My knees actually wobble. I bite my lip and shift my gaze to the open spot, silently asking for permission to sit.

He doesn't respond, instead he says, "That dress looks even better than I remember."

"Thank you." The demure tone of my voice at complete odds with the depraved need rioting inside me.

He takes a sip of his drink, which I now know is Glenlivet. His throat works as he swallows and I can almost feel his skin under my mouth. The way he smells when my face is buried in the curve of his neck.

My grasp tightens on my small purse.

The longer he makes me stand here, watching me, making me wait, the wetter I become. My thighs feel slick, my nipples far too tight. Like they'd be painful to touch, but it's that good pain. The pain I've been longing for, but can't ask for.

The night crystalizes into sharp focus.

I'll be asking him tonight.

It will be my choice, but he'll push all my buttons to get me there. Just like he's been subtly pushing those buttons over the last week.

He puts down the glass and props his arm on the back of the booth, still assessing me. "Are you wet?"

Heat infuses my face. It feels as though he's announced the question over a microphone. I nod.

"Say the words, sugar."

Implacable. That's what he is. "I'm wet."

"Good."

I glance once again at the booth.

He takes another sip of his drink. "That dress still

evokes the same response in me. I want to bend you over this table, yank up the fabric over your hips, and pound into you. I don't care who sees."

I gasp in shock. In lust. Because I can see it. Like it's my destiny.

"You'd like that, wouldn't you?" His voice—Jesus his voice—it's thick and full of power.

"Yes," I say, pressing my thighs together.

"Men stopped eating when you walked through the room." His fingers play over the edge of the glass, circling deliberately, the way he sometimes touches my nipples. "I want to show them that you're mine. That you belong to me. That I can touch what they can't."

I can't help it, I lean forward, hypnotized by his words. The possession in his tone, it's like crack to someone like me. "Yes."

He smiles then, and it's so sinful Mother Theresa herself wouldn't be able to resist. "Do you know why I picked this place?"

I shake my head.

Another long, slow deliberate drink. "The bathrooms. They are big and private. Designed to fuck."

A trickle makes a track down my legs, and I press my thighs together.

His head tilts and he eyes me with speculation. "You already look on edge. Already clenching those pretty thighs together." He scrubs his hands over his permanently stubbled jaw. "So many options to choose from. Should I make you wait? Take you there now?" His gaze flicks down my body. "Or I could make you stand there and come before I allow you to sit down."

Distress and arousal wage a battle. It's hard to tell what's winning. I gasp out, "You wouldn't?"

He laughs. "Wouldn't I? I'm sure you could manage it." He takes another slow sip of his drink.

"There are ways. You could press against the edge of the table." His gaze flicks down my body. "Or you could just stand there and rub your thighs together until you create enough friction to get off."

It is in this moment the full weight of how Michael understands me sinks in. This is not some idle threat. I'm scared, exhilarated and every part of me is alive. I bite my lip, unable to breathe as I wait.

His long, strong fingers tap against the glass. "Tell me, Layla, what should I choose?"

I sense some sort of a trap, but I'm unable to stop myself from falling right into it. "Now?" The word comes out as a squeaky question.

His lips curl into an evil smile. "Be more specific."

I shift on the balls of my feet. I wish I could play it cool, but that's impossible. I'm as needy as he suspects, maybe even more so. Because I've been craving something just like this, and it's finally happening. "Please take me to the bathroom."

"To do what?" He never makes it easy.

I clear my throat, leaning in so my hips press against the table. "Fuck me."

Most men, once you say those two little words will do whatever you want. But Michael doesn't appear swayed. He nods, his expression speculative, as though contemplating. "Anything else?"

The trap springs closed as comprehension dawns. My attention flies to his and his hazel eyes flash in silent acknowledgment.

My heart beats wildly in my chest even as my thighs slick. There are really only two choices here: I ask to be spanked in that bathroom, or I don't sit down at this table until I've come.

Neither will be easy for me. It's merely a matter of if I want to continue to hang on to my stubborn refusal to ask for what I need. Those are my choices. End of story.

Under the raging lust and demanding need, something eases inside me. He understands me. Understands I need to be pushed this way in order to be free.

I press my lips together, unable to quite say the words.

Casual as can be, Michael waits, as though we have all the time in the world.

My gaze skips around the restaurant, crowded with people. To an observer, it probably looks like I'm an acquaintance that has stopped to talk at his table, but logic still doesn't change my perception of exposure.

I can't help one last ditch effort, one test to see if I can get out of this. I laugh, and it sounds as nervous as I feel. "Umm, no?"

One dark brow cocks. "That's your final offer?"

"Isn't that good enough?"

He shrugs. "I suggest you up your ante, girl."

I suck in my breath. This is it. My moment of reckoning.

He's laid it all out for me. Given me the vehicle to ask him for what I've been wanting. All I need to do is take the bait he's handing me. I open my mouth but the words clog in my throat.

He offers no assistance other than his sure, steady gaze. Those hypnotic, hazel eyes that have captivated me since I first saw him. I've traveled a million miles since then. I've taken the steps myself, but he's a hell of a motivation.

I know how lucky I am. Girls like me search their whole lives for someone like Michael and never find him. And for the first time since John's death I don't feel cursed.

Gratitude washes over me, cleansing something twisted and wrong that's been broken. The noise of the restaurant, the patrons, my surroundings all fade away. I slowly exhale into the silence. "I'm ready,

Michael. Please, hurt me. Not in punishment, but to make me whole again. I need it, and I need it from you."

21.

I clutch at his hand as we wait in silence for the stall to empty. There are people milling about, a couple talking close, while a gaggle of girls dressed in party clothes sing a chorus of giggles and oh-my-gods.

I hang my head, my breath fast, my heart a heavy beat.

It's going to happen. I'm a mess of nerves. A bundle of raw emotions.

Once I made my plea, he didn't hesitate. Just stood, told the waitress walking by that we'd be back, and led me down the stairwell to the restrooms. In silence, we stand, waiting. His hand holding mine.

The door opens and my heart lurches, and I clamp down on his fingers like he is my lifeline and I am drowning. Which isn't actually far from the truth.

He squeezes back. "I've got you, sugar."

I nod and he pulls me inside.

Everything he described about the bathroom is right. It's designed for fucking. The stalls are more rooms, the lights lit low and pushing up to the ceiling like candles flickering their shadows against the walls. The colors are warm, the floor bamboo, and it looks more like the bathroom at a spa retreat than for a crowded restaurant.

But all that's forgotten as Michael comes up behind me, one arm sliding around my waist, and his other hand curling around my throat. I swallow hard and meet his gaze in the mirror.

He's all hard danger and my body thrills and sparks with excitement. He leans down and his tongue flicks across my neck before he bites. His teeth scrape over my flesh and I groan as electricity sparks through me. He moves up and his lips brush my ear. "I want one more thing, Layla. And you're going to give it to me. Understood?"

He's hardly touched me yet and I'm already aching, wet, ready and willing to give him whatever he desires. "All right."

He straightens and meets my gaze in the mirror and a smile of pure evilness spreads over his lips and I know whatever I'm envisioning, my price will be much higher. Panic jolts through me but I can't move, not with his grip so sure, his hazel eyes so compelling.

"Jillian's birthday party. You're going to go with me."

It's the hardest thing he could ever ask from me and he knows it. I've been rejecting any suggestion of family events. Not ready to take that next step.

I shake my head. His parents will be there, his sisters and niece. I can barely act normal around my own family let alone his. It's too much pressure.

His hands fall away. "Are you sure about that?"

The struggle wars inside me as I watch his hard, implacable face. He will not relent. I understand this. He can't relent. If he does, it would ruin the whole power dynamic between us. That he asks me something that is so hard, and risks it affecting the rest of the evening, is a testimony to how much he wants me to go with him. How much he's willing to fight to make this real, despite my desire to keep it in a safe little box.

I have no one to blame for this predicament but myself. As he's stated before, this is what I signed up for. I can pretend all I want, but it is the truth. And the thing is, under the fear racing through my blood, I want to go.

My throat is closed so tight I'm unable to speak so I offer my body in acquiescence. I place my hands on the sink and arch my back.

A lesser man would take it as the offering it is, but of course, Michael isn't that easy. Which is why he is so irresistible. He crosses his arms over his chest and flicks a dismissive glance over my body. "Is that a yes, Layla?"

I grit my teeth and nod.

He shakes his head. "Not good enough. Say the words. I want to hear them."

My fingers clutch the granite countertop, so hard my knuckles turn white. I lick my dry lips and say, "I will go with you to Jillian's party."

"Good girl." He steps behind me and places his palm on my back.

I shiver all over and watch with rapt attention, all other thought gone.

He grips my waist and slowly moves his hands down my hips. It's torture. Agony. Ecstasy. All rolled together. With excruciating slowness he lifts the hem of my dress and the slide of the fabric against my overheated skin is like a caress.

My breath quickens.

My heart slams against my ribs.

He trails a finger over the base of my spine. Slowly. Oh so slowly. And soft.

I want to scream at him to hurry but I clamp my mouth shut. If I do that, he'll stop and I can't have that. He smiles at me, that cruel smile that's captivated me from the moment I saw him. "You're a good girl, sugar, staying still." He leans over my back and I feel his pants brush against my sensitive thighs. "You can beg though. You can always beg."

A whimper escapes my throat and my clit pounds to the rhythm of my heart. I am on fire. Near desperate and nothing has even happened yet. His thumb trails over my stomach and I jerk as a strangled gasp leaves my lips.

"Mmmm..." he mummers in my ear. "That's a good sound."

His erection presses against my ass and I fight the urge to press back, afraid one wrong move will make him stop. He grips my chin. "Give me that mouth."

I crane my neck and he's there. His lips on mine.

I try and turn but he holds me still, not allowing me to move as he takes me.

It's a raw, dirty kiss filled with promise and heat that threatens to consume me. I am possessed. I feel it everywhere. Sweeping across my skin. Settling into my bones. Sinking into my skin.

I am home.

He takes me and I surrender.

I start to shake, terrified that a kiss can consume me so.

He breaks away and runs a hand down my back. "Easy, sugar. You're safe."

Tears well in my eyes and I can only whisper, "I hate you."

A small smile lifts his lips. "I know you do." Then he taps my legs. "Spread them."

I instantly comply, pushing my feet farther apart. The obscene stance only makes me hotter. More needy.

His hand glides over my ass, over my hip and he slips his fingers between my legs. His touch is an electric shock and I bite my lip to keep from crying out.

He shakes his head. "None of that, I want to hear you."

I jerk and gasp as his hand slides effortlessly over my exposed mound.

"So wet," he says, then lifts his fingers to my lips and paints them with my own essence.

The scent of sex and desire instantly fills the bathroom. I meet his eyes in the mirror. He gives me a sharp nod. "If you need to stop, say the word red. Understood?"

"Yes." A need-soaked plea.

"No coming until I say otherwise."

"Yes." My whole body is on fire, I brace myself for the first slap.

"Relax, Layla, you know it's easier when you relax."

I force my muscles to relent because he's right. Tension only makes it hurt more. Although arousal makes it hurt less, so I don't know what to expect. I just wait, suspended in breathless anticipation and intense desire.

He raises his hand.

I watch in the mirror.

He strikes. So hard it brings tears to my eyes and I cry out in pain and relief as I clutch the sink to keep from falling forward. Despite my request to be hurt, I'd expected soft. Expected easy.

I'm blissfully wrong. I need hard. I can't explain why.

He slaps me again and fiery heat explodes over my skin. I jerk forward and he catches me by the hip with one hand to hold me steady.

And then it begins in earnest. Over and over. Alternating between hard and gentle. Blows land over every inch of my rounded cheeks and upper thighs until I am panting for breath.

It hurts. Hurts in the way it used to and not in the punishment it's become.

He knows exactly what he's doing and it isn't long before I am desperate. I push back against the blows. Wanting them to stop. Needing them to continue. Sensations crest over my skin and I lean my head down, closing my eyes as I get lost.

I don't think about John. I don't think about anything. Finally, at long last, my mind is blank, my heart is open, and I am free. Free from everything but this man at my back, his palm striking me, and the indescribable pleasure and pain heating my skin.

The small room fills with the sound of his hand on my flesh, my gasps and moans and our mingled heavy breaths. Suddenly, he has a fistful of my hair and I'm being yanked. Our gazes meet in the mirror and he's got that look in his eye. All mean lust and brutal strength. He hits me again.

Once.

Twice.

Three times.

I flinch as each strike sears through me even as wetness slides down my thighs.

He steps forward, the fabric of his pants a delicious irritant against my skin as he slides his hand down my quivering belly and strokes my clit. The orgasm immediately swells like a tsunami. Relentless in it's greedy desire. "Oh god. Stop."

He shakes his head, still holding on to my hair so my head can't slip forward and hide my reaction. "Don't come, Layla."

I bite my lip and think about anything but the monstrous climax building inside me. "Please, Michael."

"No." His fingers slide effortlessly inside me. He

pumps in and out, hitting my G-spot.

A cry tears from my throat. It's too much. It's not enough.

The heel of his hand grinds against my clit. His grip tightens in my hair.

I become a pinprick of focus. My whole world narrows to this room, this man, his ruthless fingers and my sore, red skin.

He leans close, whispering into my ear, "You ready?"

"Yes, god, yes," I choke out, hanging on by a thread.

"Ask me for it."

I'm frantic and I don't even hesitate. "Please let me come, Michael."

He presses against my ass and I can feel his hard cock and I want it. I need it. "Don't hold back."

Then he shifts, pulls my hips back from the sink, and slaps my clit. Hard enough I see stars as the orgasm tears through me like a violent storm.

He strikes me again.

And again.

And again.

I come harder than I can ever remember coming in my entire life. My body shakes as the spasms rack through my frame. Everything is a quivering mess. My knees and thighs tremble, my arms shake. My body keens as he works every last bit of my release from me and I collapse in an exhausted heap.

It's like something has splintered apart inside me, breaking through the hard knot of tension, cleansing me.

All of my muscles relax, melting in a way that's a distant memory. My eyes close. My spine eases and when he releases his hold on my hair, my head drops forward.

Gentle now, his hands slide over my back,

smoothing down my hips.

I'm boneless. I could sleep for a week. He straightens my clothes, strokes down my back, and smooths my hair all while treating me like the rag doll I am. He lifts me. Gathers me close and turns me into his warm chest. He kisses my temple. "Feel better?"

I nod against him. After all this time, I finally have the relief that I've been craving and it is pure heaven. A peacefulness I'd almost forgotten settles into my bones.

He tilts my chin and runs his thumb over my cheeks because, of course, I was crying. Part of me wants to curl into him and cry a river but another part of me, a stronger part wants to be done with my tears. I blink away the wetness. "Thank you."

His expression flickers and he shakes his head. "Did anyone ever tell you that you're a complete heartbreaker?"

I shake my head. That's one thing John never said to me.

"You are." He leans down and brushes his mouth against mine in the sweetest of kisses. "We need to go."

"Okay." There's something different in my voice, it's lighter.

A smile flickers over his lips. "I see a lot of spankings in your future if they make you this compliant."

I laugh. An honest to goodness belly laugh.

He smiles. "What am I going to do with you?"

"I'm sure you'll think of something." I straighten and look at Michael. My mind is mush, and I'm more relaxed than I've been in forever. "I'm ready."

We start to walk but at the last second he swings me around and pushes me up against door. His mouth is on mine and he is devouring me. I moan and throw my arms around him, hanging on for dear life as he consumes me. His hands roam down my body. I twine my fingers through his hair, holding him close. I never want this to end. I could kiss him for days and never grow tired of it. His tongue tangles with mine as our breathing turns heavy. He growls, a low vibration that sends shivers through me. His grip tightens on my waist. He shakes his head. "See, what you do to me."

I open my mouth to speak but no words come out. I'm at a loss.

"I intended to wait." His voice is low and deep as he grips the nape of my neck. "But I can't. I'm going to fuck you right here, right now."

My breath catches. Yes. I need that. I manage a soft, "Please."

With quick, sure hands he unbuckles his belt then undoes his pants. That expression that makes my blood surge slides over his features. His gaze flickers over my mouth. "On your knees, girl."

Without hesitation, I drop, and then tilt my head up. His fingers work into my hair, and he says in a soft, rough rasp, "You wreck me, Layla."

My heart skips a beat, and something intangible shifts the air. In that moment, I'm completely his. I have no other thought or desire but to please him.

He rubs his thumb over my jaw.

My attention never leaving his, I part my lips.

His cock pushes against my mouth as his grip on my hair tightens.

I don't suck. Don't lick. I just let him fill me. Open and willing, completely compliant, I surrender.

It's hard to explain the power that comes from being used for his pleasure. Being taken. He thrusts, and I relax all my muscles as his cock kisses the back of my throat. Our eyes locked as I gag on his next pass but make no effort to pull away, and his eyes flash and he growls low in his throat.

Arousal flames like wild fire as I fight the urge to

improve on his behalf. But that isn't what he wants, or what he needs. No, he wants my submission. My acceptance that I will let him take control.

A muscle in his jaw ticks as he once again pushes past my body's barriers and slides down my throat. There he pauses, and time suspends as he blocks my airway.

And all the while, I don't resist. There is no struggle, only acceptance.

He pulls out, lifts me off the floor, presses me against the wall, and impales me.

I cry out, gasping for breath. He jerks my legs around his waist and I hang on as he pounds furiously into me. The stillness from mere seconds ago is gone, replaced by the storm that rages between us.

My head bangs against the wall as I clutch at his shoulders, desperate to hang on and ride out the fury. He fucks me like he's starving. Like a feral beast.

My muscles contract at the first telltale sign of orgasm.

He leans down and sinks his teeth into my neck.

A fierce climax rips through me.

"Goddamn it," he bites out, thrusting hard and fast. Then he buries his mouth in the curve of my shoulder and shudders in release as the waves carry us both into oblivion.

I have no idea how long we stay like that, but finally my legs drop and he pulls out of me. He straightens his clothes as I pull at my dress until we are reasonably put back together again. When we're through, he kisses me, just a soft brush against my lips. "I'm going to enjoy dinner even more knowing my come is dripping down your legs."

I flush, I'm sure ten shades of scarlet, but I can't help laughing. It rings through the air, the tone different from before, like it's lost all its rough edges. "You're depraved."

He flashes that smile I love so much. "And you're the most gorgeous girl I have ever laid eyes on."

"Thank you," I say, my voice husky and soft.

He takes my hand and I glance in the mirror, freezing at my reflection.

I look exactly how I feel, wild and free, just like the girl I used to be. I want to reach out and touch my reflection to assure myself she's real.

And I finally accept the truth. I want this. Want him and everything he will give me. I want to be whole.

Now that I've touched that girl I want her back.

And I'm willing to fight for her.

22.

I twist a tissue, staring down at my lap as I sit on Dr. Sorenson's couch. She's in her normal spot, in her standard, neutral knee-length skirt and white blouse. She waits, pen and pad at the ready, but I have no idea where to start.

I feel like I've lived a lifetime since I last saw her.

Since that night in the restaurant, I've stopped pretending I'm not in a relationship with Michael. It's begun, the process of healing, and slowly I'm starting to put together the fragments of my broken heart.

I cry less, and I laugh more. I haven't had a panic attack in over two weeks. Haven't woken up screaming. I called my mom just to say hi, went out with Ruby without her begging me, and said good morning to my coworkers.

I also spent every second I had with Michael. My apartment is starting to feel cold and deserted, a place that's no longer home.

Even when he worked late, I started going to his

house to walk Belle, not because he asked, but because I want to. Something about that ugly dog's affection—the happy, excited wag of her tail, the way she dances around in circles, tongue lolling to one side in uninhibited joy at my arrival—heals something deep within me.

I need that dog. Almost as much as I need Michael.

And this Saturday is his sister, Jillian's, birthday party. Where I'd meet everyone. His family. People who mattered to him.

I was a nervous wreck about it.

I feel Dr. Sorenson's patient gaze on me and I raise my head. On a deep breath I blurt out, "It's happening."

She tilts her head to one side. "What's happening?"

"Michael." I twist the tissue again into a tight spiral. "He's becoming a part of my life."

The scratch of ballpoint over paper. "Go on."

I bite my lip. "I can feel it…feel myself moving on. I'm starting to think about Michael in all the spaces John used to occupy."

"And how does that make you feel?" she asks in her calm, pleasant voice.

The confession wells in my throat. I want so badly to push it back down, but it refuses to be repressed for one second longer. "That's just the thing. I know what I should feel. I keep waiting for it—the guilt, the stab of betrayal, the grief, and loss. But I don't."

She tilts her head to the side, nodding again. "And how *do* you feel?"

I exhale from my tight lungs. "Free. Good."

The smallest ghost of a smile lifts the corners of her lips. "That's a very good thing, Layla."

I shred the tissue I've been holding and the tattered remains fall crumbled into my lap. I pluck another one from the box. "I'm meeting Michael's family on Saturday."

"I think that's wonderful. You're healing."

I look past her, staring at the ocean print on the wall, the blue of the water calming, as I'm sure is its intention. "I remember the first time I met John's mom. It was just the two of them and we were home from school for the weekend. We went to a little neighborhood diner for breakfast. They'd been going there since he was a boy, and everyone knew them. That morning they fussed over him, talking about how handsome and grown up he was. He introduced me, and they insisted on making me their famous banana shake."

I smile at the memory, realizing it no longer rips me open and makes me bleed. "It was in this gigantic glass the size of a big gulp, heaping with whipped cream and extra cherries. They hovered over me, watching as I took my first sip so they could witness this awesome moment in my life. I looked over the glass at John and he grinned and winked at me, and I knew. In that second, I knew he was 'the one' and that I was going to marry him and spend my life with him. It was a happy morning."

There's a moment of silence while she waits to see if I'm going to continue, but when I don't, she prompts, "Tell me more."

I shrug, not quite sure where I'm leading. "It was a good memory. I don't have any other meeting-the-parents stories and that's a hard one to live up to."

"Are you afraid meeting Michael's parents won't compare?"

I shred another tissue, and she leans over, shifting the garbage can closer to me. I gather up all the little bits of cotton and dump them into the container before brushing the lint off my beige work pants. Work pants Michael had declared not interesting enough, and insisted my panties be removed for the rest of the day. My lips quirk, it's something John would have done too. The similarity between them is pleasing instead of frightening. I think John would have liked Michael. In a different life they would have been friends, devising evil plots to drive girls wild.

I shake my head. It would be easy to nod and let that be the reason for my unease, but it's not the truth. "No, that's not it."

"Then what is?"

"Michael." His name on my lips comes out as a croak and I clear my throat. "I feel that same kind of happiness with him that I did with John."

She nods. "Go on."

I take another Kleenex and once again begin my restless twisting. "I was wrong. That day in the diner. I didn't end up marrying him. I didn't spend my life with John."

I let the words hang, not finishing the rest of the thought. Because there was no need.

I could love Michael. In a truth I could barely admit to myself, I probably already did. I'd lost my happy ending once. I no longer took happiness for granted. A future shimmered right beyond my reach, bright and glittery with promise.

But I didn't trust the shadows not to steal it away.

23.

Clutching Michael's hand, I stand on the front porch of his stately, neoclassical childhood home and will myself not to faint. He'd taken pity on me before we'd come, picking out my outfit, my shoes, how to wear my hair and makeup. I huffed, pouted, and stomped around my bedroom, until he'd turned me over his knee and given my ass quite the beating and I settled down. While I put on a good show, we both knew I was thankful he'd taken away my ability to fret.

With my rampant nerves, I would have spent hours agonizing over what to wear and worked myself into a frenzy. Michael's way may not make me a candidate for feminist of the year, but it calmed and soothed me as nothing else could have.

I wore what he told me. A brown suede A-line skirt and a soft cream, fine knit, scooped-neck sweater, and the same knee-high boots from the night of our first date. I begrudgingly have to admit he picked out a good outfit. It's trendy, flatters my dark, chestnut hair, and hugs my curves.

Of course, my ass still burns from the palm of his hand, the bare skin rubbing against the silk of my underwear. Today, my ass isn't the only thing that's pink. My cheeks now glow with health and their natural rosiness has returned as the hollowness has disappeared. There are no shadows under my eyes. My hair is down, shiny and flowing in soft waves down my back. I look good.

Probably better than I have in a long, long time. I look like the girl I'd been, mixed with something else I can't define. In the last eighteen months my face has lost the round softness it used to have. I look like a woman instead of a girl.

Now that I've lost the haunted look of grief, suddenly, men have a renewed interest in me. Everywhere I go, men seem to strike up conversations. In the morning line at Starbucks or Walgreens. At work, the new guy asked me out. And I couldn't help noticing the heads turning as I passed. After spending so much time living like a ghost, it's an odd, strange experience.

It's all because of the man next to me, who doesn't even flinch at the way my nails are digging into his hand. He gives me a little wink as the door starts to open, sweeping down to quickly whisper into my ear, "Don't worry, sugar, they'll love you."

And, then, it's happening. I'm meeting his family.

An attractive, older woman—a sleek brunette with expertly placed gold highlights in her chin-length bob—is smiling at me. No, beaming is more accurate. She holds out her hands like she's going to embrace me and says, "You must be Layla. I've heard so much about you."

I smile back and toss a furtive questioning glance at Michael, who shrugs. "Hey, Mom. Yes, this is Layla Hunter." He gives my palm a squeeze. "This is my mother, Miriam Banks."

I extricate myself from Michael and hold out my hand. "It's a pleasure to meet you, Mrs. Banks."

"Oh, none of that," she says and pulls me into a hug before pulling back and studying me closely. "Call me Miriam."

She shifts her attention to Michael. "Jillian was right, she's very pretty."

Michael shakes his head. "Of course she is."

A flush heats my cheeks. "Thank you, and thank you for having me."

"Come on, everyone is out back. Didn't we get a perfect day?" Miriam leads us through a large open foyer with high ceilings and an intricate winding staircase that could only be original. Expertly restored, of course.

She's right about the weather. One of those unexpectedly warm fall days that sometimes graces Chicago right before the weather turns cold for good. I nod in agreement. "It's lovely."

The house is beautiful, rich with charm and history. It's big, sprawling actually, with wide-open spaces and big windows. A mix of old and new. In today's market, in the heart of Evanston and close to the lake, it has to cost a fortune.

For the first time it dawns on me that Michael comes from money. I try to picture him roaming through this house as a boy and find I have no trouble. It both looks exactly like Michael and nothing like him at the same time.

"Your house is gorgeous," I say as we stroll through the massive kitchen right out of a luxury designer catalogue with its massive, clearly custom cabinets, commercial appliances, and warm, brown-and-cream countertops.

"Thank you, dear, we just had the kitchen remodeled."

Michael takes my hand again as we're led through French glass doors out to a big backyard, complete with an outdoor kitchen. There is a group of people sitting around a large, long table, all looking at me with wide grins on their faces.

Michael gives me a little squeeze, and I'm thankful for his silent reassurance.

I recognize Jillian and her boyfriend, Leo, but the rest are strangers to me.

Jillian jumps up and runs over to me, hugging me like we're best friends. "I'm so glad you came."

I pat her back and say, "Thank you for having me. Happy Birthday. I feel bad crashing your party."

She pulls back and waves a dismissive hand. "Are you kidding me? We're thrilled."

She hooks her arm through my elbow and tugs me toward the rest of the group. She points toward an older man that looks just like Michael. "That's our dad, Richard."

Before I can say anything to Michael's father, she continues, "You know Leo, that little girl is our niece, Amy. That's our sister, Sarah, and her husband, William."

"It's nice to meet you." My voice is polite and cordial, as they all start shouting out hellos.

From behind us, Michael says, "Do you mind, Jillian?"

Jillian cranes her neck and gives him a sassy smile. "Yeah, I do, you've been hoarding her for weeks and we need a chance to grill her before the rest of the party starts."

I swallow hard, looking back at him with pleading eyes.

"There will be no grilling." Michael gets that hard set to his jaw I've come to recognize means business, but of course it has no effect on his family, who just laugh at him.

Michael juts his chin at Leo. "Can't you control your woman?"

Leo grins and winks at me. "Well, yeah, but this is way more entertaining."

"Ignore them," Jillian says, pulling me over to an empty chair next to her.

This separates me from Michael, who sits down across from me, giving me a shake of the head and an eye roll.

My heart gives a tiny flutter at the silent communication between us. Such a couplely thing to do.

"We're glad you could come, Layla," Michael's father says. He's not quite as tall as his son, but the two of them are obviously from the same gene pool.

"Thank you for having me. Your home is beautiful."

"Thank you," Richard says with a warm smile. "And where did you grow up?"

"Winnetka." I know enough about Michael's dad to know he'll be pleased that I'm a North Shore girl. "My parents still live there, but my sister and her family live in Barrington."

"Good, good," Richard says, before nodding at Michael in what I can only assume is approval.

The little girl, Amy, who named Belle, comes running over to me, her brown pigtails bouncing. She giggles, her Banks' hazel eyes shining. "Are you Uncle Michael's girlfriend?"

I blink, at a loss as to how to answer the question.

"Yes, she is," Michael says, no stress in his tone at all.

Michael's other sister, Sarah, shakes her head, laughing, her blue eyes dancing. "Sorry, she hasn't learned to censor her questions yet."

Next to her, William snorts. "Please, you put her up to it."

Michael lets out an exasperated sigh, and I press my lips together to keep from laughing. And for a moment I marvel at how far I've come, it's been forever since I had to repress laughter instead of tears.

Sarah swings around and gives him an appalled look. "I most certainly did not!"

William grins at me. "She totally did."

Amy nods her cute little head. "She told me to ask."

A blush stains Sarah's cheeks.

Jillian gasps, putting a hand to her chest, her eyes wide and filled with mischief. "Sarah, how could you?"

The older sister sputters, cheeks pink, but before she can explain herself, Amy chimes in, "Aunt Jillian told me to ask you when you're going to get married."

Michael shakes his head. "God help me."

Jillian narrows her gaze on her niece. "You little traitor."

And then they're all off, talking all over each other, taking the pressure and attention off me. Michael shrugs as if to say *See, I told you they were crazy.*

I grin back, and try not to think about the fact that they mentioned the M word.

It's been a long, happy day and we're sitting on Michael's couch after the birthday party. I'd done it. Even more startling, I did more than suffer through it, I had fun. Nobody had looked at me like I might break. Nobody had avoided my eyes as they searched for a way to avoid the murder of my fiancé.

Michael's family had accepted me with open arms, and after the party had died down, we'd sat in the great room while they'd told me embarrassing stories about him, and his mom brought out the family photo album. The pictures of Michael as a child had fascinated me. It was hard to reconcile the innocent-looking boy in the pictures with the man he was today.

And through it all, Michael had just shaken his head, laughed and was generally good-natured about the whole thing. Oh sure, he put on a good show, but it was clear he came from a loving, supportive family.

Belle pushes her way between Michael and me on the couch, interrupting my thoughts. With a little whine, she puts her head on my lap, staring up at me with excited *pet me, pet me, pet me* eyes. I can't deny her anything, and I stroke her soft fur, and play with her floppy ears. I smile down at her. "You are a con dog, aren't you?"

She wags her tail and presses her head harder into my lap.

"She loves you," Michael says, his arm over the back of the couch.

Belle rolls over so I can pat her belly and I laugh. "I love her too. My mom was allergic to dogs growing up, and I always wanted one. I couldn't wait to get one."

"Why didn't you?" Michael asks, expression curious. He's sitting there, relaxed and gorgeous. We'd changed into comfy clothes when we'd gotten home. And we both wore sweats and T-shirts. How the man manages to still look dangerous in a T-shirt that reads *Hmmm... Beer* is beyond me, but he manages it.

I clear my throat, and pay rapt attention to Belle, who keeps squirming farther and farther into my lap. "We were going to as soon as we got home from our honeymoon."

The grief is still there, but it's lost all its sharp, jagged edges. I can think of John now without crying. Without it being an open wound.

"I'm sorry, Layla." He covers my hand. "Do you have pictures of him on your phone?"

I do. In a locked album. I also have his last voice and text messages. I'd refused to update my phone for fear I'd lose those parts of him that made him real. I nod.

"Let me see."

I shake my head.

He squeezes my fingers. "I'm not asking."

My head snaps up. "Hey, that's not fair."

In this way he's different from John, who kept his dominance about sex, whereas Michael tends to exert it in everyday interactions.

He laughs. "Who said anything about fair?"

"I'm not ready." While I'm better, that part of our relationship still feels private.

"I believe differently."

"What does it matter?"

"It matters because he was a part of you and we're not going to pretend he doesn't exist. It's not healthy for you, and it doesn't help you heal. He sounds like a good man, and I know how much you loved him. I want to put a face to the name. I don't think that's unreasonable."

I scowl, giving him my fiercest glare. "You can't pull *that* out whenever you want to get your way."

"I don't see why not." His tone is laced with amusement.

"Because it's not fair."

He shrugs. "The pictures, Layla."

I puff out my bottom lip, still not ready to concede, even as I feel my body responding. "We need to lay down some ground rules."

"The rules are you do what you're told. You don't dig in your heels over a simple request, or deny me a chance to get a deeper understanding of who you are, then or now."

Damn it, I hate when he's all reasonable. It leaves me so few options for revolt. And the more solid I become in both our relationship, and myself, the more I desire to test us, and me. To figure out who I am. Now that I'm no longer just existing, I need to rediscover what makes me tick. My likes and dislikes. My wants and needs. How far I want the bounds of our relationship to extend.

At my hesitation, he prompts again. "The pictures."

I'm feeling slightly dangerous. I raise a brow. "Or what?"

His eyes narrow and his jaw hardens. "Do you really want to test me and find out? Over this? Something I'll probably see anyway when I meet your parents next week?"

He's right. There are pictures of John and me at my parents' house, but I don't back down. "I don't think it's right for you to demand something so private and personal."

"It's a picture. I'm not asking for anything hard."

"He's mine. I won't share him with you." My tone is snappish and belligerent. Full of petulance. I don't know where this is coming from, or why. I don't want to ruin our day, but I'm struck with a burst of stubbornness.

He stares at me for a long time, his gaze hard and unreadable.

I hold my breath, unsure of what he'll say or do. What I hope for and what I fear.

After what feels like an eternity, he says in a flat tone, "Suit yourself, Layla. This isn't a battle I choose to fight with you. I'm going to bed."

And with that he stands up and walks down the hall. A second later the door to his room closes softly behind him.

I sit motionless on the couch, Belle's head still in my lap. This wasn't the result I'd anticipated—it's far, far worse than the fight I angled for.

I've put a wedge between us. I've disappointed him. Worse than any punishment he could have exacted on me. The kiss of death for a girl like me and the weight of it crushes me.

I stare at my phone on the table before picking it up. The metal is cool under my hot fingers. I unlock the private photo album and scroll through the pictures of John and me, stopping on my favorite taken a couple of weeks before he died. We were at a friend's house, standing hip to hip, our arms locked around each other's waist, and we're laughing. We look happy. There's no hint of our tragic future. No sign of what's to come. I flip to the next one, a shot of John in profile while he watched the water lap against the lakeshore. It was a candid shot, and it captures the essence of him perfectly. His easy charm, his boyish good looks, and the barest hint of the devil lurking beneath.

I run my thumb over his face, trying to remember what the line of his jaw feels like under my fingers. But instead of John's smooth skin, I feel the roughness of Michael's stubble that never quite disappears no matter when he's shaved.

With a heavy heart I close the album and press the voice mail icon, scrolling down and down, until I finally reach it. I click on the arrow and put the phone to my ear. A second later, John is on the line.

Hey, LayLay, I'm running late, but I'll be home by seven. It's been a hard day and I need to do filthy things to you. So be a good girl and be naked and ready when I get there.

It's not quite the last message, which I've saved, but never play. This message is from a week before he died. Again, I replay it, my lashes drifting closed at the rich timber of his voice. So achingly familiar.

I remember that night. The sex. The laughter. Curling up in his arms after. But there's a distance there now. I can no longer quite make him real in my head.

Instead, I think of Michael. Flesh and blood. The man whose palms I picture skimming down my body. Who's cock I feel deep inside me. The man who's single handedly pulled me back from the dead.

The message ends and I stare down the hall. I put a wall between us.

I shift my attention to the front door. I have two choices. I can leave and let the wall between us harden and set, or I can go to him and rip down the barrier.

In the end, there's no real contest.

I turn and walk down the hall. To life.

24.

I open the door and step inside to find him lying on the bed, reading a book. His expression is unreadable as he looks at me. He is silent, but his raised eyebrow speaks volumes.

My lashes flutter as my heart speeds up. I am suddenly nervous. "I'm sorry."

He nods. "All right."

I don't know what to do. I've been fighting my instincts and nature for so long, I don't trust them. I do the only thing I can think of—something I have never done with him. Something I've never even given to John. I open the locked folder on my phone, and find the picture of us as a couple I'd looked at moments before. It fills the screen, and I walk forward until I'm at the end of the bed. Then, I drop to my knees, lower my head and extend the phone, raising it high for him to see.

There is only silence, and the sound of my breath filling the room.

Finally, I hear him move. I resist the urge to lift my head, instead waiting in offering. It's the most submissive gesture I've ever made, and it is hard.

So very hard.

A moment later he slides to the edge of the bed and his bare feet enter my line of vision, resting on either side of my thighs. The phone is plucked from my hand, but instead of studying it, he places it next to him, and runs his hands through my hair. His fingers tangle in the soft waves, and then he tugs.

In answer, I lift my chin.

Those hypnotic hazel eyes burn into mine and a fire starts between us. I want to move, to rise to meet him and fan the flames until it rages like an inferno between us. But I don't. I sit still and I wait for him to take the lead. His thumb runs over the length of my jaw. "Thank you."

I blink, my throat tight. "You're welcome."

"I don't want to take him from you, Layla. I want you to claim him."

The full weight of his words sink in. Out there in the living room, wasn't about exerting his dominance. I was the one that turned it into a test. His motivation wasn't a power play, but to help me remember the good memories of John, instead of the nightmares.

His fingers skim down my throat. "You're mine, but being mine doesn't mean you weren't his."

"Yes." My tone is just a fraction above a whisper. They aren't mutually exclusive. My needing Michael doesn't negate my love for John, or our relationship. And for the first time I understand that. Really understand it, deep down in my bones.

"Do you think there's room in your heart for both of us, girl?"

There is no longer any question about this. I nod. "Yes, Michael."

In answer, he leans down and kisses me, a hard,

passion-soaked kiss full of promise and magic. Then he's pulling me off the floor, and rolling me onto the bed. His big body covers mine as he licks at my mouth, and his teeth scrape along my lower lip. I moan, needing to feel the full weight of him, needing him to claim me. To make what I offered on the floor real and strong. His and mine.

Separate from what I shared with John. Not better. Not worse. Just different.

His hands skim down my arms, bypassing my wrists to tangle my fingers with his. His mouth still on mine, he raises my hands next to my head, and presses them into the mattress.

But it's no longer enough. I need more.

I want his fingers wrapped around my wrists so I can't free them. I want to feel trapped. I want his hand to cover my mouth so I can't scream.

I want afraid. Scared. Needy and desperate.

Things I don't understand, but I need. Michael knows this but is forced to deliver it in a safe way to avoid triggering my past.

Suddenly, a great well of inner strength sweeps through me, followed quickly by a rush of hot, jagged rage.

I will not let that *one* night win. Not anymore.

The empowerment is like jet fuel in my blood and my movements become frantic. He raises his head and gazes down at me, that hard, commanding menace I'm addicted to, written across his face.

"How much do you hold back because of me?"

He releases my hands, and his expression clouds as his beautiful, cruel mouth dips. "I'm a patient man, Layla. And as far as I'm concerned we've got all the time in the world."

My thumb brushes over his lower lip. "You didn't answer my question."

His palm covers my stomach and the muscles there

quiver. "I'm careful not to do anything that might trigger memories of the attack. That's not the same as holding back."

I look at him, hoping my gaze is full of the trust I feel for him. "I need it all. And I think you need it too."

Something flares in his eyes, and he sucks in a breath. I know he's trying, but he can't quite hide how much he wants it, or the price it costs him to always be on guard around me. "I can wait until you're ready. However long that takes, I'm in, Layla."

It occurs to me that, in this, he needs my permission. It's the safe, caring, responsible thing. My emotional wellbeing, my mental health, it matters to him. *I* matter to him. But it's also another wall between us.

One I created that now needs to be eradicated.

It was there for a reason, I realize that, but I need it stripped away. Because finally, at long last, my need to be whole is greater than my need to feel safe.

I curl my fingers around his neck. "I'm ready."

I can see the hesitation in his expression, in the press of his lips and set of his jaw.

I hope my face conveys the depths of my sincerity, my certainty. "I need it. With you."

When he still remains contemplative, I give him my most seductive, sassy smile. Hoping to alleviate his concern, I tease, "Shall I beg for it?"

The hazel in his eyes flares to bright gold, but instead of the attack I'm anticipating, he rolls over and puts his hands behind his head. "That's a good idea."

I blink, lifting up on my elbows. "Excuse me?"

That cocky, mean look slides across his features and my belly dips and heats. "You asked if you should beg for it. And yes, you should."

My throat is dry. "I was teasing."

His cool, slightly dismissive gaze glances down my

body. "I told you that you were going to have to start paying for all your little challenges, and now seems as good a time as any to start. You want it, work for it."

It's been so long I've forgotten this part. The part where he doesn't come free just because I want him.

I eye him, biting my lower lip. I'm out of practice. I haven't begged for anything in a long time, and even back then, John typically only made me beg when I was already in a fevered state. When I was well past my fears and inhibitions and it was so easy I'd promise the world.

But this isn't John. It's Michael. He's harder. More exacting.

I want what he will give me. And I'm so damn tired of being afraid all the time. The knowledge and understanding doesn't stop the nerves and I laugh, a high-pitched titter that conveys my discomfort. "I don't know what you want me to do."

Another glance before he shrugs. "That's for you to figure out, but naked is probably a good start."

It's a concrete action I can take and I nod, slowly pulling my top over my head and dropping it to the floor before flicking open my bra. After that's discarded, I stand up on the bed, and remove my sweats and panties.

Now that my nakedness is complete I find myself once again unsure. I stand there, towering over him, at a loss. I decide the only course of action is to follow my heart. I move, lowering myself, as I straddle him. My exposed core rubs along his erection and the slight friction of the cotton sweats remind me how aroused I am. How wet.

How much I want this and him.

His expression is intent on my face, and he lies still, making no move to reach for me. I work my hands under his T-shirt and scrape my nails over his stomach. The muscles flex under my touch.

I roll my hips, my nerves slipping away as I remember why I love this. How addictive it is. Turning my brain off, I let the lust take over. I slip my hair from its ponytail holder and it falls around my shoulders. I run my fingers through the length, the motions grinding my clit against his erection.

It feels so good. *He* feels so good. I get lost in the sensation, my back arching, my nipples exposed to the air, my hair a silky cascade over my skin, soft cotton against my overheated flesh.

I gasp as pleasure races through me only to jerk back to awareness when Michael says dryly, "That looks more like masturbation than begging to me."

A hot flush spreads over my chest, rolls up my neck and splashes on my cheeks. "Oops."

He smirks, raising one brow. "Oops indeed."

I slither up his body, pulling his shirt as I go, resting my bare wetness against his belly. I grab ahold of his wrists and look down at him. His eyes are dark on mine, burning with that passion that's always been a live, tangible thing between us. I rub my slickness over his skin and watch in fascination as his jaw hardens. I squeeze my fingers around his wrists, loving the strong flex of muscles under my touch. I lean close and my breasts brush his chest, sending my nipples tingling.

And then I get serious. I get real. I lay my heart, and all my secret yearnings at his feet, because he deserves that from me and I'll give him nothing less.

"Michael." My voice trembles with emotion.

"Yes, Layla." His own voice is filled with a husky smoke that leaves me breathless.

"You're the best thing that has ever happened to me." My eyes fill with tears but I go on, refusing to stop what needs to be said. "You have pulled me back from the dead, kicking and screaming, and I can never repay you. But this is something I can do. Something that I can give you that will never belong to anyone else. Only you can help me lay those ghosts to rest, to help me overcome the past. I trust you. More than I ever thought possible. So please, I am begging you, please take me. Hold me down, restrain me, possess me and make me yours. I'm incomplete without it. Without you."

Then I roll off him and lay, arms wide, legs splayed in offering. I turn my head to speak the last words, to find him staring at me in a kind of stunned awe.

I smile, my heart breaking and filling back up again with something new and light. Something fresh and clean and pure that's for him. And *only* for him. "I am at your mercy. Do with me what you will."

He moves fast, like a panther that has been sitting too long in the brush and is now impatient for the kill. He springs on me, trapping me under him.

"Layla." My name cracks in his throat.

"Yours, Michael." I arch, offering myself completely and wholeheartedly. "Please make me yours."

He sucks in a breath, and lightly brushes his thumb over my wrist and my whole body shakes. "Any hint of panic and I expect you to tell me right away."

I blink, nodding eagerly.

His hand skims up my arm, over my neck until he grips my jaw, tightening his hold until it aches and forces me to meet his eyes. "I'm serious, girl. Any hint. If you don't communicate, I promise you will pay dearly for it. And it won't be with one of those spankings you love to hate. Understood?"

"Understood." I arch again. I'm sure. Sure in the way I was about John. Sure in the way I never believed I'd be again.

In offering, I hold out my wrists. I need the bad memories replaced.

Releasing his hold on my jaw, he encircles my outstretched hand. Twining his fingers around the fine bones, studying me as his hold tightens.

Instead of fear, instead of dread, my body rages to life.

He's watching me closely, too closely, when all I want is abandon, but I understand him. He's protecting me. Keeping me safe, even from myself.

I nod in reassurance. "I'm okay, I promise."

He tightens his hold further. His fingers like a vise. He waits.

Again, I feel no panic, only greedy desire. I nod again. "I know it's you. I won't forget. I want this. Please, it's been so long and I want it so badly."

I finally seem to satisfy him and his expression transforms from concerned and watchful to beautiful cruelty. He yanks my hands above my head and I gasp as excitement rips through me.

His fingers manacles my wrists, and my breath quickens.

Then he looks down at me, his mouth twisted into an evil smile. "That was beautiful, sugar. I loved every word of it and it means the world to me." He leans down, and bites my neck; hard enough I'll have a mark tomorrow. "But I think you can beg harder."

His teeth scrape over the curve of my breast and he licks over my nipple. "I don't think you're nearly needy enough."

Oh god, yes. This is what I so desperately need. No more kid gloves. No more easy. No more nice.

Just hard, delicious mean.

The next morning, Michael is still sleeping and I'm stretching to reach the coffee, the dress shirt of Michael's I'm wearing riding high on my thighs. Every muscle in my body aches in the best way. Last night, Michael took me in every way possible. So completely, so irrevocably, I woke up changed. My body is marked.

My wrists are bruised. My ass is sore, my knees ache, my breasts feel too full, and my skin is oversensitive.

I've never felt so wonderful in my life.

I hear the bedroom door open and turn to look over my shoulder. He walks into the kitchen wearing his sweats from last night, no shirt, his hair rumpled. "Morning, sugar."

"Morning." I can't help it, I beam at him, my smile so wide it hurts my cheeks.

He chuckles and walks over to me, slipping his arms around my waist. "I'd ask you how you feel but it's written all over you."

I laugh, and it rumbles in my belly. "Don't brag."

"I don't need to brag, I know how good I am."

I roll my eyes, and smack him in the shoulder. "You're so arrogant."

He leans down and gives me a toe-curling kiss. "You love it."

I do. Not that I'd admit it. "I took Belle out already."

He curls his hand around my neck. "You know, you can't leave me, Belle will never forgive me."

It's fast becoming clear that I can't picture my life without him, but I'm not quite ready to own it yet. Instead, I tease, "Now why would I leave, like, the best lay ever?"

He lifts me up and places me onto the counter, and then runs his fingers down the buttons of his shirt I'm wearing. "Best ever, huh?"

I open my legs, and lean back, smiling and seductive. "Absolutely."

He shakes his head and sighs. "Do you have to be wearing one of my favorite shirts?"

It slips down my shoulder. "I like it."

He grabs the fabric, pulls and rips, the buttons flying.

I gasp, the cool morning air hitting my skin. "You

ruined it."

He doesn't speak, just makes quick work of the fabric, tying it so my arms are imprisoned behind my back, and my breasts thrust out.

I'm trapped. And instead of the panic it would have invoked, all I experience is a delicious shiver racing down my spine.

"That's better. I like you open and exposed to me." He rubs his lips over the curve of my neck. "Maybe I should make it a rule."

I lick my lips as everything heats. "You know you could have accomplished the same thing without ruining your shirt."

He shrugs, and plucks my nipples, hard enough I squeak at the pain. "I could have, but aggression turns you on in a way slowly stripping you of clothes never will."

This is true. He understands me.

People take for granted the art of being understood. A mistake I'll never make again.

25.

"How long since you've had a panic attack?"

I push my hair back and smile at Dr. Sorenson, a real smile, like one I probably haven't given her before. "It's been at least a month."

"That's wonderful, Layla."

I look at the box of tissues on the table between us. I haven't taken a single one. "Michael is going to meet my parents."

She nods. "Go on."

My lashes flutter and I find I'm almost embarrassed to say it, but I do. I've been doing that a lot lately. Forcing myself to rejoin the land of the living, and it's working. Every day I feel more alive and the numbness fades away into the distance, like all my bad dreams.

I've started sleeping at Michael's, even when he's working, and with Belle curled into my side, the nightmares have finally gone away. I'm catching up on eighteen months of lost sleep and wake up each morning full of vigor and hope.

I take a deep breath. "I'm happy. I want them to meet him."

"I'm proud of you, Layla. This is a big step."

I feel a moment of hesitation, like a hitch in my chest. I clear my throat. "You don't think it's a betrayal?"

Her eyes narrow fractionally, and she tilts her head to the side. "Let me ask you, if you had died instead of John, what would you have wanted for him?"

Of course, I would have wanted him to move on, to have a life and happiness. I'd want him to have every single one of those things we'd planned together. But, it's different when you're not the one that died. When you are the survivor, rationality doesn't matter. "I would have wanted him to meet a nice girl who loved him the way he deserved to be loved."

"And don't you think he'd want that for you?"

"I do." It's unquestionable he would have hated how I'd been living. And if he had to share me with someone, he'd have wanted it to be someone like Michael. "It's just, hard, you know."

"But you're doing it anyway, and that is tremendous progress."

The words I've barely been able to admit to myself hover on my lips. They are words I should say to Michael but can't, words that are bursting to get free.

Dr. Sorenson is the one person who knows all my secrets, both the good and the bad. She's the one I tell when I can't face them myself. "I—" I sputter on the word and try again. "I love him. Michael, that is."

A weight lifts from my chest as I finally admit the truth out loud.

"I know, it's written all over you." She smiles at me, and her eyes sparkle and I see her, not just as a therapist, but as a person. This woman who has listened to me for countless hours rant and rage. Cry. Panic. And scream. I've dismissed her more times than

I care to admit. Scoffing at her advice, mocking her tools to help me. But she has, if it wasn't for her and our sessions, god only knows what would have happened to me. If it hadn't been for her, maybe one of those times I'd held that razor over my wrist, I would have just sliced and let my blood drain away into the shower until there was nothing left.

"Thank you." I can hear the sincerity in my voice. "You saved me, even when I didn't appreciate it."

She shakes her head. "I held your hand, but, Layla, you saved yourself."

"Maybe." I smile at her, the gesture somehow inadequate for all her hard work. "But I will forever be grateful."

26.

Ruby and I are sitting at The Whisky listening to an Indie Rock band play a kind of neo-soul. It's a mellow jazzy soul mix that's easy to listen and to talk over. Michael is on call tonight but instead of staying in, I use it as a chance to catch up with my best friend.

It's good to rejoin the land of the living. To have a life that doesn't revolve around grief.

Ruby nods at the lead singer, a tall skinny guy with shaggy black hair, dark eyes, and a mournful voice. He's dressed in black jeans and a T-shirt with some sort of band insignia on it and his bare arms are covered in tats. He's just Ruby's type. The kind of guy she always goes for. I smile. "He's cute."

"He is." Ruby gazes at him with an expression filled with longing. "We made out the other night."

I laugh, smacking her on the arm. "You slut!"

Ruby giggles, giving me a suspicious perusal. "Me? Really? You're calling *me* a slut?"

"Yeah, you."

God, it feels so damn good I can't even describe it. To laugh. To sit with a friend and talk about boys and life, and listen to music while you get buzzed on house wine. People always think it's the grand gestures, but it's really not, it's the little moments. The tiny snippets that you remember forever.

Ruby scoffs and rolls her eyes. "Please, on Friday after the show, we kissed. There was tongue, some groping and a little friction. But, I have a feeling you were much sluttier on Friday night than I was."

I try to repress my smile, but it spreads over my lips and stretches across my face. She's right. I was doing many depraved things on Friday. Things that would probably shock Ruby. I shrug. "Maybe."

Ruby throws her head back and laughs. "Well, it wasn't anything like that. But he has potential."

"Really now?" I glance at the singer again, and knowing Ruby's past relationships, I'm pretty sure where this will end. Ruby has terrible taste in men. She picks tortured, starving-artist types with Peter Pan complexes.

Ruby holds up her hands. "I know what you're thinking. But he didn't recite any poetry."

I raise a brow, eyeing her with disbelief. "Hmmmm... But did he play you his newest song and serenade you on his guitar?"

She presses her lips together and a pretty blush stains her cheeks. "That doesn't count."

"It totally does!"

"You just shut up."

I chuckle. "Are you seeing him tonight?"

Ruby sighs heavily, glancing at her dream boy, who meets her eyes and sings right to her. Ruby practically swoons in her stool and I can't help but shake my head. How we ever became best friends I'll never understand, but I'm happy we did. She's the best and I vow not to take her for granted again.

"So?" I prompt, when she seems to have gotten lost in the singer's music and forgotten my question.

"Yes," she says in a wistful voice.

I hold out my hand. "Ten bucks says his bed is on the floor."

She laughs, shaking her head. "Like you're one to talk. What about you? Michael probably has some sort of dungeon and wears leather pants."

"He most certainly does not!"

"No?" Ruby's expression sparks with interest. "That's disappointing."

"No. He's not a prop guy." His only real homage to his predilections is his bed, with all that interesting iron scrollwork that terrified me that first night, but now invokes nothing but heat.

Ruby takes a sip of her wine, glancing furtively at her rocker boy before tilting her head to the side. "What's a prop guy?"

I run my hands through my hair. "Some guys like instruments, crops and floggers, spanking horses, suspension cords, and things like that. Part of their enjoyment is setting the scene, and mood. Establishing the protocol and ritual of the act."

Ruby twists the stem of her glass. "But Michael isn't like that?"

I shake my head and I can't help the shiver that runs through my body in remembrance of his hands on me. Rough and demanding. Taking what he wants while he possesses me so completely I forget my own name. "No."

"So you don't have to call him 'your lordship'?"

I laugh at the very notion. "Hardly. You've met him, does he seem like someone who'd want to be called a lord?"

"True," she says. "So what do you call him?"

"Michael."

"How boring."

I roll my eyes at her and she grins. "So..." she trails off, biting her lip. "What kinds of things does he do?"

I study her closely, trying to gage the motivation behind her interest. It's not the first time she's asked me questions, passing it off as curiosity, but there's something there that goes beyond girl talk.

I'm not sure what to confess. It's not something I've ever shared and I don't quite have the words to explain the dynamic to someone who's unfamiliar with the kind of relationship Michael and I have. Or why I like the things I do. It's a fine line to walk, even within myself. I decide to put the question back on her and see what she does with it, assuming she'll draw her own line. "Since I'm not sure what you mean, ask, and I'll tell you yes or no."

She glances at the object of her affection, and then down at her wine. "Do you have, like, rules and stuff?"

I smile. "Not anything formal. If he wants something, he expects me to give it to him."

"So, what, you can't say no?"

I mull over how to explain, taking a sip of my wine as I think. "In a way. Everyone has limits. But not being able to say no is part of the appeal."

The corners of Ruby's mouth dips as her forehead furrows. "I don't understand."

I decide to try an example. "Remember in college when we went on that camping trip and they were daring us to cliff dive?"

She nods.

"We were terrified and didn't want to do it. Do you remember how hard we tried to get out of it?"

"Yes, you went first after John whispered something in your ear."

I laugh, a good happy sound, as I remember. The memory no longer shreds me with grief. Yes, I feel the loss, and I miss him with that ache that will never go away, but it's not crushing anymore. "He made me do it. Said if I didn't I'd pay."

Ruby blinks, and fingers the choker at her neck. "And to think I always thought he was such a nice boy."

"Everyone did. And he *was* a nice boy." I wink, grinning as I recall with vivid clarity that day at the cliffs. "With a mean streak."

She gapes at me, before nibbling on her bottom lip. "And the cliffs?"

I toy with the stem of my wine as I recall the sun on my face, the terror rushing through me as I stood on the ledge and John waited to the side, that telling smirk on his face.

I focus my attention back on Ruby. "We jumped, right? I went first and then you went. It was scary, but the second after you plunged safely into the water and came up for air, it was pure exhilaration, wasn't it?"

"Yes, it was," Ruby says, her tone contemplative. "I only did it after you did but we jumped for the rest of the day."

I nod. "Just to get that feeling again, right? That mixture of terror and ecstasy all rolled together."

Ruby looks at me, her eyes bright. "And that's what it's like."

"That's what it's like. It's why John forced me to jump that first time. He pushed me because he knew how much I'd love it. I didn't say no because under all my fear, it's what I really wanted but was too afraid to take the risk. When he gave me no option but to jump, it's like the fear couldn't get the better of me."

Comprehension lights up her face, and she tosses a furtive look up at the singer. I suspect she's more than curious, but I don't call her out on it. Nor do I have the heart to break it to her that, despite his bad boy edge, her indie rocker doesn't have a dominant bone in his body.

Instead, I just wait, sipping my wine and letting it

roll around in her head.

She catches me watching her, and a faint stain of pink warms her complexion. She clears her throat. "And how does it feel? After?"

I smile. "Like freedom."

I watch from the kitchen as Michael makes small talk with my parents and Derrick on the couch. In a white button-down and gray pants, he looks beautiful and slightly cruel, but so hypnotic, with his hard jaw, and strong features. When I'd first met him I'd thought him not quite handsome, and he's not really, but he's compelling and interesting to look at. His presence far more intoxicating than someone merely pretty.

I think of this morning in the coffee shop, the way the barista flirted shamelessly with him, and the fierce stab of possessiveness that had rushed through me. It had startled me. Thrown me off balance, and when he'd come back to our small round table and sat down with our coffee, I couldn't seem to help the sulky jealousy. I tried to fake it, but it sat between us, until he'd smiled and raised a brow. One look at the smirk on his face and all my sassy instincts kicked in, and I knew I was about to talk myself into a lot of trouble.

And I did. I shiver at the memory. So. Much. Trouble.

As if sensing my depraved thoughts, his head rises, and he catches my gaze. A sly expression slides over his features as his vision flicks over my body.

A look of promise.

I give him my most bold, come-and-get-me smile, and flip my hair.

He grins and turns back to whatever my mom is saying to him.

"Wow." April's voice breaks into my thoughts, and

a flush heats my cheeks as I realize I've been caught staring.

I take a stab at innocence. "What?"

She puts down the pan of muffins fresh out of the oven and removes her potholder mittens. "You've got it bad."

I turn to my sister, this woman who used to be one of my best friends. I have a choice. I can deny, or I can bridge the gap. And it's no contest. I glance at Michael. "I do."

A wide smile spreads over her face. "I'm so happy for you."

"Me too," I say, and clear my throat, still not comfortable with the emotion that has been so long absent in my life. "I never thought it would happen."

April's eyes flicker toward Michael. "He's different from John."

"He is." It's the same thing Ruby said, and that my parents are probably thinking. Some explanations aren't appropriate for family.

"I like him."

"I'm glad." I give her a genuine smile and her whole expression lights up.

She presses a fingertip against one of the muffins to test their doneness, nodding in apparent satisfaction. "I wasn't sure at first because I was so surprised, but after the way he handled the panic attack I couldn't help but be won over."

All the things left unspoken between us hangs in the air. It's time. I tilt my head toward the stairs that lead to the bedrooms on the second floor. "Can we talk?"

A spark of hope flashes in her big eyes. "Of course."

As we turn, Michael says from behind me, "Everything okay?"

I crane my neck and offer him a brilliant smile,

sinking into the safety I feel by his careful observation of me. "Everything's great, April is just going to show me some new shoes she got."

Michael gives me a nod so slight it is barely perceptible, but it still hits me right in the solar plexus. The subtle permission. The reminder of what I am and how this works, that power flows from him to me, and not the other way around.

Until him, I never knew I needed that. Now, I do.

April and I walk up the stairs and head into her large master bedroom, professionally decorated with cream, blues and grays. April plops down on the bed and crosses her legs, looking young and fresh as her blonde ponytail swings. "What's up?"

Nervousness skitters through my veins and I take a deep breath. This is good. I know I need to do this, but it's still hard. "I've been wanting to talk to you since the night at the restaurant but I haven't known how."

She tilts her head to the side. "I'm your sister, you can tell me anything."

Tightness closes my throat, and I swallow it away. "I know, but it's been hard between us for so long I didn't know how to start."

"It is." She picks up a dove-gray pillow from her bed and hugs it. "Every time I try, I screw it up."

"No you don't." I take a deep breath and let out the secrets I've been hiding. "I'm sorry, for lots of things, but mainly I'm sorry because I've been mad at you for something that's not your fault."

Her lashes flutter, and a frown mars her pretty face. "You have nothing to be sorry about, Layla. What you've been through, it's unthinkable, and you coped the best way you could."

It would be so easy to let myself off the hook she's given me, but I can't do that. She deserves better. When I speak, my voice is a bit shaky. "You have the life I thought John and I were going to have. I've been angry about it. And jealous."

She looks down at her bedspread and starts tracing the pattern on the fabric with her nails. "You have every right to feel that way."

"But I don't *want* to feel that way, not anymore." I walk over to her and sit down on the bed next to her. My sister, this woman I love and need in my life. I take her hand and our fingers intertwine.

I'm struck by a vivid memory of us, hand in hand, skipping along in our white dresses, our hair shiny in the sun. "I want us to be close again, but I don't know how."

Her eyes turn bright and she nods. "Me too. I miss my sister."

"I miss you too." I swallow, my chest heavy with the emotions that have been weighing me down. "I'm not sure I can go back to the person I was before."

Her fingers squeeze mine. "You don't have to, I just want you to talk to me again."

"It's been hard, April. So hard."

"I know."

I glance at the bedroom door that leads down the stairs to the man that's been my salvation. "But, Michael, he's helping me."

"Then I will love him forever."

I will too, just as completely, and devotedly as I loved John. It turns out my heart is big enough for the two of them. I look at April and there are tears in her eyes that match my own. I croak out, "Do you want to do lunch next week?"

She laughs. "I'd love to."

And, just like that, we're sisters again.

27.

Michael is on call and I'm going to a hot new club with Ruby to dance the night away. I haven't gone dancing in forever and when she asked me, I jumped at the chance. More than ready to experience life again.

I could have gotten ready at my house, but I didn't because it would be time away from Michael. And I like it, the comfort of getting ready while he lounges on the couch with Belle's head on his thigh. Neither one of us says it, but we are practically living together. My clothes are draped over the chair in Michael's bedroom, my toiletries are in the bathroom. It's the future I'm not quite ready to discuss, but that I roll around in like a glutton.

I slip on my black sky-high heels, smooth my hands over my new electric-blue dress, and appraise the results in the mirror.

I look good. Like, really good. I practically glow with good health.

Gone are the haunted shadows under my eyes, the

pasty skin, and the hollowed-out jut of my bones. The silky fabric of the dress flows over my body, stopping at an indecent length at my thighs. The top scoops down low, revealing the swell of cleavage, and the thin spaghetti straps crisscross over my bare back.

It's like wearing sex.

While my body has come alive, it's my face that holds my attention. My eyes are bright, my lips a glossy pink, my hair a wild mess of waves down my back. And she's there, staring back at me, the girl I used to be. The one I'd been so sure I'd never see again. She's more a woman now, but she's there, a part of me. Like the wounded, scarred girl that mourns the loss of her beloved will always be a part of me. Only, I've learned they don't have to be mutually exclusive.

I pick up my purse, straightening my dress one last time before making my way out into the living room. Michael is lying on the couch, just as I'd left him, reading a book. At the click of my heels on the hardwood, he raises his head, and I come to a stop at the foot of the couch.

He gives me a long, slow once-over before lifting one brow.

I know, for a fact, I'm rocking this dress, and I'm ready to own it. I put a hand on my hip and give him a cocky smirk. "What do you think?"

His eyes darken as he closes the book and puts it on the table. "I think you're lucky I'm not a jealous man."

"Not even a little?" I hold my finger and thumb an inch apart, full of sass.

He crooks a finger.

My blood heats. No matter how many times we have sex my desire for him is like a live, needy thing. I smooth my hands over the silky fabric and frown. "You're not going to ruin me, are you?"

He chuckles. "Like you wouldn't be disappointed if

I let you walk out of here untouched. Who do you think you're dealing with?"

I know exactly whom I'm dealing with.

He's right, of course. If he lets me walk out looking like this without a word, I'd be supremely disappointed. Not like I'm going to admit it. "I spent a lot of time getting ready."

"I can tell." His gaze hot as he looks over my body.

"So I don't want you to ruin me." I sweep a hand down my frame. "'Cause this took a lot of work."

He sits up, leaning his elbows on his knees and lacing his fingers in front of him. That stern, evil expression that makes me crazy, settles into his features. "I suggest you don't make me get up."

I gulp and my nipples bead into hard, almost painful points. Even though I'm going to end up right where he wants me, I have to make a big show of it. I sigh, and huff before rolling my eyes. "Are you sure you're not jealous? Because this sounds jealous."

"You're already going to be sorry, Layla, I suggest you don't make it any worse." His voice reaches inside me like a vise, pulling me close. The line of his jaw tightens. "I'm not telling you again."

He's different from John this way. John would have come got me, thrown me over his shoulder and had his way with me. We would have laughed, and play fought, until things turned serious and he got down to business.

But Michael isn't like that. Every day he finds ways to remind me that this, and him, are a choice I'm making. He always makes me take the steps that lead to him so I never forget the power he holds over me.

It makes me stubborn, but not stupid.

I walk to him.

His big hands curl around my knees, and he strokes over the soft, sensitive skin there. "You look like a girl that needs to be fucked, and I always give you what you need, don't I?"

Throat dry, my pulse kicks into over drive. "Yes."

His palms skim up my legs, over the swells of my thighs, before his fingers wiggle under the edge of my panties. My breath catches in mid intake and hangs there, suspended.

Those hazel eyes roam all over me as he squeezes the curve of my ass. "Let's get rid of these."

My panties slide down my legs.

He taps my thighs. "Open."

I do as I'm told but he's not satisfied. "Farther."

I splay my legs farther apart, so far it's uncomfortable, but it doesn't stop my nipples from beading or the welling desire.

He runs his knuckles over my inner thighs before brushing my soft, moist flesh.

A tiny moan escapes my throat.

He cocks a brow. "Already wet, I see, why am I not surprised?"

"Because I'm always wet for you?"

"You are." He shifts the hem of my dress until it gathers at my waist, leaving me bare. "I think it's only appropriate you have a proper reminder of who you belong to before you go, don't you?"

Pulse hammering away in my throat, I nod.

"And why's that?" He slides a finger inside me while his thumb makes slow maddening circles around my clit.

I lick my lips, tasting the gloss there. "So I can think of you all night."

"And?"

He rarely lets me go with my first answer.

I gulp. "So I can be marked by you."

"How?" He pumps in and out, apparently in no rush.

I know what I want. What I crave from him, but it's still hard to say the words. To ask. My mind searches for a way out, but with the cool air brushing my ass, my need only builds. I break, unable to help myself; the words tumble from my lips. "A spanking?"

His lips curve into an evil smile. "You want the brand of my palm on your ass all night while you make men sweat, is that it?"

"Yes, please." My voice is hoarse and whispery with lust.

"How are you going to earn it?"

"What do you want?" Michael makes me work for everything. But the truth is, secretly I love it. It's a challenge.

And I've discovered I need challenge in my life.

"Make me an offer." His thick voice is the only evidence of my effect on him.

Well, that, and the hard bulge in his jeans. "I could suck your cock."

"You are good at that." He tilts his head to the side, as though considering. "But that seems a little easy."

In sheer frustration, I growl. He just laughs and shakes his head.

"I could beg." Another offer that's hard for me, I like to cajole, but that doesn't work on him. The bastard.

He pulls away and I immediately miss the heat of his big palm. He reaches up and slips the straps of my dress down my shoulders until the fabric dips below my breasts. He rolls my nipples between his thumb and forefinger, gradually increasing the pressure until pain pricks and I let out a gasp.

"That's a good sound," he murmurs, before nodding. "On your knees."

I drop like a stone.

"Good girl." He unbuttons his jeans, slowly unzipping before pulling down his boxer briefs.

My mouth practically waters at the sight of him,

and I lean forward.

He shakes his head. "Tell me how you feel, Layla."

I'm greedy and hungry and needy. I want my ass smacked, his cock at the back of my throat, and then to be fucked so I can feel it for days. But all those thoughts clog in my throat and I blink up at him. "What do you mean?"

"How do you feel?" he repeats.

"Like I want you. Like I'll do anything."

He curls his strong fingers around his shaft, and slowly strokes up and down as I watch, hypnotized. "Good. Keep begging, girl."

I lean forward, ready to take him in my mouth, but fast as lightening, he reaches around and jerks me back by the hair. "I said beg."

"Please let me suck your cock?"

"And then what?" His lids hood and that mean expression fills his face.

I'm so wet it trickles down my thighs. "Then please spank me and fuck me."

"Why?"

"To remind me that I'm yours."

"Good girl." His voice is tinged with dark, hungry lust. He releases his hold on his cock and still gripping my hair, tugs me forward. "I'm going to fuck your throat. You just sit there and take it. Understand?"

I nod, so eager my mouth opens. I can't explain it, the why, but I love being treated this way. I need it. Need him.

He guides my head and fills my mouth, holding me still so I can't move. He lifts his hips, pushing in deeper until I'm stretched full. And then he begins.

In and out.

Over and over again.

Until my mind empties and my only base desire is to please him.

It's messy. I gag. Struggle. Dig my nails into my

thighs to keep from reaching for him.

At last, he pulls out. When he speaks his words are edged with the same dark need that drives me. Opposite sides of the same coin. He tugs my hair. "Over my knee."

I scramble from the floor and fall helpless over his lap. He shifts my hips until my legs splay open over his thigh, and I rub against his jeans. In a sudden frenzy, I groan. I grind my clit against him and he strikes me hard. Delicious, fiery pain explodes over my skin.

"Stop." With that one word I freeze.

He does nothing, just allows my desperation to fill the air between us, mixing with his iron will. The room practically crackles with the tension.

His palm presses against my back. "Stay still."

I bite my lip. It's so damn hard. I'm so needy and the denim against my sensitive, aroused skin is so tempting.

He slaps me and I jerk.

He rubs my ass, and then slaps me again.

Each time he does, my clit presses against his thigh, and it's electric. The pain mixes with the pleasure and transforms it into something right and perfect. I close my eyes and give in.

Surrender until I'm nothing but need.

Everything falls away but the sounds of his palm striking my flesh, our heavy breaths, my pounding heart.

And I can feel it, the orgasm building inside me. Waiting to explode.

Just as I'm about to go over he stops. There's no fight left in me, no sass, or stubbornness. I am his to do with as he pleases.

He moves, and pushes me to the floor, jerking my hips up, he positions his cock to enter me. In a gruff, rasp, he asks, "Who do you belong to?"

My answer is automatic. "You, Michael."

And then I am claimed, and he's pounding into me. A rough, angry rhythm that has me screaming and moaning his name. His fingers dig into my ass, setting off a new, different pain.

It pushes me over the edge. My release shakes my entire body as waves of pleasure crash through me, blinding in its force and power.

He's right behind me. On a feral growl, he comes, pushing deeper and deeper until I can no longer tell where he ends and I begin.

Panting for breath, I collapse in a heap on the floor, my muscles still quivering.

A soft kiss brushes my shoulder, and then my neck as he murmurs against my skin, "I've ruined you."

A soft laugh bubbles from my lips. "You have. Forever."

He moves, and rolls me over, and I lay sprawled obscene on the floor. "You've never looked more beautiful."

I blink at him, taking in his gorgeous face, and I can't help reaching for him. I trail my finger over his jaw and suddenly, from out of nowhere, I can no longer hide my feelings from him. Can no longer deny him what is rightfully his. When the words come, they are a whisper, "I love you, Michael."

His expression softens, and he kisses me. A deep, soul-changing kiss that promises everything I never thought I'd have again.

He lifts his head and whispers back, "I love you too. I've been waiting."

"I know," my voice soft. "Thank you."

"I want it all with you, Layla."

"Me too." There is no more pretending, no more walls between us.

I am finally home.

The music pulses through me and I'm happy. Really happy. I feel safe. Alive.

And I'm in love.

Ruby and I dance to the blaring beat of techno music in the packed club and I let it all go. My muscles ache from the exertion but I'm having too much fun to stop.

That sassy, flirty Layla is back and I let loose on the dance floor.

Ruby shakes her hips with abandon, and she looks like a rogue pixie princess in a short, black dress. She waves a hand over her sweaty face and screams over the crowd and music. "You ready for a break?"

No. Never. But I nod and we make our way through the dance floor. The night is young and I have all the time in the world.

As we weave through the crowd, I can feel the eyes on me, the slow perusal of my body. Maybe, if I was another type of girl, I'd be demure about the looks I'm getting, but I'm not, and never will be, so I smile and let my hips sway.

A man grabs my wrist, and I meet his heavy gaze. His eyes flick over me. "You want to dance?"

Laughing, I pull Ruby close, letting my arm drape over her shoulders. "Sorry, I'm taken."

Ruby giggles and we flit away, finding a quiet place in the corner to catch our breaths. She shakes her head. "You're the worst."

I wave, and take a sip of my drink. "It's easier than explaining I have a boyfriend."

For a moment I pause, realizing how easily the word boyfriend slips over my tongue.

Ruby points at me, waving her finger up and down. "Speaking of your boyfriend, I'm surprised he let you out of the house in that dress."

I laugh, after our hard, furious fucking, he'd put me back together again. Taking his time to lick and suck my nipples, squeeze my ass, and generally make me crazy all over again. His last act before he sent me on my way was to pull up my panties, and grind the heel of his hand over my clit wearing that dangerous expression as he growled, "Consider yourself properly marked."

I wink at Ruby. "He thought I looked nice."

She looks me up and down. "Nice?"

I shrug.

She rolls her eyes. "Come on! I want to know!"

As our friendship has strengthened, Ruby has taken quite the interest in my relationship and as a result become more and more bold in her questions.

I smirk. "Are you sure?"

"Yes!" Her eyes are excited, and she leans forward, expectantly.

I blow out a breath. "Well, if you must know, he said, I needed to be marked. So he spanked me until my ass burned, took me on the floor, and sent me out with come dripping down my legs."

Ruby's mouth falls open and she blinks in rapid succession. "Wow."

"I can assure you it was very *wow*."

"Can you still feel it?"

"Oh, yes." And it's delicious torture, the constant reminder of him branded on my skin.

"Laylay, that is kind of hot."

I laugh, as my phone buzzes in my small purse. "It *was* hot."

I reach to grab it, and look down to see a text from a number I don't recognize. I frown and flip open the lock screen on my phone. *Layla, this is Jillian, Michael's sister. Can you call me?*

The icy dread, so familiar, rushes through me, and I can feel my skin pale. Panic makes my heartbeat pick up and I gulp it down. There are other reasons she could be calling me. It doesn't mean anything happened. The reassurances don't work though.

My gaze flies to Ruby. "It's Michael's sister, she wants me to call."

Ruby blinks, her heavily mascaraed lashes fluttering. "I'm sure it's fine."

But she looks as uncertain as I feel. I point to the door. "I've got to call."

She nods. "I'll come with you."

We make our way to the door, my stride no longer seductive, but purposeful. My pulse is hammering in my throat as my palms turn sweaty.

It will be okay. It has to be okay.

It's nothing. It has to be nothing.

The second we step into the cool Chicago night, I press the call button. Emotions clog my throat as the phone rings and then Jillian picks up. "Layla."

Her voice. I've heard that voice before; it's burned into my brain and heart and follows me into my nightmares.

I can't speak. If I don't answer, maybe she'll never say the words.

"Layla?" Her is voice high and frantic.

"Yes," I manage to choke out.

There's a heavy pause over the line and I close my eyes, I don't want to hear.

Not again.

Her voice cracks. "It's Michael...he's in..." She trails off and starts crying.

I sag against the wall as the panic rushes over me.

No. No. No. No. I can't do this, not again.

This cannot be happening.

Ruby grabs my arm, her expression as stricken as I feel. "What's wrong?"

I shake my head. The memories of John, lying in that alley, blood seeping over the sidewalk, consume me. The whole nightmarish scene rushes through me until I can hear nothing but the sounds of my sobs, both echoes from the past and brand new.

A male voice comes over the line. "Layla, this is Leo. It's Michael. He's been shot."

The phone drops from my hand and I hear the crack of glass on pavement.

And then, everything goes black, and I'm once again a shell.

28.

I sit on the hard chair, my head resting against the wall, as Ruby's hand clutches mine. I don't have any memory of how Ruby got me to the hospital where Michael is already in surgery. I only know my worst nightmares have come true.

Ruby squeezes my fingers and when she speaks, her voice is filled with fear. "He's going to be okay, Layla. The bullet didn't hit any major organs or arteries. They're going to remove it and he'll be okay. I promise."

She keeps saying this to me. As does Michael's sisters, parents, and Leo as they watch me with wary, tearstained faces.

I hear them. They might even be telling the truth. But I can't respond.

I can't do anything but stare into the too bright, neon lights flickering overhead. Inside I'm screaming, ranting and crying and cursing the heavens, but I can't speak. The words will not take shape. So I sit here, numb, waiting for my life to end.

I cannot do this. Not again. It's too much for a person to bear.

Life can't be this cruel. But I already know that's a lie. Life can, and is, that cruel. I'd started to believe, if only in the deep corners of my mind, that happiness could once again be part of my life.

I was wrong.

As if sensing the darkness of my thoughts, Ruby squeezes my hand again, hard enough for me to flinch, even though I remain motionless. "Layla, he's going to be okay. Do you hear me?"

This time.

Michael might pull through this tonight, but what about the next time? Or the time after that? What will happen to this homicide detective of mine whom I love more than life itself?

Stupidly, I've put his dangerous job out of my mind. How could I have made such a terrible mistake? After John, I should have learned my lesson. My jaw clenches even as my hand lays limp in Ruby's. I know why. Because, I'm selfish. His job made me feel safe and I ignored the rest. I'd focused on how that gun he wore strapped to his body protected me. He's so big and strong; he's invincible in my eyes.

How could I have forgotten, even for a second, how fragile life is?

I swallow, my throat so tight it aches. I didn't want to let him go. Now I'm paying the price.

I'm cursed. Destined to have the men I can't live without, die.

I stare off into space, reliving all the awful memories of that night in the alley. This must be my punishment for my culpability of that night. That's all I can think. The only thing that makes any sense.

In vivid Technicolor, an image of John, lying lifeless, his head on my lap, fills my mind. But when I look down, it's Michael I see, eyes sightless and blank.

I repress the urge to start screaming. I can't, if I do, I'll never stop.

Michael's family is sitting across from me. When I'd walked in they all crowded around me, hugging me as they cried, too distressed to notice my lack of response. They'd made room for me next to his mom, but I removed myself from their warmth to stand apart.

"He's going to be okay," Ruby says again, her tone laced with concern.

This time.

Or maybe not. What if something goes wrong in surgery? Or what if the damage is more extensive than they thought? He could have an allergic reaction to the anesthesia. There are a million things that can happen that will take him away from me. I glance out at the dark night, visible through the sliding glass doors of the hospital.

There are a million things that can happen to him out there.

It's just a matter of time before he's taken away from you. If not tonight, then another.

I can feel Ruby's gaze on me, the weight of her worry and fear for me. I know I'm scaring her, and I want to reassure her, but I can't. All my energy is spent on not collapsing into a heap on the floor.

I have no idea how long I sit like that, in the cold, overly bright florescent lights, while endless minutes tick by and we wait for word that Michael is out of surgery. But I remain still as a statue, lost to anything but the dark, dangerous thoughts in my head.

A hand falls on my shoulder and I jerk back, my head snapping up.

It's April, her skin too pale, her eyes too bright, her mouth pinched.

She looked exactly the same way when she rushed

to see me when I was in the hospital that other night when my world collapsed. Only then, I was the one lying in a bed, bruised and bloodied, broken.

This is worse. Much, much worse.

Everything inside me implodes.

I break into hysterical sobs. April starts to cry too, and bends down, gathering me up to hold me close. I bury my face in her hair as the tears finally get the better of me and she holds me through the shaking. I squeeze my eyes shut, and let her hold me as the storm rages. I feel for her, my sister, whose greatest unhappiness comes from me. My tragedies. My despair.

She's sunshine and innocence to my darkness.

She strokes my back and whispers nonsense, assuring me that everything is going to be okay.

It's a lie. Nothing will ever be okay again.

I can feel them all watching me and through some inner reserve, I force myself to calm down, but I can't seem to attain that level of zoned-out numbness. Now I'm all raw emotions, straining at the seams, needing to be unleashed.

April sits down beside me, and takes my other hand, just like Ruby.

We wait.

Finally, after what seems like a million years, the doctor comes out. He faces us, collectively, that impassive expression medical people seem to wear, affixed to his bland face.

I hold my breath, waiting for him to tell me Michael has died. Just like John.

He consults his chart, and then addresses us. "The damage was a bit more extensive than we thought, but he's going to pull through." He goes on to explain the bullet placement and the shards they needed to pull from Michael's strong body. "He's in the ISU and hasn't woken up yet, but as a soon as he does, we'll let you know. He can only have one visitor at a time until he comes out of recovery and is moved to a regular floor. But he's going to be okay."

There is a collective sigh of relief that everyone feels but me.

He's going to be okay. They're all saying it. All hugging each other, with relieved smiles I can't share. Maybe he'll be okay today, but what about the next time? And the time after that?

While Michael has been careful not to push me, I know he wants a future. He's never denied that. Our life stretches out in front of me. The fear I'll experience every time he goes to work. The worry that will sit in my stomach like a rock when he gets called to a scene in the middle of the night. The endless hours I'll endure, waiting for *the call*. The one that will someday come and tell me he's dead. Murdered. Like John.

I can't take it. I can't go through this again.

I speak for the first time, my voice too loud amongst all the relief. "I have to get out of here."

They all turn and stare at me.

With a furrowed brow, April releases my hand to stroke my hair. "Honey, did you hear what the doctor said? Michael is going to be fine."

I rip away from April and Ruby, jerking up from the chair. I ball my hands into fists, fighting the tide of panic threatening to consume me. I feel wild and out control, at the very edge of my sanity.

"I can't be here," I say, my tone shrill.

Michael's parents frown, and I can see by their puzzled faces they have no idea of my past. That Michael has shielded them from the ugliness that lives inside me.

They'll hate me after this. I blink back tears,

remembering sitting next to Michael's mom on her couch, looking at her family photos. She won't remember that. No, she'll only remember how I deserted her only son in his hour of need. I'm driving the first nail into the coffin of my relationship with Michael. I swallow hard.

Michael's father clears his throat. "He'll want to see you when he wakes up."

I start to shake, uncontrollably and my teeth start to chatter. "I'm sorry. I need to leave."

His mother opens her mouth, but Jillian covers her hand and shakes her head, before turning to me. I can see it written in her face, the truth of my past. "It's okay. Leo, can you take them home?"

"No, I'm fine." I can't stand to be around them one more second.

April worries her bottom lip, and takes both my hands. My fingers feel ice cold in hers. "Layla, are you sure about this? Michael is going to be fine. Don't you want to see him?"

More than my next breath. I pull away from her and wrap my coat tight around me. "I want to go home."

I see April exchange a worried glance with Ruby who's standing behind me.

"I'm leaving," I shriek and turn away from all of them. Don't they understand? I can't be here. I can't be with Michael. I'm not strong.

I need to walk away. It's the only way.

Leo takes my elbow and looks down at me, brown eyes narrowed. "I'll take you."

April shakes her head. "No, I'll take her. I don't want her to be alone."

"I'll go too," Ruby says.

Leo's jaw hardens, as though he's about to protest, but then he nods. "All right."

I glance toward the sliding doors, and all the

sudden, I remember Belle, the mangy dog that now feels like mine. I give Leo a pleading look. "Belle."

He nods. "I'll take care of her."

No! She's mine. I need her. The words a scream in my head but I say nothing. My nails dig into my skin. She doesn't belong to me.

"Please, she'll be scared," I say, and my voice breaks.

Leo's brow furrows and a muscle ticks at his temple. "We'll make sure she's taken care of."

Them. Not me.

It's wrong, but I don't know how to stop the series of events. And in the end, I'm a coward. I can't do this. I can't stay and go through this torture over and over again.

I can't live every day waiting for a call that will tell me Michael is dead.

April curls her hand around my elbow and says softly, "Are you ready?"

Michael's mom stares at me, incredulity written across her tearstained features. "What should I tell him?"

This is it. Leaving right now will sever us. I will be cut off, cold turkey. I swallow down my despair. "Tell him I couldn't do it. He'll know why."

Her expression twists and I know what she's thinking. How can I be so cruel? Her son is lying in a hospital bed after being shot, and I refuse to see him. I must be a monster. And, perhaps, I am. Maybe that night in the alley changed me too irrevocably to ever recover.

More than anything, I want to explain, but I can't. I don't want her understanding and sympathy. I need her to hate me. To be happy I'm gone.

I turn away, before I can do anything stupid like beg for forgiveness. The only thing that makes my feet move toward the door is the knowledge that my actions will not surprise Michael.

Something tells me this is exactly what he'd expect. It's the only peace I have as my dreams for a happily ever after, once again, die a slow, painful death.

29.

They won't stop talking. Ruby and April tag team me, taking turns speaking and trying to reason with me. I have no idea what they are saying. I can only stare into space, numb as they spew streams of words that make no sense to me.

I shift on the couch, clutching my Kleenex, eyes swollen, throat raw. I've changed into yoga pants, and an old T-shirt of John's but it's Michael's touch I feel on my skin. My condo is as cold and abandoned as I feel, and sitting here, it no longer feels like my life. I don't want to be here. I want to be with Michael.

I miss him already. It's a near desperate ache that sits heavy in my chest.

I wish I was strong. Wish I could go back to the hospital. I want to put all this behind me and forget it ever happened. To focus on the fact that he'll be okay. That he'll recover. Survive. It would be so easy to pretend this will never happen again. That he'll be safe from danger.

But it's a lie.

It will happen again. Michael is a homicide detective. He deals with death and violence on a daily basis. It's just a matter of time before he's killed. Shot dead in the line of duty and I'm once again standing over another grave.

I can't do it.

It's too much. I can't survive another loss.

April and Ruby are still talking and I look at them, my hand clenched tight. "Please stop."

April frowns. "What can we do to help, Layla?"

Ruby says, "Do you want to go back to Michael?"

Yes. I press my fingertips to my temples. "Stop talking. Please, I just need you to stop." I need to escape. "I have to go to the bathroom."

Before they can speak, I stand up and race down the hall, slamming the door to the bathroom and locking the door. I slide down the wall, falling to the cold, tile floor.

I don't want to be here. I can't stand it here. It's lonely. Filled with grief and despair, fresh and new again. Unbearable in its crushing weight. A violent rage sweeps through me. I want to scream. Throw things. Break the mirror with my bare hands. Trash the place. But I can't do that. Not while Ruby and April sit in my living room, worried and fretful. I'll scare them.

Instead, I curl into a ball on the floor, and cry.

I cry for Michael. For John. And lastly, I cry for myself. I was wrong. I dared to hope, and I was so, so wrong.

Deep, wrenching sobs shake my body until finally there is nothing left.

I have no idea how long I stay like that, but there's a knock on the door. April's voice quickly follows. "Layla, are you okay?"

No, I am not okay. I want to scream at her to go away. To leave me alone, but I don't. I scrub my hands over my face. "I'll be right out."

I get up off the floor and dry my tears with a towel before looking into the mirror. I look as horrible as I feel. I need quiet. And Belle.

The dog slips into my mind and it suddenly becomes a frantic, panicked notion that will not let me rest. I need her and she needs me. I need to bury my face in her shaggy fur. I need her head on my lap. Her comfort. Michael would want her with me.

Rescuing her from Michael's gives me something to do while I wait for the cold numbness I'm so familiar with to reclaim me once again.

I rush out of the bathroom and into my living room where April and Ruby are huddled together, talking in whispered tones.

They look up at me. Ruby's brows furrow. "Oh, Layla."

I ignore her worry and say, "I need my dog."

Ruby and April glance at each other as if unsure what to do.

I repeat the words. This is an action I can take. "Belle. I need her."

Ruby bites her lip. "Layla, it's Michael's dog."

"She's mine," I say, full of stubbornness. "She needs me to take care of her."

April clears her throat. "Honey, Michael's family will take care of her."

I shake my head. "No. I will. I need to get her. She's alone and she's going to be scared."

April and Ruby share another one of those concerned glances I've received hundreds of times and I can't take it one more second. I scream, "I need my dog! If you want to do something for me, take me to her. Get me Belle."

They stare at me, eyes wide, mouths open.

I become restless under their stunned silence and I hand Ruby my cracked phone. "I have a key, but call

Jillian and tell her I'm taking her."

"I don't know," April begins and I cut her off.

"I'm getting her. I don't need your permission, or your help." I walk to the hallway and grab my coat in the front closet. "Call Jillian, I'm getting my dog and there's nothing you can do to stop me."

Then I turn and slam out the door. I race to the elevator and jab the down button repeatedly, staring up at the blinking numbers and cursing under my breath. Now that the idea has taken hold I can't get to Belle fast enough.

The elevator chimes, and I step inside, and just as the doors start to close, Ruby slips in. "I'm going with you."

I'd rather be alone, but shrug. Some battles aren't worth fighting.

Several beats of heavy silence pass before Ruby turns her head to look at me. "She's not yours to take, LayLay."

I want to shriek at her not to call me that, but I say, in what even I recognize as an eerily calm voice, "She's alone, and she needs me."

She touches my arm and I jerk away. She blows out a deep breath. "I don't know what to do."

"There's nothing to do."

"Layla," Ruby says, putting her arm around me and not letting me flinch away. "Don't do this to yourself. Don't throw away your happiness. Not when you're getting a second chance."

A second chance? He's been a cop for all these years without incident, he meets me and within hours of telling him I love him he's shot. How can that possibly be a coincidence? He's not *my* second chance—I'm *his* curse.

Why don't they understand this?

I ball my hands into fists.

When I don't speak Ruby continues, "He makes

you so happy, please think about this."

I am thinking about it. It's why I have to leave.

Ruby's voice softens. "I'm jealous, you know?"

I laugh, a brittle bitter sound, and then, full of sarcasm, I say, "Oh sure, that's me, living every girl's dream."

The elevator shudders to a stop and I step out, heading toward the door, but Ruby grabs my arm. "Actually, in a way you are. I've never had anyone look at me the way Michael looks at you. It's special. Some of us never get that, Layla, and you've gotten it twice. You've been given a second chance, don't let it go."

She's trying to jar me into some sort of perspective, and I can't deal with it right now. I can only focus on my mission. "I'm going to get Belle. Are you with me, or not?"

Expression creased in concern, Ruby nods. "I'm with you."

I open the door of Michael's apartment and the second I do, Belle bounds out, her tail wagging wildly as she plants her paws on my stomach and practically knocks me to the ground. Relief storms through me and I drop to my knees, hugging the dog to me as she whines excitedly. I close my eyes and start to cry, thankful I'm finally with her.

"She loves you," a female voice says from above me and I look up to see Jillian standing there, Leo behind her.

"Michael?" His name is a hoarse croak on my lips.

Leo puts his hands on Jillian's shoulders and gives her a little squeeze. "He's awake."

"He asked for you," Jillian says.

Belle squirms in my lap as I pet her. I know what they want, for me to go to Michael, but I can't. I clear my throat. "Why are you here?"

"Your sister called," Leo says, his gaze searching my face, for what I don't know.

Probably for signs of humanity. They can't possibly understand my actions are the only way I can save him. To protect him. "I'm sorry."

Jillian, her coloring so like Michael's I want to turn away from her, gestures into the doorway. "Why don't you come in and we can talk."

I peer past her, biting my lip. Everything I desire is down that hall. My hopes and dreams, the future I'd started to believe in, Michael and all his strength.

In a flash of insight, I realize that's why I'd come. Yes, I need Belle, but also want to escape the cold, desolation of my apartment. I want to soak up his warmth, one last time, before I'm forced to close this chapter of my life forever.

But I understand now that's impossible. If I walk into his home, I'll never have the strength to leave. I shake my head.

"Layla," Ruby says, her tone pleading. "Let's just go talk."

I bury my face in Belle's fur, wrapping my arms around her. I need her, but Ruby was right, she's not mine to take. I squeeze her tight. At least I got to see her, to say goodbye.

Because that's what this is. A goodbye.

Tears stream down my face as I suck in her scent, all that goodness. In this one thing I can be strong. "I can't."

Jillian bends at the knees, forcing me to meet her eyes. "You've been through a lot, and I can't begin to understand how you feel, but Michael needs you now. Please don't abandon my brother."

It's a low blow, and the strike hits me right in the chest, but I don't blame her. "Tell him I'm sorry."

"You can tell him," Leo says.

Jillian cranes her neck to look up at him, and

shakes her head, before shifting her attention back to me. "Michael loves you."

"I know."

"And you love him."

I nod.

She takes a deep breath. "Sometimes it's really that simple."

I gather all my inner reserves. "I used to believe that too, but it's a lie."

"All I'm asking, all he's asking is that you go and talk to him. Give him that one thing. That's all he wants."

Of course that's what he wants, and what he deserves. But he has hidden motives Jillian doesn't understand. He knows, once I see him, I'll never be able to leave. Since the moment we met, I haven't been able to deny him anything, and this will be no different.

But leaving is my only option. It's the only way we'll both survive. The only way to stay safe.

I can see the hope shining in her eyes and it's cruel for me to let it linger. Tears well in my eyes as I stand. "You'll take care of Belle?"

The light drains from her face. "Michael said you could keep her."

More than my next breath I want to take her, it was my purpose in coming here. It was also a trap I set myself, a connection to Michael, a way back in. Because, of course, once he's out of the hospital, he'd come to get her, and by default me.

Even my subconscious is against me.

I can't even look at Belle, still standing next to me, wagging her tail.

None of them understand, because none of them know the whole truth. Not even Michael knows my deepest secret, the one I won't permit myself to think about.

If they knew, they'd understand why leaving is the only option.

A tear slips down my cheek and I shake my head. "No, she belongs with her family. Not me."

Then, for the second time that night, I turn and walk away.

30.

It's been five days since that night.

Five days since I saw Michael.

Five days since I told him I loved him.

Five days since I, once again, began measuring time in minutes and hours. Watching the clock tick by as I sit on my couch and sink into misery. My sadness and grief is like a long lost lover, comfortable and familiar, with no surprises.

My nightmares have come back, but they no longer alarm me. After all, I know what to expect. I've been free of panic attacks, and maybe I'd view that as an accomplishment, but I haven't left my condo.

I've called into work, pleading a horrible flu that would keep me out of the office at least until the end of the week. I've turned off my phone, my cell, and refused to let anyone up to see me.

I've shut them all out.

They're worried about me. I don't blame them, and I'm sorry for the distress I'm causing, but I ignore them anyway. It's wrong, but I can't talk to anyone right now. I'm too susceptible, too vulnerable, because I live with the truth.

More than anything, I want to go to Michael. Every single moment I'm awake, it's all I want. This isn't like John, who no matter how much I want him, is never coming back.

No, in a strange way this is much worse, because I know full well I could see Michael. All I need to do is get up, get dressed, walk out the door and go to the hospital. As Jillian said that fateful night, sometimes it's really that simple.

I know he's out there, waiting for me. Illogically, I convince myself I can feel his frustration at not being able to come for me. It nags me all day, pulls at me. I struggle not to concede to his silent demands every second. The only way to maintain my shaky resolve is to stay holed up in my apartment, locked away from the world.

At some point, I understand I'll have to work up the strength to manage life without him. I'll need to get up off this couch, get dressed, go to work, and call my family and friends. And I will. Soon.

Just not today.

I curl the blanket tighter around me, pressing into the back of the couch, and close my eyes. If I concentrate hard enough, I can almost feel Michael behind me, his arm draped over my waist as he holds me. I remember the exact weight of him, the slide of his palm over my belly. I lean harder against the cushions in an attempt to recapture the warmth of his body.

I replay the last time I was with him, his total destruction of me, the bone-deep satisfaction. The way my heart swelled with happiness and contentment. The look in his eyes as I whispered I loved him. The sound of his voice as he whispered it back. The belief that I would hear those words from him thousands of times.

When it's over, and I've reached the end and I'm walking out the door, that sassy smile flirting back at him, I freeze frame on the grin he gave me. And begin again.

Over and over, until I fall into a restless sleep.

Loud banging rings through my apartment, and I jolt awake, disorientated.

I blink, my gaze flying to my front door as someone pounds furiously away at it.

Michael.

My heart gallops at the mere thought. I'd been dreaming of him, vivid carnal dreams, and not my normal nightmares. I hate the hope that swells in my chest, the desperate, silent prayer that it's him at my door.

But that's impossible. He's still in the hospital. I've called every day, including this morning. I ask for his room, only to hang up during the transfer. I've also Googled gunshot wounds to the shoulder, typing in any key word I can remember from the doctor that night at the hospital. From my reading, I figure he'll be in there for at least another couple of days.

More pounding, as someone beats their fist against my door. But who could it be? I've refused to answer the buzzer, ignored calls from the security guard on duty. It's been so long since I answered, I'm sure they believe my condo is deserted.

I shake off my daze, and rub my eyes, praying whoever it is will give up and go away. That hope is dashed when an unfamiliar male voice, yells, "I know you're in there, Layla, now open the fucking door."

My pulse doubles in speed as fear races through my blood. Should I call the cops? But the man on the other side of the door knows my name. So who? All

I'm certain of is that it's not Michael. His voice haunts my dreams, and I'd recognize it anywhere.

On shaky legs, I get up and peer through the peephole, sagging against the wall when I see who stands there.

"I'll kick the door down if I have to, but you will be talking to me. Now open the door." It's a bark of a command, unrelenting.

I weigh my options, and don't see any. Or, at least, none that I want to see. I take a deep breath and slowly open the door to Leo. He's standing there, all hard eyed, looking every inch the cop he is with his crossed arms, set jaw and menacing expression. Nothing like the affable guy I'd met before.

I can't fathom what he's doing here. Suddenly, the most horrible thought enters my mind. What if something happened to Michael? What if he got an infection? Or had complications? Dread, panic and a horrible, unrelenting fear almost bring me to my knees. I croak out, "Michael?"

He shakes his head. "He's recovering just fine."

Relief. Thank god. In this moment I come face-to-face with the power of my love for him. How desperately I need him and want to go to him. How a world without Michael is no world at all.

I place my hand on the wall to steady myself as a spinning vertigo overtakes me. I close my eyes against the dizziness as sickness twists my stomach.

Leo grips my elbow and when he speaks his voice is calm and clear. "Are you going to pass out?"

I suck in deep lungfuls of air and shake my head.

"Are you sure?" he asks again.

The steadiness of his words focuses me and I gasp out. "I'm okay."

He doesn't let go. "When's the last time you ate?"

I open my eyes. I can't remember. "I don't know."

He sighs and frowns. "Why am I not surprised?"

Now that the spell has passed, I lick my dry lips. "What are you doing here?"

He juts his chin toward the entrance. "Let me in."

I peer beyond him. "Is Jillian here?"

"No. It's just me."

I'm not sure if I'm grateful or not. Stronger now, I ask, "How'd you get up here?"

"I'm a cop. I flashed my badge."

"Oh."

We stare at each other for several long moments.

He narrows his eyes. "Do you want to have this conversation in your hallway, or in your living room? Your choice."

I glance up and down the length of the corridor, buying time, even though it's a lost cause. Leo clearly won't leave until he's said what he needs to. And deep down, I don't want him gone. I'm too greedy for news of Michael, and Leo is a way to feel close to him. I stand back and let him in.

Leo's not as tall as Michael, probably around six feet, but his shoulders are broad in his distressed gray jacket, his legs long in jeans. I close the door, and ask again, "Why are you here?"

He points to the couch. "Sit."

I bite my lip, unsure how to handle this situation or him. He was so good-natured the times I've met him, but he's nothing like that now. In the end, I don't have the energy to fight, so I sit down, huddling into the corner of the couch.

Leo moves with purpose through my small condo, acting as though he's been there a thousand times before. He opens my fridge, scrounges through it to pull out orange juice, before riffling through my cabinets. When he locates a glass, he fills it to the brim and returns to me, holding out the juice. "Drink it. Every last drop."

He reminds me so much of Michael, tears well in

my eyes. I take the glass and a small drink.

He sits on my coffee table, right across from me, and places his elbows on his knees. "More."

I hate how good it feels, to be looked after, to be cared for. The liquid is cool on my dry throat and I realize just how thirsty I am. I take a bigger gulp, draining half the glass.

"Now the rest," Leo says, his voice a bit softer now.

If I close my eyes, I could pretend it's Michael across from me, but that's a dangerous notion. I don't resist though, and swallow the last of the juice and hand the glass to him.

He takes it and puts it on the table next to him. "Better?"

Surprisingly, yes, I hadn't realized how weak I'd become and the sugar races through my blood stream, waking me up more than I've been in days. I nod.

Leo laces his fingers and pins me with a steady gaze. "I was there, when he went down. The shooter was a young kid, scared out of his mind, and he took a wild, aimless shot. Michael was in the wrong place at the wrong time."

"I don't want to hear this." Irrationally, I want to slap him across the face. I don't want the image of Michael's shooting in my head. I've had enough violence to last me two lifetimes.

Leo doesn't appear impressed with my plea. "As soon as he dropped, he shook his head and said, 'Layla's never going to forgive me.'"

His first thought had been of me. "I'm sorry."

"You should be," he says, and my head snaps back at his harsh tone.

I'm used to gentle. Used to being handled with kid gloves. I'm ill equipped for hostility. I stiffen. "You don't understand."

"The fuck I don't."

Anger fills my chest, and I can't deny it feels good. So much better than the sickening knot of despair. "How could you possibly?"

"I became a cop because my twin brother was murdered. I met Michael the first day of the academy and he's been like a brother to me. So I sure as hell understand."

Instantly contrite, I look down at the floor and tuck my feet under me, as though if I try hard enough I could curl into a ball. "I'm sorry. I didn't know."

Leo moves closer to me, and waits in silence. When I finally lift my lashes to meet his gaze, he says, "You're tougher than this. He needs you and you need him. So stop this shit and go to him."

Tears spill onto my cheeks. "I can't."

Leo's gaze doesn't leave mine. "Don't let them win, Layla. He deserves better than that."

I can't look away and I blurt out, "I'm cursed."

He smiles, a soft understanding twist of his lips. "Maybe you are, but you're a fighter, now fight."

"I don't know if I can, not again."

"You can and you will."

I shake my head. I'm weak. "I'm not a fighter."

"Yeah, you are."

"He deserves better. Someone who's not damaged and broken. Someone better than me. Don't you understand? Don't you want that for him?"

"I want him happy. And you make him happy," Leo's voice is full of stubbornness.

"But you can't deny you'd want someone better for him." Somehow, I think, if I can get him to admit that Michael deserves better it will shore up my resolve to do the right thing. That, if his friends and family want a different girl for him, I can stay strong.

Leo sighs, long and heavy. "I'm not playing this game with you. I'm prepared to wait you out all day if I have to, but you're coming with me."

My shoulders sag. I want to give in. I can't even begin to describe the strength of my desire. Unable to speak, I shake my head.

Leo studies me for long, uncomfortable moments, before he finally says, "Michael was pissed as hell when I started dating his sister."

My brows pull together at the change in the conversation, and I shift restlessly on the sofa until Leo grips my jaw, shocking me still. "And you know why, don't you, girl?"

I suck in my breath as my eyes go wide with understanding. Leo's gaze is direct, hard and unmistakably commanding as I come to the truth about him.

He doesn't allow me time to process before he ruthlessly continues, "That hole inside you right now, that ache in your chest, that's how Michael feels. He's suffering. Not because he's been shot. Not because he's had surgery. Not because he's in pain." He lets go of my jaw, and points at my chest. "But because of you. Because he knows what this is doing to you, and he's fucking helpless to do anything about it." Leo narrows his eyes. "And you know how he feels about being helpless."

It's tough love. And I'm riveted, unable to pull away. Because it rings with truth. I'm killing Michael right now. He's suffering at my hands, and no one else's.

"You know what you need to do, Layla." He tucks a lock of hair behind my ear. "You've fought through more than most people ever will in one lifetime. Now you're going to fight through this. Understood?"

I want to fight, but don't. I'm too weak. I need Michael too much and the idea that I'm hurting him is more than I can bear. Alone I could pretend, but with Leo here, forcing me to confront the truth, the last of my resolve crumbles away. I nod my agreement.

"Good girl," Leo says.

I remember the last time Michael said those words. His hands had been all over me, rough and firm just the way I like, as he whispered them into my ear. A shudder races through me.

Leo smiles, and straightens. "I'll take you to the hospital now."

When I speak, my voice is filled with worry. "What if I can't?"

"You can." Leo points down my hallway. "Now get dressed."

I stare at him for a full twenty seconds before I rise from the couch and do what I'm told.

***

Nerves riot in my stomach as Leo hand delivers me to Michael's hospital room. Holding me by the elbow as though I'll try and escape if he lets go. My throat goes dry as I walk into the room.

Michael is sleeping, and the room is silent except for the whine and beeps of the machines monitoring his vitals. Everything goes still at the sight of him lying there, skin pale, his beautiful eyes closed. I fight the urge to run, to turn around and leave this place and all it's bad memories.

John never made it to a hospital bed. He went straight to the morgue. I'd been the one lying in that bed, my loved ones hovering over me. I remembered how I had stirred to consciousness only to remember what happened and pray to be swept back under.

"Are you going to be okay?" Leo asks.

I don't know. But I'm here. I don't have the strength of will to walk away again. I nod.

Leo releases his grip on my arm. "I'll leave you alone with him."

I offer a shaky smile. "Thank you."

"You're welcome." He turns to leave but at the last

second spins back around. "Your wrong, you know."

My gaze is on Michael. My fingers twitch with the need to trace his jaw. To place my palm over his heart and feel it beat under my touch. To assure myself he's alive. I shift my attention to Leo. "About what?"

"You're deserving of Michael. If I didn't think so, I'd have let him suffer."

I bite my bottom lip. "I'm glad you think so."

"I do. Not that he wouldn't have come for you himself the second he got out of here." His lips lift in a small smile. "But you already know that."

I nod, and he's gone, leaving me alone with Michael.

I take a deep breath and turn back to find Michael awake and watching me. He might be in a hospital bed, but his gaze is intense and as mesmerizing as ever. When he speaks, his voice is still the same strong voice I remember. "He's right. I would have come for you the second I was released."

My heart beats double time and I resist the urge to fling myself into his arms and beg for forgiveness. Instead, I offer a trembling, "I'm sorry."

He shifts, and then angles the bed upright with a remote. The harshness of the motor an irritant to my ears. When he's positioned to stare directly at me, he says, "The second I went down I knew you'd leave."

I swallow hard, clenching my hands into fists. "I wish I could have proved you wrong."

"I understand you."

I lower my gaze to the cold smooth hospital floor. "I don't know if I can do this."

He points to the chair next to the bed. "Come sit down."

My feet feel like concrete blocks are attached to them. Unable, or unwilling to move in my paralyzing fear of what my future holds.

I think of that last night I saw him, how it was

between us. How I felt, that fun, sexy dress that made me feel reborn, and the way Michael looked at me. Maybe I can't escape the girl I've become. Maybe I was wrong to even try, to risk it.

Maybe I'm not meant to be happy.

"Come sit."

I nod, take a deep breath, and walk over to him, sitting down in the chair.

"It's going to be okay, Layla."

I lick my lips. "Are you in a lot of pain?"

"Look at me."

Throat tight, I blink, raising my gaze to meet his.

"We're going to get through this."

I clutch my jacket tight around me, pressing back into the chair. "I…don't…"

He holds up his hand, his left one, the arm not attached to his injured shoulder. "I can't lose you. I won't."

I nod. "It's not what I want, but I'm afraid."

He reaches out. "I love you so much."

I take his hand. "I love you too."

He squeezes my fingers. "We'll work it out."

I want to believe.

"I'm so fucking sorry." His voice is hoarse and broken sounding.

"It's not your fault." Tears well in my eyes and I can't stop them from spilling down my cheeks. "Concentrate on getting better."

"It was a fluke."

"That's what Leo said." I believe them. Michael's been a detective for a long time without incident, but that's the thing about flukes, they don't happen often but when they do they lead to tragedy. He might go another ten plus years without another one, but when it happened again, I could lose him forever.

He shifts restlessly, and I can see the strain of the exertion at his mouth. The fatigue in the lines at his eyes and shadows under his skin. He hasn't been sleeping or getting the rest he needs, because of me. He's not recovering as quickly as he could because he's too worried about me. I make a silent vow that I will stay until he's recovered. I squeeze his hand. "Please, you need your rest. We can talk when you've slept."

He searches my expression. "Promise you won't leave."

"I won't." I pluck the remote from his fingers and start to lower the bed. "You need to sleep."

"But..."

I shake my head, standing and hovering over him. I trace the line of his jaw. "We'll talk later. Sleep."

His lids start to flutter. "I'd fight you, but the drugs are kicking in."

I don't want him focusing on when, or if, I'll desert him. I want him at ease, so I smile and say, "Leo's...you know...one of us."

He laughs and winces. "I know."

I stroke over his forearm, tracing the veins in his skin with my fingertip. "That must have gone over well."

He takes a deep breath. "It did indeed."

"He ordered me back here."

He looks at me and a shadow of a grin ghosts over his lips. "Then I will forgive him for violating my sister."

I want to see it again—the glimpse of the man I know—so I tease. "I guess we won't be going to the club with them."

His brow furrows. "God no, woman, are you insane?"

I laugh, and watch as he drifts into sleep.

I'm unsure of where our future will lead, unsure if I have the strength to stay, but leaving him while he needs me is unthinkable.

For now, it's enough.

31.

Michael has been home from the hospital for one week, and I watch him carefully, warily. My gaze scans over him, searching for signs of discomfort, as he lies asleep on the couch.

Real shoulder gunshot wounds aren't like you see in the movies where the hero springs up from the ground, and shakes off the pain to run after the villain. From what I understand, with all those muscles, bones and tendons in that region, Michael is lucky he'll regain full use of his arm.

He stirs in his sleep before settling again. He had his first round of physical therapy today. It had been a frustrating, exhausting experience for him. When we'd come home his face had been drawn with strain, the corners of his mouth etched in pain. I forced him to take a painkiller he didn't want.

He'd been too tired and in too much pain to put up much of a fight.

I sit on a chair across from him, the room silent

except for his breathing. Belle's gone, staying at Jillian and Leo's while Michael is recovering, and I miss her terribly.

I try and focus on the book in my hand, a light chick lit type read that's supposed to be "laugh out loud funny", but I can't concentrate on the words.

No, instead, I study Michael and contemplate my future.

Every day I think about leaving. Every day I stay.

I can't quite explain the war inside me. How I've worked myself into a corner. I feel selfish for staying, and selfish for thinking I should leave. With Michael not strong enough to do anything but recover, I've had nothing to do but take care of him and think.

And the more I think, the more twisted my thoughts become.

I'm convinced I'm cursed somehow. That if I stay with Michael, I will be his demise. As crazy and irrational as it sounds, I can't help the thought from battering away, filling my head.

I'm once again afraid. Because it *must* be me. Something about me must attract violence. After all, I do love danger. And damaging the men I love *must* be the consequence.

I wish, more than anything, Michael could take me in hand and calm all these volatile emotions. I'm a horrible person for even wanting it, for being frustrated that he can't do that for me. Maybe, if things weren't so rocky, it wouldn't eat away at me.

But things are not good. There's a strain between us that never existed before, not even at the beginning of our tenuous relationship when I fought so hard to stay away. We know why, but it remains unspoken.

For the first time, I'm not the only one that's afraid. Michael is too.

I can feel it in the way he looks at me. The way he holds his tongue when I say something he doesn't agree with. He's scared one wrong move will send me running, and he doesn't have the strength to chase me.

In other words, the power dynamic between us has shifted.

And neither one of us knows how to shift it back.

Our conversations focus on the mundane. I take care of him, making sure he follows all the doctor's instructions. I scour the Internet looking for books and movies he'll enjoy to keep him busy while I'm at work. I cajole him into taking his pain meds, get him blankets and make him chicken noodle soup. Sometimes he tries to argue, but he doesn't have enough stamina to win.

Shamefully, I can feel my cravings creeping in on me, threatening to spin out of control. When I find myself bursting with the desire to push him so that he'll take control, I leave the room and do my breathing exercises and journal the way Dr. Sorenson taught me. Writing endless pages that I rip free from the notebook and burn after I'm done. I hate myself for wanting things to go back to the way they were so voraciously. Ironic, considering how hard I fought to stay away from him.

I've been very careful to hide my dark, selfish desire. But he knows.

And the more it remains unspoken between us, the more I have the urge to unleash the brattiness building inside me. It's a pattern I'd long established with John to get what I wanted. Habit. One I never instilled with Michael because, truthfully, I never had to.

Before, he exerted his control and it was unwavering, leaving little room for resistance. I've grown to love it, to need it. The more he controlled me the more peaceful I became. I don't know how to explain, or even why, but it soothed the damaged part of me and set me free.

I miss it.

And he's not strong enough to give it to me.

On the couch, he stirs, shifting to turn his face toward me. The sun from the window falls across his hard face, highlighting his strong jaw. Dark lashes closed, his face is relaxed, although his pallor is not quite right. My eyes skim over his body, every delicious inch of him, and rest on his bandaged shoulder. It's hidden away under his T-shirt, but I know it's there, taunting me. It brushes against my skin at night, reminding me, of what has happened, and what might happen in the future.

It's like fate has played a cruel trick. He's right across from me, so close I can touch him, but the essence of him has been taken away from me.

He stirs again and his lids flutter. He'll wake soon.

I can't help the thought that floods my mind. That maybe I should stand up, and leave. Walk out of that door forever. That it's the only way to protect him.

He opens his hazel eyes, disoriented at first, but then fixing on me.

I stand up, but instead of walking to the door, I walk to the couch, sitting on the edge. His hand covers my knee and I smooth over his brow. "How do you feel?"

"Tired, but better."

"Are you sore?"

A muscle works in his jaw. "Yes."

That simple word tells me what I need to know. Michael downplays his pain. Hiding it from me, the way I hide from him. He's hurting badly. I glance at the clock. "You can't take another pill for at least an hour."

He shakes his head. "No more pills."

"We'll see," I say, a slight smile on my lips.

"I'm serious, Layla, they make me so damn numb."

I nod. I will not rise to the bait. "Just rest."

He opens his mouth to speak, then closes it again.

His fingers squeeze my knee, and my belly jumps with traitorous desire. I ignore the heat, and ask, "What do you want for dinner?"

His gaze drops to my lips and tension fills the space between us. "I'll get my strength back soon."

I'm not sure if he's reassuring me, or himself. Probably both. "Of course you will." His eyes narrow and I stroke over his flat, hard belly. "It will be faster if you get your rest."

He gestures in a motion that I can only describe as helpless. "I'm worried about you."

"Michael, I'm fine," I say in a hard, stern voice. Adopting his persona, shoving my own as far down as I can muster.

He goes to say something, but the words die as his lids close. "Can we talk later?"

The pain meds working their magic, stealing his consciousness. I tuck the blanket he's kicked to the floor around him. "How about pasta for dinner?"

"Sure," he mumbles.

Five minutes later he's breathing deeply and I'm once again on the chair, pretending to read words I don't comprehend.

I peer at Michael before glancing at the door.

How am I helping him? His worry and anxiousness about me distracts him away from his recovery. He needs to focus on what's important and he can't do that with me.

As much as I try and talk myself out of them, the dark thoughts persist. They whisper in my ear, playing into all my deepest fears in the most compelling and convincing way.

Go. Leave. It's for the best. If you don't, you'll be his demise.

I look back at Michael. I promised him I'd stay.

I remember how it was between us the night he was shot. The way he ground the heel of his hand between my legs and said in his harsh, demanding voice, "Consider yourself marked." Then he kissed me, told me to have fun, and pushed me out the door.

Into life.

I glance one last time at the door, and then back at him.

I stay.

32.

I'm in Dr. Sorenson's office, sitting on her bland, nondescript couch, while she sits across from me in her bland, nondescript therapist's outfit.

I find myself wondering what she's like outside the office.

Does she like her life? Is she afraid? Does she believe in her work?

Since I haven't spoken, she prompts me, probably conscious of our fifty minutes drifting away. "How is Michael's recovery going?"

I glance away, focusing on the calm seascape painting on the wall. "He's getting better every day." I pause, sucking in a breath. "He wants me to move in with him, officially that is."

A small smile curves her lips. "And how do you feel about that?"

I bite my lower lip. I've been so busy putting on a happy face for everyone, and it's exhausting me. With her, I don't have to hide. "I don't want to live without him, and I don't know how to live with him walking out that door every day."

She nods, and writes something in her note pad. "That's to be expected. Did you give him an answer?"

I shake my head, unsure how to explain how it's been between us. It's like by some unspoken rule, we've decided not to talk about anything significant.

She nods, as though contemplating her next words. "Forget everything else. Do you want to live with Michael?"

"More than anything." I'm scared though. I don't know how to keep him safe.

"But?"

I exhale. "His job, it's dangerous. I'll have to learn to live with it every day for the rest of my life."

She doesn't speak for a minute, but then she puts down her pen and paper and pins me with a direct stare. "Life is full of peril and risk. Safety is an illusion."

For the first time I feel I'm talking to the real Dr. Sorenson, and not the therapist. Somehow, it eases me. "But you can't deny his job is more dangerous than the average person's."

She clasps her hands in her lap. "True. But even the safest of lives—if you truly want to live—suffer loss. Parents take their children to the doctor because they have a headache and leave with a child diagnosed with cancer. Someone looks down to read a text message while they're driving and dies in a car accident. Life is risk. Unless you want to go off by yourself and live in the woods, disassociated from all your loved ones, you will experience loss and sorrow again. Grief is inescapable."

I bite my lower lip. "This is an interesting therapy technique."

She tilts her head to the side. "After a year of seeing you, I understand sometimes you need things laid out before you in black-and-white. I'm not going to insult your intelligence and tell you that your life will always be full of sunshine and rainbows. Because, after what you've experienced, you know that's bullshit."

My eyes widen at her language, and I blink.

She smiles, not her normal professional one, but a real one that lights up her whole face. "As sure as we are sitting here, our lives will change. Sometimes for the good. Sometimes for the bad. That's life. But, I've been a therapist for a long time, and the human spirit never ceases to amaze me. I've seen people go on to do some pretty awe-inspiring things in the face of tragedy."

I take in a deep breath. "So what are you saying?"

She opens her hands in a gesture of surrender. "I'm saying life is interesting. Filled with joy and sorrow. Good and bad. Peace and agony. It's part of the package. If you choose to accept it. Or you can go live out your life in isolation."

"I'm afraid." So very afraid that it's me, and not his job.

She leans forward, placing her elbows on her knees. "Here's a secret. We all are. The question is if Michael is worth the risk."

"He is." He's everything. I don't want to live without him.

"What path do you want to take, Layla? The choice is yours."

She's right. I have a decision. Do I want to live the rest of my life afraid? Alone? I try and picture walking out of Michael's life, and never seeing him again. I find I can't. A world without him, a world of isolation, is unthinkable. I take a deep breath. "I choose Michael."

She smiles and sits back in her chair. "I think that's wise."

33.

As we sit at the table from our first date it feels as though we have traveled a lifetime. Full of smiles, the beautiful Gwen has brought me one of her delicious drink concoctions, and promised us another fantastic meal.

I'm trying to get into the mood of the evening, but it eludes me. Although, I've gotten quite good at pretending.

Next to me, Michael holds up his Glenlivet in a toast. "To good news."

"To good news." I clink my glass, although this isn't a celebration for me. After a month of intensive physical therapy, where Michael has worked tirelessly, he's been cleared for desk duty.

He returns to work Monday. He's been going crazy on bed rest, and he can't wait to get back to the job he loves. I, on the other hand, can only think this means he's officially one step closer to being confronted daily with murder and violence.

I can't stop worrying about him.

I had my first panic attack since that night we went to dinner with my sister in the bathroom of the doctor's office after we receive the "good news".

I hid it from Michael.

I don't want to ruin his happiness when he's worked so hard to recover. More than anything, I want to be a good, supportive girlfriend. But I've grown used to keeping him safe in the house. Once he's out in the world, how will I handle it? I'll go crazy with fear every time he leaves for work. When he's called away in the middle of the night, I'll never sleep for worry.

But, I've accepted I can't live without him, so I'll have to find a way to cope. I won't lay that burden at his feet.

He takes my hand, pulling me away from my troubling thoughts. Determined to give him a night he deserves, I plaster on a bright smile on my lips, only it dies when I catch his expression.

He's not happy.

He searches my face and then he shakes his head. "We need to talk."

Instantly on alert, I lean forward, frowning. "Are you all right? Is it your shoulder?"

He lets go of my hand and pinches the bridge of his nose. "My shoulder is fine, but we are not."

My pulse kicks up, and a flush of heat that has nothing to do with desire and everything to do with panic. *No, not now.* We've been avoiding our relationship and I need to stay in this bubble. It's the only way. I swallow hard. "Everything is fine."

A muscle jumps in his jaw. "Everything is not fine. We need to get back to normal."

I bite my bottom lip. It's what I've secretly been desperate for, but I can't do it. I need to keep him safe. I pretend to misunderstand. "We are getting back to normal. You're going back to work in a few days."

He narrows his gaze. "And you're not happy about it."

I flash what I hope is a brilliant smile, but feels more like a grimace. "Of course I am. I know how stir-crazy you've been and how you can't wait to get back to work."

"You know, I did think about it."

"Think about what?"

He scrubs his hand over his jaw. "I'm well aware my job upsets you, especially with my injury."

He's careful never to say the word *shot*. I'm compelled to correct him, because it's not unreasonable or illogical to be afraid of his job. That's one thing I'm sure of. "You were shot. Wouldn't you be upset if I was shot?"

"Yes, but—" A muscle jumps in his jaw when I hold up a hand and cut him off.

"But it's not the same, is it? After all, I'm a communications manager." I point at him. "While you are a homicide detective."

All my emotions are stirring inside me, threatening to spiral out of control. I take a deep breath to push them back down.

His fingers tighten on his glass, whitening his knuckles, but he says in a calm tone, "I'm aware of that. Which is why I thought about quitting for you."

Shocked, I can only stare at him wide eyed while my brain concocts a million reasons why I want him to quit. I twist my necklace and push back the desire to beg him to do just that. Only I can't, because that's not something a good, supportive girlfriend would do. So, I speak the truth, his truth, even though the words taste like dirt. "You love your job, and I want you to be happy."

"You are such a liar," he says, tone tinged with exasperation. "At least be honest."

"I am. I'd never ask that of you." I might think it five hundred times a day, but I refuse to say it.

Michael shakes his head and takes a sip of his drink. The liquid sloshes when he puts it back on the table. "Do you honestly think I can't feel your constant worry? That I don't know how anxious you are?"

I look away, studying the crowded restaurant. I remember the first time we came here—how the tension between us was all about sex and chemistry, and not this mess we have now. I take a deep breath. "What do you want me to say, Michael?"

"Tell me you wish I wasn't a cop."

I give him a sharp glance. "Fine. I wish you weren't a cop. Are you happy now?"

"Not really," he says, and the words cause a riot of panic. When he speaks again, he sounds resigned. "I love you, but I can't do it, Layla. Not even for you."

I bite the inside of my cheek so hard I taste a hint of blood. "I don't expect that."

He laughs, hard and brittle. "Do you know why?"

"Because you love it." I shift my attention over his shoulder, watching the chefs in the open kitchen as I fiddle with the stem of my glass.

"I do love it, almost as much as I love you. But that's not why." He shakes his head. "If I quit, in the end, it would be our undoing."

"I'm sure you're right." It's what I'm supposed to say, but I don't feel it. Instead of contrite acquiescence, I want is to scream, *If you love me so much, you won't do this to me.* It's selfish and unfair, and I won't say those ugly words. I won't sacrifice his happiness for mine. Because he's right, in the end, he'd grow to resent me.

In silence, we both look past each other, gazing out at the crowded restaurant. This is nothing like our first date. All I want to do is go home, watch TV and forget.

Michael sighs. "We can't go on like this."

Bile rises in my throat. He's going to leave me. I put my hands under the table to hide their shaking. "Everything is fine."

Maybe if I say it enough, I'll start to believe it.

"Look at me." The tone is achingly familiar and my heart skips a beat.

I face him and my chest swells. He's back to normal. All gorgeous and dangerous in his black sweater and matching pants. I can almost convince myself that things can go back to the way they were, but it's a lie.

He takes my hand. "We need to get back to normal, and we can't do that while you're worried I'm going to break. It's not what you need and it's sure as hell not what I need. It's driving us both crazy. I need to get back in charge, and that's what you need too."

I should feel relief, but I don't. We are at a standoff. I can't go back, no matter how much I want to. In my head, it's become part of the problem. "I can't."

"Explain it to me."

How can I explain the responsibility I feel without telling him about that night? My secret. I shake my head.

His jaw hardens, but before he can speak the waitress comes over and gives me a momentary respite.

She places her wooden board of homemade breads and spreads on our table. "Gwen said she's making something special for you guys."

My stomach twists because I fear we won't make it to dinner. I'm terrified this is it.

The end of us.

"Can you give us some time?" Michael asks.

She nods and points to the menu. "Just turn it over when you want me to come back."

I swallow hard as she walks away.

"I expect an answer," Michael says in that do-not-fuck-with-me tone.

I shiver. It would be so easy to give in. I want to so badly I can taste it. I stare at the bread on the table, remembering how he fed me that first date. How his big palms slid up and down my thighs.

Tonight, we haven't touched at all. We haven't been together since that night, and with each day that passes, it's harder to bridge the gap.

I say the words that go against everything I want. "I just don't think I can."

"Why? When it's what we both need."

"Because..." I search my mind for an excuse, but only the truth to blares in my head. I settle on the obvious. "You need to focus on work and your recovery. Not me. Not our relationship. You."

He releases his grip on my hand and takes my jaw in his strong grasp. "You forget how this works, girl. I decide. Not you."

Those words I've longed to hear. They ping every one of my senses, heat my belly, make my thighs clench. But as much as I long to give in, I can't. Not with the stakes so high. "It's not time."

"You think I'm not paying attention, but I am. You think I can't feel all that need and desire coiling tight inside you? You think I don't feel your restlessness? Because you're wrong. It's pounding away at me." He juts his chin toward the crowded restaurant, with its swarms of people and clatter of plates. "Why do you think we're here? Because you need the reminder of what you are, who I am, and what we are."

Hope and lust flutter in my chest, beating in time to the rapid beat of my heart. "You're not strong enough."

"I am." His grip tightens on my chin. "I need it too. Don't deny me."

His hand falls away, leaving me cold. I don't know

how to explain, how the shooting has gotten all tangled up in my head, so I feel responsible. How I can't help but think that he'd gone all these years unscathed, until he met me. "Please, stop."

"No. It's time to get this out in the open. Now tell me why."

Again, I shake my head. My heart is beating fast, my skin warm. I'm out of the habit, and it's overloading me.

"I'm not asking you. I'm telling."

When I say nothing, he encircles my wrist. "You have two choices here: Tell me or we head to the bathroom and I'll show you exactly how strong I am."

Everything inside me stills and I gulp, my gaze flying to his injury. "Your shoulder."

His head tilts, his expression turning hard and arrogant. "Go ahead and test me, because I'm itching to prove you wrong."

"Michael," I breathe his name and it sounds like a plea, instead of firm as I intend.

He holds up a hand. "What's it going to be?"

I bite my lip. If I was good, I'd stop this, but the words are all dried up.

His lids hood, and his lips curl into that cruel twist I love so much. "There are plenty of ways to torture you and I'm not above using them all to get my way. I haven't changed. You need to be reminded and so do I."

I close my eyes; the words to end this madness stuck in my throat. Because, in the end, I crave it. As I've always craved it. Sheer selfish, demanding need for what will happen leaves me breathless, paralyzed to do the right thing.

He nods. "The bathroom it is."

And before I can protest any further, we're on our way. He's weaving fast through the crowd. Gwen, her beautiful red hair in a ponytail, looking model perfect in black skinny jeans and tank top with her restaurants logo embalmed across her chest, starts toward us.

Michael shakes his head and barks, "Later."

Her eyes go wide, but she nods and I offer a smile of apology as he drags me downstairs to the restrooms. I can feel the danger emanating off him in waves, reminding me so much of the night we met. All my hopeful, panicked desire.

It's wrong. My survival instinct kicks in, begging me to stop him, but that other part of me I've been shoving away since he was shot, is far too loud.

Far too consuming in its desire to get fed. Satiated.

When he reaches the bathrooms he frowns at the lines, and growls in what I can only guess is frustration. "This won't work."

I grip his wrist. "Michael. Stop."

"No." He walks down a corridor opening doors until he finds an office. He pushes me inside, slamming the door. "Gwen won't mind."

He doesn't wait, doesn't talk, he just shoves me against the wall and claims me. His mouth is sheer possessive, unrelenting force.

Oh god, I've missed it.

He devours me, his tongue stroking past my lips, forcing its way into my mouth, and lighting me on fire. All our intensity, our chemistry, comes rushing back, pushing away all the comfort that's been wearing away at us.

My hands curl around his neck and he rips them away, shoving them over my head and shackling them with his strong fingers. I give one fleeting thought to his shoulder, but then it's gone as all his repressed dominance unleashes on me like a tsunami.

Yes. Yes. Yes.

I need this. My drug of choice. My fix.

It's been eating away at me and now that he's finally taken the control away from me and I understand what he was saying. Why it's been so hard for us. Why I've been restless and agitated. It's not only my fear, and irrational worries. Not just his profession. It's the struggle against my nature.

And as he claims my mouth, taking complete ownership of me, it finally, irrevocably, sinks in.

I will never escape.

There is no way to manage this away. It is me.

It will forever be me.

One hand encircles my wrists as he slips the other under my silky top. With a flick of his fingers, my bra falls away, and he pinches my nipple, hard enough I gasp at the bite of pain. A fiery ache radiates from my breast and spreads heat through my body. I buck my hips against his straining cock, and he growls in warning.

I'm past caring.

Heedless to his injury I bite at his lip, and he rips away. "You're going to pay for that."

Before I can respond, he's twisted me away from him, pushing me back against the wall face first. His arm, presses against my shoulders, pushing me into the wall, trapping me.

It's a mad, crazy rush of lust-filled frenzy.

I fight to turn around, needing to mark him somehow. Needing to fight and struggle and resist so that he can exert the full force of his power over me. It's wrong, we should be careful, take it easy, but I can't help it.

I need the proof.

He shoves his thigh between my legs, and his hips press against my ass, making movement almost impossible.

But I don't care; I'm like a wild, untamed beast.

Using all my strength, all my pent-up adrenaline and fear, I fight.

Somehow, he rips my panties away, and he smacks

my ass, sending sparkles of pleasure-filled pain through me.

There's no warm up. No easy, getting me prepared strokes. He wails on me, and I push into the blows, my head thrown back in unbridled ecstasy. He kicks my legs apart, his slaps stilling as he roughly shoves his fingers between my legs.

He pinches my clit before ruthlessly pushing into me.

I'm soaking wet.

He whispers low in my ear, "You need this, Layla. You'll never be happy without it."

He's right.

He pulls away, and I go to move, but his palm lands on my neck and he pins me to the wall. I strain and buck, but it's useless. I'm immobilized and I love it.

I hear the sound of his belt being unbuckled, the swish of the leather releasing from the fabric of his pants. Before I can process what he's doing, the whip of the belt rings through the air and strikes my flesh. The contact sends a new, unfamiliar pain lashing through my body.

I've never been hit with a belt. John always used his hands. So had Michael.

I let out a scream as it strikes over me. Again and again.

I cannot describe the release I feel, the exquisite, almost unbearable pain.

The heat.

The lust.

The need.

As I'm pinned to the wall, my cheeks smashed against the surface, my skin on fire, something inside me breaks.

Splits wide open, and explodes. Obliterating all my fears and doubts and setting me free.

The belt drops to the floor.

Then he's inside me. Pounding into me.

One hand around my neck.

The other gripping my hip.

His fingers digging into my sore, painful flesh, he reclaims me. Owns me, body, heart and soul.

I come, my orgasm ripping through me as I claw at the wall under my palms.

Behind me, Michael snarls, thrusts hard, and follows me into oblivion.

Everything quiets and stills, the room turning silent. I close my eyes and listen to the sounds of our heavy breaths.

He leans over me and kisses the side of my neck. "I love you, Layla."

"I love you too." And I do, more than words can possibly convey.

"I refuse to lose you, so we're going to have to work it out."

"Yes." A tear slips down my cheek. I can't hide for one more second.

I lick my lips and say the words I have never spoken out loud, the ones I need to say if I'm ever going to find peace. "That night…he didn't want to go."

Michael's big, strong palm settles in the curve of my spine. "Let's go home, sugar, and you can tell me all about it."

Back in our comfy clothes, we're settled on the couch. I'm nestled in Michael's lap, Belle on the chair watching us, right where I belong. I don't want to have this conversation, but I need to. It's the only way, because leaving isn't an option.

Life is too precious to throw away what we have out of fear. I understand that now.

I rest my head on his shoulder, and his arms curl around me. I feel safe. Protected. Like I can make this confession that's been weighing heavy on my soul and finally forgive myself.

Michael kisses my temple, squeezes me tight, and says in that voice that holds no argument, "Tell me."

It's like coming home.

The tears well, and my chest squeezes, but I'm no longer fighting. No, I left all my fight back in that office.

All I have left is surrender.

It's hard. There's nothing easy about it. But I do it anyway. Because he deserves it, and so do I.

I clutch his arm, but he doesn't protest the digging of my nails into his skin. Calm now, after the release of all our pent-up tension, he brushes his lips across my hairline and gives me another tight hug. "It's okay, Layla."

I let it free. The last secret that lies between us. The one that haunts me and is tangling me up inside. "He'd had a bad day at work. Several client meetings had gone badly, and they were in damage control. He had to go to an early-morning strategy meeting the following day. He called and left a message saying he didn't want to go the club."

I swallow hard and take a deep breath. "It's the last message I ever got from him. It's still on my phone."

When I falter, Michael prods me on. "Go on, let it out."

"I was mad. I was in a mood and not willing to be pacified. The club was new to me, and I'd been on a real public kick. It was fun and exciting and I wanted to go."

I remembered John walking in the door, looking exhausted, but I didn't want to see it. I thought, if we just got out of the house, he'd forget all about his workday. In fact, I believed I was doing him a favor.

"When he got home from work, I begged him to go. I pulled out every trick I knew." I looked up at Michael, my eyes watery, my lip quivering. "We'd been together since our freshman year of college, I knew how to flip his switch. I knew how to play him and get what I wanted."

Michael smiled down at me, wiping the tears from my cheek. "Somehow that doesn't surprise me."

"He said no. But I persisted and in the end, I won." I twisted the fabric of Michael's sweater, needing something to do with my restless hands. "He wasn't like you that way. You wear your dominance much closer to the surface than he did. He was more a bedroom-only type."

Michael nodded. "I understand."

"Nobody would have ever guessed the way he was, whereas, with you..." I trail off, and sweep my hand over him.

He tucks a lock of hair behind my ear and smiles. "Subtlety's never been one of my strong suits."

I would have laughed, if the subject matter weren't so serious. I do manage a wobbly smile. "We went to the club, but I don't know, his heart wasn't in it and it wasn't enough for me. We'd started, but I wasn't satisfied. I needed something edgier. More dangerous. When we left the club, I dragged him into that alley, despite his protests. I told him I needed to feel the scrape of bricks against my bare skin. That I needed to be hurt."

I start to cry in earnest, all the loss, and tension, and crushing guilt spilling out of me like bile. "It was because of me. I did it. I made him go and he died because of it. Because of me."

Michael doesn't say anything, he just holds me close as the sobs rack my body. Shaking all over, I whisper my secret shame.

It was my fault. All my fault.

The ugliness I've carried around inside me demands release and I grant it. I let it all out. I have no idea how long I cry, but it's hard and exhausting, and I don't stop until there's nothing left.

When I finally still, Michael reaches under my chin and raises my head. He gives me a searching look before brushing a kiss over my lips. "He didn't die because of you, Layla. He died because some drugged-out, crackheads thought it would be fun to torture someone. *You* didn't kill him. *They* killed him."

I press my fingers to my temple. "It's not logical, I know that, but I feel responsible."

He nods, his jaw hard. "You do understand you can play it the other way, right? If you'd died instead of him, don't you think he'd have gone over that night with a different lens?"

"But it was me that started it."

"And he could have said no. He could have put you over his knee and gave you the spanking you were asking for. He could have put tape over that mouth of yours to get that sassy attitude under control. He could have tied you to the bed until you calmed down. If it had been him that lived, he would have played over in his mind a thousand ways he could have saved you. That's how survivor guilt works."

I bite my lip. "He's not to blame."

Michael's voice softens. "No, he's not, and neither are you. That's the point. Like you, there are a million things he could have done to stop the sequence of events that played out that night. Yes, you could have relented. And he could have said no. But neither of you is responsible for the actions of those men in that alley that night."

I push past my arguments and guilt and let the words sink in.

He grips my chin and holds me firm. "Do you understand?"

It would be easy to agree, but suddenly, I don't want to. I don't want to hide anymore. Or pretend. I want him to know it all. "I feel responsible…for you getting shot."

His gaze goes wide before he narrows. "What?"

I turn my head and he releases his hold. I swallow hard. "I know it sounds crazy, and I don't know, maybe I am, but you can't deny I'm the common denominator."

He shakes his head. "I'm lost."

I clasp my hands tightly together. "You went all that time without anything happening to you, then the night I told you I loved you, someone shoots you."

"Shit," he says, the word a bark of agitation. "I'm such an idiot. I should have known."

"I didn't want you to."

"I should have pushed you to talk to me."

I look past him, to Belle resting on the chair, her head in her paws. "But you didn't."

He strokes down my arm. "I'm sorry, can you forgive me?"

I swallow hard. "Of course."

"On our first date, I told you I was bound to fuck up sooner or later."

To my surprise, I find a smile lifting the corners of my lips. "I remember."

He trails a path down my jaw, and I shift my attention back to him. He kisses me, a slow brush of his lips over mine. "I was afraid, Layla."

"I know." I put my head on his shoulder. When I first met him I couldn't imagine him being afraid of anything. He'd seemed like a god, not flesh and blood, but he's real now and all that comes with it. Yes, it's his job to take care of me, but it's also my job to take care of him. Love. Relationships are two-way streets, he gets to be imperfect too.

I've been unfair to him. And I'm going to make it

up to him, starting now.

"All this time, I didn't want to push because I was too scared you'd leave. And I meant what I said at the restaurant, I seriously considered quitting for you."

I'm laying it all on the line, because that's what needs to be done if I want to be free. "I'm selfish. I know it's wrong, but I wanted you to."

"Do you understand why I can't?"

I'm growing stronger by the minute and like a light bulb going off, I get it. It's like when John made me jump off that cliff all those years ago. "Because my fear can't win."

He smiles and tucks a lock of hair behind my ear. "Exactly. It wouldn't work, Layla. It's not what's best for me, you, or us."

"Your right." Because, of course, he is.

"I should have pushed you. I won't make that mistake again."

I shudder, knowing someday I'll be on my knees both loving and hating those words. "And I won't hide my feelings from you." I flutter my lashes up at him, a lightness that wasn't there before taking hold. "Although I can't promise I won't need a little gentle coaxing from time to time."

He laughs, and it's like music to my ears. It's a sign that everything is going to be okay. That we haven't lost who or what we are. "Gentle coaxing, huh? Is that what you call it?"

"Yep," I say, grinning.

He kisses me, long and deep, and when I'm breathless and moaning, he pulls away. "You're going to move in with me."

I raise a brow. "Is that an order?"

"It is." Another hard press of his lips.

"Then I have no other choice." My tone is light and teasing. And it feel so good to have fun again. "I guess it's a good thing I'm so in love with you."

"It is lucky how that works out." His fingers snake under my top. "I love you too."

34.

I'm standing over John's grave, dusting my hands off after having cleared the leaves away. I run my hands over the stone, tracing his name, the dates of his birth and death with my fingers, before sitting down in the grass. I love him and I miss him. But, it's time to choose life.

And I'm ready. Ready for all the joy and heartache that goes with it. Ready to rediscover who I am now, instead of trying to recapture who I used to be.

I pick up a leaf and study the grave where my beloved now lays. Before he died, I never really understood the purpose of a cemetery. But, I do now. It's a way to connect. To remember. To talk to the dead. It's for peace. Closure.

I take a deep breath and begin to speak. "I met someone. Maybe you already know that, I'm not sure. I suppose, someday, I'll see you again and find out. You'd like him. His name is Michael, and he's brought me back to life. He's helped me heal, and even though it's hard, I believe you want that for me. You always had my best interest at heart."

I twist the leaf between my fingers. "I love you. I will always love you. I miss you every day. And I'm sorry. So sorry I didn't listen that night. I should have. If I had, you'd be here right now. But I can't change the past. I just have to learn to live with it. I know if you were here, you'd tell me not to blame myself. And I will try. For you. I will honor your life, by living mine. I will laugh and love, cry and grieve, and I will do it because that is what you deserve. And I do too. Michael has helped me understand."

I brush away my endless fall of tears.

I smile to myself, to John. I pick up my cell phone, scroll through my messages and come to that last one. Without listening, I delete it. His tired voice, telling me he wants to stay in that night is not the last time I will hear him. Instead, I play the second to last one.

His low, smooth voice, filled with amusement comes over the line. *LayLay, I'm running late, but I'll be home by seven. It's been a hard day and I need to do filthy things to you. So be a good girl and be naked and ready when I get there.*

I play it again.

And again.

And finally, one last time.

Through my tears, I whisper, "When I get to where you are, I'll be ready for you. Although I don't know how I'll handle you both. Neither of you likes to share."

I swipe my finger over his name. That name that is as familiar to me as my reflection. "I love you."

I delete it.

The wind picks up, blowing over my cold cheeks and ruffling my hair. For a split second I feel him. Alive and vibrant, filled with joy and laughter, just like he used to be. I lift my head to the sky, the air kisses my lips and, then, it's gone.

Real or imagined, it doesn't matter. I felt him, and at long last, I am at peace. All my tormented, angry, fearful emotions finally smoothed over into something fresh and clean.

The contentment that has eluded me for so long settles deep into my bones. I stand, brushing off my pants and turn, raising my hand to shield my eyes from the sun.

Michael is standing by the car, waiting for me, wearing dark sunglasses, looking dangerous and strong. Capable and alive. My heart fills with love for this man that dragged me back from the dead and taught me how to live again.

I walk toward him, my future unknown, but with him. Always with him. For as long as life allows. Because, in the end, we have no real control. We only have choices.

And I choose him.

But more important, I choose me, and the life we will build together.

Get a taste of Sinful...

"Is *he* going to be there?" My roommate Heather Cowan asks, carefully studying her bright, glittery pink nails. She's been painting them on my nightstand table as I've been tearing through my bedroom like a mini tornado to get ready for this evening's festivities.

The *he* in question is my brother's best friend, and tonight, I'm going to put an end to our extended game of cat and mouse, once and for all. I grin at Heather in the mirror. "Oh, he'll be there."

In answer, Heather gives me a long suffering smile.

The party is for my older brother. Its his birthday, *and* he's recently been promoted to the next rank of homicide detective in the Chicago Police Department. He's one of those over achiever types and my parents couldn't resist the urge to throw him a big bash.

I survey myself in the full-length mirror, twisting and turning in my minuscule dress. I turn to my roommate. "So what do you think?"

Heather flicks a glance over me. "I think you're going to give your poor brother a heart attack."

"Don't you worry about Michael, he'll be fine." Yes, he's annoyingly overprotective, but I'm twenty-eight, and there's not much he can do but grumble and scowl. Since he can't help himself, I take it in stride. I don't deny him his big brother privileges; I just smile, nod and do what I want. See, a win-win for both of us. "You didn't answer. "

Heather sighs, and flops down on my bed, holding her hands in the air as to not ruin her manicure. "You look like I hate you and I'm glad I don't have to stand next to you all night and watch men drool all over you."

"Perfect." I've achieved the intended effect, although the man I want to drool all over me refuses to bend to my seductive will.

"Please, Jillian, I'm begging you, let this go." Heather's voice is a pleading whine.

We've had this conversation before, but I'm nothing if not determined.

"Not going to happen. So just deal." I twist once again in the mirror. I'm not normally this vain, but tonight I have to look perfect. Impossible to resist. "And the dress?"

"You look like a very expensive escort."

"Excellent." I beam, my lips extra full and pouty with the dark crimson gloss I've slicked on. It goes with my light olive skin, long, dark wavy hair, and hazel eyes.

I must say, I do look spectacular. Yes, my red dress is painted on, short on my long legs, extra slinky, and maybe a bit slutty. But I'm going for show stopping here.

Subtly is not one of tonight's words.

No, I'm going for hit-you-over the head bold.

Heather rolls her eyes. "This will only end in disaster, and I'll be gone this weekend and unable to pick up the pieces."

I step away from the mirror and put on a pair of nude, stiletto heels. "Yep, it will probably be a disaster. But, I've tried everything else, I'm running out of options."

Most girls probably would have taken no for an answer a long time ago, but I've been told I can be a bit stubborn at times.

Heather rolls off my bed and stretches her long, lean frame. She's a ballerina at the Joffrey Ballet, and with her platinum blonde hair, fine classical features and clear blue eyes she looks the part. Dressed in black yoga pants and a tank top, she reaches for her heel and stretches her leg to the ceiling. Her flexibility is something to marvel.

I tilt my head at her. "Are you sure you won't come tonight? Even for a little bit?"

"As much as I'd love to watch you make a fool out of yourself, I've got to be up at the crack of dawn tomorrow."

"I know," I say, and as much as I'd like her there to support me, which she would despite her belief that I'm being dumb, I'll know plenty of people at my brother's party.

My father had rented the back of the hot new Irish pub featured in all of Chicago's what's trending magazines. Michael protested the celebration, but my father refused to budge. His only son being a homicide detective wasn't what my investment banker father wanted, but he was proud and showed it. At least my older sister took pity on him and married a partner in my dad's firm.

I was the last hold out. After college I gave it a try, taking a low-level entry job in my dad's office, but I hated it. I'm not cut out for corporate life. I lasted three months before I quit. Since then I've flitted around in various careers, abandoning each one much to my parent's worry.

I'm what is affectionately known as a free spirit. Aka, I have no idea what I want to do with my life.

Something artistic and free— in other words— poor. But I'm not worried. When I finally hit upon that elusive "thing" I'll know. And I'll give it everything I've got. In the mean time, I support myself by waitressing at my best friend Gwen's trendy restaurant.

With a six-month waiting list to eat there, it's a great gig, but I'm a mediocre waitress and the restaurant business isn't my passion. The best I can say about my job is I use my relationship with Gwen for the best shifts, and didn't have to work out much.

I smooth down my dress and walk into our tiny

living room. I'll figure out my career another time, tonight is about pursuing my other elusive passion.

Leo Santoro.

My brother's best friend and partner. Object of my lust-filled fantasies.

And general pain in the ass.

Heather follows me down the hallway that leads to our living room. "You've been practicing in those heels."

I laugh. There is an art to walking around in too high stilettos, and it's not innate. "I have."

"Your legs look fantastic."

"Why thank you." They did. I'm tall, five-nine to be exact, and I've been told by men and women alike that my legs are endless. I consider them one of my best assets.

I move to the kitchen and start transferring necessary essentials from my big purse to my small evening bag.

Heather slides onto the stool and watches me. "Do you think it's smart to wear heals that put you eye level with him?"

I toss my hair over my shoulder and search for my powder before emptying the contents onto the counter. "He can handle it."

Four-inch heels are part of my strategy.

I want him looking me straight in the eye when he rejects me.

ABOUT THE AUTHOR

Jennifer Dawson grew up in the suburbs of Chicago and graduated from DePaul University with a degree in psychology. She met her husband at the public library while they were studying. To this day she still maintains she was NOT checking him out. Now, over twenty years later they're married living in a suburb right outside of Chicago with two awesome kids and a crazy dog.

Despite going through a light FM, poem writing phase in high school, Jennifer never grew up wanting to be a writer (she had more practical aspirations of being an international super spy). Then one day, suffering from boredom and disgruntled with a book she'd been reading, she decided to put pen to paper. The rest, as they say, is history.

These days Jennifer can be found sitting behind her computer writing her next novel, chasing after her kids, keeping an ever watchful eye on her ever growing to-do list, and NOT checking out her husband.

Printed in Great Britain
by Amazon